Shepherd's Prayer

**katja
willemsen**

www.katjawillemsen.com

Published by Katja Willemsen
www.katjawillemsen.com

ISBN-13   978-1479369010

Cover design by Elsabe Gelderblom – www.farmdesign.co.za

This book is for my parents,
for their unwavering belief.

Acknowledgements

Seven people make up Team Willemsen, and without them you wouldn't be reading this. So heartfelt thanks to:

Mam and Pap, my parents, for not batting an eyelid when I dumped a lucrative marketing career to write, and for never trying to talk me into being More Responsible.

Dave, my husband, for being the sole breadwinner while I wrote and wrote and wrote. Your atelier is one step closer!

Laura Boon and Rana Eschur, my beady-eyed editors, for their belief in me all those years ago.

Elsabe Gelderblom, friend and designer extraordinaire, for planting the publishing seed and for the spectacular cover.

Helen Fripp, for that first hot day in Collioure, when Shepherd's Prayer was just a few scribbles on a flipchart.

1

You could bake bread in the scorched heat of the mountain. Even the low stone wall next to the path seemed to buckle under the sun that blazed through the last of the morning shadows. A brown snake flashed across the pepper grey surface. Raisin froze. Up ahead, her brother disappeared over the crest with Pi, the rust-coloured mutt he had rescued in Andorra.

She eyed the snake, wary but unafraid. *Don't move. Don't give it something to attack.*

It looped into the path and stopped just ahead of her, arrow head raised, fangs close enough to puncture her leg. A black line zigzagged like a biker tattoo down its back. She wished she knew more about snakes in France.

'Geoffrey!' she called.

Sweat dribbled between her breasts and her shirt clung to her back. The snake's baleful stare unnerved her. It looked thuggish and far too confident.

She took a slow sidestep off the path. The grass crackled. The snake snapped its tail into fat coils and lunged. She threw herself over the wall, pulled in her legs and waited, chest heaving. Nothing. She sat up as noiselessly as she could and peered over the wall.

Still there, still staring at her.

Damn Geoffrey. He was a loner at the best of times but a hundred times worse in the mountains. She still couldn't believe he was here. He had come to her after a long-dreamed-of hiking trip in Andorra. To spend some long overdue time with her... or so he said.

Where was he then, when she was in a face-off with a snake that was protecting its turf like a cocksure bouncer?

Its amber eyes bored into her. The sun seared her London-pale arms.

'Geoffrey!' she shouted angrily.

The snake didn't move and her brother didn't appear. She fanned herself with her hat and looked longingly at the cork oaks on her right. Path or shade? Who knew how long it would take Geoffrey to realise she wasn't behind him. At the pace he walked, she would never catch up to him anyway. His problem. He would wake up soon enough. As long as the snake was there, the path wasn't an option, and she needed to get the hell out of the sun.

The snake's head hovered sideways. She scrambled back. *Damn you, Geoffrey.* Then she kicked her way through thick scrub towards the trees, pausing at a bush that fizzed with hot pink flowers. Matt was a botanist, and if he were with her, he would be reciting their name and healing properties to her. She turned and kept walking. He was in London and she was in France, and she wasn't here to think about him.

The sun lost its fierceness the minute she moved under cover. She rubbed her arms irritably. By nightfall her skin would be bright red. What was she thinking, hiking on a boiling hot day?

She looked for a place to wait. Enormous boulders lounged about like toppled sculptures on the shale-strewn terrain. The forest looked forsaken by the gods. Up ahead, a rocky shelf rose above the ground. Perfect. From it she would be able to see the path and watch out for Geoffrey.

She clambered onto it easily enough, leant back on her elbows and let out a contented sigh.

No skyscrapers. No crowds. Just silence so intense it felt sacred. Her only companions were the cork oaks, bent and crooked as old men with their wizened branches and gnarled bark. Matt once showed her how corks were hand-punched from their thick spongy underlayers. She balled her fists. No more damn Matt. That had been the whole idea, hadn't it? But she couldn't stop herself. It seemed like just yesterday that he had said so casually, while repotting his cacti, that it was high time they got married.

Six weeks later she was gone. Found a potential buyer for her catering business, put a tenant in her home, and booked her trusty Golf on the Eurostar and driven eleven hours to Collioure in one stretch. There were worse places to forget someone than a small fishing village on the Mediterranean.

Except she hadn't forgotten him, and Geoffrey's surprise visit had been a godsend. Although she had almost choked when he told her he was planning to stay until the 10th of July. Three weeks. A bloody lifetime. Right up until the moment he loped towards her at Perpignan train station, she didn't have a clue how they would survive together that long.

Years ago, they were close, but not anymore, and she could count on one hand how many times they had seen each other in ten years. They didn't even look related. He was grim reaper thin with Dad's olive skin. She was farmgirl buxom with unbrushable red curls she loved as much as she hated.

But so far, so good. Six days down, nineteen to go, and they hadn't fought yet.

A bird squawked overhead. Raisin looked up. A black and white magpie bounced on a branch close by. She was probably near its nest.

'Your chicks are safe from me,' she laughed.

It flitted to a lower branch, bobbing and screeching. She smiled at its indignant huff. It was heaven being in nature again, a million miles from London's car-clogged streets. And Matt's hurt eyes. Even the air here tasted like summer.

She lay on her back and fanned her arms over the rock. It felt solid. Reliable. If she came back in a hundred years, it would still be here, waiting for her. She shut her eyes and explored its scars and grooves with her fingers. Here was a cross buried in its surface. Here a small crater. Another cross. This was more fun than finding shapes in clouds. Her fingertips traced a cone-shaped hole, another, then a cluster of crosses near her waist. She rolled onto her side for a closer look.

A jumble of crosses and small pitted circles splattered the rock's surface all the way to the edge. She crawled to the side. They disappeared behind a thick tangle of ivy. She pushed aside the long green branches and frowned. The rock was hollow underneath. She squinted into the darkness. It wasn't just a small burrow created by an animal, but an open cavern big enough to hide a dozen people.

She slid off the rock and circled it, intrigued to see it was actually a massive stone slab perched like a lid on a mound of raised ground. Long creeper branches snaked up the sides and bright fern fronds sprouted from its base. She grinned. Geoffrey would kick himself for not being with her. Curiosity was one thing that coursed through both their veins.

She scanned the path. Perhaps she should wait for him. She prodded the greenery again. A soft draft whispered out. Gooseflesh tingled. She shifted the ivy curtain and squeezed inside. Just a quick look.

It was dungeon-cold and not quite high enough to stand upright. She crouched uncomfortably and waited for her eyes to adjust.

The sides were flat slabs of scabrous rock, easily a metre and a half high, and over two metres long. The back wall reminded her of the low stone walls that stuttered in uneven rows down the terraced vineyards around the village.

She was in a shelter of sorts. How strange. Had terrified Jewish escapees from the Rivesaltes concentration camps hidden here? Or Catalan dissidents, running for their lives from Franco?

She touched the grey granite. Whoever it was, their presence still thickened the air. Her eyes searched for a clue about who they might have been: a name etched into the rock, a date. She found nothing, not even a scratch.

'Raisin?'

Geoffrey. A *worried* Geoffrey. She squinted at her watch. Forty minutes had gone by. She stifled a laugh and kept still, but Pi spoilt her fun and wormed his way through the overhang towards her. He nuzzled her with his bearded snout.

'Raisin? Where the hell are you?'

She shielded her eyes against the glare and wriggled out between the branches.

'So you finally remembered you had a sister,' she grinned.

'How was I supposed to know you weren't behind me? What happened?'

'A snake.'

'Really? What kind?'

Trust him to be more interested in the snake.

'The long and scary kind.'

'You should've waited closer to the path. If it wasn't for Pi, I wouldn't have found you.' He looked past her. 'What's in there?'

'I'm not sure... I think it's some kind of hideout...'

He nodded but didn't move closer to look. She looked at him uncertainly. Was he still so afraid of the dark?

'Your eyes will adjust to the light,' she said quietly.

He slid his backpack to the ground. 'Is it worth a look?'

'I couldn't see much, but it could be anything... maybe even a refuge from World War Two.' She saw a spark of interest in his eyes. 'It's manmade though, and I don't think anyone's been in it for years.'

He unzipped the side pocket of his backpack and took out a small red Maglight.

'Such a boy scout,' she smirked, pushing aside the foliage and going back inside.

He followed her, head bowed low.

'Wow...' he whistled. 'This goes back in time... *way* back.'

'What do you mean?'

'I think it's a dolmen, Raisin.'

'A dolmen...?'

He scanned the walls with the yellow light.

'It's very typical of prehistoric tombs. Flat granite slabs positioned on their sides with a huge capstone balanced on top of them... all of it camouflaged on the outside by earth and stones.' He held a palm against the roof. 'Complex bit of engineering...'

'How could they have made it without modern equipment? These slabs must weigh a ton.'

'More like *tons* with an s. No-one knows how they did it… probably some kind of leverage system with logs. Interesting… this back wall here doesn't belong in a dolmen.'

He jostled a loose stone near the top and jumped back. Part of the wall crashed to the ground, leaving a gap the size of a small porthole. He shone the Maglight through the gap. They exchanged glances.

'Looks like another chamber,' he said.

'What's that thing on the right…?'

She started pulling away more rocks but he caught her wrist.

'Don't. We should report it.'

'Don't be a granny. Be useful and shine the torch inside.'

The light revealed a small statue in a shallow recess. She nudged him out of the way, reached inside and ran her hands over it. It was no taller than a school ruler and her palms easily cupped its base.

'It's cold… and wet.' She tried to lift it. 'It won't move.'

'Leave it, Raisin.'

She ignored him and explored the ledge it stood on with her fingers.

'There's something here.'

He shone the torch around her shoulder. She bit back a wisecrack. So much for wanting to discourage her. He was as intrigued as she was. She drew out her arm and showed him the objects in her hand.

A small pink clamshell. Something curved and sharp that gleamed like a crescent moon on her palm. And a flat round stone the size of a large coin.

She rolled the shell over.

'What's this doing in a cave?'

He picked up the sharp object.

'This looks like an animal tooth.'

'What about this round thing?' she said.

He twisted the coin-shaped stone under the light.

'No idea, but we really shouldn't be touching anything. There are laws protecting prehistoric sites.'

He carefully replaced the tooth and the round disk. She pulled her fist away when he tried to take the shell from her.

'Put it back, Raisin.'

'Later. No-one will know. And we don't have to report it straight away. Don't you want to see what's on the other side of the wall?'

'I came here to hike up to Massane not to break the law.'

'It's because it's dark, isn't it?' she said shrewdly. 'Look... it's not even nine in the morning. We can easily get to your tower, go home for a bigger torch, *and* be back here by mid-afternoon. Please...?'

He glanced at the broken wall. She knew that look. He was hooked. *Hobbiting* they had called it as kids.

'Okay, but don't take the shell.'

'I'll put it back this afternoon.'

Outside in the light, she inspected the shell. Fine ridges rippled in curves from its base to the outer edge. It looked identical to the earrings her first boyfriend had given her. She prised it open with a fingernail, vaguely surprised to find it empty.

'How do you think it got here?' she asked.

'Probably left by the same person who hid the statue... and the statue's obviously not prehistoric.'

'I like the idea of owning something really old.'

'Old or not... you're not keeping it. We're leaving everything the way we found it.'

'Once a maths prof, always a maths prof,' she needled.

He didn't rise to the bait and ruffled Pi's shaggy fur.

'*Dean*, Raisin, I'm a dean now, and adopting a lost dog ten thousand kilometres from home is hardly what you'd expect from a prof *or* a dean,' he laughed.

Pi covered his face with grateful licks.

'Have you thought about how you're going to take him back home with you?'

'On the same SAA flight as me. I'll just throw money I don't have at it. He would've died if I'd left him on that mountain. Besides, it's high time I had a dog again.'

She studied him quietly. 'Do you miss the farm?'

'Not one bit.'

'That came out too fast to be true. We *both* loved growing up there.'

He stood up and began to leave.

'Maybe, but I don't miss it. Come… we're wasting time.'

At the path, she hopped onto the wall and looked for the snake. Gone. Pity. She would have liked Geoffrey to have seen it. She stepped down and manoeuvred herself in front of him. The only way to make sure she didn't lose him again was to force him to walk behind her. She looked up at the sun and wiped the back of her neck. What had possessed her to hike on a boiling hot day like this?

They climbed for an hour along a narrow track that took them past a jagged wall of rock towards a forest of beech trees. She groaned in relief. Shade at last. This was the last time she was hiking with him. Ever.

The cool shadows soothed her skin but did nothing to ease the heat. The branches were sparse and sabre sunbeams still stabbed at her through the leaves. All too soon, the forest ended and they were in the scorching heat again and approaching a wide clearing at the top of the mountain. The stubby Massane Tower was perched high on a steep outcrop just to the right of them. Grassy terrain flowed from the tower as though poured from heaven. It was meadow-like and more what she would expect on a hilltop than a mountain crest. Nowhere near as majestic as she had imagined it to be.

The tower itself looked both grand and frail, as if a nudge might send it tumbling off the cliffs behind it. She was disappointed that they weren't alone.

A small group of people sat in a semi-circle not far from the path, facing a man with wild white hair. Their stiff-necked posture and stern faces looked more suited to a London boardroom than the Pyrenees. She tried not to stare when they walked past, but the white-haired leader turned towards her, and his eyes were so fierce, she lost her footing. The whole group looked up when she fell. She glared at them, furious with herself for wanting to apologise. It wasn't their damn mountain. She made a show of rubbing her ankle then hurried after

Geoffrey.

'What a cheek… they look pissed off that we're here,' she fumed.

'They're lucky we're not a Spanish tour group,' he shrugged.

She followed him up the stone steps to the base of the tower. The mountain top itself might not be majestic, but its 360° views were. Blue-black peaks serrated the skyline towards Spain, and seawards, the Roussillon plains baked in the summer haze.

'Apparently this tower dates back to medieval times and is part of a surveillance system that stretches from the Mediterranean to deep in the Pyrenees,' Geoffrey said. 'They used fires to communicate between them. If you look carefully you can just see the one closest to the coastline. It's called Madeloc Tower and is just above Collioure… on that mountain there. Can you see it?'

She nodded and sighed.

'Doesn't being in a place this beautiful make you think there must be a God?'

'Hell no. If there is a God then this beauty is probably just his way of sugar-coating reality for us. And damn right too.'

'You don't really believe that!'

'What kind of a god allows babies to starve… children to get hurt?' he said morosely.

She pointed her camera at him.

'Say cheese, Mr Cynic.'

He blocked the lens with his hand.

'I'm hardly a cynic. These mountains aren't the real world.'

'But you *love* them!'

'Only because they're my escape… I never forget what's back home.'

'What's there that's so awful?' she teased.

He gave an irritated snort and jumped down the steps. She photographed his back then impulsively zoomed her camera over his shoulder onto the seated gathering.

The leader swung round.

She quickly directed the camera towards the sea and when she glanced back, the group was already leaving. They walked fast, in single file, with their leader in front, his white hair gleaming in the sun. Good riddance. Their creepiness unnerved her.

'That's a good camera,' Geoffrey said.

'It was a Christmas present from Matt.'

She bit her tongue. *Damn it. Get out of my head, Matt.*

'You don't talk about him much, do you? How does he feel about you being in France?'

'Haven't a clue. We're not together anymore.'

She hated how blasé that sounded.

'Oh? I thought you two would be together forever.'

'So did he.'

'So what happened?'

'He wants marriage, white picket fence, nappies…'

'And you don't?'

'Definitely not.'

'Not even *one* little Raisin?'

She paused at a feathery fennel bush and plucked a head of tiny yellow flowers. She broke off one of the slender stalks. *Tell him.* She snapped off another. *Don't tell him. Tell him. Don't tell him.* She crushed the last flower and held it to her nose. Liquorice. *Tell him.*

'I can't have kids,' she mumbled.

He stopped, face white.

'That's awful. Are you okay? You aren't sick, are you?'

Too many questions. She should've kept her mouth shut.

'No,' she said carefully.

'I'm so sorry, Raisin. How long have you known?'

'Since I had my tubes tied at twenty-one.'

He winced. 'Tubes tied? *Why*, for fuck's sake?'

'I didn't want kids.'

'I don't understand. You're only thirty-five, you can change your mind. It's not too late.'

'I'm thirty-*three*. And I don't want to change my mind.' She threw the barren flower away

'I don't see *you* rushing to have any.'

'It's different for guys. Twenty-one?' His voice softened. 'Do you want to tell me what happened?'

Tears pricked. She packed her camera away.

'Nothing. I was scared to be a mum… responsibility and all that. It's no big deal.'

'Is that why he left?'

'He doesn't know. And anyway, *I'm* the one who left, not him. Have you seen enough of your tower? Can we go and get the torch now?'

2

THE HOUSE RAISIN had escaped to after leaving London was squeezed into a row of old fishermen's homes in *rue Mirador*, a narrow cobbled street near the cliffs overlooking the sea. It was three storeys high with just one room on each level. The steepest staircase she had ever climbed zigzagged between them.

She pushed open the red front door. Her Swedish landlord had proudly told her that the house was over eight hundred years old and that he himself had painted the walls pink, and the shutters indigo blue. She hated all the bright colours. They reminded her of cheap toffee wrappers.

'I'll throw some lunch together quickly,' she puffed at the kitchen level.

Geoffrey refilled their water bottles and packed a second torch while she prepared anchovy bruschetta. Once a foodie, always a foodie. She wasn't about to compromise on a meal because they were in a rush. Lunch would be tasty. Rushed or not.

'Where can we buy more batteries? I don't want to take any chances,' Geoffrey asked.

'The newspaper shop will have some,' she said.

The memory of him sobbing in her arms flashed before her. She licked anchovy bits off her fingers and arranged the toasts on a plate as she remembered his night terrors. She was four years younger than him, a lifetime for children, and yet she had been the one to hold him in her arms and distract him with stories about hobbits that lived on the farm. She wondered if he remembered.

They ate quickly and by 1.20 pm they were ready to leave. Her little lane was almost deserted, but *rue Pasteur*, the wider cobbled street out of the old town, was swamped with sweaty half-dressed holidaymakers. Every few metres, she dodged another pushchair, and stepped past another aspirant Pulitzer prize winning photographer snapping underwear fluttering from a washline. The chaos worsened at the end of the pedestrian zone. Cars were backed up as far as Raisin could see. What the hell was going on? The village was grid-locked with people and cars. She pointed to the narrow bridge that once kept the fisher-folk away from the wealthy side of the village.

'We have to cross there,' she shouted to Geoffrey.

But two gendarmes blocked their way. One jerked a thumb over his shoulder to a group of demonstrators behind him.

'*Désolé*, sorry, the bridge is closed. There's a protest coming,' he said.

The marchers were moving in a silent block towards them. Red and white no-entry signs jabbed skywards over their heads and large drums hung from the waists of the men in front.

'They don't want the *Grotte des Loups*... Cave of Wolves... to be opened to the general public,' the second gendarme explained with a yawn.

'Bloody France and their protests,' Raisin grumbled as they walked away. 'All this bedlam for twenty people who look too damn ordinary to care about anything.'

'Don't be fooled by ordinary. I've seen student protests turn ugly in less time than it takes to write a slogan. We should be careful. Where's the newspaper shop?'

'Opposite the post office, near where the demonstrators are.'

He shortened Pi's lead.

'Let's wait next to the railing by the river. Pi will get trampled on in this madness.'

Angry drivers jammed fists out of their windows and roared abuse at the gendarmes, who yelled straight back. A nearby tourist bus opened its doors and the crowd swelled dangerously. Raisin stood her ground as two men bulldozed past her. The taller one shouldered her so hard, she stumbled against his friend. She clutched his arm to break her fall. He glared at her and shook her off. Venomous eyes. Wild white hair. Then he was gone.

'How weird… that was the guy from the tower!'

'Which guy?'

'The one from this morning. I'll never forget those eyes. What a jerk… he crashed right into me. And he damn well knew what he was doing.'

'Nonsense. Why would he remember you?'

She grabbed a handful of her red curls. 'How many redheads do you see here?'

They found a quieter spot and watched the protestors advance across the bridge and stop next to the fountain under the plane trees. The gendarmes followed at a discreet distance, two-way radios pressed against their mouths. A tall bare-footed woman in a long muslin dress stepped up onto the fountain wall. Her blond hair was pulled into a tight bun and she had the strong chin of someone used to getting her way. Large freckles smudged her translucent skin. She held up her palm for silence. Anticipation rolled over the curious crowd.

'I hope she slips and falls into the water and everyone goes back to the damn beach where they belong,' Raisin muttered.

'We are outraged!' the woman cried. 'Our forbearers worshipped in the *Grotte des Loups*… man communed with the gods there. Now scientists steal rock samples and desecrate the cave art. We say *no*!'

'We say *no*! We say *no*!' the demonstrators echoed, punching their no-entry signs high.

'*No* to destruction. *No* to profiteering from sacred art.' Her words flowed in steady waves. '*Nowhere* in the world do wolves appear in cave art! Keep the caves safe! Keep the caves closed!'

'*Keep the caves closed! Keep the caves closed!*'

The summer crowd joined in, clapping enthusiastically. Drumbeats pulsed. Palms slapped thighs. Feet stamped the sweltering tarmac.

'*Here*… in the foothills of the Pyrenees, wolves once roamed. *Here*… deep in the *Grotte des Loups*, our ancestors consulted the wolf spirits. *Here*… we honour their power.'

'*Honour! Honour! Honour!*'

The clapping became intense. More holidaymakers thronged

towards the noise. Someone began to sing the *Marseillaise*. Geoffrey scooped Pi up in his arms.

'The crowd's too worked up. Let's get out of here!' he shouted.

'Let me take some photos first.' She rummaged in her handbag. 'Where's my camera, damn it? I *know* I brought it!'

The marchers linked arms and hummed and swayed as one. The woman raised her arms above her head. A dark blue tattoo blazoned from her wrist:

'Let Quirinus determine who enters the cave,' she chanted. 'Not man, not money, not politics. Dishonour Quirinus and face his wrath.'

'Who the fuck is *Quirinus*. Let's go Raisin! You probably left your camera at home,' Geoffrey shouted.

'*Quirinus… Quirinus… Quirinus,*' the protestors murmured, eyes lowered as if in prayer.

Geoffrey grabbed Raisin's elbow and steered her through the throng and over the bridge.

'I wouldn't be surprised if this turns ugly,' he muttered.

At the shop, Geoffrey bought a third torch and enough batteries to last a month. She held her tongue, shocked that his fear of the dark was still so bad. She would have to tread carefully.

They left her Golf at the start of the footpath leading to the Massane Tower, and by four o'clock they were in front of the dolmen.

Raisin shook her head. It looked like a natural rock elevation, nothing more. That was probably the point, no-one was meant to find it. Death was sacred, no matter what millennium you were in. Maybe she and Geoffrey were wrong to explore it, but she couldn't resist the pull of the unexplored. Her curiosity had never been dictated by shoulds and shouldn'ts.

'I'd never guess it was a dolmen from the outside. Do they always hide it like this?' she said.

'No, not always. One of the theories is that covering the sides with earth made the placement of the capstone easier.'

'And you know all this because…?'

'The prof who taught us number theory did his best to convince us that maths was in our genes. He showed us slides of bones with scratch marks on them as proof that man was already counting 30 000 years ago. Prehistory has fascinated me ever since.'

She wished she had known that about him.

'How old do you think the dolmen is?' she asked.

'Five… six thousand years. And every slab would have been chiselled out of the ground by hand. It's an amazing feat.'

He gave her his Maglight then unwrapped the new torch and switched it on and off. She eyed it irritably. It was a huge black thing that could probably light a house. But she wasn't about to complain. Better too bright than not exploring.

He held back the ivy branches and she squeezed through. The slabs of stone looked even bigger than before. She ran her hand over the moss-mottled surface, awed by the human hands that had put the shelter together. It must have taken forever.

'How many people do you think are buried here?'

'Twenty, thirty, maybe more. This front section might have been the ante-chamber. It's this wall that's really odd…'

He jammed a stick between the loose stones and made the hole big enough for them to climb through. Raisin went first and Geoffrey followed with Pi.

The chamber on the other side was cramped and tapered into a narrow corridor at the back. The roof slanted sharply and Geoffrey was forced into a crouch.

'So there could be bodies under my feet?' she asked.

'Technically yes, but there wouldn't be anything left of them. The real mystery is why this wall and shrine are here.'

Raisin shone the Maglight on the silver grey figure of a man in a cowl-necked robe clutching a cross across his chest. Thick calcified streaks of brown ran down his body and dribbled over the ledge onto the wall. She touched the statue's bare feet.

'He looks like a monk.'

'Now would be a good time to put the shell back,' Geoffrey said.

She patted her jeans pocket.

'I'm keeping it right here as a good luck charm so we get out in one piece!'

'Raisin, you promised…'

She gave him a playful nudge. 'I'm not one of your students.'

'But you are my kid sister…'

'…who respects and obeys you at all times.'

He rolled his eyes back. 'Just don't forget.'

'I won't,' she lied.

He pointed the torch to the fissure at the back. 'Ready to look further?'

She nodded, feeling closer to him than she had in years. They edged through the gap and found themselves in a wide tunnel with uneven ground that fell into a steep slope. Geoffrey tried to touch the ceiling but couldn't reach it. She rubbed her arms.

'I wasn't expecting it to be so damn cold.'

'Do you want to stop?'

'I'm fine.'

The bedrock was slippery and she had to grip the wall to stop herself from skating forward. A cone of light beamed past her from Geoffrey's torch, so solid she could almost lean on it. Thank God he had it. She wouldn't have dared go further with just the small Maglight. Where had her childhood courage disappeared to?

Loose stones made walking difficult. She moved carefully, testing her foothold with each step. The walls began to crowd into them, as if challenging their right to be there.

'If it gets any tighter, we'll have to go back,' Geoffrey said.

'If it gets any tighter, I won't fit.'

Pi tried to overtake her but she pushed him away.

'Hold onto him, Geoffrey.'

'Want me to go in front?'

She didn't answer. Even with the new torch, the darkness ahead disappeared into nothing. She wished she had brought something warmer to wear. What on earth were they getting themselves into? She was nervous, but also unable to resist the pull of going further. This was how they had explored the untamed coastline of the Eastern Cape. Curiosity always pushed them to walk onto the next cove, find the next beach, and before they knew it, they would be trapped by the rising tide. It was always so damn hard to know when to stop.

The tunnel suddenly grew wider and released them into a towering cave that was as still and shadow-filled as a chapel. They stared at each other, stunned. Only Pi's rhythmic pants rattled the silence.

Raisin beamed the torch skywards. Slender stalactites glistened above them like inverted candles. Crags and fissures scarred the walls. This was an otherworldly place. Had the men and women who had built the dolmen been here? Her skin prickled. They definitely weren't the first people to stand here.

'The tunnel continues on the other side,' Geoffrey said softly.

She saw its dark entrance but didn't follow him. No-one knew where they were. What if they got lost?

'Come and look at this… someone's carved a face on the wall!' Geoffrey called.

Raisin narrowed her eyes and studied the rock then shook her head.

'I can't see anything.'

He stroked the surface with his fingers.

'Look here… and here,' he said. 'It's the shape of a face, long and thin, and they've added black paint into these holes to highlight the eyes. This outcrop that sticks out here is the nose…'

She grimaced. A gaunt mask with angry eyes.

'I don't think we should go any further,' she said nervously.

'We can't stop now, Raisin.'

'I don't like it. What if it's a warning not to go further?'

'It's more likely to be here for protection.'

'What if the torches stop working?' she snapped.

His jaw tightened but he ducked into the new tunnel. Why couldn't he be scared when she needed him to be? Pi trotted after him, stopping and starting at each new smell. She reluctantly followed, zigzagging the torch over the walls and ceiling as she went along.

A flash of red caught her eye. She stopped, retraced her steps, and swept light over the surface.

Two red handprints. Human handprints.

Black spots spun before her. Cold air breathed over her neck. She shrank against the opposite wall, pulse quickening. She wasn't alone.

A woman appeared in front of the handprints. Her sun-seared hair swayed in tangled tresses over a suede animal skin that draped her small frame like a robe. Grass plaits bundled the hide together at her shoulders, leaving her sinewy arms free. She was close enough to touch. Raisin raised her hand then drew back. A man was with her. Raisin held her breath.

Thick brown hair covered his arms and chest, and a matted beard sprung like a small animal from his broad jaw and neck. He held up a limestone lamp. The smell of burning fat filled the tunnel.

Raisin stayed in the shadows. Where was Geoffrey?

The woman paused, lifted her head, then looked over her shoulder at Raisin, green eyes glittering below her sloping brow.

Raisin's heart raced. Had she been discovered?

The man whispered in the woman's ear; her face softened and she turned away. Raisin lifted her hand. *Don't go.*

The man removed something from a small leather pouch and placed it on the woman's outstretched tongue. She chewed steadily, grimacing at the taste, then dropped her head back and he dropped red berries into her mouth.

Raisin looked down. It felt too private. Should she leave?

The woman churned the mixture from cheek to cheek then spat some into her hand.

Raisin stayed, riveted.

The man brought the flickering light closer and rolled his thumb into the paste. The woman watched, shoulders tense. He drew a vivid red streak on the inside of his arm, inspected it closely then gave a satisfied grunt. Her face lit up. She moved slowly towards the tunnel wall and stretched up onto her toes then ran her fingers along the top of the rockface and grazed the surface all the way to the bottom, dropping onto her haunches to probe a small outcrop near the ground. She stood up, still chewing, and repeated the process further along the rockface. The only sound was the clitter-clatter of shells around her neck.

The man followed patiently, raising and lowering the lamp to match her movements. Raisin took a tentative step towards them. What were they looking for? The woman's hands darted forward and caressed the wall. She turned to the man, but he shook his head.

She sighed and spread her fingers wide, drifting them upwards, downwards, sideways, then she stopped and her eyes sought out the man again. He studied the wall, touched it briefly and gave a quick nod.

She spat the mixture into her hands, smeared it over her palms then pressed them reverently against the wall.

Raisin glanced into the dark tunnel. Where on earth was Geoffrey?

Tears coursing down her cheeks, the woman gazed at the red handprints then cupped her hands against her forehead and smeared the remaining paste over her face. Shiny clumps stuck to her hair and tiny teardrops of red slid onto her chest and shoulders.

'Raisin? Where the hell are you?'

Geoffrey. The beacon glare of his torch blinded her. She blinked, looked for the tribeswoman. Her heart sank. The woman was gone.

'I'm sorry… I… I must've been daydreaming… look what I found,' she said.

'Handprints! I've read about these…'

'Could they belong to the people who made the dolmen?'

He shook his head.

'No, I don't think so. It's hard to imagine, but cave art in this part of France is even older than dolmens… we're talking thirty thousand years ago versus a mere six or seven thousand years for the dolmens.'

His voice was filled with awe. He tugged her arm. 'There's more... I found an underground river at the end of this passageway.'

He disappeared again but she couldn't tear herself away. Thirty thousand years ago someone had stood in this tunnel and pressed their hands against this wall. Was it the woman she saw? She hovered her palms over the prints. *Who are you?*

'Raisin?' Geoffrey shouted.

She joined him in a small cave that curved around them like a cauldron. A storm of white froth ripped along the back and disappeared under a ledge in the rockface. Hundreds of glistening mushrooms covered the river edge closest to her.

She grimaced at the noise. After the silent sacredness of the tribeswoman's ritual, the water's angry turbulence sounded louder than a jackhammer.

Geoffrey pocketed a handful of mushrooms.

'Be careful with those,' she warned. 'You never know if...'

A high pitched howl tore through the cave. Raisin screamed. What the hell? Pi cowered against Geoffrey's legs. Geoffrey dropped to his haunches and grasped his collar. The wailing became crazed. Raisin covered her ears and began to back out of the cave. Pi broke free and raced up and down the length of the water, barking and snapping at the surging spray.

'Geoffrey, let's go!' she shouted.

'Wait... it's stopped.'

She dropped her arms in disbelief.

'What the *hell* was that?' she gasped.

'Probably just some kind of wind tunnel phenomena. The cave network opens to the surface somewhere, and the wind must create...'

The howling started again, wild and frenzied.

'Geoffrey, that's not wind,' she said hoarsely.

Pi whimpered in terrified yelps.

'It's okay, boy,' Geoffrey soothed.

Pi leapt against his chest and knocked him off his feet. Geoffrey shot his arms forward but grasped thin air and plunged into the water.

'Geoffrey!' Raisin screamed.

The howls rose into spine-chilling cries. The torrent pulled Geoffrey under. Pi pawed the water, barking feverishly. Geoffrey's chest slammed into the rockface, his legs disappeared with the current under the ledge. He pounded his hands against the wall for something to hook onto. Pi sprang into the torrent and crashed into him.

'Pi, *no!*' Geoffrey yelled.

Raisin latched onto Geoffrey's rucksack and heaved it towards her.

'Get Pi first!' he shouted.

'Don't be stupid!'

'Get my dog out of the fucking water.'

She angrily let go of the rucksack and yanked Pi out by his collar.

'Stay!' she yelled, pushing him behind her.

Geoffrey's body was under the ledge, just his shoulders remained hooked against the rockface. His arms were splayed like a crucifix against the wall, fighting for leverage. Blood streamed from his face and hands. Spumes of foam splintered over him. His rucksack glistened on his back like a black seal. Raisin grabbed it with both hands.

Inch by slow inch, she strained and pulled him to the edge. Her arms burned, her body shook. He hauled first one leg, then the other onto the bank. Pi clambered over him.

'God, that was close,' she panted.

'I lost my torch.'

'That's the least of our bloody worries. I've still got mine, and there's a spare one in your bag.'

'The batteries will be wet...'

He rocked on his heels. She knew that look.

'Geoffrey, *don't*... stay calm. Not now. *Please.*' She shone the torch in his face. 'Look, it works.'

'It's dark...'

'It's not. We have the torch. Get up.'

'Too dark. Too dark.'

'Stop it, for God's sake.'

'Craigy's scared,' he wheezed, eyes blank.

She tried to hold him but he pushed her away. She shook him angrily.

'Who the hell is Craigy? You're frightening me.'

'It's dark...' he whispered.

'What about Pi? He's terrified... we have to get him out of here,' she coaxed.

His eyes flickered to his dog. Pi nuzzled him with a whine. Geoffrey buried his face in Pi's neck then hugged him hard and staggered to his feet and stumbled past her towards the tunnel.

In her heart, she knew the embrace had been meant for her.

3

RAISIN PAUSED AT the red handprints on the tunnel wall and scanned the darkness for the tribeswoman, but all she saw was Geoffrey disappearing around the corner. She waited a little longer then ran after him, disappointed. Had she dreamt it all?

Her skin crawled when they passed the face on the rock. Geoffrey had been wrong to think it was there for protection. She should have listened to her instincts and refused to go further. He had almost drowned because they had ignored its warning.

She followed him across the cave into the tight passageway. It was the only time he waited for her, and as soon as he saw she didn't get stuck, he rushed off again, leaving her to struggle up the steep slope on her own.

His phobia shocked her. It seemed worse than when they were kids. She would have to find the right moment to ask him about it. At last she stumbled into the chamber with the statue. She touched its face. Was it also a warning? She didn't think so. The saint's serene expression was welcoming and nothing like the vacant chill of the carved face in the rock. Her fingers brushed against the figurine's shoulder. She frowned. It was rough and jagged, as if something had broken off there. She longed to explore it further. Another time. Geoffrey would kill her if she took any longer.

Outside, the wind caterwauled through the trees and shredded clouds across the sky. Geoffrey was pacing around the dolmen and refused to let her take a break.

'Just a few minutes,' she pleaded.

He sneezed and jogged towards the path.

'Geoffrey, *please* don't go so fast.'

He ignored her. She had no idea whether he was angry or upset. Either way, she felt guilty.

'Where did this bloody wind come from?' she grumbled.

He kept walking.

'It's cold. I hope we don't get sick,' she muttered.

No reply.

'Damn it, Geoffrey, talk to me!'

'Stop being so goddamn needy.'

'That's not fair,' she stammered.

'I almost fucking drowned.'

'I know, I'm sorry.' She was silent for a moment. 'Who is Craigy?'

'Shut up.'

'But...'

'Drop it, Raisin.'

'Why?'

'Just leave me alone.'

'Please don't be like that. I just...'

He swung around, face glowering. She jumped back in fright. He flung the car keys at her.

'Go at your own pace. I'm walking back to the village.'

'Geoffrey, don't. It's too far. I'll shut up, I promise.'

He grunted and broke into a run. Pi paused, looked at Raisin in confusion, then trotted after his master. She stood rooted to the spot, fighting the impulse to follow him.

Where was the old Geoffrey? The one who never kept secrets from her, looked out for her, protected her?

Pi's high-pitched bark drifted further and further away, and she imagined Geoffrey tearing down the hill, regretting his visit and making plans to leave. Damn him for shutting down. He was as out of reach as ever. Their whole bloody family was out of reach.

One of her earliest memories was toddling after Geoffrey as he ran to Mum in the kitchen, and the delighted look on Mum's face when she swung him in her arms. It was the first time she understood how much more Mum loved him than her.

Damn him. Let him run off if he wanted to. She checked her watch. Not even eight o'clock and the sun was still high... time enough for another look at the statue.

No matter how hard she tried, she couldn't move the stone figure. Someone had made darn sure it would never be stolen. She took a step back and studied it. Small shrines like this were dotted all over local villages and vineyards, usually with saints she had never heard of. Some stood on low stone pillars, others were tucked away in small alcoves embedded in walls of old houses, often with bright plastic flowers attached to wrought-iron swirls that protected them. There were three she knew of on the way up to the Consolation Hermitage alone. So why was this one hidden for no-one to bow their head in front of? It didn't make sense.

She looked around her. Unless it was protecting something. Foreboding filled her. Had Geoffrey's near drowning been a warning? And what about the awful howls they had heard? She had never heard anything like it. She took the clamshell out of her jeans pocket and replaced it on the ledge, glad no-one could see how superstitious she was being.

Had whoever built the shrine known it was an ancient burial site? She was sure he or she had. It was impossible not to be affected by the tomb's silent sacredness.

She shone her torch on the objects on the ledge. They were probably talismans of some kind. A small shadow behind the statue caught her eye. *Another* talisman? How had they missed it? She gently lifted it out.

A delicate carving of a baby bird lay in her palm. It had no legs and its underbelly was rough and jagged; its beak was parted as if chirping for its mother.

She looked at the statue then back at the bird. What if…? She leant forward and balanced it on the broken shoulder. Perfect fit. The bird belonged there. Her fingers explored the cold stone and found another rough area on the left leg. What else had broken off? She shone the torch behind the statue but all she saw was the silver glint of spider web.

She swaddled the little bird in her jersey and carefully nestled it in the bottom of her backpack, glancing guiltily at the statue and silently promising to return the bird once Geoffrey had seen it. Maybe it would persuade him to stay.

She squeezed through the ivy barrier and began the long trek back to her car. The wind whipped her from behind as if chivvying her away. At last she glimpsed her red Golf through the trees and walked a little faster. Air conditioning was moments away.

Her heart lurched when she saw a fine sprig of wild jasmine tucked under her window wiper. Geoffrey's apology. Thank God for that. She plucked it free and scrambled for her phone to call him.

Two missed calls. From Matt.

She brushed the jasmine against her lips. Why was he calling? He had phoned often in the beginning, but she had never answered any of his calls. Not even when she desperately wanted to. Then he had outsmarted her and written to her old London address, knowing his letter would be forwarded to her. But she hadn't had the faintest idea how to explain why she had run away and so never replied.

Only curiosity made her listen to his voicemail now.

I'm coming to Collioure, and have my own transport and somewhere to stay. We need to talk, sweetheart. I'll call you when I get in on the 26th.

Five days away. She threw the phone onto the passenger seat, angry tears burning her eyes. How dare he come here? Collioure was her safe haven. The gears screeched as she raced down the dirt road. Damn him for crashing into her life. She gripped the steering wheel, knuckles white, and fumed the whole way home.

Village traffic hadn't eased since the morning chaos and after half an hour of trawling for parking, she finally managed to squeeze her car into a small gap between a farm truck and the cemetery wall. If the truck driver opened his door too wide, he would hit her car, but she didn't give a damn. The Golf was eight years old and another scratch wouldn't make any difference.

Inside the cemetery, towering poplar trees bowed like green monks in the wind. She felt tired and lonely, and on impulse drifted into the graveyard's open gates, pausing in front of the wide grey slab of Antonio Machado's tomb. Flowers and handwritten notes from his Spanish compatriots covered the grave.

Now here was someone who had been forced to run away, narrowly escaping Franco's hit squads, only to die within days of finding safety in Collioure. She had read his poems and one in particular still haunted her. Something about a heart that was filled with bees making honey from past failures.

Did her relationship with Matt count as failure? Would bees make honey from it? She doubted it. Nothing could sweeten the cowardly way she had left Matt.

She found a stone bench that was sheltered from the wind and watched a young man place a pot of white geraniums on a new grave. Freshly churned mounds of soil in cemeteries always moved her. She felt inexplicably tender towards the unknown grieving family, and faintly envious of the silent peace of being deep in the earth.

If only she could stop Matt from destroying her haven.

The village beggar's scraping shuffle broke into her thoughts. She had seen him here before, snoring on the bench, belly bursting out of his shirt and arm trailing on the ground. It was obviously nap time and she was on his bed. She stood up, nodded hello to him, and left.

She took the long way home via the wisteria-lined cobbled street where Jürgen and Catherine's studio was. The couple were the only friends she had in Collioure and were always ready with coffee, or a glass of champagne if Catherine had anything to do with it.

Jürgen was German but looked Italian with a wiry body and expressive face. Limp black hair drooped on either side of his red-rimmed glasses, and Raisin was always tempted to offer him a clip from her own hair to pin his back.

Catherine was a head taller than her husband and as boisterous as he was quiet; her guffaws barrelled up from her toes when she laughed. He painted, she marketed his work. He was busy with a painting of Collioure when Raisin walked in, his face so close to the canvas, it was a miracle he wasn't covered in paint.

'*Salut!*' Catherine greeted. 'We were just talking about you. How about dinner this weekend? Bring your brother. I want him to meet Annette, my friend from Paris. Where is he?'

'We hiked up to the Massane Tower but he was tired and wanted to go home,' she lied.

'Massane... I like it there,' Jürgen murmured, stippling fine red dots onto an indigo sky. 'There's a prehistoric cave in the valley next to it called *Grotte des Loups*.'

'They've been preparing it forever to make it safe for people to visit, but they're six months behind schedule and have decided to hold a special opening this Thursday for locals and the media to try to get more funding. We got you an invite... you're a local too, aren't you?' Catherine bubbled and gave Raisin a bright purple card with a golden wolf crest.

'That's wonderful, thank you. We saw the protest this morning, and I'd love to see what all the fuss is about,' Raisin said.

'Collioure hasn't seen an event like this in *years*. Mon Dieu, I could be on TV and become famous. The *Théâtre du Capitole* from Toulouse will perform La Bohème!' Catherine rolled her eyes back. 'But they're only doing that because the mayor's wife is the theatre director's sister, otherwise believe me, they wouldn't be seen dead in a small village like ours.'

'Won't the protest affect the launch?' Raisin asked.

'Not a chance. You know the French... red wine, baguette... a protest and they're happy,' Jürgen muttered.

Raisin was tempted to tell them about Geoffrey's fall in the river but didn't. He probably wouldn't want them to know.

'I should go. I've done more hiking today than I've done in ten years, and I desperately need a shower.'

'Don't forget to tell Geoffrey about Annette, and bring the invitation with you on Thursday. Without it, you won't get in,' Catherine said.

'What time and where should we meet you?'

'It starts at four, so come to the studio at three.'

At home, Raisin was disappointed to find Geoffrey's door closed. Was he still angry with her after all? She hoped not. It was half past nine and she was starving. She tapped on his door.

'Geoffrey?'

'Yes?'

'Can I come in?'

'Sure.'

She twisted the handle and pushed but the door wouldn't open.

'It's stuck,' she called.

She heard him walk across the room and turn the key. Pi squeezed out and leapt up against her.

'You *locked* it?'

'Sorry, I didn't realise.'

She held up the jasmine. 'Thanks.'

He smiled, eyes vulnerable and wary.

'Have you eaten?' she asked.

He shook his head. 'I'm not hungry.'

'Well I am. Come talk to me in the kitchen.' She showed him the invitation. 'It's from Catherine and Jürgen. They also asked us over for dinner on the weekend. She has a friend she wants you to meet.'

'No, Raisin.'

'Don't be silly! What if her friend is Ms Right?' she teased.

'No.'

'Suit yourself. But will you come to the cave launch with me?'

'As long as it isn't an excuse for a blind date.'

'Geoffrey...'

'I don't want to meet anyone.'

'You don't have to, but... can we talk about today... please?' she asked.

'There's nothing to talk about.'

She knew that look. He was switching off.

'Fine,' she sighed.

4

DESPITE SAYING HE wasn't hungry, he ate two slices of her spinach and feta quiche. She didn't tell him about the bird sculpture in her backpack.

'I left my cap in the cave,' he said.

'We can go back and look for it if you like.'

'No thanks, I'm not exactly in a rush to go there again. It's just a bloody hat anyway.'

She studied his shuttered face and longed for the easy closeness of their childhood, before Mum and Dad's divorce and Geoffrey went to live with Dad. Their sudden disappearance had created a hole so big she could still feel the fog thick pain.

'Shall we go for a walk? With all the clouds coming in, the sunset will be beautiful.'

She willed him to say yes.

'Okay,' he shrugged.

Gossamer clouds draped the sky in watermelon pink as they strolled along the narrow peninsula that stretched out into the sea from the beach. They sat with their backs against the warm stone wall of the little chapel and watched the day disappear. Pi barked at the seagulls that cackled above them on the belfry.

Geoffrey pointed to the mountains behind the village.

'There's a hike up to a peak called *Pic de Sailfort* that I'm keen to do. It goes over the ridge behind the towers there…'

'Sounds a bit too far for me,' she laughed.

'Well… uhm… actually Raisin, I was thinking of doing it alone.'

She didn't want to do the damn hike but hated that she wasn't invited.

'Okay,' she murmured.

'It'll mean spending the night in a hiker's hut and mountain refuges are usually pretty grim. Believe me, you wouldn't like it.'

'So much for being here to spend time with me.'

He whistled for Pi.

'Don't be like that, Raisin. You know me and mountains. And anyway, we were together today.'

'*Today* was a disaster.'

'I've got two more weeks here. There's loads of things we can still do together... like go to that *Grotte des Loups* thing.'

'What about going back to the dolmen?'

'That too. It's just the caves I'm not keen on.'

She smiled at him, unsettled. How could he shift so quickly from shutting down to being so nice to her?

'We should get back so I can start dinner. It's tuna, your favourite,' she said.

Laughter and holiday excitement bubbled from the crowded cafés and walkway along Boramar Beach. Two toddlers chasing each other almost crashed into Raisin. She laughed and sprang out of their way.

'I didn't tell you. Matt called today... he's coming to Collioure.'

'*Here*? I thought you said the two of you had broken up?'

'We have.'

'Maybe I'll do the hike the day he arrives so you can be on your own with him.'

'Don't you dare. I'm going to need you right next to me.'

'You'll be better off without me; and quite frankly, if things are going to be strained, I don't want to be around.'

'What if I ask you to be there... for *me*? Or is that too needy for you?'

'It is a bit but...'

'Damn you Geoffrey!'

He caught her arm.

'Before you throw a tantrum, let me finish what I was going to say. Maybe it *is* a bit needy, but not *too* needy. I'll be there. I can do that for you.'

She gave him a crooked smile. 'I hate it when we fight.'

'We don't fight; we read different books.'

'Yours must be *Gone With the Wind*…'

'And yours *Catch-22*…'

'*Catch-22*? How do you get to that?' she grinned.

'You do *and* you don't want Matt here…'

'Ouch.'

'So why is he coming here anyway?'

She linked arms with him. 'Can we change the subject?'

He looked like he was about to pull away but then he relaxed.

'Glad I'm not the only Radcliffe who isn't an open book.'

'So when will you do the hike?'

'Don't worry, I'll do the walk tomorrow… long before he gets here,' he promised.

'Four days is hardly *long*,' she groaned.

Fresh croissants poked out of a torn packet on the counter, and a spluttering stove-top espresso machine oozed coffee aromas into the kitchen when she came down the next morning. A large hiking map covered the table.

'Nice touch,' she yawned, eyeing the bakery bag.

'I also bought baguettes for our hike.'

'Our?'

He traced his finger over the map.

'We go past the Massane Tower then head for the refuge. It'll take most of the day, but we'll have lots of stops along the way. How does that sound?'

Her heart leapt. 'But I thought…?'

'So did I, but I changed my mind.' He smiled sheepishly. 'So? Can those short legs of yours walk that far?'

'You're serious? Of *course* they can. They'll walk a whole *week* if they have to!'

'Good. The weather fundis say it's going to be hot, so use sun block and wear a hat. Go get ready!'

They set off with enough food for three meals and four bottles of water. Even though it was thirty-two degrees with a cloudless sky, he made her pack a jersey.

'If the wind comes up or it rains, you'll need it. We can't risk it, not even in the middle of summer,' he warned.

An hour later they were on the footpath below the Massane Tower. Purple flowers on spiky stems burst onto the track, and the biggest bees Raisin had ever seen hovered above their stamens. If Matt was here, he would be describing how light or dark the colour of their honey was. She groaned and pushed him out of her mind.

Just after midday, they crossed the scrubland that sprawled up to the grassy shoulder of *Pic de Sailfort*. A hawk dipped and twisted in the sky and small unseen animals scurried in the undergrowth.

The sun scorched her skin through her shirt and her legs ached. So much for having lots of breaks, she was exhausted and they weren't even halfway.

The path ran parallel to a rickety fence whose poles veered at zigzag angles. A small sign announced they were on the GR10 hiking path, 980 metres above sea level. She grunted with relief when Geoffrey stopped to take photos. She wiped her face and gulped down lukewarm water.

Toffee coloured cows grazed on the other side of the fence; their clanging bells made her feel she was in a Swiss postcard. Geoffrey looked up from his camera.

'It's beautiful here. When I show my students these shots they'll never believe this kind of wildness exists in France.'

'I wish I hadn't lost my bloody camera. You'll have to give me copies of your photos before you leave.' She pointed to a building in the far distance. 'Is that a ruin?'

'Looks like an old farmhouse.' He zoomed his lens closer. 'There's washing on the line… someone must live there.'

'Damn isolated. I can't even see a road.'

'Strange… there are cages. Maybe they're breeders.' He gave a wistful sigh. 'They're living my dream. Remember how we used to set up camp near the river and stay there for days?'

'You see! You *do* miss the farm! Remember when we stayed at that bush camp near Cape St Francis for two weeks?'

'Our last holiday together,' he nodded.

'Our *only* holiday together. Remember that Afrikaans girl you met there?'

'What about the boy from that posh family you fell for? You carried on seeing him in Cape Town, didn't you?'

'The whole summer, then he wanted me to move in and I bolted.'

'Why don't you want kids?'

'Where did *that* come from?'

'You've never stopped bolting, Raisin. Is that what happened with you and Matt? Too much commitment?'

'I just don't want kids.'

'But why? What happened to make you like that?'

'Nothing *happened*.'

'Having yourself sterilised is pretty drastic.'

'You make it sound terrible.'

'Then explain it to me.'

His expression was haunted, and her chest tightened at the fragility she saw there. She swallowed a flippant reply.

'It just frightens me,' she admitted.

Pi nuzzled Geoffrey's hand. He pushed the dog aside.

'Why?'

'I'm scared I won't be able to protect them.'

His face twitched then he looked away and dropped his backpack on the ground.

'It's one o'clock… let's stop and eat.'

His switch-off felt like a slap. She watched him unpack their picnic things, his back hunched away from her. What had she said now? She despaired of ever understanding him. He gave her half a baguette. Pi ran up to her, tongue lolling. She laughed despite herself and threw him a chunk.

'Greedy bugger.'

Geoffrey glanced at her and smiled. Raisin hid her hurt.

Challenging him would only push him further away. She lay back and reached up to touch one of the bright yellow flowers that flared from the paddle-shaped leaves of a dense tangled cactus next to her.

'*Opuntia maxima*,' she murmured.

'He was good for you, you know.'

She knew exactly who he meant. 'Who was?'

'Here's a clue... he taught you the names of trees and plants. Do you miss him?'

'Why are we talking about *my* love life? What about yours?'

He sliced the cheese and layered pieces on his baguette. Pi thumped his tail in anticipation.

'I'm a numbers man... my life's boring. How are your legs?'

'My legs are sore but my ears aren't. Tell me about your love life.'

A deep growl broke their banter. They both jerked upright. A flash of brown flew past the cactus. Pi yelped and ran away.

'Goddamn... a fucking wolf. Don't move!' Geoffrey hissed.

They stared open-mouthed at the emaciated animal. It stood firm, fearless eyes fixed on them. It looked dangerously hungry. Geoffrey inched towards it.

'Geoffrey, for God's sake! What are you doing?'

The wolf snarled. Geoffrey dropped to his haunches. The wolf arched its back, growling angrily.

'Move away, Raisin.'

'*You* move away! Are you mad?'

'Shut up... you're making it worse.'

The wolf lunged forward. Geoffrey retreated a step then remained still. Raisin held her breath. What on earth was he doing? The wolf didn't move, panting heavily. Geoffrey lowered both hands to the ground and held eye contact with the animal. It began to pace, eyes fierce, jaws snapping in agitation.

'Get the hell away, Geoffrey!' Raisin whispered furiously.

He glared her into silence then slowly opened his hand, left his sandwich on the ground, and crept back two steps. The wolf pawed the ground, eyes on the food.

'Take it,' Geoffrey urged softly.

It darted forward, snatched the sandwich and bolted off, tail flying like an arrow.

'Wow…' he gulped.

Raisin crumpled to the ground, head on her knees.

'It could have killed you.'

'Did you see how thin it was? It wouldn't have had the strength to take me on. It probably hasn't eaten in days.'

'And starving animals are safe? Let's get out of here.'

Before they left, Geoffrey cut a plastic bottle in two and filled the bottom half with water. Pi slunk out from his hiding place and nuzzled the bottle. Geoffrey pushed him away.

'Drink from your own bowl, boy.'

'I had no idea there were wolves here,' Raisin said nervously.

'Me neither. I wonder where the hell it came from?'

'Do we have much further to go? I hate the idea of that thing being out here with us.'

He opened his map and showed her the route they still had to walk.

'We go through a forest then along a contour path till we get to the next peak, *Col des Emigrants*. After that we walk along this ridge to the refuge. I don't think it'll follow us.'

'I damn well hope not.'

They helped each other put on the backpacks then set out again. Craggy peaks crinkled the skyline, and down in the valley, soft waves of forest folded into each other. The only sound was the whirring cric-crac of cicadas, even the birds seemed to be resting in the heat.

Pi patrolled up and down, yapping at nothing, then running back to Geoffrey for comfort.

Raisin jumped at every crackle and kept a sharp eye on the bush. Being confronted by a wild animal was what she expected back home, not here in civilised France. She poured water onto her front to keep cool. The refuge couldn't come soon enough.

They reached it just before eight thirty. Their accommodation was a poor man's hut with a billionaire's view. The Mediterranean shimmered like molten gold on the horizon.

'This is spectacular,' she sighed.

'Wait till you see where you're going to sleep before you get too excited,' he warned, pushing open the door.

Inside were two metal bunk beds without mattresses and a melamine table with matching blue chairs. Graffiti, mostly names and dates, covered the walls and ceiling. Raisin pulled a face. The hut stank of urine. What the hell was she doing here? Pi jumped onto a bunk, curled up and dropped his head on his paws.

She took out the picnic dinner she had prepared at home while he dragged two chairs outside.

'I hope the wolf survives,' he frowned.

'Do you think there could be others?'

'I don't think so. Maybe it escaped from somewhere. It certainly didn't look like an animal thriving in its domain.'

'You're weird... the dark frightens you but a rabid animal doesn't.'

'Hardly rabid.'

'How come you still hate the dark so much?'

'How come you still ask so many stupid questions?'

'Why can't we ever talk about you, without you getting defensive?'

'I'm going to join Pi.'

She watched him leave, angry with herself for goading him. Why couldn't she be satisfied with what he could give her?

Because he was like the wolf, not thriving in his domain, and she was worried about him.

5

THE *GROTTE DES Loups* cocktail party was on a wide deck that smelled of freshly cut timber and that stretched out in front of a massive cavern that looked gouged out of the mountain by the gods. A white tarpaulin sagged above the guests, protecting them from the sun but not from the heat that clung to their skin like molasses.

Raisin bundled her hair in a high ponytail. 'I'm hot.'

'I'm thirsty. It's ridiculous that we've only got water to drink,' Catherine grumbled.

A slender red ribbon prohibited access to the shade of the gaping overhang, and worse, to the drinks table. A tall woman with a peacock feather hat strutted between the guests, reassuring everyone in a high-pitched voice that the mayor would arrive soon.

'Can't bear that woman,' Catherine muttered. 'She's the mayor's secretary and her father owns the village butchery. She thinks she runs the village.'

She edged next to the ribbon and tested it with a quick tug.

'Don't even think about it,' Jürgen warned.

'It was supposed to start an hour ago. They should at least let us stand in the shade. These ridiculous tarpaulins do nothing against the heat.'

'We all know it's the champagne you're after, *chérie.*'

Agitated drumbeats and strident cries rumbled in the background. The protestors had arrived long before the guests and blocked the way to the cave, each with a red no-entry sign painted on their foreheads. A double row of gendarmes, elbows linked, did their best to keep them away.

'Raisin said you saw a wolf on Monday and that you tried to feed it. *Quelle horreur!*' Catherine said to Geoffrey.

'It was just as terrified as us and looked on death's door. I had no idea there were wolves here.'

'There are some on the Spanish side of the Pyrenees but they probably know that a French shepherd would shoot them in a heartbeat,' Jürgen said.

'Is there anyone I can contact to help save it? An animal rescue organisation like the SPCA?'

'No chance of that. No-one's going to bother to help a wolf in this area. Be happy it's not winter and hunting season.'

'*Monsieur le Maire* will be here in fifteen minutes!' the secretary clucked.

'He's *always* late. It's a French thing,' Jürgen muttered.

The promised deadline dragged into thirty minutes then forty. Someone snapped the ribbon in two and scooped up glasses and a champagne bottle. Catherine was quick to follow.

'Hallelujah!' she laughed.

Two red-faced gendarmes jostled past the demonstrators. The mayor's secretary teetered towards them on her silver heels and they exchanged urgent whispers. The news spread quickly. The mayor was late because his young son wasn't home from school.

'*Ridiculous* reason,' Catherine scoffed.

'It's late, I'd also be worried,' Raisin said.

'Raisin's right. I hope he's okay,' Geoffrey said.

'Of course he is! It's summer... he's out playing football with friends. Believe me, the *real* reason our beloved mayor is late is because he's lingering over lunch.'

At last Monsieur Pujol arrived with an entourage of five people, waving his arms in apology and thrusting his belly out as he swept onto the deck.

'*Desolé! Désolé!*' he called.

'He doesn't look very *désolé* to me,' muttered Catherine.

The mayor took a pair of golden scissors from the secretary and made a show of snipping the already broken ribbon. The guests laughed politely and corks rocketed into the air.

'I'm beginning to feel dizzy. I don't know if I should have more champagne,' Raisin giggled.

'A girl can *never* have too many bubbles. It's good for our skin,' Catherine admonished. 'Oh look... they're getting ready to let us in.'

They were herded into eight groups and told to wait their turn near a grey steel door that looked more suited to protecting a Swiss vault than a Pyrenean cave. Catherine couldn't hide her irritation when she realised the groups were leaving at ten minute intervals.

'At this rate it'll be *another* hour before it's our turn,' she grumbled.

'Patience, *ma belle*, patience,' Jürgen sighed.

'More champagne anyone?' Raisin asked.

'I thought you said you'd had enough?' Geoffrey said.

'Didn't you hear Catherine? Champagne's good for me. Would you like a glass?' Raisin asked an elderly woman in their group.

'Thank you dear, I will. It's my grandson's birthday today.'

The youngster squirmed in embarrassment. Catherine waved her glass at Raisin.

'Marc and Etienne here are at university with our delicious guide and they have nothing to drink! *Quelle catastrophe!*'

'Happy to help,' Raisin said with a flirty flourish of the bottle.

'They play rugby for Toulouse. Say *bonjour* to our new friends.'

'*Bonjour*,' Raisin parroted.

'*Enchanté*, I'm Marc.'

'Hello Marc. Kiss my hand otherwise I won't believe I'm in France,' she bantered.

She filled their glasses, grinning cheekily, then offered champagne to a blond Nordic-looking couple.

'Thank you,' they said in unison.

Raisin eyed the last member of their group, a thin man with thick greasy hair who was picking his fingernails. He looked up and scowled. She hurried away. If he wanted champagne, he'd have to be a lot more pleasant than that. Their guide began to hand out small green torches.

'*Bonjour*, I'm Jean-Philippe. Please use these only when I say so, and *s'il vous plaît*, no photos... not even without a flash. *On y va?* Let's go.'

A sharp chill nipped Raisin's skin as he pulled open the metal door to a long dark passageway that disappeared deep into the rock. Raisin glanced at Geoffrey. He was fiddling with the copper bangle on his wrist. *I'll be fine*, his frown said when he caught her eye. She hoped so.

Curved chisel marks covered the walls in tiny half-moons. The door slammed after them and they were plunged into darkness. Jean-Philipp's torch snapped on.

'Thank fuck,' Geoffrey muttered under his breath.

Raisin moved closer to him and prayed there would be enough light along the way for him. Their footsteps were soundless as they walked through the icy tunnel.

'This access stays closed to maintain the temperature inside at a certain level. Too much variance will damage the paintings. It's also why we'll be controlling how many visitors are allowed inside every day,' Jean-Philippe explained.

A second door opened onto a small cave that was barely big enough for the twelve of them. Thin stalactites hung like lances from the ceiling.

'Well what do you know? An ancient execution chamber,' Etienne the student joked. 'Imagine if they broke off and impaled us.'

Geoffrey stiffened. Raisin began to worry. If the rest of the visit was also in dark confined places, Geoffrey would never last. The greasy-haired man stood close by, looking bored. She edged away. He smelled as unwashed as he looked.

'There are four kilometres of tunnels and caves in the Massane subterranean system but only very little of it will be available to the public when the caves are officially opened,' Jean-Philippe explained. He aimed his torch at the black opening in the opposite wall. 'The tunnel we're about to go into was only half a metre high before we made it bigger. That means our prehistoric predecessors crawled into it on their stomachs.'

Raisin couldn't imagine anything worse. The passageway she and Geoffrey had struggled through at the back of the dolmen had been claustrophobic enough. She wondered if Jean-Philippe knew about the dolmen.

'How would cavemen have known where to go?' Marc asked.

'A cavewomen probably showed them the way,' Catherine grinned.

'We believe they went underground to connect with the spirit world, and that they knew the way intuitively,' Jean-Philippe replied. 'There were no maps, no compasses. Their only light source was probably a receptacle carved out of stone and filled with animal fat for fuel.'

'Do any maps exist of the tunnels today?' Raisin asked.

'They're still in the early stages of being drawn up. But the plan is to chart every nook and cranny down here.'

Raisin exchanged glances with Geoffrey and shook her head. She had managed to talk Geoffrey out of reporting their dolmen, and now wasn't the time to bring it up.

'What's on the wall next to the tunnel?' Catherine asked.

'The first example of shamanic activity. You may approach it but please don't touch,' Jean-Philippe said.

Clusters of red handprints covered the rockface in a riot of wide-splayed fingers. Raisin lifted her hand. Would it match any of the prints?

'He said don't touch,' Geoffrey whispered.

'Why shamanic activity?' the Nordic man asked.

'The most recent theory is that cave art was made during deep trance, and that it represents what shamans saw and experienced while hallucinating.'

'The hands look like they're reaching for something,' Raisin murmured.

'Except there's no *they*,' Jean-Philippe said. 'We believe the prints were made by one person… a woman.'

Raisin went cold. Had *her* woman done them? She wanted to linger but Geoffrey insisted that she stayed with him. They walked in single file down a tunnel that curved to the left then fell into a steep descent. The steel handrail was damp and cold. Geoffrey's laboured breathing chugged in front of her. She hadn't realised they would go so deep into the mountain.

Ten minutes later, the tunnel flared open into a cave so big it didn't seem possible they were still underground.

'Welcome to the *Galerie des Mains*... Gallery of Hands,' Jean-Philippe announced.

Rock ledges fanned out like horizontal pleats up the cave wall, and ivory columns of hardened calcium soared around them like an enchanted forest. Soft orange lights played tricks with shadows and shapes.

'Are you okay?' she asked Geoffrey.

He nodded but didn't make eye contact. She kept close to him and hoped the lights would stay on. A pungent stink from the sullen outsider wafted her way. She gave him an irritated glance. Her eyes widened. He was taking photos. It was the first time he had shown any interest in the visit.

'We will now go up the stairway to see the paintings,' Jean-Philippe said.

The man slicked his hair behind his ears and casually slid the camera out of sight. If she caught him doing it again, she would say something.

Aluminium steps zigzagged up the rockface like a modern fire escape. The man pushed past Raisin and Catherine.

'*Manners*,' Catherine snapped.

Raisin waited until his filthy sandals and cracked heels were out of sight before she followed. Halfway up, the group stalled and she caught up with him. She gasped in shock. A tattoo blazed on his ankle:

He was one of the protesters. How the hell had he slipped past the police at the cocktail party? As though sensing her attention, he whipped his head back. She turned and pretended to say something to Catherine. The group began to move again and he was swept up with them, his carcass stink trailing after him. She breathed through her mouth and followed nervously.

They climbed onto a wide balcony whose gleaming metal looked out of place against the craggy underground rock. Two thin railings shielded them from a twenty metre drop.

'As you can see, there are many animals in this panel of paintings, but the cave is called the *Galerie des Mains* because the handprints outnumber the animals,' Jean-Philippe explained.

Raisin edged towards Geoffrey to tell him about the tattoo. He waved her away.

'I'm fine,' he whispered.

Before she could say anything else, Jean-Philippe asked them to switch off their torches and warned that he would temporarily be briefly switching off the cave lights.

'I want you to feel the full impact of what early man experienced.'

One by one torch lights snapped off. Water dripped somewhere close by. The man's stench enveloped Raisin like dirty smog. Geoffrey squeezed her hand.

Soft blue light flooded the rockface in front of them. Animals teemed over its surface... bison, horses, goats and deer. Some floated alone, others were layered on top of each other like ancient echoes. Three figures with tiny beaked heads and human torsos clustered together on the right. Long parallel spikes stuck out of their bodies like arrows. Red dots and black spirals swirled in between.

There were red handprints everywhere, alone, interlinked, overlapping, covering a flank, a face, a limb.

Raisin moved closer, entranced. Which of the hand prints belonged to her tribeswoman?

'Thanks to the presence of charcoal in some of the pigments, we've been able to carbon-date the work to twenty-five thousand years ago. That's five times older than the pyramids.'

The young boy whispered something to his grandmother.

'My grandson would like to know how they got this high without stairs?' she asked.

'Good question, but no-one knows,' Jean-Philippe replied.

The soft whir of a camera lens buzzed over his voice and Raisin was blinded by a bright flare. The tattooed man again! Taking photos without bothering to hide what he was doing.

'No photos! No flash! It's very bad for the paintings,' Jean-Philippe shouted.

Angry murmurs spread through the group. Raisin leant close to Geoffrey.

'I was trying to tell you that he's got a tattoo like that woman we saw at the protest,' she whispered.

Jean-Philippe held out his hand for the camera.

'I'll take that from you.'

The man gave a belligerent scowl and tried to leave but Jean-Philippe blocked his way.

'Camera, please.'

'Make me,' he sneered.

'Photos are forbidden for the protection of the paintings.'

'You think they belong to you?'

'He's taken other photos,' Raisin murmured.

'Shut up, bitch.'

'Hey!' Geoffrey said.

'Butt out, fuck face.'

The grandmother gasped and scrambled to the stairway with her grandson.

'Give me the camera,' Jean-Philippe said quietly.

'Fuck you.'

'He took other photos,' Raisin repeated loudly.

'Who asked you, bitch?'

Geoffrey strode up to him and gripped his shoulder.

'That's my sister you're talking about.'

'Fuck her.'

Geoffrey punched his face. The man crashed to the ground; his torch rolled over the ledge, smashing on the rocks below. Geoffrey kicked him manically.

'Geoffrey! Stop!' Raisin cried.

Jean-Philippe pushed himself between the two men.

'Please, *stop*! We're too high up.' He turned to his friends. 'Marc, Etienne, get everyone down.'

'Make him apologise,' Geoffrey snapped.

'It's fine Geoffrey… I don't *want* an apology.'

The man lunged for Geoffrey. 'Fucking prick!'

Geoffrey hammered his torch against the man's head but Jean-Philippe's arm shot up and broke the blow. Raisin yanked Geoffrey away. The man punched Jean-Philippe. The guide doubled over, dragging the man's wrist down with him. They wrestled frantically, bouncing against the flimsy barrier. Geoffrey groped for the man's ankle but he slammed his heel forward and pulled away. Jean-Philippe rolled free. Geoffrey and the man tumbled dangerously close to the edge.

'They're going to fall!' Catherine screamed from below.

'Geoffrey! Stop! For God's sake! *Stop*!'

Geoffrey gripped the man's shirt and head-butted him. Once. Twice. Three times. The man collapsed, arm sliding under the railing and over the edge. Geoffrey heaved for air, then he straightened up and kicked the fallen man. He floundered like a ragdoll. Jean-Philippe staggered to his feet and grabbed Geoffrey's waist.

'Calm down,' he panted.

'Leave me alone!'

'Marc! Etienne! Help me!'

Tears streamed down Raisin's face. If this was Geoffrey's way of protecting her, she didn't want it.

'Apologise. He must apologise,' Geoffrey ranted.

'I don't want him to,' she sobbed.

Marc and Etienne ran up the stairs and rugby-tackled the man.

'Go down with your sister,' Jean-Philippe instructed Geoffrey.

'Come with me,' Raisin begged.

Geoffrey wiped his forehead and stared at the blood on his hand. He removed his belt and threw it on the ground.

'Tie him up. He's dangerous.'

Only when Etienne had tightened the belt around the man's wrists did Geoffrey agree to let Jean-Philippe escort him and Raisin off the balcony. Raisin refused to look at him. This raging lunatic wasn't her brother. What the hell had happened to make him so out-of-control angry?

'Fucking donkey faggots! You have no right!' the man yelled as Marc and Etienne pulled him down the stairs.

The young boy buried his head in his grandmother's waist. The Nordic couple looked terrified. Raisin stood nervously behind Geoffrey and Jean-Philippe.

'Please can we leave? My grandson's scared,' the grandmother asked shakily.

'I'm sorry but we can't break up the group until the next guide arrives. It won't be long.'

The man screamed in protest. He aimed a wild karate kick at Geoffrey.

'You and your whore-bitch sister will rot on Earth!'

Marc hooked his foot around his legs and threw him to the ground.

'Enough, *tais-toi*! Shut up!'

'Quirinus will condemn you to *hell on Earth*!'

'Okay, that's it,' Marc snapped and yanked him to the other side of the cave.

'I'm going to have to reduce the lights to control the temperature in here, just until the next group arrives,' Jean-Philippe announced.

The young boy sobbed hysterically. Tears burned Raisin's eyes. She glanced at Geoffrey sitting on the bottom step, face in his palms.

For the first time in months, she longed for Matt.

6

THE SUBDUED LIGHTING bathed the crags and crevices of the rockface in soft amber and turned the metal stairway into shimmering gold. A magical underground palace. Under any other circumstance, Raisin would have been enthralled but she was desperate to leave. The drip-drip of water somewhere in the back worked on her nerves, and even though the man's belligerent cries had dwindled into angry mumbles, she wished Jean-Philippe would ram something in his mouth to keep him quiet.

'I can hear the next group,' someone whispered.

Torchlight danced in the tunnel opening then swung into the cave and a young woman appeared. She stopped when she saw them, startled. Her group clustered behind her like curious schoolchildren.

'*Mon Dieu*! Why are you still here? Jean-Philippe…?'

He moved out of the shadows. 'I'm here, Angeline.'

'What's wrong? Why haven't you left?'

'We had a problem with a… uh… guest who needs to be taken to the gendarmerie. Please could my group go with you to the main cave? I'll be back as soon as possible.' He signalled to Geoffrey. 'You should come with me to have your injuries seen to.'

'That's okay. I'm not hurt.'

'No, you should go. I'll come with you,' Raisin said.

'I'm fine.'

'You're still bleeding.'

'Surface cuts… I've had worse.' He glanced at the man. 'If I leave, he wins.'

'I need to get out of here, Geoffrey.'

'If you go that *connard* will have ruined our evening,' Catherine said.

Raisin reluctantly let herself be persuaded. Geoffrey refused to make eye contact with her. She didn't know if he was angry or embarrassed.

'Attention everyone!' Angeline called. 'Please notice the ground and the walls of the next tunnel... they were worn smooth by an underground river hundreds of millennia ago. We will eventually put a wooden walkway here so please be careful as it will be slippery. Follow me, *s'il vous plaît*.'

They entered a wide oval passageway whose ceiling bristled with tiny stalactites. The colour of the rock reminded Raisin of the clamshell in the dolmen. She lagged near the back with Geoffrey.

'Are you okay? How is your face?' she ventured.

'Fine.'

She didn't know what else to say. Would she ever see the smiley, jokey big brother she had worshipped again?

They arrived at an intersection of several dark passages and Angeline counted their heads as she shepherded them into the widest tunnel on the left. They began a rapid plunge into the mountain. Raisin wrapped her arms around herself and hoped their young guide knew the way. The ceiling split into a deep fissure but closed up again around the next corner then dipped so low the Nordic man and Geoffrey had to stoop. The passageway twisted past another junction and ended abruptly in a wall of rock.

'Are we there?' Catherine asked hopefully.

'*Non, non!*' Angeline said, putting her hand on a wide metal rung. 'We've reached the Sanctuary Steps.'

'More like Steps to Hell, if you ask me,' Catherine muttered.

Thirteen rust-red rungs formed a ladder straight up the rockface. Raisin was tempted to ask why they weren't new like the platform and stairway in the *Galerie des Mains*. Angeline ran her torchlight up the ladder.

'The *Grotte des Loups* isn't far from here. These rungs stop at a deep ledge that opens into the tunnel that will take us right to the main cave. I'll go first.'

The little boy stopped halfway up and broke into sobs.

'Come *chéri,* just a little further,' his grandmother cajoled.

'I can't,' he whimpered.

Raisin watched Geoffrey scoot after him and coax him to the ledge, one slow rung at a time. At the top, his grandmother bundled him against her and all three disappeared from sight. Raisin put her hand on a cold rung and paused. Behind her, the tunnel vanished into blackness, and above her, just an eerie glow burned from everyone's torches. No friendly face appeared to see if she was alright. She scowled nervously and slid her torch into her jeans pocket. The rockface came alive in the broken light. Small outcrops turned into beetles. Cavities darkened into eye sockets. The air felt thicker, colder. She climbed up the rungs, breathing hard. Damn Geoffrey. She heard a burr of voices and climbed faster. What if they forgot about her? She grinned sheepishly when she reached the ledge and found them crowded around the youngster. Angeline looked up.

'*Bon,* we're all here. Let's go,' she said.

'Would you like a piggy-back?' Geoffrey asked the child.

He nodded gratefully. Raisin felt a pinch of envy when Geoffrey hoisted him onto his shoulders.

They walked along a narrow high tunnel that smelled of stale water. Slimy moss made the ground difficult to walk on and Raisin had to grip the walls for support. A long line of heads stretched out in front of her but barely anyone spoke. Even Catherine seemed to have lost her voice.

'Ladies and Gentleman... the *Grotte des Loups!*' Angeline announced.

Raisin gaped at the candlelit cave. It was bigger than the biggest cathedral she had seen. A secret sanctuary hidden in the earth. Her anxiety eased. No wonder ancient man sought out this magical place.

Three young women in floaty dresses of pale gold lace played flutes next to a stalagmite as thick as a baobab tree. Most of the back wall was hidden behind purple velvet drapes. Raisin's pulse quickened. The wolf paintings were hidden behind. She squeezed Geoffrey's arm.

'I'm glad we didn't leave,' she whispered.

Part of her longed to talk to him about his attack on the tattooed man, but his eyes were wary and she was still too upset to broach the subject. At least he was smiling. They joined the other groups under an elaborate filigree gazebo. Fruit baskets and large wooden platters with anchovy toasts, *saucisson* and olives filled a table covered in purple organza.

Raisin accepted champagne from a loin-clothed waiter and let the cave's splendour wash over her.

'It's beautiful, isn't it?' Catherine murmured.

'I'm amazed anyone ventured this deep into the mountain, without the security of a single piece of modern equipment!'

'Courage is relative, *chérie*.' She pointed to Geoffrey with her champagne flute. 'Is he okay?'

'Honestly? I haven't a clue. I've never seen him like that before.'

She felt close to tears.

'He was protecting you. That's what brothers do. The man was a pig and deserved what he got.'

'He scared me, Catherine.'

'Wait until Annette hears what a hero he is!'

'He's not a hero and please don't say anything to him about her. He doesn't want to meet her.'

'Leave it to me. He won't even know he's meeting her.' She linked arms with Raisin. 'Looks like they want us to sit down. Where are the boys?'

The flautists played their last notes and voices turned into whispers. Flickering candles were the only lights. As the mayor marched solemnly to the front, the musicians picked up their instruments again.

'Chopin,' Geoffrey murmured.

The music spun into an excited crescendo. Raisin's heart pounded. Love, fear, anger faded in and out. She felt lightheaded and fearful. The music escalated, exploding in her ears. The cave grew and grew until it reached eternity. She shut her eyes and let it swallow her.

Orange, purple and yellow lines whirled around her, curving into snakes with flared heads and gaping mouths. The serpents twisted into circles, then planets. Solar systems hurtled through her body. She saw blurs of purple and gold then the mayor's face pulled into focus. She clutched the chair as his face became the dishevelled face of a woman. Something touched her knee. She blinked hard, panicked.

The tribeswoman knelt at her side, green eyes burning. Her blond hair curtained her face and she crouched low under a bulky brown pelt. Raisin glanced around anxiously. No-one had noticed her. The woman beckoned with a dirt-streaked hand and loped to the front. Raisin stood to follow. Geoffrey pulled her down.

'What the *hell* are you doing?'

She stared at him. Bright stage lights flooded the cave wall and the purple velvet slowly sank to the ground in thick folds. She slumped in her seat. Chairs scraped. People jumped to their feet. The applause was deafening. Raisin dug her fingers into her temples. The woman was gone.

'Ladies and gentlemen, *voilà* the *pièce de résistance* of the *Grotte des Loups!*' the mayor shouted.

Animals and handprints covered the rockface in front of them. Raisin's eyes locked onto a single black wolf in the middle of the fresco. Its legs were stretched in full running stride, its jaws wide, tail high as it leapt over a dark cave-like hollow. Smaller wolves ran below and above it, heads tilted skywards and howling. Red handprints shivered with energy as if trying to catch them.

Raisin went cold with certainty. The hands belonged to her tribeswoman. She scanned the cave. *What do you want from me?*

'Feel free to look but please don't touch. The paintings are fragile,' the mayor cautioned.

Raisin stumbled closer, mesmerised.

'I know it's you,' she whispered.

You, you, you, the cave echoed back.

Her body felt on fire. Drumbeats and voices rang in her ears. She lifted her hands and gently pressed them over the prints on the rockface.

'Are you mad?' Geoffrey snapped.

She jumped back, rubbed her eyes.

'Yes... no... I... I think these handprints were done by the same woman who did the ones in the dolmen cave.'

She traced their outline with her finger. He yanked her hand away.

'What woman? You're pissed.'

'No, I'm serious. I keep seeing the face of a woman... give me your notebook, I'll draw her for you.'

He muttered under his breath, but flipped it to an empty page and gave it to her. She pulled a pencil from her handbag.

'Her forehead is broad, like this, but it doesn't slope back like you see in books.' She saw curiosity flicker in his eyes. 'She has long ragtag blond hair. Her nose is normal... thin like mine, but her jaw is square and juts forward. Her teeth are much bigger than mine. She seemed so damn real...'

Catherine plucked the drawing out of her hand.

'*Who* seemed real, *ma belle*?' she laughed.

Raisin took the notebook back with a casual smile.

'It's nothing. I was just describing... a dream I had.'

'Dreams have meanings. They are messages from your subconscious and you should *always* try to understand them. What was it?'

Raisin hesitated.

'Come on... I'm good at interpreting them.'

'It was nothing. I saw a woman put handprints on a cave wall. Then later I saw her again, but she ran off before I could speak to her.'

'Ah *mon dieu*, that's easy! It's your inner wild woman telling you to express yourself to the outside world!'

'Don't listen to her. She always does this when she's had too much champagne,' Jürgen said.

'Now if it was *my* dream... a wild-haired caveman would be seducing me in a rock shelter filled with candles and furs,' Catherine said dreamily.

'And when he drags you by the hair?' Jürgen teased.

Raisin slipped the drawing into her handbag. Catherine was right, she badly needed to understand what it meant but she didn't have a clue where to start.

'Is that Jean-Philippe coming towards us?' Geoffrey said. 'Why has he brought the police here?'

The guide looked worried as he introduced the two gendarmes with him.

'These are Officers Cardona and Fabre. They would like to have a word with you, *s'il vous plaît*. I'm afraid our man got away.'

'How do you mean, *got away*?' Geoffrey snapped.

'*C'est pas possible*! There were *two* of you and only *one* of him!' Catherine exclaimed.

'He said he was sick and when we stopped for him, he broke free and disappeared into a tunnel. God only knows if he'll ever come out of there alive. It's a maze down here. But I did get his camera off him.'

He held up a small Canon digital.

'That looks like *mine*!' Raisin exclaimed.

'It can't be. I took it from him myself,' Jean-Philippe said.

She looped her fingers through the silver strap. It looked and felt exactly like hers. She flicked through the images the man had taken of the cave then held up a photo of Geoffrey and Pi.

'Look… my brother and his dog! It's definitely mine.'

'How on earth did he get his hands on it?' Fabre said.

'I lost it on Sunday during the protest.'

'Do you see him there?' Cardona asked.

'No, we didn't. But he has an ankle tattoo that is *identical* to the one a woman at the protest had on her wrist. They obviously know each other. If you find the protestors, you'll find him.'

Raisin searched for the photo of the group at the Massane Tower and pointed to the white-haired leader.

'I don't think he was at all happy that I took this photo. We saw him later that day and he crashed into me. I don't want to seem paranoid, but what if *he* stole the camera?'

'We're going to need you to come to the station and file a report,' Fabre said.

'But they can't! The party isn't over yet,' Catherine said in dismay.

'I'll bring you back on a private visit,' Jean-Philippe promised. 'This is too important. There have been death threats about this cave being opened to the public, so if you're right, we might be able to trace where they came from.'

The office in the gendarmerie where Geoffrey and Raisin were told to wait stank of stale cigarettes. She couldn't believe the French were still smoking indoors. Three desks were crammed into the small space and a large fan covered in worms of dust did little to relieve the heat. All three phones rang unanswered. Geoffrey paced between the desks, hands deep in his pockets. Raisin wished she had asked for something to drink.

'Where *are* they?' Geoffrey groaned.

Twenty minutes later, a small man barrelled into the room carrying a green folder. Cardona and Fabre followed, red-faced and flustered.

'I'm Brigadier Guillaume. I was having dinner.'

He signalled to the gendarmes to leave then snapped open the folder, adjusted his spectacles, and scanned the handwritten document inside. His left leg bounced restlessly. When he finished, he glared at Geoffrey.

'Tell me what happened.'

'It started when the man took a photo of the cave painting and Jean-Philippe...'

'Which painting?'

'The one on the platform in the *Galerie des Mains*,' Raisin said.

'Why didn't Jean-Philippe stop him?'

'It was too late, he'd already...' Geoffrey replied.

'What happened next?'

'He swore at my sister...'

The brigadier looked Raisin up and down.

'Why? What did you do?'

'Nothing!' she said furiously.

'He refused to apologise,' Geoffrey said.

The brigadier spun a pen between his fingers then added a note to the document.

'According to what's written here, the man was aggressive...'

'Yes, he also attacked Jean-Philippe. He was a dangerous lunatic,' Raisin said.

'Did you feel your life was threatened?' the brigadier asked Geoffrey.

'No.'

'Yes! They could have fallen off the platform. It was *terrifying*!' Raisin said.

'Yes or no?'

'He wouldn't apologise,' Geoffrey mumbled.

'So you hit him.'

'I think so... I can't remember...'

'He hit my brother first,' Raisin insisted.

'Where?'

'In the stomach... he hit him in the stomach.'

'Did he?' the brigadier asked Geoffrey. His palm shot up to silence Raisin.

'No, I hit him first.'

There was a long pause as the brigadier read through the report again. Raisin tried to catch Geoffrey's eye to warm him to stop volunteering information, but he refused to look at her.

'That matches Jean-Philippe's statement,' the brigadier said at last.

'We have photos of the man on my camera.'

'Camera?'

'Surely it's in the report?' she said rudely.

'Fabre!' the brigadier shouted.

The gendarme ran into the office. '*Oui*, Brigadier?'

'Where's the camera?'

'In the car.'

'Bring it. It's late and my dinner's getting cold.'

The minutes dragged by. Raisin walked to the door. Why did everything take so damn long in this place? The brigadier stretched his legs and lit a cigarette. She was tempted to pull it out of his mouth and throw it out of the window.

Fabre rushed in, waving the camera in the air. Raisin snatched it from him and found the photo.

'This is him… the man with the tattoo.'

'Lots of people have tattoos,' the brigadier drawled.

'Not like this one.'

She picked up a pen and drew the tattoo on the inside of the folder. The brigadier ignored it.

'Are you going to press charges?' he asked Geoffrey.

'No.'

'*Of course* we are,' Raisin said.

'Only Monsieur Radcliffe was attacked, only he can press charges.'

'Raisin, I leave in a fortnight, there's no point.'

'He *will* be pressing charges. We'll come back tomorrow and do it,' she said.

Officer Cardona came into the office.

'Sorry to interrupt but we have news of Nicolas.'

The brigadier leapt up and jabbed a finger towards Geoffrey.

'Are you going to press charges or not?'

Geoffrey shook his head. Raisin groaned and leaned across the desk for her camera. The brigadier caught her wrist.

'Sorry, evidence.'

'Even if we're not pressing charges?'

He nodded curtly, slid the camera across the table to Cardona, and left. Cardona followed him with an apologetic shrug.

'You can go. Nothing more is going to happen tonight. The mayor's son has been kidnapped,' Fabre said.

'*Kidnapped*?' Geoffrey said.

'Yes. By the same people who want to keep the cave closed. They're using him as leverage,' Fabre said.

'Why isn't anyone listening to us? The man with the tattoo *knows* these people.' Raisin turned to Geoffrey. 'You damn well *can't* refuse to press charges now.'

7

GEOFFREY WAVED FABRE back.

'Don't go. I've changed my mind.'

'*Trés bien.* Good. I'll take your statement,' Fabre said.

'Actually, I'd rather the brigadier hears it directly from me. Would it be okay if we did it tomorrow?'

'No problem,' Fabre said.

'Do it now, Geoffrey.'

'What time should I come?' he asked Fabre.

'The end of the day would probably be best. Five o'clock?'

'You're not going to do it, are you?' Raisin snapped when they were outside.

'Jesus, Raisin, what do you take me for? These arseholes kidnapped a child... *of course* I'm doing do it.'

'Why wait then?'

He patted his backpack.

'I didn't want the brigadier getting his bureaucratic hands on my camera too, not before I've had a chance to download the photos. I don't trust him one bit.'

'Nor do I, but you're going to have to tell him about our dolmen.'

'That's fine. You're the one who didn't want to.'

'I'd really like to go there again before everyone hears about it and all hell breaks loose.'

'That means tomorrow.'

'We didn't take any photos of it,' she pleaded.

'Okay,' he agreed grudgingly.

At home, Pi was asleep under the kitchen table with a half-chewed book under his head.

'Oh no!' Raisin wailed.

He thumped his tail and rolled onto his back. Geoffrey ruffled his belly and rescued the book.

'*Last Lovers*... sounds depressing. Although speaking of lovers... if Matt's coming tomorrow, how can we go to the dolmen?'

'We're going. He hasn't bothered to let me know what time he gets in.' She snatched the book from him. 'I carted this halfway across the world!'

'I'll get you another one.'

'It's out of print.'

Geoffrey opened the fridge and took out a bottle of wine.

'Want some?'

'Better make it a big glass,' she said, furiously rubbing the teeth marks on her book. 'Damn your dog.'

'What's it about?'

'Love. Nothing a cynic like you would know about.'

'At least I'm not a bolter like someone else I know.'

'You're bolting from Catherine's Annette.'

'That's hardly love.'

She narrowed her eyes.

'Wait... what are you saying? Have you met someone?'

'Believe it or not, I have.'

'Crap.'

He held two fingers in the air with a tense smile.

'Scouts' honour. We met about four years ago in London during a maths symposium.'

'*Four* years ago?'

'I know, I'm sorry.'

'Please don't say this person lives in London?'

He nodded miserably.

'Things weren't that serious in the beginning because we lived so far apart, but then... I don't know... we stayed together and I just never got round to telling you.'

If he had slapped her, it wouldn't have hurt more. Only his vulnerable eyes stopped her from being catty. He prodded Pi with his foot.

'Come mister, we're going for a walk.' He raised his palm in defence. 'It's been a hell of day and I need fresh air.'

'*Geoffrey! Tell* me about her.'

'I will, but it's a long story. There's time enough.'

She touched his arm. 'I'm happy for you.'

'Thanks.'

She tried not to feel resentful when the door slammed behind them.

The next morning, while Raisin drove, Geoffrey scanned the newspaper headlines. He slapped the front page angrily.

'Fucking bastards. They're demanding closure of the cave or they'll kill the boy! People are animals. Go ahead, kidnap the bloody mayor to make a point, but why the hell bring a kid into it?'

'God, his parents must be frantic. Anything about *why*?'

'Same bullshit we heard at the protest… that the cave art is sacred and they don't want hordes of tourists trashing it. Hmmm… here's something interesting. There's been a wolf sighting near the Massane Tower.'

'Isn't that quite far from where we saw it?'

'Not far for a wolf. We should go up there today and leave some of our food for it.'

Pi sat between his legs in the footwell and nudged the newspaper aside. Geoffrey scratched his head but kept reading. Raisin stole a glance at him. He hadn't breathed a word about his girlfriend, and she was dying to ask. Four years they had been together, which meant he must have visited her in London without telling her. It hurt, really hurt. Patience, she chided. If she pushed for answers, he would shut down.

They left the car under the oak tree next to the forestry track and an hour later they were close to the top of the mountain. A smooth oval cloud hovered overhead like a flying saucer. They broke through the tree line, ignored the narrow path to the tower and walked across the scrubland. Pi didn't leave Geoffrey's side.

'He's nervous… probably smells the wolf.'

'He's not the only one who's nervous,' she said, scanning the area.

A man zigzagged between the low bushes as if searching for something. He noticed them and screwed up his eyes against the glare to look at them. A shaggy beard crinkled the edges of his jaw. She relaxed. Definitely not someone to be scared of. Geoffrey unpacked the *saucisson* and the leftover quiche.

'What shall we leave for the wolf?'

'The meat?'

He left the *saucisson* and half the baguette on the tower steps. The old man stormed up to them.

'That's all we need… a bloody busybody,' Geoffrey said.

Pi growled. Raisin held him against her.

'Steady boy, it's just an old man.'

'What are you doing?' the man demanded.

'Sorry?' Geoffrey frowned.

He pointed to the food. 'What's that?'

'Meat… for a wolf we saw.'

'Did you put poison in it?'

'Of course not!'

Pi pulled out of her grasp and barked frantically. The man lowered his hand for him to sniff.

'I know that wolf,' he said quietly.

'You do? Is it still alive?'

'*She.* Yes she is, but only just. I check on her as often as I can.'

'How long has she been here?'

'A week, maybe more. It's a long time since I saw wolves here and I know every inch of my mountains.' He waved at the Roussillon plains sprawled before them. 'In another time, wolves were as common here as bison. Man hunted the same terrain as them but there was never trouble between them.'

'What changed?' Raisin asked.

'Man stopped roaming and settled on farms, and the wolf became his enemy. The old people say wolves get their courage from the warm Marin wind that blows off the sea, their shrewdness from the Cers wind, and their fearlessness from the cold fierceness of the Tramontane.'

The old man twirled his beard into a spiral.

'When the wind roars, you take shelter. It's the same with wolves. A good shepherd knows how to respect them. I never killed a wolf and they never took my goats.'

He introduced himself as Henri and told them he lived in a nearby hamlet with his seven goats. He tugged at something around his neck and showed them a curved ivory tooth on a frayed black cord.

'It's from a wolf and it's been in my family for five generations.'

'Looks like the one we saw at the shrine,' Raisin murmured to Geoffrey.

'We pass it down from firstborn to firstborn as a reminder of the shepherd's credo to protect the vulnerable.'

'I could have done with one of those,' Geoffrey muttered.

'She's here...' the old man hushed.

Geoffrey snapped a leash on Pi's collar. 'Where?'

'Over there, to the right of the tower,' Raisin whispered. 'Her tail's sticking out above that lavender bush.'

Pi's hackles rose. The wolf padded into the open, muscles taut, tail flicking as she sniffed the air. Geoffrey eased his camera out. The wolf whipped round. They froze. Her head veered towards the food.

'*Allez allez*,' Henri urged. *Go, go.*

Her ears fluttered. She turned towards them, bronze eyes burning, then she lowered herself to the ground sphinx-like, and watched them.

Raisin couldn't believe her restraint. Her pelvic bones were practically breaking through her fur, and her rib cage looked too big for her body, yet she was master over her hunger. They waited, not moving. In the blink of an eye, she vaulted over the bush, snatched the sausage and disappeared. Pi gave two high-pitched barks.

'*Now* you're brave,' Geoffrey laughed.

'*Très bien.* This is good, she's eating,' Henri said.

'Should we fetch what she didn't take?' Raisin asked.

'No. She's smart, she'll be back.'

Raisin held onto Pi while the two men placed water next to the leftover food.

'Most people want to kill wolves,' Henri said.

'Not Geoffrey,' Raisin smiled. She checked her watch. 'Time to go if we're going to… to finish our walk and be back in the village for our appointment.'

Kind as the old man was, she wasn't about to tell him about their dolmen.

'We'll bring more food tomorrow,' Geoffrey promised.

Henri shook his head. '*Non.* She mustn't forget she's a hunter. Why don't you come on Sunday? I'll be up here with my goats.' He waved goodbye. 'Don't forget, the wind isn't the enemy, just your reaction to it is.'

'What was that about wind?' Raisin asked when they were out of earshot.

'Folklore, I guess. He's nice. I wish there were more people like him in the world.'

The path twisted amongst the trees and past the signpost to the Massane Forestry Station. She stopped in front of it.

'I wonder what they do here.'

He shrugged, and kept walking.

'I hope the old man comes back on Sunday,' he said.

'We should ask him if he knows about dolmens in this area and see if he mentions our one.'

'You're not coming on Sunday. Your man will be here, remember?'

'He's not my man and anyway, he still hasn't phoned. Maybe he's come to his senses and changed his mind.'

'He'll be here. What's Pi chasing now?'

'I hope it's not a snake.'

'He's too much of a baby to hunt anything but butterflies.'

'It's beautiful here,' she sighed when they arrived at the rock-strewn clearing under the trees. 'I love these chunks of mountain. It looks like someone got bored and used them as marbles.'

They studied the dolmen.

'After seeing Henri's tooth, I wonder if the things around the shrine aren't ex-votos,' Geoffrey mused.

'Ex-what?'

'They're gifts for prayers answered, usually a precious object offered to God as thanks. Traditionally, it would be from the family of a fisherman who survived a storm, or from the mother of a child who survived illness... that kind of thing.'

'Someone left a wolf tooth as a thank you?'

'If it was Henri's offering, it would have been a very big thank you. I'm glad you talked me into coming here.'

'Me too, but before we go in, I've got something to show you.' She removed the bird sculpture from her backpack. 'I went back to the dolmen after you stormed off the other day and found this behind the statue. Remember that rough bit on the shoulder?'

'No...?'

She looked at him in confusion.

'Oh? Maybe I was on my own. The thing is... I'm sure this little bird comes from the statue's shoulder... I'll show you inside.'

'A monk with a bird on his shoulder...?'

'Yes,' she nodded.

'Raisin, it's probably St Francis of Assisi.' He cupped the bird in his palms. 'Protector of animals.'

Her eyes widened.

'Didn't he have something to do with wolves? I'm sure I remember a story about him saving a wolf.'

'Me too. Let's go get a closer look.'

He held aside the ivy branches for her and she went in, excited to show him what she had found. He photographed her balancing the bird on the statue's shoulder. She pointed to the rough surface on the saint's left leg.

'Maybe there was another animal attached to him.' She looked up. 'Do you think it could've been a *wolf*?'

'Makes sense if this was St Francis of Assisi.'

'This shrine meant a lot to someone. I wonder who damaged it.'

She glanced behind her. Who had been here before them?

'I'd like to go and look for my cap,' he said casually.

'Very funny,' she laughed.

'I'm serious.'

'But that means going back to the river, Geoffrey.'

He stooped down and ruffled Pi's fur.

'It was a nice cap.'

'You're doing it to prove you can beat your fear, aren't you?' she said gently.

'I thought you'd be pleased.'

'You worry me, Geoffrey. What if you panic again?'

'I'll be fine,' he snapped and shone his torch to the back the cave.

Pi ran into the narrow passage, barking excitedly. They squeezed after him.

'Are you sure about this? What if…?'

'We've got torches, spare batteries.' He held her eyes. 'I need to do this, Raisin. If it gets tricky, we can just turn back.'

'If it gets tricky, it'll be too late.'

He shrugged and headed into the tunnel. She went after him, full of concern. It wasn't courage making him face his phobia, it was bloody-mindedness. Why the hell would today be any different from the last time? Damn him for making her do this with him.

The passageway shrank and the roof pitched. They crept along, heads bowed low, his breath laboured.

'Are you okay?' she asked.

'It's never as bad the second time. Are *you* okay?'

She didn't reply. There was no point trying to talk sense into him. When they reached the cave with the mask-like face on the rock, he stopped and traced over its features with a finger. Raisin kept her distance, hating that they were about to ignore face's warning a second time. She reluctantly went with him into the next tunnel. Her skin prickled. They were passing the handprints. Her eyes darted about feverishly. *Where are you?*

They were metres from the round cave when they heard a scream. A human scream. Nothing like the supernatural howls of Sunday. She gripped his arm.

'I heard it too,' he murmured.

Pi growled as they edged closer. The noise from the underground river was deafening. She was desperate to leave. Geoffrey motioned for her to hold Pi while he went in. She saw the tight cords in his neck and grudgingly admired him. Gritty willpower was overruling his phobia.

'Jesus!' he shouted.

She clung to the wall and followed him. A man lay face down on the ground, one leg dangled dangerously in the river. A deep flesh wound gaped through his drenched shirt and his right hand was locked over a rock. Geoffrey's green cap lay next to him.

'Is he dead?' she asked hoarsely.

Geoffrey flopped the body over.

'Jesus, it's *him!*' He booted the comatose man in the stomach. 'Fucking *paedophile!*'

Blood belched from the man's mouth. With each kick, his body jolted closer to the rapids. A shoe fell off and hurtled along the roaring water. Raisin paled. His tattoo glared like an evil eye through his shredded trousers. She tried to get between Geoffrey and the man.

'For God's sake, stop kicking him!'

He shook her off so violently, she crashed into the wall. The man's other leg slid over the edge. She scrambled across the ground to him and hooked her fingers under his belt and pulled.

'Are you insane? He's alive, damn it!' she cried.

'He deserves to fucking drown.'

The man stirred and tried to sit up. Vomit and blood leaked from his mouth. Geoffrey scooped up his cap and punched his fist inside it.

'What the hell are we going to do with him?' she panted.

'Leave him here.'

'But he'll die here.'

'He kidnapped and did God-alone-knows-what to a fucking *child*.'

'Omeg… omeg…' the man stammered.

'He's trying to tell us something!' she panicked.

The man jerked upright and grabbed her.

'Omega,' he hissed.

She pulled free and pushed him away. His head cracked against a rock. He convulsed then stopped moving.

'Geoffrey, *do* something! Get help!'

'*You* get help.'

'I'm not leaving you with him. Go. Get the police, *anyone*…'

He studied her, eyes dead. She saw his withdrawal. His shutdown was as terrifying as his rage. He took off his shirt and tore it into strips.

'What are you doing?' she asked weakly.

He knotted the strips, snapped the makeshift rope to test its strength, then kicked the man onto his back.

'You're hurting him. Be careful,' she begged.

'He hurts children.'

'You don't *know* that. He's connected to the kidnappers but we don't know how. Maybe he's never heard of Nicolas. You can't assume he's guilty.'

He ignored her and lassoed the cord around the man's wrists and yanked it closed.

She gave him her car keys. 'You'll need these.'

'If he wakes up, ignore him. Animals like this are dangerous.'

He left without a backward glance. She wrapped her arms around Pi. The river seethed beside her. The man lifted his head with a painful grunt. She buried her face in Pi's fur.

'Water,' the man groaned.

She shone her torch on him. He winced and turned away. She moved the light back to his face, took the water bottle out of her backpack, and nervously approached him. His eyes followed her. She stopped, tempted to not help him.

'Please,' he begged.

She held the bottle to his mouth. He drank greedily. She couldn't keep her hand steady. Pi growled quietly at her side.

'Omega… Omega.'

'Is that your name?' she asked.

'Yes… Omega… Omega…'

'Did you kidnap the boy?'

'Stop… wolf cave… Omega…'

She snatched the water away. Geoffrey was right. He *was* linked to the kidnapping.

'You're *disgusting*!'

His mouth curled into a sneer as he struggled onto his elbows. She edged away. He swung his feet up and pincered her legs. The bottle flew into the air and she crashed to the ground. Pi lunged at him and sank his teeth into his ankle. He shrieked in pain but Pi held on, thin legs scrambling. She wrestled free. The man arched his back, screamed then collapsed.

Raisin coaxed Pi away and huddled against a rock. Pi stood guard in front of her, haunches sturdy, body on guard. She dropped her chin on her knees and stared blindly into the raging river.

An image rose from the plumes of white foam. The tribeswoman. Raisin's heart raced. The woman stood on a barren mountainside surrounded by wolves. Her hunter's legs were tanned and powerful, and her tussled sun-bleached hair tumbled over her shoulders. She held Raisin's eyes with a bright and steady gaze.

'*Who are you?*' Raisin whispered.

The woman untied a pouch from her waist and removed an object that she kissed and held up. A tooth. Raisin pointed to the wolves. A smile spread across her tanned face. She held the amulet out to Raisin, but before she could take it, the woman changed.

Deep lines creviced her brow and cheeks like spider web. Her skin lost its lustre and her mouth tightened. The chin narrowed and the nose sharpened. Fear glinted in her eyes.

Raisin's chest constricted. '*Mum…?*'

The man snorted and kicked his legs. Raisin whipped around. He rolled onto his stomach and lay still. She turned back to the water but the woman was gone.

8

Two HOURS PASSED and still no Geoffrey. If the man attacked her again, she would get the hell out of there. What did she care if he died? Going into the slippery tunnels with only a small back-up torch terrified her, but the man terrified her more. She retied her shoelaces. Where the hell was Geoffrey? She shuddered. He would have kicked the man right into the river if she hadn't stopped him.

The man woke and begged for more water. Raisin ignored him. He swore at her and threw his body in her direction. She scrambled back against the wall and switched off the torch so he couldn't see her. The darkness was total, and the crashing river too loud, too powerful.

She fingered the clamshell. Why had the woman wanted her to have the wolf tooth? Protect the vulnerable, Henri had said. She went cold. Was it another warning? Her mother's pinched face flashed before her. The man coughed. She pulled her knees into her chest. The cave felt crowded.

Pi dashed towards the tunnel, yapping excitedly. Raisin strained for sounds of Geoffrey. Rattling rocks signalled movement from the man. She snapped on the torch. He was on his knees and shovelling mushrooms into his mouth with his bound hands.

'What are you *doing*?' she cried.

He crammed more mushrooms into himself, laughing crazily. She wielded the torch like a weapon and backtracked slowly. Time to leave. If he died, she didn't want to be anywhere near him.

'Pi!' she screamed down the tunnel.

A halo of light floated towards her through the darkness. She blinked. Geoffrey? She shaded her eyes and made out the stumpy figure of Brigadier Guillaume. He nodded coldly and brushed past her, followed by Officer Cardona and a young fireman carrying a red and white medical pack, then Geoffrey. Her legs buckled and she fell into his arms.

'Are you okay?' he whispered.

'No,' she mumbled. His embrace was so unfamiliar, she wanted to stay there forever.

The brigadier shook the man's wrist, scattering the mushrooms into the air. The fireman pressed two fingers against his neck to check his pulse. The man's eyes glazed over and he clawed the air as if trying to catch something. Cardona scooped up some mushrooms and smelled them.

'He was eating them,' Raisin said helplessly.

'Hopefully they're poisonous,' Geoffrey muttered.

'189… his pulse is out of control,' the fireman announced.

The man screamed and cowered behind his arms. The fireman frowned.

'Psilocybin?' he said to Cardona.

'*Oui*. He's hallucinating.'

Brigadier Guillaume's face was impassive.

'He needs a hospital,' the fireman said urgently.

'No,' the brigadier snapped.

'*Il est malade,*' the fireman protested. *He's sick.*

The brigadier gesticulated at Raisin and Geoffrey.

'Get them out of here,' he barked at Cardona.

The gendarme looked ready to refuse then he shrugged, removed his jacket and draped it over Raisin's shoulders.

'Let me take you both to the top.'

The wind whipped them as they climbed through the foliage of the dolmen. She slid her arms into Cardona's jacket and gazed up at the dark sky in disbelief. Just a few hours ago it had been boiling hot, now grey shafts of rain slashed the air and heavy clouds pummelled the sky. There were patches so black, it looked like night had fallen.

She filled her lungs. 'God, it's good to be outside.'

Cardona offered to drive them to the village.

'That's okay, our car's nearby,' Geoffrey said.

'This weather's turning… you'd better hurry.'

'What about my five o'clock meeting with the brigadier to press charges against that lunatic?'

'He'll never be back at the gendarmerie in time. I'll tell him you'll come the same time tomorrow… if that suits you?'

'That's fine. Is there any news of Nicolas?' Raisin asked.

Cardona shook his head.

'Did they close the cave?' Geoffrey asked.

'Of course. How did you know about this dolmen?'

'I found it by accident last Sunday. Are we in trouble?' Raisin said.

'Should you be?'

If he knew about the bird sculpture in her pocket, she would be. As it was, Geoffrey would be furious that she had forgotten to put it back.

'Stay close to the village in case we need you,' Cardona said then he gave a half-salute and disappeared back into the dolmen.

Raisin walked behind Geoffrey to the car. Was Matt in Collioure yet? Swollen raindrops caressed her skin. She stopped and raised her face. Dark clouds barrelled overhead.

'I hope it pours for days,' she sighed.

He tugged her arm. 'Hurry. The storm's turning ugly.'

Suddenly thunder battered the air and lightning cleaved the sky, so bright it blinded them. Pi fled into the bushes. Geoffrey dashed after him.

'Stay away from the trees!' she shouted.

Geoffrey's grey outline merged into the downpour. The storm clattered and crashed. She zipped up her jacket.

'Geoffrey! Hurry! It's right above us!'

He re-appeared carrying Pi. A deafening crack buffeted the air. She screamed. Flames leapt from a stump next to them.

'Jesus!'

'Run for the car!'

They sprinted down the mountain. At the car, she threw the keys to him.

'You drive!'

They tumbled into a sopping wet car with Pi cowering in a pool of water at her feet.

'I forgot to close the fucking windows!' she wheezed.

'That lightning got *way* too close.'

'Oh my God. Did you see the *flames*?'

His knuckles were white as they drove home in mist so low and thick, they couldn't see past the bonnet. Water hurtled in funnels down the side of the dirt road. The storm was shifting seawards but lightning still fired across the clouds.

'Do you believe in ghosts?' she asked.

'Ghosts?'

'*Do* you?'

'I don't think so. Why?'

'The woman I keep seeing, could she be a ghost?'

'You obviously think she is.'

'I don't know *what* she is, but she's here and she's trying to give me something.'

'Like what?'

'A wolf tooth. But Mum appeared before I could take it and...'

'*Mum?*'

'Yes, looking old and scared. It was horrible.' She gave him a frightened look. 'Maybe something's wrong with her... when did you last speak to her?'

'Ages ago.'

'How come?'

'Busy I guess.'

'Crap. You're her favourite. Did you argue about something? Come on, you can tell me. We've never had secrets.'

'You're wrong, there were always secrets.'

'What do you mean? You're being weird.'

He changed down a gear and didn't reply.

'Has your girlfriend met Mum?'

He gave a heavy sigh. 'Boyfriend.'

'*Boyfriend?*'

'Boyfriend.'

Was he joking? She tried to read his expression.

'This is your four year relationship?' she said carefully.

'Four years in November.'

She felt numb. What else was he hiding? He glanced at her, face loose with regret. She turned to the window to hide her tears.

'Do Mum and Dad know?'

'Of course not.'

'Why didn't you tell me?'

'It was never the right time and then it was too late… I'm sorry.'

She nodded silently.

'Still heard nothing from Matt?' he asked.

'No, and don't change the subject… what's his name?'

'Chris. Where will Matt stay?'

'Oh, you're *good*… I don't know, not with us. Why are we talking about Matt when you owe me four years on Chris?'

'You're insufferable,' he said, but his voice was light. 'Do you really not want to see Matt?'

Fatigue swept over her. She wanted to see him, badly. His rooted certainty about everything he did would be heaven after the chaos unravelling around Geoffrey.

'I'm not sure,' she lied.

'Does he know you can't have children?'

'No.'

'Would he mind?'

'Some men want football teams, Matt wants grape-pickers for the vineyard he dreams of having.'

Her phone beeped.

'That's probably him. His ears are burning,' Geoffrey needled with a grin.

'It's not funny.'

She scrolled through the SMS, reading it out to him.

Meet me tomorrow for lunch? 1pm at Ma Vigne *restaurant. Bring the ring. Matt xx.*

'He wants the ring back,' she said shakily.

'I'd also want it back.'

'But he's not you, and I'm not giving it back.'

'It's an *engagement* ring, Raisin. I'm making myself scarce tomorrow.'

'No, you're not. You're coming with me.'

'Nope. You're on your own, kid.'

'You can't do this to me.'

'He's taking you for lunch after months of not seeing you. It's romantic… most women would love that.'

'I don't want *romantic*.'

'Where's the restaurant?'

'Overlooking the vineyards below the St Elme fort. I'm not going if you don't come with me.'

'Being a gooseberry isn't my thing.'

'You owe me,' she scowled.

He capitulated with a grimace. You owe me a damn sight more than this, she thought.

'You better warn him that I'm going to be the third wheel.'

'I will,' she promised wanly.

The next day, Raisin opened a z-fold map of Collioure and showed him the way to the restaurant.

'We go up *rue de la République*, where the demonstrators were walking on Sunday, then at the roundabout, we pass the blue church and go up this road to the railway bridge. From there, we follow the little yellow train's route into the vineyards.'

'It looks like it shouldn't take us more than twenty minute to walk there. You did tell him I was coming?'

'Yes.'

He clipped Pi's leash onto his collar.

'Best paw forward, boy. Time to escort our reluctant bride to lunch.'

They crossed the village and walked up towards the gabled church. A bloodied Christ on a weathered cross loomed over them as they mounted the steep lane that led to the railway underpass. Raisin ducked when a train clattered overhead. The vineyard road was well-marked and easy to find. Slender vines lolled in the faint breeze, and the St Elme fort perched high above the village, looking more like a misplaced sandcastle than a citadel.

'Romantic setting,' Geoffrey laughed.

'Stop it! I'm nervous enough as it is. I wonder how he got a booking? They have the best food in Collioure but only four or five tables.'

'Sounds cosy.'

Pi raced ahead but was yanked back by the leash. Geoffrey freed him and he disappeared between the vines, tail high and quivering. The road curved to the left towards a thicket of pine trees.

'The restaurant's in those trees over there. What if he didn't book?'

'It's *lunch* not a wedding.'

'What if he brings up marriage or wants to talk about why I left?'

'*You're* the bulldozer, not him. I doubt he'll say anything with me there anyway.'

She pointed to a group of people walking in a long row across the vineyard.

'Surely they can't be harvesting?'

'No, not in June. They're probably lost hikers.'

Despite the clouds, she was sweating by the time they got to the restaurant's narrow sand lane. She wiped her forehead and ran her fingers through her hair.

'You look fine,' he teased.

'It's ten to one, we're early.'

'Enough time to get you to relax with a glass of wine.'

'Aren't you just a laugh a minute?'

As they got closer, a ramshackle stone building came into view.

'*That's* the restaurant? It's no bigger than a garage!' Geoffrey said.

Hot pink geraniums erupted from flower boxes and two wooden tables stood on a wide pebbled terrace. She stopped and stared. A family of four was huddled around one table, and Matt sat at the other table with his back against the wall, khaki hat over his face. He looked like he was sleeping. Everything about him was familiar. The shape of his body. The hat. How relaxed he was.

'Not exactly dying to see me, is he?' she mumbled.

'He's probably just as terrified as you.'

'I'm not terrified.'

Matt jolted upright, squinted at them with his hand over his eyes, then waved his hat in the air. She returned the wave. *Breathe*, she told herself. So typical of him not to hide how happy he was to see her. She felt the same, but she wasn't ready to show it.

'Hello Sarah,' he said softly.

She swallowed hard. Only Matt called her by her real name.

'Hello.' Would he kiss her?

He placed his palm against her cheek. Fine wrinkles crinkled his face when he smiled. In London, people's eyes flitted like butterflies, but Matt's eyes settled on the person he was with, and stayed there. She looked away, wincing at the love in them. He slipped his arm over her shoulders.

'France suits you. You look well... better than well.' He shook Geoffrey's hand. 'Nice surprise! What brings you here?'

Matt's arm felt good. Too good. She avoided Geoffrey's angry glare.

'My sister was supposed to tell you I'd be joining you. Would you prefer to be alone?' Geoffrey said tightly.

'Don't be silly. You don't mind, do you?' Raisin smiled at Matt.

'Of course not. I booked one of these outside tables. Two... three... there's more than enough space for all of us. Let's sit!'

She hesitated at the end of the table, not sure which bench to choose, then Geoffrey sat in the middle of the free bench, forcing her to join Matt on his side.

'So when did you get here, Matt?' Geoffrey asked.

'A week ago in France, but only yesterday in Collioure. I've been to a hamlet called Oms, visiting an elderly woman who attended a talk I gave last year. She's an expert on Catalan plant remedies.'

A young waitress came to the table with the menu, a chunk of cork bark with a scrap of paper nailed to it, on which someone had scrawled the day's three dishes.

'Xavier recommended the smoked monkfish,' Matt smiled.

'Ah... you're his friend from London! I'm his sister, Aline. *Bienvenue!*'

'You know people here?' Raisin said when Aline left with their order.

'Sort of. Her brother, Xavier, is a colleague at the Chelsea Gardens.'

'No wonder you managed to get a table,' Geoffrey said. 'And look at the service we're getting... she's back already!'

Aline hovered a large earthenware platter in front of them.

'Compliments of the house! *S'il vous plaît*... would you make some room for our anchovy speciality, *boquerones...*'

Matt moved the plant standing in the way and Raisin pulled her handbag off the table. Aline lowered the dish with a Gallic flourish. Ovals of tomato-crusted bruschetta topped with silver anchovy fillets filled the plate. Matt raised his glass.

'Who would have thought the three of us would be having lunch in Collioure this summer... *santé!*'

'*Santé!*' Geoffrey echoed. 'And I'm really sorry about barging in like this.'

Raisin studied Matt over her glass. He looked good. She was glad he hadn't grown his hair back after shaving it off two and a half years ago.

'So where are you staying?' she asked.

'Up at the Massane Forestry Station. Xavier and Aline know the zoologist there.'

'We've seen a signpost for it,' Geoffrey said. 'We also saw a very sick wolf near there yesterday.'

'There are *wolves* here?'

'Not anymore... and no-one seems to know where this one comes from. We're planning to take food up to it. Why don't you join us?'

Matt glanced at Raisin. 'Is that okay with you?'

'Fine,' she shrugged.

His face fell. 'But I can only do it tomorrow.'

'Busy schedule?' Geoffrey joked.

Pi weaselled his head towards the bruschetta. Raisin pushed him away. Matt ruffled his head.

'Did you bring him with you from Cape Town?' Matt asked.

'No, he adopted me on a hike I did in Andorra, just before I came here. I tried leaving him at the local police but they said he'd be put down if I didn't keep him.'

'Look…!' Raisin whispered.

A squirrel sat on a tree stump nearby, whiskers twitching, paws clasped together like a nun. Pi raced towards it, crashing against the table. The wine bottle toppled over, the plant and bruschetta platter tumbled to the floor. Geoffrey jumped up with the lead. Matt stopped him.

'Don't tie him up. It wasn't his fault.'

Geoffrey scraped the bruschetta into a pile with his foot and lifted the plant pot back onto the table.

'Thank God this didn't break.'

Bright green leaves circled a wizened vine stem and clusters of tiny budding grapes hung in between. Matt patted the soil down with a spoon.

'It'll survive another summer.'

Geoffrey disappeared inside to get more wine. Raisin parted the vine leaves with her fingers. A small brown box dangled from a gnarled branch.

Matt pushed it closer to her. 'It's yours.'

'Don't be silly. It belongs to the restaurant!'

'No, I brought it with me from London. It's a bonsai *vitis vinifera*.'

Raisin stared at it without touching it.

'It's just a plant, Sarah.'

'What's in the box?' she asked despite herself.

Geoffrey returned with an open bottle of rosé. Raisin held up her glass, grateful for the diversion.

'How long are you staying?' Geoffrey asked Matt.

'I'm not sure yet… and you?'

'I fly out on the 10th… thirteen days to go.'

'Aren't those the people we saw earlier?' Raisin said to Geoffrey.

Six men were walking in the vineyard near the restaurant. Two black and brown Bloodhounds, noses to the ground, led the way.

'Those are search dogs,' Matt said in a puzzled voice.

Geoffrey went pale.

'They must be looking for Nicolas.' He put his glass down. 'I've got to talk to them.'

'Where's Pi's lead in case he wants to follow you,' Matt said.

'On the bench,' he muttered distractedly.

She tried to catch his eye to make him stay, but he was already on his way.

'Who is Nicolas?' Matt asked.

'The mayor's son. Someone kidnapped him as leverage in an attempt to shut down a prehistoric site.'

'That's terrible. No wonder Geoffrey's upset.'

'This is nothing. He attacked one of the men involved in the kidnapping.'

'I don't like the sound of this. Why are you two involved?'

His concern was like a caress. She fidgeted with her napkin.

'How are you, Sarah?'

'Fine. I love it here.'

'What do you do all day?'

'I took French lessons in the beginning but stopped when Geoffrey arrived. I'll start again when he goes. There's also a pastry course at the Hotel School in Perpignan that I'm registered for.'

'You're not missing me then,' he grinned, palms up in mock despair.

Geoffrey jogged to the table and picked up his camera.

'I'm going to show them the photos,' he said and raced back.

'What photos?' Matt asked.

Raisin described the events of the past five days, ending with Geoffrey's attack on the unconscious man.

'Isn't this a police matter?'

'It is. We're supposed to go to the gendarmerie after lunch to lay charges, but Geoffrey won't leave it at that. He's been so strange. He never used to be violent or unpredictable like this… and then yesterday…'

She fell silent. Matt reached for her hand across the table. She didn't pull away.

'Yesterday he told me he's in a relationship with a guy called Chris… someone who lives in *London*. We *never* used to have secrets.'

'Everyone has secrets, sweetheart. It's not always a bad thing.'

She chewed her lip, embarrassed about the secret *she* had kept from him during the three years they were together. He raised his eyebrows. She flushed. Pi crept onto the bench next to her and dropped his head on her lap. She stroked him, trying to hide how flustered she was.

'Do you mind that I'm here?' he asked, cupping her chin towards him.

She twisted away.

'Look at me, Sarah.'

'You can't barge into my life and presume…'

'I'm not the one making presumptions, sweetheart.'

'What does *that* mean?'

'I still dream of owning a vineyard, and I still dream of sharing it with you. The vine I brought for you is in exchange for the ring.'

'Why?' she asked.

He tapped the little cardboard box.

'The answer's in here. Open it when you're ready.'

'When will that be?'

'When curiosity wins. Did you bring the ring?'

'No. I'll give it to you tomorrow.'

'Okay.' He squeezed her hand. 'There's one more thing… I start work here on Monday.'

9

'WHAT... WHAT DID you say?' Raisin stammered.

'Sarah... just let me explain...'

'This is *my* life, *my* village.'

Pi nuzzled her leg. She pushed him away, frustrated tears stung her eyes. Matt caught her fingers. She flicked him aside.

'Hear me out,' he said gently.

'I'm never going back to London so there's no point...'

'I'm not asking you to.'

'Then why are you here?'

'We were together for three years, and I'd really like to talk about that.'

His voice was low and unruffled, and he sat very still as if worried he might scare her away.

'There's nothing to say.'

'I know how much you hate talking about stuff like this, but...'

'Don't patronise me. I'm not a child.'

'Then stop behaving like one,' Geoffrey said behind her.

She spun around. 'Stay out of it, Geoffrey.'

'Oh grow up, Raisin.'

'How would you like it if Chris barged into your life like this?'

Geoffrey studied her quietly.

'You mean if he flew ten thousand kilometres to be with me? You think I'd be angry? You don't know me then.'

He held up his camera.

'They borrowed the memory card and when I told them about your camera, they said they'd fetch it from the gendarmerie this afternoon. They want us to meet up with them before we go to the brigadier.'

'Go without me.'

'Saying no to the National Police isn't really an option here.'

Matt stood up.

'I think I'd better leave you two to it. Sarah, I'm sorry about springing this on you, but when the possibility of helping them with a research program while someone was on leave came up, I grabbed it. It's temporary, not even two months, and I'll be up at the forestry station. You don't have to see me if you don't want to.'

His eyes never left hers. He looked tired, and she knew he was hurt. Her anger evaporated.

'You could have asked,' she mumbled.

'Would it have made any difference?'

She didn't answer. He touched her cheek.

'Don't look so glum.'

His tenderness made her feel worse.

'Here comes Aline with the food. Matt, please don't go,' Geoffrey said.

'Sarah...?'

'Yes, stay. I'm sorry...'

It was a relief to let Geoffrey rant on about the kidnappers while she tried to calm her thoughts. She hated surprises. It was one thing being happy to see Matt, but quite another having him right on her blasted doorstep. For two long months. She pronged a piece of monkfish into her mouth. It was firm, moist and dripping in homemade olive and anchovy pesto. She tried to identify the other ingredients. Definitely garlic, some basil, and possibly capers too. The restaurant deserved its reputation. She hadn't realised how much she had missed cooking. She turned her attention back to the men.

'Using tracker dogs is a good idea. The police obviously know what they're doing,' Matt said.

'Unlike the local idiot who's in charge. He's done more to stall the investigation than help it,' Geoffrey said.

'The village must be distraught. In a small community like this, a youngster like Nicolas will be everyone's child.'

Raisin loved how earnestly Matt listened to Geoffrey. He leant forward, head nodding, even his hands were involved. He glanced up and winked at her, eyes twinkling. Her heart lurched. She returned a nervous smile.

'What time are we supposed to meet the police?' she asked Geoffrey.

'We need to leave in about half an hour.'

'Tell me about the wolf you saw,' Matt said.

'We saw her twice. The first time was last Monday, then again yesterday. It's a miracle she's still alive.'

'Geoffrey was fascinated by her, but I found it nerve-wracking. She could easily have turned on us,' Raisin said.

'Matt… there was something down in the cave you'd be interested in. Mushrooms… hundreds of them… growing next to the river. Brown caps with long thin stalks. I was surprised anything could grow down there.'

'They usually thrive in the dark and damp, but it's unusual for their spores to travel very far underground.'

'The police thought they were hallucinogenic.'

'Based on your description, I'd say they were right. It's a plant with a fascinating history. Primitive cultures ate them to induce trance to commune with the spirit world.'

'We heard at the launch that the latest theory is that cave art is an expression of what shamans saw in trance. Maybe that's how the mushrooms got down there in the first place. Raisin found prehistoric handprints in one of the tunnels… so we know shamans have been there.'

She willed him not to say anything about her tribeswoman.

'You've gone very quiet,' Matt murmured to her.

'Just thinking about Nicolas,' she lied.

He tapped his watch.

'You should probably get to your meeting and see how you can help find him. Where shall we meet tomorrow?'

'Ask someone at the forestry station how to get to the signpost with the reserve map on it, and we'll meet you there. It's really easy to find,' Geoffrey said.

'Sounds straightforward enough. What's a good time?'

'About eleven?' Geoffrey said.

'Sarah…?' Matt asked.

'Sounds perfect.'

When he leant across to kiss her goodbye, she gave him her cheek but couldn't stop herself from touching his arm.

'See you tomorrow,' she mumbled.

He picked up the grapevine. 'Don't forget this.'

'Don't worry. It's not the restaurant's,' she told Geoffrey, too defensively for her liking.

Matt pointed to the pistachio green Vespa parked next to the restaurant.

'I rode down here with it hanging from my scooter handles.'

The picture of him bumping over the corrugated dirt roads with her vine bouncing in a bag was so typical of the man she loved. *Had* loved.

'We'd better go,' she said quietly.

'Nice one, Raisin. You said you'd told him I'd be there,' Geoffrey snapped when they were out of earshot.

'I didn't know how to,' she shrugged.

'He's still in love with you.'

'It's just a plant, Geoffrey.'

'I'm not talking about the plant and you know it.'

She wasn't sure what she knew anymore.

'Where are we supposed to meet the police?' she asked.

'They've been given one of the mayor's offices. I said we would try to get there around four.'

'Did they say how the investigation was going?'

'Just that there's been a new demand. Now that the cave has been closed, they want to trade Nicolas for the man.'

The meeting room was an airy office that opened onto a wide veranda shaded by the slender up-turned branches of a plane tree. A man leant against the railing smoking a cigarette, a mobile phone jammed between his shoulder and ear. His crumpled shirt and open-toed Crocs made him look more like a holidaymaker than a police officer.

A second man and a petite, dark-haired woman in smart civilian clothes were bent over photos scattered across an oval conference table. Raisin recognised the photos immediately. At least the new team were on the ball.

'*Bonjour.* Thank you for coming at such short notice,' the policewoman smiled. 'I'm Michelle Valette. This is Olivier, and the smoker outside is Vincent.'

Raisin liked the woman's informal use of first names. She seemed earnest and professional, and although dwarfed by her colleagues, she was clearly the boss.

'Your pictures are a big help,' Michelle said.

'I'm glad... when do you think I can get my camera back?'

'Not for a while, I'm afraid,' Olivier said. 'Michelle wants me to send it to Montpellier for fingerprinting.'

The gendarme looked twice his boss's age and unconcerned about her rank over him.

Raisin picked up a photo and stared into the angry eyes of the group's leader, then took great pleasure in lassoing him with a black marker pen. She hoped like hell they caught him.

'This man stole my camera, and the one opposite him here is the maniac from the cave,' she said.

'Any ideas why they were sitting in a circle like that?' Michelle asked.

'Looked like some kind of meeting. They pretty much acted like we didn't exist,' Geoffrey said.

'Except when I took out my camera,' Raisin said.

Geoffrey tapped another photo. 'This blonde woman led the protest on Sunday.'

'She and the man we found have exactly the same tattoo,' Raisin added.

'Yes, the tattoo. Let's talk about that,' Michelle nodded.

Olivier rifled through the flipchart sheets until he got to a large hand drawn copy of the tattoo.

'So far, the research I've done indicates that it's an ancient talisman called the Jupiter Seal that dates back to the days of King Solomon,' he explained.

Vincent sauntered inside. 'So what have I missed?'

'We're talking about the tattoo,' Michelle said.

'I know about these talismans. They're derived from something called magic squares which have been around for over four thousand years, and as widespread as Egypt and India. I teach them to my students to keep them interested in my lectures,' Geoffrey said.

'Magic and maths… that'll be the day!' Raisin laughed.

'Can't say I see a square anywhere,' Vincent snorted.

'Go on, Geoffrey,' Michelle prompted.

'In the Middle Ages, people gave esoteric meaning to magic squares and then turned them into talismans with special powers, but actually… it's all just good old-fashioned maths… the magic lies in the numbers.'

His pen flew over the flipchart.

4	14	15	1
9	7	6	12
5	11	10	8
16	2	3	13

'The numbers are always in four rows of four.' He glanced at Vincent. 'Hence the square… and they're 'magical' because no matter which row you add up… horizontal, vertical or diagonal, the sum is always the same, in this case thirty-four.'

There was silence as everyone did the maths.

'You're right… they do,' Michelle frowned.

'Now I see a square but no circle,' Vincent yawned.

Geoffrey drew a circle and two lines over the numbers.

'Voilà! One Jupiter Seal!'

Raisin grinned. He looked tempted to bow.

'Does the symbol have any other meaning?' she asked.

'Not in maths,' Geoffrey said.

'Beyond establishing its origins, and what you've just explained, we don't know anything else. The answer could be *anywhere*… maths, astrology, religion, mythology,' Michelle groaned.

Geoffrey snapped his fingers. 'Quirinus.'

'Quirinus?'

'They were shouting Quirinus at the protest, but how does that link to this?' Raisin said.

'Quirinus… Jupiter… Mars…' Geoffrey rattled off.

'I still don't get it.'

Vincent dragged his chair to the veranda door, straddled the seat and jabbed an unlit cigarette between his lips.

'Oh, but *I* do! Our cult *worships* Quirinus,' he smirked.

'Take it seriously, Vincent,' Michelle snapped. 'And don't even think about lighting that thing.'

Geoffrey paced the length of the room, massaging his temples.

'Jupiter, Mars and Quirinus were Roman gods back in 500 B.C., so he has a point.'

'But the timing is all over the place. The earliest Jupiter Seal records I found were 900 B.C., and the Roman gods are four centuries later. Both are positively modern compared to the magic squares which you say are *four thousand* years old. It's hard to believe anything links them,' Olivier said.

'The only other thing we know is that the kidnappers seem to believe the wolf rock art is sacred,' Michelle said.

'Which takes us back another few thousand years,' Olivier muttered.

'And don't forget how wolves keep featuring. Believe it or not, we even saw one this morning up at the Massane Tower,' Raisin said.

'I don't think that has anything to do with this though,' Geoffrey said.

'Coincidences are for Hollywood. It must be relevant. Where exactly did you see it?' Michelle asked.

'The first time was near *Pic de Sailfort*, but this morning she was up near the Massane Tower,' Raisin said.

'We're planning to go back there tomorrow. If she's there, I'll try to photograph her for you,' Geoffrey offered. 'I heard there's been a new demand from the kidnappers.'

'If we give in to them, we'll end up like Italy,' Vincent muttered.

'What are you saying… we mustn't take them seriously?' Geoffrey said sharply.

'Vincent's opinions are Vincent's opinions,' Michelle soothed. 'We'll agree to the exchange, but we're trying to buy time so we can extract information from the prisoner before we release him.'

'How old is the poor kid?' Raisin asked.

'He turned five in May,' Olivier replied.

'I think that wraps things up for today,' Michelle said. 'If you think of anything else, let me know.'

'There's one more thing,' Raisin said. 'He may have told me his name… Omega. He kept repeating it.'

'Isn't that biblical? Alpha and Omega…?' Olivier said.

'It's not religion,' Vincent said from the doorway.

They all looked at him.

'Certain animals have established group hierarchies, particularly wolves. The lead wolf is the Alpha and the bottom of the pack is the Omega. If this is a cult then we have their least important member,' he drawled.

'Better than nothing,' Michelle said irritably. 'Vincent, go to the hospital and see if he's well enough to be questioned. Take Olivier with you. If he's coherent, call me… and don't start without me.'

She waved him away then gave Raisin and Geoffrey her card.

'You'd better get to your meeting with the brigadier. Please call me if you think of anything, even if it seems unimportant. We're grasping at straws here.'

10

RAISIN STUDIED THE sky with a frown. Freckles of blue were sprinkled between thick clouds that looked sodden and ready to burst. Who knew how the day would turn out? The horizon over the sea was so dark, it was probably already raining there. But inland, gleaming columns of sunlight pounded the plains. It wouldn't be the first time sun and rain had tangoed together in one morning. Usually she wouldn't care but today she wanted rain. Matt was hiking with them, and being drenched by rain was better than being drenched by perspiration.

A large black and white bird soared above them. They craned their necks, palms cupped over their eyes. Its wing tips flared like a dancer's fan, and its tail swivelled from side to side as it looped and glided through the air.

'Beautiful,' Geoffrey sighed.

'Is it an eagle?' Raisin asked.

'Could be a vulture. Looks like it's eyeing something on the ground.'

'Wouldn't you love to be a bird?'

'Nope. I need earth under my feet.'

She waved her arms in the air.

'I'm a phoenix, flamboyant and in charge of my destiny.'

They laughed and continued towards the trees. She glanced at him and her heart tightened. It was lovely to see him so relaxed.

'You're a lot more easy-going than you used to be,' he said.

She looked up, startled, then grinned. They were both thinking the same thing about each other. She wished they had made more effort to spend time together over the past ten years.

'I'm dreading you going home. What on earth am I supposed to do with Matt for two months?'

'He's not here on holiday and won't need entertaining. You heard what he said, he's not even expecting to see you. Relax.'

'Easy for you to say.'

'What are you scared of? He's not going to talk you into doing anything you don't want to do.'

'I know, but I don't even want to talk about it.'

'Talking marriage and getting married are worlds apart.'

'When you ran off at lunch to speak to the police, he said he still dreamt of us being married.'

'Did he actually use the word *marry*...?'

'Not exactly, but...' She adjusted her hat. 'I came to Collioure to get away from all this pressure.'

'*You're* the only one creating any pressure here.'

'Enough about Matt. What can I drag out of you about Chris? Start with his surname...'

'Summers... Chris Summers.'

'And what makes Chris Summers special?'

'He's kind and he always...'

'I don't know if I'd like that to be the first thing someone said about me,' she teased.

'But it's him. Gentle with animals, good with kids, patient with old people... patient with me.'

'He sounds a bit like Matt.'

They rounded a large moss-flecked rock that jutted out of the mountain like a shoulder blade.

'Sarah! Geoffrey! Down here!'

They peered down the slope. Matt was on his hands and knees in the undergrowth. He clutched his khaki hat and waved. A row of plastic specimen bottles jangled from an old fisherman's belt around his hips and he brandished bright yellow flowers in the air as he scrambled up the bank. Geoffrey held out his hand and pulled him onto the path.

'Hello, you two. Damn it, I'm out of shape!' he wheezed.

A flush of warmth surged through her. His trouser legs were covered in mud, his hat was too big and his face shone. Matt believed all plants had medicinal value, and his greatest challenge was working out what a plant's contribution to the world could be. His window ledges at home were crammed with plants he was researching.

'Hello, Matt,' she stammered.

He wafted the flowers in front of her. A nutty citrusy smell filled her nostrils.

'St John's Wort... on my *doorstep*!' he beamed.

'Where *is* your doorstep?' Geoffrey asked.

'Not more than four or five hundred metres from here. Would you like to see it?'

'We haven't really got time now. We don't want to miss Henri,' Raisin said hurriedly.

'Okay, we can do it another day.'

His pots clattered as he stepped aside so they could lead the way.

'How did your afternoon finish off yesterday?' he asked.

'The new bunch from Paris are taking everything a lot more seriously. At least they looked at our photos,' Raisin said.

'Which is more than we can say about the idiot running the gendarmerie. He cancelled our meeting. It's like he doesn't want me to lay charges,' Geoffrey fumed.

'And the boy's parents?' Matt asked.

'We haven't seen the father again, but he must be going through hell,' Raisin sighed.

They fell silent. Raisin felt Matt's eyes on her and wished he wasn't behind her. Her thoughts drifted to the ring in her pocket. Matt had chosen it because it reminded him of daisies, their favourite flower. The design was a swirl of diamonds chips around a central yellow sapphire. She would never have chosen it herself but had loved it the moment he slipped it on her finger. She wished she didn't want to keep it so much.

They walked across the treeless scrubland at the top of the mountain and stopped below the tower. The sun had lost the battle for the sky and bulbous clouds churned overhead. There were now three vultures hovering together in an invisible thermal. She scanned the bushes around them and wondered if the wolf was watching. Matt pointed to a figure near the tower steps.

'Is that your shepherd over there?'

'That's him. What's he carrying?' Raisin said.

Henri stopped when he saw them, lowered a cardboard box to the ground then sank onto a step to wait for them. Pi ran up to him and snuffled the corners of the box.

'*Bonjour*, Henri,' Geoffrey greeted. 'This is Matt, my sister's…'

'A friend of ours from London,' she said quickly.

He nodded hello and nudged the lid off the box with his foot. Two tiny grey wolf cubs slept curled around each other on a faded red sweater.

'Oh my God, they're adorable! Where did you find them?' Raisin said.

'Right there… near the tower steps.'

Pi dropped his head into the box and licked the wolf cub closest to him. It stirred, rolled on its back and placed two squat paws against his jaw. Pi's tongue was almost as long as its whole body.

Matt moved Pi aside and cupped a small grey bundle in his palm. It lay still, awake but sleepy. He stroked its head with his thumb.

'I've never held a wolf cub before,' he murmured.

'It looks like a puppy!' Raisin whispered.

Small yellow eyes gazed up at her with wary curiosity.

'Did you find them in this box?' Geoffrey asked.

'No. They were in the same spot we left food and water. Their mother was the wolf we saw.'

'*Was*?' Raisin asked.

'Dead,' he said heavily.

'Damn it… I *knew* I should've come here yesterday,' Geoffrey grunted.

'*Mon ami*, there is nothing you could have done for her. She knew she was dying and left her cubs for us to find.' Henri looked up at the vultures. 'The birds led me to her.'

'Will they live? What are you going to do with them?'

'We should take them to the forestry station. René will know what to do,' Matt said.

'I'm not leaving her body for the vultures. Raisin, take Pi and go with Matt, I'll stay and bury her,' Geoffrey said.

'I'll help you,' Henri nodded.

He held his tooth amulet and drew a small cross on each cub's forehead. His lips moved in prayer. A lump formed in Raisin's throat. *Protect the vulnerable.* She would do everything she could to help the cubs survive.

'Do you think the cubs will survive?' Raisin asked Matt on the way to the forestry station.

'I hope so. If anyone can help them, René can.'

They slid in and out of comfortable silence, and it was only when they passed the signboard to the forestry station that she realised he hadn't mentioned marriage. The cubs must be worrying him more than he let on.

A flimsy fence of drooping wires and skew poles blocked their way, and a makeshift gate dangled between two wooden stakes.

'Not much of a barrier,' she laughed.

'It's only meant to stop four-legged animals from grazing on the protected side... the two-legged ones respect the no-entry sign and stay out.'

He unhooked a metal loop and lifted the gate open.

'Welcome to my home for the next two months.'

She gave a nervous smile. *Home* sounded very permanent.

'It's miles from the village. Surely you don't carry supplies up on foot?' she asked with forced gaiety.

'No, there's another access... a forestry road on the other side of the mountain.'

'What kind of research do they do here?'

'Everything. From studying the impact of cattle on the forests to cataloguing the beetle population. There are over fourteen hundred beetle species here.'

'I'm *really* glad I know that,' she grinned.

He stroked her cheek.

'It's nice to see you smile, Sarah.'

The path took them through a beech forest then curved along an almost-dry riverbed. Just a thin sliver of water dribbled between the rocks. Ten minutes later, Raisin saw something on the upper bank.

'Is that where it is?'

'Yes, let's hope Rene's home.'

The forestry station was a hodgepodge of buildings, dominated by a big double volume stone barn with square windows and faded shutters. A wrought-iron bar secured its arched double doors.

'The barn is a storeroom that turns into a makeshift hothouse in winter, and the green shack at the back of it is supposed to be the office, but we only ever use it to phone or send faxes,' Matt explained.

A low wooden house with a wide deck stood a few metres away. Raisin assumed it was where Matt and his colleagues lived. Every surface was badly in need of paint; the only bit of colour was the red and yellow striped hammock swaying between the deck's pillars. A man stood at the top of the steps with a pipe drooping from his mouth.

'René!' Matt called. 'We need your help!'

The man continued to puff without moving. He looked like a weather-worn farmer.

'*Bonjour* Matt,' he said, pipe bouncing against his chin. 'In France we say *bonjour* first.'

'Yes, of course. I'm sorry. *Bonjour.* This is Sarah. Sarah, this is René.'

Matt lifted the lid and showed René the cubs. They cowered in a corner, eyes wide, ears twitching. René jumped down the stairs with teenage agility.

'*Bordel! Des louveteaux!*'

'Their mother's dead,' Raisin said.

He dropped his hand into the box and the biggest cub lunged forward and bit his finger. He smiled like a proud parent.

'*Très bien*! If you defend yourself, you want to live. Bring them inside.'

They followed him into a large living room. A leather sofa with frayed cushions took up most of the space, and an uncomfortable-looking red armchair covered with un-ironed shirts stood next to a charred fireplace. Raisin wondered where everyone sat when all the men were home. A pile of books stopped a coffee table with a broken leg from toppling over, and a fluffy ginger cat slept underneath it.

René shook out a denim shirt from the pile and draped it over the table then nestled one of the cubs on it. His hands never left the little creature as he firmly rolled it onto its back. It growled and tried to attack him. The cat jerked awake. René swept it up and gave it to Matt.

'Can you put Chilli in the garden for me, *s'il te plaît*? I don't want to stress these little things any more than they already are.'

Matt nuzzled the cat and took it outside. Henri stroked the cub's belly.

'Alright, *ma puce*, let me have a good look at you.'

He ran a gnarled finger along its body then gave each limb a quick tug. It wrenched its paws back and tried to twist free.

'*Bien*. You have strength.'

'What do you think?' Matt asked as he came back inside.

'If we keep them warm and can make them eat, they'll be fine.'

He swaddled the shirt around the cub and gave it to Raisin. She was shocked how little it weighed. The sofa creaked when she sat down. Matt perched on the armrest next to her.

'What'll happen to them now?' Raisin asked.

'They can stay here until they're able to fend for themselves, then we'll see,' René said and gave Matt the second cub. 'Come to the kitchen... I'll see if I can rustle up something for them to eat.'

They went to the kitchen through a doorway whose door had been removed.

'How old are they?' Raisin asked.

'Hard to say... five weeks, maybe six. Old enough.'

His confidence gave her hope. She wished she could take them home. René placed a bottle of water and two bananas on the kitchen table then took a red medical pack out of the broom cupboard and removed two plastic syringes.

The cub squirmed free and stretched its little snout up to sniff Raisin's hair.

'You're cute. Are you a boy or a girl?'

René filled a syringe with water and held it out to her.

'Yours is female. One drop at a time… slowly,' he instructed.

'But I don't know how to,' she protested.

Matt pulled up a kitchen chair for her.

'You'll be fine. Sit here, hold her firmly on your lap and dribble water into the side of her mouth.'

She watched him coax his cub to drink then nervously inserted the syringe into her cub's mouth. A round pink tongue darted out and licked the water.

'René, can I give them names?'

René broke chunks of bananas into a blue plastic bowl.

'Sure. Is yours taking the water, Matt?'

'Like a fish.'

'Raisin? Matt? Are you there?'

'We're in here… in the kitchen!' Matt called.

'It's my brother. He stayed behind to bury their mother,' Raisin explained.

René sauntered over to the front door, mashing the bananas with a fork, then he dropped the bowl on the coffee table and ran outside. Raisin clutched the cub to her chest and followed. She froze in the doorway.

Geoffrey stood at the bottom of the deck's steps, face ashen, the dead wolf in his arms. She stumbled towards him. Pi flew past her and threw himself at Geoffrey. René jumped up and hauled him aside.

'Why have you brought her here? Where's Henri?' Raisin stammered.

René stopped her halfway down the stairs.'

'Keep the cub away,' he snapped.

She tried to brush past him but he caught her arm.

'*J'insiste.* Until we know what she died of, other animals must be kept away. Matt, please take the dog inside!'

He glared at them over his shoulder as he slid his hands under the wolf and tried to coax Geoffrey into letting go of the body.

'I need to examine her,' he said gently.

Geoffrey stared right through him. The last time she had seen him so vulnerable was down in the cave. Matt drew her to him.

'Come inside, sweetheart,'

She let him lead her back to the kitchen.

'I couldn't bear it if the cubs died.'

'They'll be fine… pop her back into the box and go to your brother. I'll stay here and feed them.'

She shot him a grateful smile and rushed back outside. The men were hunkered over the wolf. Geoffrey pointed to a round wound on its hip. She went cold.

'It *can't* be…' she stammered.

The livid mark was crusted with pus and blood, and had been burned into the wolf.

'The Jupiter seal,' Geoffrey said dully.

They exchanged frightened glances. She squatted next to him and squeezed his hand as they watched René examine the wolf. He probed every inch of the body then checked the eyes, ears and mouth. He grunted as he rolled her over. A large cut gaped across her left back leg. He studied it quietly then stood up and slid his pipe out of his shirt pocket, struck a match and dipped it into the bowl. White smoke surged around him as he puffed.

'No broken bones but two very serious infections. The one on her hip killed her. What do you know about the brand?'

'It's some kind of insignia used by the group who kidnapped the boy. The police are investigating it. I can't believe we're seeing it on a wolf,' Raisin said.

'What kidnapping?'

'Raisin will fill you in. I've got to get to the police.' Geoffrey's hands balled into angry fists. 'I should've pushed him into the river when I had the chance.'

'Come with me… we'll call the police from the office,' René said.

Geoffrey strode after him, back rigid. She let out a heavy sigh and went to Matt. He was on the floor, leaning against the sofa with the cubs asleep on his outstretched legs. Pi lay against his thigh. She joined them on the ground.

'Are they okay?' she asked.

'Are *you* okay?'

She bit her lip.

'Sarah, there's nothing you could have done for her.'

'It's not her… it's Geoffrey. I'm worried about him. He's acting like his own son's been kidnapped.'

Matt slipped his arm around her. She didn't resist and leant her head against him.

'Geoffrey can look after himself,' he murmured.

'I don't know if he can. One minute he's fine, the next he's so… *angry.*'

'He's just worried.'

They heard rapid footsteps and she shifted away from him like a guilty schoolgirl.

'Good. They ate the banana,' René said.

'They gulped it down. What did the police say?' Matt asked.

'They want to do an autopsy and asked me to deliver the body to the police vet in Perpignan.'

'Anything new on Nicolas?' Raisin asked.

'Apparently the Omega guy talked. Not much, but he gave them some names,' Geoffrey said. 'The man you photographed is called Romul, and the blonde woman is his second-in-command, Rema.'

'Odd names. Anything else?'

'Some garbage about planets being aligned and being saved from hell on earth. That's it. He flat out refused to tell them where Nicolas is being held. They're not even sure if the kid's alive or not. It's a good thing he's under police guard otherwise I'd force it out of him with my own bare hands. Look Raisin, I've got to do something to help. Can I use your car? Matt can get you back to the village later.'

'No... I want to come with you,' she said.

'Okay, I'll help René load the body into his truck... see you at the car.'

Reluctant to leave, Raisin stood at the door and watched them lift the wolf into the back of a green jeep. Matt came and stood next to her.

'I should go,' she said awkwardly.

'Don't worry about the cubs. I'll take good care of them and you can visit them as often as you want.'

'Thanks.'

'Sarah... I...'

She looked up.

'Raisin...!' Geoffrey called impatiently.

'Off you go,' Matt murmured.

She hid her disappointment and pecked his cheek.

'See you soon.'

She trailed after Geoffrey, resisting the temptation to look back, sure she would see Matt watching them disappear into the trees. She let Geoffrey race on ahead, her mind a whirl. Still not a word about marriage. Hardly the behaviour of a man desperate to win his girl back. Things had been a lot clearer when he was a safe thousand kilometres away in London.

Geoffrey already had the engine idling when she caught up with him. Cold air blasted her from the air-conditioner as he pushed open the passenger door; she barely had time to get in before he sped off.

'Don't drive so fast,' she said testily.

'Why am I the only one worried about Nicolas?'

'That's not fair. We're *all* worried, but we've told the police everything. What else can we do?'

'I'm going to look for him myself. I can't stand by and do nothing for another second.'

11

CHURCH BELLS RANG as she unlocked their front door. Geoffrey counted the rings.

'Damn, it's three o'clock already. I'm changing my shirt and going straight to the police.'

He climbed the stairs two at a time and dropped his backpack on the landing. She hooked her hand through a shoulder strap and carried it to the kitchen.

'Do you want something to drink before you go? What the *hell*...? Geoffrey!'

There was glass everywhere. Wind gusted in through the broken window and Matt's vine was upturned on the floor, the pot shattered. A football-sized rock wrapped in blue and white cloth lay in the middle of the chaos. Geoffrey walked past her, jaw wide.

'If that rock had hit one of us, we'd be dead,' she gulped.

'Who the fuck would do something like this?'

He pushed the rock with his foot and the cloth unbundled.

'Oh fuck, *no*! Raisin!'

A child's striped shirt lay at his feet. Dark red stains smudged the face of a grinning Donald Duck on the front of it.

'Is that... blood?' she stammered.

'I hope to God not. If it *is* his blood, I'll fucking kill them. He's just a goddamn kid, for Christ's sake.'

He picked up the shirt and flung it across the room. A piece of paper fluttered to the ground. They stared in horror. STOP was scrawled across it in bold black letters with a no-entry sign in the one corner, and the Jupiter seal in the other.

Raisin took a slow step back. Geoffrey kicked Matt's vine in anger, skittering soil clods across the tiles and exposing roots as black as witch fingers. She bit back a reproach.

'What the hell do they want us to stop?' he shouted.

'Why us?' she whispered.

'*Who* does this kind of thing?'

She didn't know if he meant the broken window or the kidnapped child.

'We have to call Michelle… she needs to see this,' she said.

'What's the point? They'll probably be tied up in goddamn meetings,' he said scornfully.

But Michelle answered after two rings and Raisin quickly explained what they had come home to.

'We'll be there in a few minutes,' she promised. 'Don't touch a thing.'

Raisin inched over the mess and plucked Matt's cardboard box off the vine branch. She poked a nail under the lid and flipped it open. A fluffy white feather quivered inside. She frowned. A feather? Its silken softness bowed away from her in a sleek curve. Her hand dropped to the ring in her pocket. If this was supposed to help her understand why he wanted it back, it wasn't working. She didn't have a clue what the feather meant. The buzzer rang.

'I'll let them in,' Geoffrey said morosely.

She slipped the ring out of her pocket and pressed it against her lips. She really didn't want to give it back. Voices echoed up the stairwell.

'*Bonjour*, Raisin. Are you alright?' Michelle asked.

'Hello, Michelle. I'm fine… just shocked.'

'*Bordel!* That rock could have killed one of you!' Vincent exclaimed.

'*Now* you take us seriously,' Geoffrey muttered.

'We have no idea why anyone would do this to us,' Raisin said.

'We were talking about that on the way over. We think it's because you can put a face to them.'

Vincent stuck his head out of the broken window.

'One storey up, quite a throw. You'd think it would be easier for them to smash a window at the gendarmerie.'

'Except no-one there has pissed them off,' Geoffrey snapped.

'And *you* have?' Vincent drawled.

'Where's the note?' Michelle asked.

'Under the table. We didn't want to touch it again. It fell out of the bundle when Geoffrey... picked it up. I'm so scared the shirt belongs to Nicolas,' Raisin mumbled.

Michelle threw Vincent a latex glove.

'Put it on and pass me the note, please.'

He snapped on the glove then held up the note and read it.

'Not exactly chatty. Is that the shirt over there?'

Raisin nodded. He crunched over the glass and hooked a latexed finger through the collar.

'Do you think it's Nicolas' blood?' Geoffrey asked hoarsely.

'We have to wait for forensics, but it's his shirt. His mother gave us a description of it,' Michelle said.

'Fucking monsters,' Geoffrey grunted.

'We're doing everything we can.'

'It's not enough. Every second in this kitchen is time lost. We should be out there looking for him.' He brushed past her. 'In fact, that's *exactly* what I'm going to do right now.'

'Geoffrey, wait. You can't, it's late,' Raisin protested.

'Rubbish. It's not even four o'clock.' He faced Michelle with a belligerent glare. 'And you can't stop me.'

'Oh yes I can. You and your sister are on their radar and they're dangerous. Don't underestimate them.'

'So arrest me. You'll find me at the top of Massane. Has anyone bothered to search the caves below the dolmen yet? Surely it'd be worthwhile to know *how* their man got there.'

'How did *you* get there?'

'From the dolmen,' Raisin said. 'But nothing had been disturbed when we went back, so he couldn't have gone that way.'

'And the area *around* Massane? Has anyone looked there?' Geoffrey demanded.

Raisin squeezed his arm. He shook her off. Michelle contemplated them silently.

'*Bon.* Point taken. I'll have both areas checked out. Does the no-entry sign on the note mean anything to you?'

'It was on their placards at the protest. It probably refers to the cave,' Raisin said.

'I'm off,' Geoffrey said.

'While he sniffs around for the Alpha male, I'll see if I can persuade our Omega to be a bit chattier,' Vincent said.

'While you're there… ask him for a map of the underground caves,' Geoffrey said sourly.

'Vincent, wait. I'm coming with you,' Michelle said. She stopped at the door and stabbed a finger at Geoffrey. 'Stay out of trouble and leave the police work to us.'

When they were gone, Raisin tried to dissuade Geoffrey from going to Massane. He refused to listen.

'No-one's bothered to go there. What if Nicolas is up there somewhere?'

'Didn't you *hear* what she said? They're dangerous.'

'And smart. They're probably over the border in Spain by now. But I want to be sure. Maybe, just *maybe*, I can find some sign of him.'

'Then I'm going with you.'

'No, Raisin.' His voice softened. 'Michelle's right. It *is* dangerous and I don't want anything to happen to you.'

'And I don't want anything to happen to *you*. If you go, I go.'

Two and a half hours later, they were the only people on the steps of the Massane Tower. She half-expected Henri to show up. A bank of clouds lodged thick and grey against the horizon, and a hot breeze swirled leaves around their feet.

'I hope we're not in for another storm,' she shivered.

'Were those rocks always down there?'

'There are rocks *everywhere*, Geoffrey. Which ones?'

He pulled her next to him so she shared his line of sight.

'Those below us… over there…'

Grey-white stones the size of clenched fists formed an untidy circle near the path the group had taken a week ago.

'That's near where they were sitting. Maybe they do weird rituals here,' she joked nervously. 'What if they're watching us?'

'Relax, will you?'

When they got to the rock circle, they saw a second circle further up.

'Same stones…' Geoffrey brooded.

'What do you think it means?'

'I don't know.' He studied the narrow track that disappeared down the hill. 'That's where they went when he caught you photographing them. I think we should check it out.'

'It's not even a proper trail, Geoffrey.'

'So go home.'

'Don't be like that. No-one will know where to look for us if we get lost.'

He waved impatiently at her and headed for the path. She hesitated then went after him. Within a few metres, brambles choked the ground and the trail disappeared. Geoffrey snapped off thorny branches and stamped on bushes to make it easier for her to pass. They carefully picked their way between massive boulders and soaring pines. The forest became denser and the heat eased. She flinched at every crackle in the undergrowth. Were they being watched? When a tree stump the size of a small car blocked their way, she stopped.

'This isn't going anywhere. *Please* let's go back.'

'Look over there. I think we're getting close to the end of the forest.'

'This is madness.'

'Who else is going to look for him? The police are too damn busy making notes on flipcharts.'

Pi squirmed out from under the fallen tree and bolted ahead, nose to the ground, following a scent. Geoffrey held out his hand to help her over.

'Coming or going back?'

She scrambled across on her own.

'I wouldn't put it past you to leave me here,' she grumbled.

Heat wrapped around them like a thermal blanket as the sun began to filter through the sparser foliage. The forest came to an abrupt end.

'Wow...' he whistled.

They were on a clearing that overlooked a rolling valley. She billowed out her shirt to cool herself, too anxious to take in the view. He passed her a bottle of water. She pulled a face at the lukewarm taste.

'Now what do we do?' she said.

'There's the farmhouse we saw on our second hike.'

He pointed to a stone house down in the valley.

'Are you sure it's the same one? Didn't it have cages?'

'They must be behind the building. It shouldn't be difficult to get to. We can ask whoever lives there if they recognise anyone in the photos.'

'You're kidding, right?'

'It's worth a try, Raisin.'

His voice was steady, but she didn't miss the pleading in his words. He looked at her with unwavering eyes. This was the brother she remembered, driven by conviction rather than fury. How could she say no?

'Okay, but I don't like it,' she sighed.

After an hour she begged for a break. He tossed her a small packet of dried fruit.

'Have some, but we can't stop for long. It's already 7.30pm. We've only got about another three hours of light left.'

'What will you do when we get there?'

'I told you, I'll show them our photos.'

'You can't just go barging up to someone's house.'

'Unless you have their phone number, that's *exactly* what I'm going to do.'

'I *really* don't like it, Geoffrey.'

She checked her watch. They would never be home by nightfall. Following an unmarked trail was one thing, but trying to find their way home in the dark was sheer lunacy. She fumbled for her mobile and stared at the screen. Just one bar of network. Right, that would be the deciding factor. The minute her phone lost signal, she would make him turn back. She kept the phone in her hand and followed him down the hill. Her heart jumped when she saw a yellow trail mark on a boulder.

'Geoffrey, stop! There's a proper path here! You walked straight past it.'

'No, I saw it. It's not the right way.'

'It is. Look at the yellow mark!'

'That's going east, which isn't the right direction. We're going to the farmhouse, not following a trail.' He held up a palm. 'A car...'

'What if it's them?'

'Stop being such a bloody baby.'

'Just get me home in one piece.'

She struggled down the bank after him. Her foot hooked over a root and she flew forward, crashed onto her knees and careened downhill on her stomach. She screamed, lurched for a branch, missed it, rolled onto her back and plummeted to the bottom, landing at Geoffrey's feet, mobile still clutched in her hand.

'I'm *sick* of this!' she yelled.

'It's over. Here's the road.'

He helped her up.

'You owe me,' she grunted.

'Are you okay?'

'Like you care.'

'Do you want to stop for five minutes?'

'No, I want to get it over and done with and go home. Which way?'

The road was a dirt track fractured by long furrows and potholes but wide enough for two cars.

'Only a 4x4 could get anywhere on this,' Geoffrey said.

'It's quiet. I wonder where the car went.'

'Hopefully to the house.'

'You're really just going to walk up to it?'

'Stop fretting. People who live in beautiful surroundings like this can only be nice.'

'And that from Mister Cynic.'

The clouds had taken possession of the sky, but heat still shimmered off the earth. Her shirt clung to her skin and her back hurt. She rubbed her scraped hands, feeling close to tears. If only Matt was with them. Maybe he would be able to stop Geoffrey's craziness.

They almost missed the driftwood sign with the house's name, *Mas de Puixança*. It hung at an angle from a nail in the tree and looked close to falling off. They walked along a narrow lane that funnelled them into an overgrown driveway that yawned across a neglected field. Four cars and a truck, all without wheels and doors, slumbered in the grassland like sleeping beasts. The downstairs shutters and doors were closed, but the upstairs windows were open and a pale blue curtain fluttered from a corner room.

'We'd better leave Pi here,' Geoffrey said.

'Why?'

'In case they have dogs.'

He clipped the lead onto Pi's collar and tied him to a tree. He yelped in confusion when he couldn't go with them. Raisin took refuge behind Geoffrey as they walked up to the front door, cringing at the noise when he pounded the heavy metal knocker. No-one answered. Geoffrey rapped again. She looked up just in time to see the blue curtain being yanked inside and the sash window drop shut.

'There's someone in there,' she murmured.

The front door creaked open and an old woman squeezed her face into the gap.

'*Bonjour*,' Geoffrey smiled confidently.

The woman's eyes darted to Raisin.

'*Bonjour*,' Raisin echoed.

'We're lost… could we have some water please?' Geoffrey asked.

The woman shook her head and began to close the door.

'Just a glass of water and we'll be on our way again,' he pleaded.

The woman hesitated, nervously tucked stray grey curls under her black headscarf, then opened the door.

'*Merci*,' he said.

They followed her down an unlit corridor. Green paint peeled off the walls and they had to side-step rotting floorboards. All three doors along the way were shut. A steep staircase led up one side of the passageway.

'It stinks in here,' Raisin whispered.

The kitchen was at the back of the house, and light streamed in through two barred windows that looked onto an overgrown garden. A faint smell of jasmine hung in the air. Electrical wires dangled across the ceiling and an uncovered rubbish bin wedged the outside door open. Raisin declined the chipped glass of water the woman offered her. Geoffrey took out the photos.

'Have you seen any of these people in the past week or two?' he asked the old woman.

She flinched and turned away. Raisin's mouth went dry. The woman was afraid.

'Geoffrey, let's go. Right now.'

'You've seen them, haven't you?' he persisted.

'*Now* Geoffrey...'

Raisin sidled closer to the door to look outside. A row of wide metal cages big enough for someone to stand in ran along the back corner of the yard. There was movement inside, but she couldn't make out what it was. The woman elbowed Raisin aside, pushed the bin out of the way with her foot and tried to close the door.

'Can I help?' Geoffrey offered.

'*Non, non*! You must leave!' she said hoarsely.

'What's wrong, Maria?'

A man with a shock of white hair stood at the window; his hooded pig eyes glared at her. Raisin's skin crawled. Romul.

'And you are...?' he demanded.

He spoke with the precision of a broadcaster and had a warm, deep voice that belied the menace on his face. When the face disappeared, Raisin grabbed Geoffrey and tugged him towards the corridor. He hid the photos but stood his ground. The man reappeared at the door. Despite the heat, he wore a thick fisherman's jersey and heavy boots.

A pitchfork seesawed in his hand. The old woman scuttled towards him, spluttering explanations in Catalan. He vaulted over the bin and waved her away.

'Get Thomas,' he snapped.

She hurried out of the kitchen, clearly terrified. He kicked a chair next to the table.

'Sit.'

'I'll stand, thank you,' Geoffrey said.

'I said *sit.*'

His backhanded blow knocked Geoffrey off his feet and onto the chair. Raisin lowered herself onto the neighbouring stool, panting in panic. Romul leaned on the pitchfork handle and twisted the black prongs between his boots.

A squat man with a high Neanderthal brow entered the kitchen. He was completely bald and a wild black beard hung from his jaw like a small animal.

'Master?'

Romul thumbed at Geoffrey. 'He has something I want.'

Raisin squirmed in her seat. The photos.

Thomas unfurled stocky fingers in front of Geoffrey. He fumbled in his jeans pockets and took out his wallet. Thomas laughed then slammed his boot into Geoffrey's crotch. He flew across the kitchen floor, landed with his head against the corner of an open cupboard door, and slowly curled into a foetal position, hands jammed between his legs.

'Geoffrey!'

A vice-like hand clamped her shoulder.

'Total obedience,' Romul growled. 'Search them... then throw them into the cages.'

12

RAISIN JUMPED UP. 'Leave me alone!'

Thomas struck her hard then grinned lazily as his hands wandered over her body. He found her phone and tossed it in the bin. Geoffrey didn't resist when it was his turn to be searched. Blood streamed from his forehead and one hand was still squeezed between his legs. She tensed when Thomas gave Romul the photos. He shuffled through them.

'You're certainly persistent. Why are you here?' Romul snapped.

Raisin didn't reply.

'Explain yourselves,' he said softly, stepping closer.

She focussed on his thuggish black boots. Just one kick would break her leg. Coarse fingers caressed her cheek.

'Speak when you're spoken to you, Princess,' Thomas murmured.

She kept still, heart pounding.

'Lock them up, Thomas,' Romul said in a bored voice.

'Be my pleasure, Master.'

Thomas yanked Geoffrey up by his shirt and shoved him towards the door then propelled them both across the garden.

'No,' she screamed.

Six mahogany wolves paced inside the enclosure, silent and watchful. Raisin wrenched out of Thomas' grasp. He laughed and caught her easily. Geoffrey twisted sideways, smashed his heel into Thomas' shin and pulled Raisin towards him. Thomas snapped out a gun and pistol-whipped Geoffrey.

'Okay, big boy... so you want to fight,' he jeered.

Geoffrey fell back, hands to his face, blood spurting through his fingers. The wolves raged between the bars. Raisin sank onto her knees next to Geoffrey. Thomas kicked her aside, hauled her to her feet and stroked her chest with his gun.

'This is how we'll do it. You walk and big boy here follows or...' He cocked the gun. 'I shoot. Do you understand?'

Tears streamed down her cheeks. 'Please, I...'

He lowered the gun and prised open her top button.

'Do you understand?' he yelled.

She clutched her shirt closed and nodded.

'Do you?' he shouted.

'Yes...' she stammered.

'Now walk in front of me. And you...' He glared at Geoffrey. 'Don't do anything stupid or your girlfriend gets shot.'

She stumbled towards the cages with Geoffrey hobbling behind her. Would she ever see Matt again? The wolves looked starving. She and Geoffrey would be torn apart in seconds. She searched behind her for an escape route. Romul waved from the kitchen doorway, pitchfork swaying in his fist. They were trapped.

'Get in!' Thomas yelled.

He held open a metal door. Raisin's eyes widened in shock. The cage was empty. She almost fainted at the reprieve. Thomas nuzzled her hair as she squeezed past him.

'You're a chubby little thing, aren't you?' he breathed.

The padlock clunked shut and he yanked it twice to check. The wolves became an explosion of bodies, crazed eyes and slashing jaws.

'Shut the fuck up,' Thomas yelled.

The wolves hammered into the bars. Thomas caressed Raisin with a last leer and left. Geoffrey shook the gate.

'What have you done with Nicolas?' he screamed.

'Geoffrey, *don't!*'

Thomas turned and slowly raised his gun.

'Obedience is what the master wants. And what the master wants, the master gets.'

'Go to fucking hell!' Geoffrey roared.

'You'll get us killed!' Raisin cried.

Thomas guffawed and lowered the gun. She groaned in relief when he slammed the kitchen door behind him.

The wolves growled next to them, tails flicking flies off the festering Jupiter Seal wounds on their haunches. A large male strode along the divide, assessing Raisin and Geoffrey with steady eyes. The rest of the pack hunkered down behind him.

Geoffrey crumpled onto the concrete bench at the back of the cage. The alpha wolf followed him with his eyes.

'We have to get the fuck out of here or Nicolas will die. They've got him here. I *know* it!' Geoffrey muttered.

'What about us? You'll get us killed!'

'*Someone* has to help him.'

'But why does it have to be you?'

He stared at his bloodied hands. A frightened yelp pierced the air. His head shot up.

'Pi!'

Seconds later, Thomas and a tall thin teenager appeared with Pi flung over the youngster's shoulder.

'*Fuck* no,' Geoffrey whispered.

The wolves swung around, bodies arched, hackles bristling. The alpha male let out an angry snarl. The boy swaggered up to the cage and flung Pi on the ground. The wolves hurled into the bars. Pi raised his head and whimpered. Thomas booted him closer to the cage.

'Your mutt?' he smirked.

'No,' Raisin said quickly.

'Yes,' Geoffrey said.

'Choice time, people. He can be wolf meat or I can shoot him. We're democratic here, so you get to decide.'

They gaped at him. He jangled the cage door.

'Choice is yours,' he sneered.

The alpha male lunged at him through the cage wall.

'Stupid fucking beast,' he laughed.

'Please don't hurt our dog,' Raisin begged.

'*Please don't hurt our dog,*' he mimicked. 'You decide then, my chubby little princess. Wolves or bullet?'

'Please, you *can't*!'

121

'Wolves it is. Eric bring the mutt.'

The teenager dragged Pi to the cage door. Pi's paws scrambled against the ground as he tried to wriggle free. The alpha wolf slowly sat down, dropped his head back and howled. One by one the others joined in. Thomas glanced over his shoulder to the house then angrily kicked the wolf's cage. Raisin wondered what he was scared of. The wolves howled louder. The teenager shuffled his Nikes nervously in the sand. Pi gave a feeble yelp and flopped onto his side. Geoffrey buried his face in his hands. Thomas inserted a key into the padlock of the wolf cage.

'No, don't. Shoot him,' Raisin said hoarsely.

Thomas cupped a palm to his ear. 'Why's Big Boy so quiet?'

Geoffrey stared at him with dead eyes.

'For God's sake, Geoffrey! He'll throw Pi in there! Tell him to shoot.'

'Listen to the princess, Big Boy.'

'Shoot,' Geoffrey said dully.

'Shoot *what*?'

'Shoot, *please*,' Raisin begged.

'Big Boy…?'

'Please.'

They recoiled at the gunshot. Raisin hid against Geoffrey. He gripped her to him. The men crowed with laughter. The youngster skipped over Pi's body and strutted alongside Thomas back to the house.

Blood pooled thick and red under Pi's head; his eyes were open and blank.

'Don't look. There's nothing you can do,' Raisin said gently.

He stretched for Pi between the bars, fingers just reaching him. She tried to coax him away but he refused. The wolves quietened but remained alert and restless.

Raisin winced as the kitchen door slammed a second time. If they didn't get out, they would die like Pi. But the cages were built like a prison against a high fence. There were five pens in all; they were in the middle one. The two on their right were empty, and the far one on the other side of the wolves was packed with rusting farm equipment and old furniture. A fig tree poked finger-spread leaves between the roof bars. She climbed onto the cement bench at the back and tested the bars with both hands. They clanged but had no give.

A small drinking trough curved across the front corner of their enclosure. Twigs and leaves clogged the stone basin in a black rotting mess. She hadn't drunk anything in hours.

There was movement near the house. The wolves swung around and growled. She refused to look and focussed on trying to persuade Geoffrey to move away from Pi. He hunched into a ball on the back bench and stared blankly at Pi's body.

She took Matt's feather out of her shirt pocket. Thank God she didn't have the ring with her. The feather nestled white and weightless in her palm. She clutched it to her heart. Was he looking for her?

Daylight was fading fast and the sky glowered red with danger. She heard a car leave then silence blanketed the house. A few birds still twittered as they searched for scraps of food before night hid everything from sight.

She glanced at Geoffrey. He was sprawled on his back and sleeping, or pretending to. She couldn't tell but envied his escape.

A gloomy carpet of clouds rolled overhead and the sky slowly lost its pinprick stars. Blackness devoured the house.

She was hungry but her thirst was worse. What were Romul's plans for them? Was Matt frantic, or did he think she was playing hard to get? She gulped back a sob. She didn't want to die.

She moved closer to Geoffrey, exhausted but unable to sleep. Mum and Dad didn't even know she was in France. Not that she stayed in regular contact with either of them. Years ago, Dad had pretty much vanished into his second marriage, and Mum... well Mum would probably only notice that Geoffrey had disappeared. She gazed at his sleeping figure. What had happened between him and Mum?

A creaking door splintered the night. She jolted upright. The wolves sprang awake, heads high and alert. Light poured from the kitchen and a dark silhouette walked towards them. Her chest tightened. The wolves growled. She huddled against the cage wall.

'Maria?' Raisin said in a hushed voice.

'Shhh...' the old woman replied.

Three tomatoes, a torn-off baguette, and a chunk of cheese tumbled into the cage.

'Water?' Raisin pleaded.

A metal spout poked between the bars and filled the trough with water. Raisin cleaned out the debris in frantic handfuls. The woman turned to leave.

'Don't go,' Raisin croaked.

Maria ignored her, but paused briefly over Pi's body.

'They'll kill us too if you don't help us.'

The old woman shrugged helplessly then rushed back to the house. What horrors had the old woman witnessed inside the house?

The alpha male continued to pace. Raisin dropped her head against the cold bars. The only person who could help them was paralysed with fear. She bit into a tomato and sucked it dry. A light went on upstairs then blinked off immediately. Somewhere close by an owl hooted. She tore the baguette in half and inhaled its breadishness. It smelled of France and freedom. Hot tears burned her cheeks. After two bites she lost her appetite and hid everything under the cement bench.

The night turned talkative. Something scurried behind the fig tree, leaves rustled in the mild breeze and the owl gave another mournful hoot. An engine rumbled in the darkness. She tensed then quickly lay down, eyes half-closed.

Minutes later, a flashlight appeared around the side of the house and low voices approached. Thomas and the teenager. She held her breath.

'Mind the mutt,' the teenager sniggered.

'Get rid of it. Rema will do her nut if she sees a dead body so close to her precious wolves. It's bad enough we lost the pregnant one,' Thomas muttered.

Their torches washed over the animals.

'When's the big night?' Eric asked.

'Friday. It's full moon and Jupiter will be ready at midnight. Romul and Rema are there every day to prepare.'

'Do you think the wolves are ready?'

'They'd better be...'

Their boots crunched away and she exhaled. Geoffrey muttered in his sleep and kicked the wire mesh. The men paused, looked back, then ambled off again.

She clenched her fists. Being ignored was as terrifying as being groped. What the hell was being planned for Friday? She rolled over and eyed Geoffrey. Still asleep. Loneliness and fear swamped her.

What were the wolves for? All six animals sat motionlessly watching the house, as if sensing the danger inside.

Thomas had talked about full moon and Jupiter. Scenes of ritualised devil worship invaded her mind. She gave a frightened sob and twisted onto her side. Just five days between now and Friday. Would Matt have found them by then?

13

HER BODY WAS stiff and sore, her clothes damp. She rubbed her eyes. Ribbons of sunrise-coral draped the morning, sliced by the black bars of their prison. Her heart sank. They were still caged.

Geoffrey was crouched next to the door, staring at Pi's body.

'Geoffrey?' she whispered.

He didn't move. She reached under the bench for the food and stumbled towards him. The wolves watched her in broody silence. She wondered if they were ever fed.

'We're in deep shit,' he muttered.

'I know. They were here last night. I almost woke you.'

'They?'

'Thomas and the kid who killed...' She couldn't finish her sentence. 'They were only interested in the wolves and some important event scheduled for Friday... something to do with the wolves.' She gave him the food. 'Here... Maria brought it.'

He took a tomato from her.

'What exactly did they say?'

'Nothing that made sense. Something about whether the wolves were ready or not. And something about full moon and Jupiter.' A hunted feeling filled her. 'I'm scared, Geoffrey.'

'Me too. If anything happens to you...' He squeezed the tomato so hard, it burst. 'I'll never forgive myself.'

She bit back an I-told-you-so and tore off a piece of bread. It was stale and tasted like sawdust.

The wolves settled back on the ground, heads cushioned on each other's bodies. The sun inched higher, blazing into their confined space. Flies clustered like fat ticks on Pi's head. Geoffrey threw twigs at them to chase them away. She grimaced. If the body stayed in the sun much longer, it would bloat within hours.

Time stood still and the stifling heat seemed to sap their will to survive. By late afternoon, the last of the water had evaporated and the wolves' laboured panting choked the air. Geoffrey broke off a fig branch and threw it at Raisin.

'Here… use it to cool yourself with.'

She fanned herself listlessly as he swatted flies and swept them into a black pyramid next to him. Hours after nightfall, they heard a car leave. Maria didn't come with food and the house remained dark throughout the night. A vicious fight between the wolves woke them the next morning.

Raisin pushed herself upright, instantly alert.

The alpha male's jaws were clamped over the throat of a small brown wolf. It squirmed on its back, paws barely moving. Raisin banged the wire divide.

'Stop it!' she yelled.

Another wolf leapt onto the trapped wolf and bit its exposed belly. The three remaining wolves circled the fighting wolves like watchful gladiators. She blocked her ears.

'Geoffrey, *do* something. They're going to kill it!'

He gave a weary shrug and half-heartedly kicked the metal divide. The wolf under attack twisted its head towards them, eyes terrorised. She couldn't look at it. Would this be their fate too? Torn to shreds for food?

The kitchen door flew open and Romul burst out, followed by Thomas, Eric and a woman.

Raisin froze. The wolves abandoned their torture and threw themselves at the bars, saliva flying from their jaws.

'Rema,' Raisin mumbled, edging backwards.

Rema wore a flowing white dress, and her blond hair, freed from its tight bun, shimmered around her waist. She looked more angel than captor. Only her arrogant chin betrayed the firebrand from the demonstration.

'Are the animals ready?' she asked Thomas.

'Yes, Mistress.'

She signalled to the teenager.

'The cage stinks. Clean it out.'

'But what about the wolves?'

She pincered the soft flesh of his cheek and savagely dug her nails into him. He stared at his feet, slack-jawed and shocked. Blood dribbled down his chin.

'Do it now.'

'Yes. Sorry.'

Thomas kicked Pi. The flies buzzed angrily.

'I told you to get rid of this,' he snapped.

'But where must I…?'

'*Now*,' Romul growled.

Eric paled and dragged Pi away by his hind legs. Raisin slid her hand in Geoffrey's. He pinched tears from his eyes. The alpha male padded to the front of the cave, thrust his jaws between the bars and drew back his lips into a fanged snarl. His pack growled and paced behind him.

Romul and Rema talked in low voices then Romul waved at Thomas and gave an instruction Raisin couldn't hear. A smirk uncurled over his face as he sauntered to their cage.

'Ready to answer the master's questions?'

'Yes,' Raisin said, nudging Geoffrey.

'Yes,' Geoffrey said dully.

'Ah, Big Boy's found his voice.'

'Why did you come to our house?' Romul asked.

'For the boy,' Geoffrey said.

'What boy?'

'The mayor's son… we thought he might be… nearby…'

Romul tapped the photos. 'Why did you take these?'

Geoffrey and Raisin exchanged nervous glances. Her stomach churned.

'No reason. We took them while we were hiking at Massane,' Geoffrey said neutrally.

With an angry swish of muslin, Rema headed back to the house, leaving a whiff of jasmine in her wake. Raisin relaxed a fraction. The woman was more frightening than Romul.

'Really? We'll see,' Romul yawned.

A child's high pierced scream came from inside the house. Raisin and Geoffrey ran to the front of the cage. Rema strode out of the kitchen, dragging Nicolas. The blood drained from Raisin's face. This was bad. Really bad. Rema was capable of anything. She placed a cautioning hand on Geoffrey. They exchanged horrified looks.

Rema stopped in front of their cage. A grey t-shirt with a white 007 swamped the child's small frame. His legs were streaked with dirt, his hair unwashed and knotted. He was sobbing hysterically.

'Fucking *lunatics!*' Geoffrey screamed.

'Tsk tsk… mind the child,' Thomas drawled.

'Let's try again, shall we? *Why* do you have photos of us?' Rema asked, digging her nails into Nicolas.

He screamed, terror-stricken, and tried to pull free.

'You're *hurting* me,' he whimpered.

'We heard Nicolas was missing and wanted to help find him. Please let him go. It's not his fault. Don't hurt him,' Raisin begged.

'How many people have seen these photos?' Romul growled.

'Two… maybe three,' she stammered.

'She's lying. We need to be careful,' Rema said to Romul.

'Five days is a long time to be careful,' he replied.

Rema flung the squirming child in Thomas' direction. Nicolas scrambled away from her on all fours. The wolves were silent, their amber eyes on Nicolas. Thomas waved his gun in the air.

'I believe you already know how this works, Big Boy. It's *choice* time again.'

'For God's sake, Geoffrey, stay calm,' she urged hoarsely.

'Your hand, Princess. Between the bars, palm up.'

She clenched her fists at her sides.

'Out with it,' he snapped.

She held out a trembling hand. He cocked the gun and pressed the tip into her palm.

'Hold it, my chubby little princess. Hold it.'

Her fingers circled the muzzle. He rotated it obscenely, leering at her breasts. Tears streamed down her cheeks. He guffawed then raised the gun and gave it to Nicolas.

'Take it, kid.'

'I don't... want to,' he sniffed.

Raisin shut her eyes. His wobbly courage reminded her of Geoffrey as a boy. Thomas manoeuvred Nicolas' index finger over the trigger and pointed the weapon at Raisin.

'*Bang bang* and she's dead!'

Geoffrey jumped in front of Raisin.

'What do you know... Big Boy's a hero,' Thomas sneered and shoved Nicolas against the bars. Geoffrey slipped his hand onto the child's shoulder. Thomas jabbed the gun at Raisin.

'Choice time, Big Boy. Who's it to be? Your girlfriend...?' He veered the gun towards Nicolas. 'Or the brat...?'

Nicolas looked up at Geoffrey with frightened eyes. Thomas pivoted the gun between Raisin and Nicolas.

'Where's the hero now, huh? Girlfriend or brat? Girlfriend or brat?' he snarled.

'Don't,' Raisin pleaded.

'Shut up! I can't fucking hear myself think!' Thomas yelled.

Rema fiddled with her dress strap as if bored. Romul returned Raisin's panicked look with raised eyebrows. His dead blue eyes paralysed her.

'Shoot me,' Geoffrey said firmly.

'No, *me*,' Raisin cried.

Thomas stroked the gun over Nicolas' cheek.

'They're fighting over you. Isn't that nice? The thing is, Big Boy, you don't feature in the choice. Last chance or I get to decide... girlfriend or brat?'

Geoffrey gave Nicolas a last reassuring pat then sank to his knees, arms high.

'Shoot *me*. Please.'

Thomas plunged the gun between the bars and into his neck. Raisin screamed. Nicolas ran along the cages towards the back fence. Rema sprinted after him, dress whipping her legs. The wolves sat motionless in a tight pack, watching. The alpha male rose and trotted up and down the front of the cage. His eyes never left Nicolas. Raisin was mesmerised. The raging animal was calm, as if he knew what had to be done. Then he lowered his haunches and began to howl.

'Thomas, enough,' Rema called.

Thomas frowned, confused, but withdrew the gun. Rema turned on her heel and dragged Nicolas with her. Raisin gripped the cage bars, trembling. The alpha male's howls reached deep inside her. The image of the tribeswoman flashed through her mind. She stared at the alpha male. Its body was rigid, its head thrown back, jaws parted as howl after howl spiralled skywards. No-one spoke. Nicolas' screams tore through the air.

Maria scuttled out of the kitchen. Rema's palm shot up to stop her. Maria lowered her head and a stream of pleas flew out of her. Rema shrugged and let Nicolas go. The old woman bundled him inside. Raisin didn't know whether to be relieved or scared. Could they trust Maria?

Without another word, Romul and Thomas turned and followed Rema into the kitchen. The alpha male fell silent, settled on his haunches, his eyes remained riveted on the house.

'I really thought he was serious,' Geoffrey panted.

'Me too. Oh God... they're back...'

Eric was carrying a heavy black bucket, and a large rifle was slung over Thomas' shoulder.

'Looks like a tranquiliser gun,' Geoffrey muttered to her.

She watched in horror as six sharp cracks whipped through the air, and one by one, the wolves keeled over. What the hell was happening? Thomas unlocked the cage and pushed Eric inside. The youngster stood paralysed, barricading the gate. Thomas yanked it free and slammed it shut after him.

'Start cleaning!' he yelled.

Eric toed one of the bodies and sprang back. Thomas howled with laughter.

'Bloody baby. Get to fucking work.'

Eric heaved the animals to one side, poured water on the cement floor and scrubbed frantically. Thomas whirled the gun like a baton. The alpha male stirred. Eric yelped and fled to the door.

'Let me out!'

Thomas handed him the tranquiliser gun through the bars. 'Shoot it again.'

'Me? *Really*?'

Eric snatched the gun and shot the wolf in the abdomen. It jerked and fell back.

'What about the others?' he grinned, face flushed.

'Fucking *child*. Give me the gun and finish before they all wake up and you become lunch.'

Eric fell to his knees and continued cleaning. A second wolf raised its head and struggled to its feet. Eric picked up the empty pail and brush, and raced to the door.

'I'm finished. Let me out!'

Thomas took his time to unlock the cage door and Eric stumbled out.

'Stay here and monitor them. Only call me when they're all awake,' Thomas snapped.

'Can't I come inside with you?'

Thomas backhanded him. '*When* will you learn to do as you're fucking told?'

'I'm thirsty and I...'

'Jesus, Eric! Do you have rat shit for brain?'

Eric flinched, scooped up the cleaning materials and disappeared around the side of the house. Thomas sauntered towards the house. Seconds later, Maria appeared with meat for the wolves. She tossed it into their cage and furtively thrust two brown bananas between the bars of Raisin and Geoffrey's cage.

'Some water, *please* Maria.'

She stopped, scuttled back with a watering can and splashed water into the trough. Raisin drank greedily. They hid the food just as Eric returned. He kicked the wolf enclosure.

'Get up!' he yelled.

They growled lethargically but didn't move. He rattled the door. They barely reacted.

'Why are they so docile?' Raisin whispered.

'They probably realise they're not fit to fight.'

'Shut the fuck up,' Eric shouted.

They retreated to the bench at the back of the cage. The wolves slowly became more alert and started to pace shakily, just the alpha male stayed unconscious. The others circled it, snuffling their pack leader. Thirty minutes later, Thomas appeared.

'They're all up, except the big one. It's hot and I'm hungry. Can I go?' Eric wheedled.

'Get me a stick,' Thomas barked.

'How long?'

'A *stick* Eric. To wake the fucking wolf up. Start praying you didn't kill it.'

'But you *told* me to shoot it.'

'Stick, Eric.'

The wolf showed no sign of waking when Thomas prodded it. He struck it hard but it stayed motionless. The rest of the pack began to growl.

'Call the Master,' Thomas ordered.

'But...'

Thomas whipped the stick across the boy's legs.

'The only reason you're here is because he's your fucking father. *Piss off* and go and fetch him.'

Geoffrey put his arm around Raisin. She glanced at him, grateful for the comfort. Romul and Rema strode across the yard towards them. Her white dress fluttered around her ankles.

'What happened?' she growled.

'Eric over-drugged it,' Thomas said smugly.

'But you...' Eric protested.

Rema glared at him. 'Get in and check.'

'It wasn't my fault,' Eric whimpered.

Thomas smirked and removed the padlock. Romul yanked Thomas forward so their faces were inches apart. Thomas went deathly pale.

'Maybe *you* should go in.'

The staccato thud of a helicopter rattled the air. Romul's head shot up. He shoved Thomas aside.

'Move them. *Now!*'

Raisin gripped Geoffrey. 'He means us!'

14

THOMAS SHOVED THE gun into Raisin's back and forced them across the kitchen into the dingy passageway. The helicopter's dull rat-a-tat still circled somewhere close by. Were Michelle and her police team looking for Nicolas? Did they even know that she and Geoffrey hadn't returned home? Thomas stopped at a wooden door under the staircase and brutally knocked Geoffrey to the ground.

'Don't do anything stupid,' he growled, then caressed Raisin's cheek with his thumb. 'You too.'

'Leave her alone,' Geoffrey snapped.

Thomas pushed Raisin up against the door.

'Or you'll do *what*?' he smirked, licking her mouth.

She twisted away. He chuckled and stretched above her, grinding his hips into her as he unhooked a large black key from the wall. He threw it at Eric.

'Do the honours, kid.'

Eric rattled it in the keyhole but struggled to turn the lock. Raisin held her breath. Don't open, she willed. She eyed the corridor. Thomas grabbed a handful of her hair and yanked her face within inches of his. Her stomach lurched. He stank of stale fish.

'I told you to fucking behave,' he said softly.

'It's stuck,' Eric whined.

Raisin pushed Thomas away with both hands.

'Geoffrey, *run!*' she yelled and sank her teeth into his arm.

He swiped her head away and hooked her feet out from under her. She screamed in pain and fell to the ground.

'Stupid fucking bitch!'

'Don't hurt her,' Geoffrey begged.

'*Don't hurt her*. Is that the best you can do, Big Boy?' He slid his hand between Raisin's legs. 'She's got more balls than you. I'll give her that much.'

The latch gave a loud clunk and Eric heaved the door open. Raisin propped herself up against the wall and nursed her cheek with a trembling hand. Their last chance of escape had just disappeared. Geoffrey stood rooted to the spot, looking stricken. Thomas tugged a cord and blue light flooded the stone stairwell. Her blood ran cold. She would rather die than go down there. The drone of the helicopter chugged in the distance. She glanced at the ceiling in despair. It was leaving.

'Get down there,' Thomas shouted.

She shook her head. He pointed the gun at Geoffrey's knees.

'You're probably a good fuck, but right now, you're a pain in the arse. Get in, or your boyfriend spends his life in a wheelchair.'

'He's not... he's my brother,' she stammered.

'Like I give a shit. Now get in there.'

Her fear of steep stairs paralysed her.

'I can't,' she whimpered.

'Oh for *fuck's* sake.' He cocked the gun. 'Your brother's going to love you for this.'

'Shall I help her?' Eric giggled.

'Go, Raisin,' Geoffrey urged.

Their eyes locked. He gave a firm nod. She crawled to the doorway, crouched onto her haunches then began to bump down the steps on her backside. Thomas flung Geoffrey against her and they plummeted further, crashing into the curved wall. He hugged her to him.

'I'm sorry,' he mumbled.

Thomas loomed above them, waving his gun.

'This isn't a goddamn sight-seeing trip,' he barked.

They helped each other up. She grappled her way downwards, repulsed by the damp grit on her fingers. The steps were dangerously narrow and the air fog cold. Yet she was sweat-drenched and hated how rancid she smelt. A shot rang out and the light died. She screamed and froze.

'Raisin!' Geoffrey yelled.

She felt his arms around her and clung to him.

'Are you okay?' he whispered.

'Are *you* okay? Why did he shoot?' she panted.

'I don't know what happened. The guy's a dangerous fucking maniac.'

A light bulb flared on at the bottom of the stairwell. She winced at the glare. It went off then flashed on again. She was too scared to move. The door slammed shut above them and she heard the iron bolts thud shut. *No.* She wrenched free and raced back up the stairs and threw herself against the door, tugging the handle with both hands. It broke off in her fist.

'Let us out!' she screamed.

Thomas slapped the other side and guffawed. Geoffrey coaxed her away.

'He'll shoot through the door just for the hell of it.'

She shook the handle then limply let it fall to the ground. Defeated, they crept back to the bottom and stood side by side on the last step, horrified by the long stone chamber before them. It stank of mould and dust. Geoffrey walked inside and kicked the rubble and earth on the ground.

'It's like a goddamn crypt in here!'

'Who *are* these people?' she choked.

There were cardboard boxes scattered everywhere, along with piles of abandoned household equipment. She dully ran her eyes over them and counted three vacuum cleaners. A brick shelving structure against the wall was stacked to bursting with buckled tin cans and cracked plastic containers.

'*Spaghetti... peas... pilchards...* most of the labels are so old, I can't read them. It's like a World War II safe-room,' Geoffrey spat.

He kicked over the metal ladder next to him and it fell on top of four earthenware pots, shattering them into fragments.

'Geoffrey, *don't*! What if they hear us?'

'We could scream blue-fucking-murder and no-one would hear.'

The light went off. Geoffrey jerked back and tumbled against her.

She groped for his hand. The light fluttered on again.

'Thank Christ,' he grunted.

He walked into the middle of the room and stared at her.

'I got us into a pile of shit, didn't I?'

'You did,' she said bleakly.

He nudged a box onto its side, tore it open and held up a packet of peanuts. He ripped open the box next to it and showed her a carton of mould-covered tomato soup.

'What in God's name are they stockpiling for?'

'Stop breaking everything. What if he comes back?'

He picked up a broken spade.

'I'll attack him with this. What more have we got to lose? What *more* can he do to us?'

She shuddered.

'A lot more. You're scaring me.'

He fell silent, a haunted look on his face.

'I can't stop worrying about what they're doing to Nicolas.'

She grimaced. Rema was capable of anything.

'I don't think they'll be hurting him. They need him in one piece if they want that tattooed guy back.'

She almost believed her own lie. The bulb flickered. Geoffrey's eyes flashed towards it.

'It won't go out,' she said gently.

'Thank God Matt's out there looking for you.'

'Except no-one will think to look here. We told them we were going to Massane.' She sank to the step and dropped her head on her knees. 'I hope the wolf pups are okay.'

'You still love him, don't you?'

'I don't know.'

'You don't know or you don't *want* to know?'

'Give the psychobabble crap a break. It doesn't suit you.'

'Don't write off something you haven't tried.'

'Like you have.'

'Actually, I have. Chris's idea.'

'That'll be the day.'

He shrugged, broke open another box and held up a tin of dog food.

'Motherfuckers,' he roared and hurled it across the room, then another, and another.

One ricocheted against the ceiling and catapulted past her head.

'Geoffrey, *stop!*'

He overturned the box then crumpled to his knees and hid behind his hands.

'They killed Pi.'

'Geoffrey...'

'What if they kill Nicolas?'

The light dipped, flashed on again then snapped off. The abrupt darkness and silence drowned them like a tidal wave. She crawled towards him. His shoulders felt boy-thin.

'They won't kill him,' she said.

The light crackled on again.

'Matches. We need fucking matches,' he croaked. 'And anything that'll help us get out of here.'

He got up slowly, as if his body hurt, repositioned the ladder against the shelves and climbed up. The roof was so low, his head touched it after three rungs.

'I'll look up here, you go through the bottom shelf,' he said quietly.

'What exactly are we looking for?'

'Anything that can help us. Matches, a knife, rope.'

She caught the tremble in his voice and nodded half-heartedly, dizzy with panic. They might as well be buried alive. She squared her shoulders and tried to relax, but her breath rasped painfully. Desperation overwhelmed her. They had to survive. She had things to say to Matt. A life to live with him. She jerked a plastic container onto her lap, tears stinging her eyes. If she was going to die, she would die fighting.

The box was filled with fabric pieces, patterns, and balls of red wool. Rusting pins and needles rattled around its base. She pushed it back and flicked through damp maps in the next container.

'Road maps, hiking maps, maps on Spain, Italy... fat lot of use these are down here.'

She slapped the lid shut. No-one had been in the cellar in years. They would never find anything. She jostled the box back into place and pulled out its neighbour. Toiletries. She listlessly checked the sell-by date on a tube of Mentadent P. More than seven years too old. She dropped it back into the box and ran her tongue over her teeth. What wouldn't she give to brush her teeth? She opened the second to last box and hiked up an expanse of white fabric with two fingers. A long tunic-style garment with red velvet braiding and a white leather glove spilled onto her lap. She picked up the glove and turned it to the light. Her heart missed a beat. The Jupiter Seal was embroidered on the front in barely visible thread.

'Geoffrey,' she whispered.

He jumped down and took it from her.

'And look at these...' she murmured.

She shook out a second tunic and a small object rolled onto the floor. Geoffrey stamped his foot in front of it to stop it rolling under the trolley and stooped to pick it up.

'A signet ring with the *Jupiter Seal*?'

'And what does the writing mean?' she asked.

'Haven't a clue. Could be Russian for all I know.' He gave it to her in a daze. 'If they make rings with their own insignia, it means they have money. We're in even more shit than I thought.'

The door at the top of the steps screeched open and men's voices crashed down the stairwell.

15

RAISIN HID THE signet ring in her pocket and bundled the garments and glove into the container.

'Hide those damn packets under the trolley and tidy the boxes,' she whispered.

Footsteps drummed down the stairwell. Raisin paused, nose in the air. Jasmine. That meant Rema. She slid the plastic box back, leapt up and scanned the room in panic. Would Rema notice the pots Geoffrey had broken? She hoped to God the woman didn't go to the back and see the dog tins he had thrown there. Geoffrey kicked the last of the packets out of sight.

'My finger's on the trigger,' Thomas shouted.

Rema's slippers appeared first, small and dainty on the rough stone. Geoffrey lurched for her but Raisin yanked him back.

'Don't be stupid!' she begged.

'Fuck it, Raisin. *Let go of me!*'

Rema's feet froze. Geoffrey ripped free but Raisin grabbed his shirt and held on. They were no match for Thomas and his gun. If they were going to fight to escape, they would have to use their brains. Thomas' thug-black boots overtook Rema and he gradually appeared, gun balanced on his hand. His bald head gleamed in the blue light and danger crackled from him like an electric storm. Geoffrey tensed, ready to pounce. Raisin clung to him.

'Separate them,' Rema ordered.

Thomas jabbed the gun in Geoffrey's direction.

'Get to the back.'

Geoffrey moved in front of Raisin. Thomas smirked, welcoming the challenge, raised his thumb and slowly cocked the hammer, eyes small and mean. Raisin elbowed Geoffrey.

'Do as he says,' she whispered.

'*Move!*' Thomas shouted, waving the gun to the back.

'What do you want from us?' Geoffrey snapped.

'A little cooperation would be good,' Rema murmured.

'Bring us the boy and we'll cooperate.'

'Really? You want a little boy in such a cosy place? Are you sure?'

'Then let him go.'

'I'm afraid not.' She smiled at Raisin. 'Do you have everything you need?'

Raisin glanced nervously at Geoffrey. What the hell was this?

'Towels and soap might be nice,' Geoffrey sneered.

Thomas jerked Geoffrey to him and head-butted him three times in quick succession. Geoffrey swayed unsteadily then crumpled to the ground like a ragdoll.

'Geoffrey!' Raisin screamed.

Rema's arm whipped up and stopped her from helping him.

'I asked if you had everything you needed.'

'What have you done to my brother?' she cried.

'Thomas, hold her.'

'My pleasure, Mistress.'

He kicked Geoffrey brutally as he went to Raisin. Rema skipped forward and struck him across the face, gouging a bloody tear in his cheek with her ring.

'Control yourself. We need them in one piece. Now lower her head.'

He pushed Raisin down, pinching her shoulders cruelly in revenge. Her head dropped and her hair fell forward, exposing her neck. She saw a glint of metal. A knife. She kicked back against his shin and tried to twist free. He snorted angrily and jerked her arms higher. Pain tore through her shoulders. Cool fingers grazed her bare neck. She almost vomited at the intimacy.

'Please don't hurt me,' she sobbed.

Thomas bunched her hair together and pulled, immobilising her against his thigh, her mouth inches from his groin.

'Don't move, and it won't hurt,' Rema said.

There was a sharp metallic snip and Raisin tumbled to the ground, free. Cold air breathed over her neck. She looked up warily and saw Rema lower a bush of red hair into a cream muslin bag. Her hand flew to her head.

'My hair...'

Rema stroked her cheek. 'Thank you.'

Raisin watched in horror as Rema knelt next to Geoffrey and sliced off fistfuls of hair, then gently, reverently, arranged it on top of hers in the bag. Raisin went cold. Rema wore a signet ring identical to the one burning a hole in her jeans. Rema cradled the bag against her and gave Raisin a thin smile.

'Thank you,' she nodded.

'Wait! My brother needs a doctor!'

Rema waved dismissively and disappeared into the stairwell, followed by Thomas. Raisin fell to her knees next to Geoffrey.

'Wake up! For God's sake, *wake up!*'

He was clammy and deathly pale. A gritty scab covered his temple from his fall against his cupboard, his lip was split open, and his nose looked broken. She tried to stem the blood flow and carefully shook his shoulder. His head flopped sideways. She checked his pulse, searching desperately for signs of life. Nothing. Her heart pounded. He couldn't be dead. She saw movement under his eyelids and slapped him hard.

'Geoffrey, damn you! Wake up!'

His eyes fluttered open. She collapsed on his chest.

'Thank God!'

He grimaced and pushed her off.

'What happened?' he grunted.

'Thomas.'

He struggled to sit up. 'Are... you okay?'

'Yes... no.' She turned her head. 'They cut your hair too. They're going to kill us. I know it. Those things in the container... this shit with our hair. And Rema was wearing one of those rings.'

He touched his nose. 'Jesus, it hurts.'

'Is it broken?'

He gingerly moved it and winced.

'Don't think so. There'd be a lot more blood.'

'I wish you'd stop goading him like that. You're not going to survive another one of his attacks. Did you hear what I said about the ring?'

The light dimmed and his eyes flew to the bulb.

'Do you think Thomas is doing that?'

She shrugged helplessly.

'We need matches,' he said.

'We need a plan to get out.'

'Matches first.'

'How often do you get these panic attacks?' she asked softly.

He stared at her, jaw clenched.

'I need to know what to expect, Geoffrey.'

'It hasn't happened in years. I've learned to… manage it.' He flicked his hand impatiently. 'But this… I'm not prepared for this.'

'So tell me what to do if it happens.'

He wobbled to his feet.

'It won't. We need matches… or a torch…'

'Sit down. You're still bleeding.'

There was a sharp crackle and the room went black. His fretful breathing rasped through the air. She edged towards him with outstretched hands and collided into him.

'It'll come on again,' she mumbled.

'It's so fucking *dark* in here,' he wheezed.

She heard the knife-edge hysteria in his voice and tried to distract him.

'The hike to Massane… what time did we leave?'

His laboured panting clattered like a jackhammer.

'Why?' he stammered.

'Just answer me… what time?'

'Don't know… early.'

'How long was the drive there?'

'Twenty… twenty-five minutes.'

'No. Half an hour. How long was the walk to the forestry station

144

signboard?'

'Forty, fifty...'

'What was on it?'

'A map. Flora... fauna.'

'How far to the tower from there?'

Light erupted around them and he hugged her fiercely. She dropped her head against him, swamped by hollow familiar guilt for not protecting him. As kids, they had controlled his phobia by weaving it into their hobbit adventures. It was the monster they had to beat. Now the monster was back and she had no plan of attack. She scanned the room. He was right. They had to find another light source. Or at least try. It was worth turning the place upside down to see what else they might find to help them escape.

They opened every box, searched every container, tore through every pile of junk. An hour later, dusty and thirsty, they surveyed the mess.

'I hope they don't surprise us with another visit,' she coughed.

'Food, toiletries, even bottles of fucking water, but no matches. No-one hoarding on this scale forgets matches or candles.'

He was bent over and fearful like an old man. She shivered. His phobia was too big. It shrank their prison, chased out the air, tightened the walls. She sank down on the steps and stared at the light. *Stay on, stay on.*

'Tell me how I can help you if it happens again,' she begged.

'It won't.'

'Just tell me anyway.'

He sat down on the edge of the trolley and buried his face in his hands. She longed to go to him. Years ago, when needing help wasn't a sign of weakness, he had accepted her help so readily, but now she didn't dare approach him.

Her mind drifted to the day when a crazed warthog had attacked them in the bush. Geoffrey couldn't have been more than eleven years old, but he had sprung between her and the animal, and was so badly gored that he couldn't walk. So she half-dragged, half-carried him home on her back. The homestead's outline was pitch-black against the flaming sky and she would never forget the flock of birds that exploded around them as they collapsed in front of the farm gate at sunset. Nor Mum's anger and her fierce blaming eyes.

Geoffrey had been raced to hospital, and for years afterwards, she imagined a different scenario: the warthog ripping *her* flesh and sending *her* to hospital to be fussed over by Mum.

Raisin sighed miserably. Mum would probably also blame her now. She dropped her head on the step behind her and stared bleakly into the black stairwell above her. She frowned and twisted around. A dark cavity punctured the curve of the wall about a metre away. She clambered towards it and saw a rusted metal box at the back, the kind grandfathers kept cigars in. Dust ballooned in her face when she flipped open the lid. She sneezed then gave a wild laugh. Matches. Hundreds of old café matchboxes, and seven very dry candles, wrapped in creased brown paper. She headed back down the stairs and gave him the open tin with a happy grin.

'I knew it,' he grunted.

He propped two candles between food cans and struck a match.

'I'll light one to try it out,' he said.

The flame flared briefly but died. He tried again. The match head crumbled. She held her breath. He scraped another match against the small black strip on the matchbox. It didn't light. He struck it again. The light bulb crackled and went off.

'Damn it!' he mumbled.

'Try a different box.'

The next match ignited at first strike. It trembled in his hand. The flame jumped to the wick, quivering.

'*Burn*,' she begged.

It shrivelled into an orange ember. He held the burning match closer but it fizzled out. He threw it on the ground, chest heaving. She scrambled through the tin container, willing the right matchbox to find her hand.

'Raisin, I…'

'You almost lit it, Geoffrey. Focus on that.'

'It… happened… in the dark,' he panted.

'What did?' she said, striking match after match.

'To Craigy… '

'Who the hell is Craigy?'

He lashed out at her with his hand.

'Are you *crazy*?' she cried.

He collapsed into wracking sobs.

'Geoffrey? You're *scaring* me.'

'I was five,' he choked.

Dread seized her. 'I don't understand.'

The bulb flickered. His face shimmered like a ghost. She scraped alight another match.

'What happened?' she whispered.

'Chris said… to tell you.'

She moved her foot against his. He didn't pull away.

'I'm here, Geoffrey… talk to me.'

'Sometimes… in the day, but… mostly at night.'

She blinked rapidly. *No*, she screamed silently. *Yes*, her heart yelled, *you know*. Tears streamed down her cheeks. The match went out. She lit another and caught his hand.

'*Who*?' she asked hoarsely.

He groaned. Relief, fear… she didn't know. She blurted out the name of a relative they both hated.

'Uncle Fred?'

He shook his head. She remembered an overweight manager at her mother's favourite haberdashery store.

'Jack… Jack Borbal?'

His eyes burned into her.

'Pete Visserman? The guy with the limp… from the corner shop?' The flame singed her fingers. She dropped the match and struggled to light another. Deep inside, a memory stirred. 'Damn it, Geoffrey. *Who*?'

He didn't answer. She clenched her fists.

'*Dad?*'

She held her breath.

'No,' he groaned.

She sank against him in relief. Light bled over them as the bulb sprang on. She winced at the glare.

'It was… Mum,' he stammered.

16

'No, it can't be... you're her *favourite*. She'd never do anything to hurt you,' Raisin mumbled hoarsely.

He held her frightened gaze then looked down. Her mind reeled. All Mum's love had poured into him, leaving barely a trickle over for her. It didn't make sense. She was desperate for it to be a lie.

'You don't believe me. I knew you wouldn't,' he said dully.

I do, her heart shouted. She stared helplessly at the ground, unable to meet his eyes, reassure him. Bewildering memories trembled inside her.

How many times hadn't she woken to an empty bed in the room they shared... and found him asleep with Mum? Another bad dream, she was told, then shooed back to her own room.

The pain of her rivalry with him hit her again. Her tug-of-war for Mum's love started at breakfast when she tried with desperate pleading eyes to be served before Geoffrey. But no, every morning, even on her birthday, the Rice Krispies bowl glided past her to him. The sticky envy that had clogged her young girl's heart oozed up like pus. *No*. She didn't hate him. He shuffled past her and she half-heartedly reached for him.

'Geoffrey...'

He stopped, waited, but her words wouldn't come. He was hand-reach close, and yet a lifetime away. She dropped her arm. Was he lying? Mum had loved him so much.

He looked at her, eyes hard and accusing, then shrugged and walked away.

She took a bottle of water with her and retreated to the far corner, a jumble of fear and dread, and found a pile of cement bags to sit on. She opened the bottle, not daring to check its sell-by date. What did she care if it was old? Water was water. She gulped thirstily, peering across the cellar to Geoffrey. A chasm wider than hell separated them. She wiped her mouth and put the bottle down. If she believed him then even the morsels of love she had scrounged from her mother like an urchin were worthless, tainted.

She rocked to and fro, cringing at the flaky residue crumbling over her from the wall. The candle flickered between them and she could just make out his shadow crouched on the step. She hated how vulnerable he looked.

Stop shutting me out, she longed to scream, but remorse silenced her. She was also shutting him out. Every breath burned her lungs. Mothers didn't hurt their children. *Mothers didn't hurt their children.*

'Why now? Why tell me *now*?' she murmured, more to herself than to him. But her whisper came out as loud as a shout.

'What does it matter? You *knew*!' he said angrily.

'How can you *say* that… how *could* I have?'

He didn't reply. More childhood echoes rumbled through her mind, but she cut them off, heavy-hearted and cold. Minutes turned to hours, still neither of them spoke. Her body grew numb and somehow, head against the hard wall, she dozed off.

Deep in the night, she woke to the low splutter of stifled sobs. She groaned and tried to loosen the stiffness in her neck. Across the cellar, the candle stroked long shadows over Geoffrey's buckled figure.

'Geoffrey… are you okay?'

No reply. She sighed in frustration and rubbed her neck and shoulders. He could damn well stay in his black hole. She was sick to death of feeling responsible for him.

Out of nowhere a memory exploded.

Mum. Kneeling next to the bath tub. Washing Geoffrey. Her hand sliding between his legs. Rubbing… rubbing. His blank eyes drilling into her over Mum's head as she, just four, stood rigid at the door, bewildered, terrified. And jealous.

She jerked upright. *No.* Her heart smashed through her chest. She tried to breathe, fought for air. Then she scrambled onto her hands and knees, gagging. Her head pounded, her face burned.

Sturdy hands gripped her shoulders and Geoffrey pulled her to him. Her body shook as she retched sour bile.

'I remember. Oh God, Geoffrey. I remember. I'm sorry… I'm so sorry,' she whimpered. Tears poured down both their faces. 'I didn't *know* I knew.'

He squeezed her to him.

'You have to believe me,' she panted.

'I do. It's alright, Raisin. I do.'

'Why didn't I help you?'

'You were little… it wasn't your fault.'

'Did… did Dad know?'

'No.'

'Why not? Why didn't you *tell* him?'

'She said he'd go to jail… we'd all go to jail. You too.'

She crumpled against him, safe in his comfort.

'Whenever we passed a policeman talking to a child, she'd say the kid was going to be locked up… because he couldn't keep secrets,' he mumbled.

She stared at him, open-mouthed.

'How old were you when it…'

'Five or six… I can't remember exactly.' He searched her face. 'Did I do the right thing telling you?'

'Yes,' she shivered.

He stood up.

'You're freezing. There must be something here we can use to keep us warm.'

Their precious moment fissured apart. She cocooned herself into a bundle while he yanked open the container with the strange garments. Vulnerable Geoffrey was gone, replaced by coping Geoffrey. One step towards truth, a hundred steps back into secrets. He held up the white dress.

'I can't, Geoffrey. Not that. I'd rather freeze than have it near me.' She hooked the ring out of her jeans pocket and flipped it across to him. 'I almost fainted when I saw that bitch was wearing one.'

He slid it onto his finger and studied it.

'Don't you wish we knew what the insignia meant?'

No, she groaned silently. *I don't give a damn. I want to know what happened to you.*

'Geoffrey… just put it back.'

He began to pull apart an empty cardboard box.

'What the hell are you doing?'

'Making us something to lie on. It'll be warmer.'

He spread the box out on the ground next to him and patted it flat. She dropped down on to it and touched his arm.

'When did it stop?' she asked sombrely.

He tore apart another box and for a moment, she thought she had asked too much.

'When I went to live with Dad.'

'Did you tell him then?'

He looked at her, haunted.

'I couldn't. I was twelve and… embarrassed. I didn't think he'd believe me, and I was terrified.'

'About jail?'

'Not for me. For *her*. If she'd gone to jail, *everyone* would've known why. I couldn't face it, Raisin. I just couldn't.'

'What if she'd done it to someone else?'

'I was a kid… that's how adults think.' He paused and swallowed. 'Whenever it happened… I became someone else. She didn't do it to me, she did it to Craigy.'

Her heart splintered into shards.

'Craigy…' she repeated sadly.

'He was as real as you and me,' he nodded.

'Don't you feel desperate that she got away with it?'

'It's too late for talk like that.'

'It's never too late.'

'I don't want revenge, Raisin. I want freedom.'

'What about talking to her and getting an apology?'

'It's hard enough talking to you.' He gave her more cardboard. 'Put this around you. It'll help.'

'So when you see her, you pretend nothing ever happened?'

'I don't really see much of her anymore.'

'*I'll* report her for you.'

'No. This is *my* thing, Raisin.'

'But...'

'Stay out of it.'

'If you wanted me out of it, why tell me? You're crazy not to do something.'

He blinked rapidly. She realised she had gone too far and took his hand.

'I'm sorry, you're right.'

'I didn't want to burden you with it, but Chris thought I should, and so did Paula, my therapist.'

'Does *she* think it's normal for you not to talk to Mum about it?'

'She says I should do what's right for me.'

'But she's a child molester... a blasted paedophile.'

He jerked back. She winced as a red flush crept over his cheeks. Shame burned there. Craigy may have become the victim, but the suffering was all Geoffrey's.

'It may not seem like I've getting over it, but according to Paula, I'm doing well, better than before. It's hard to talk about it. You're only the third person I've ever talked to about it, and you... knew already.'

'Please let me talk to Mum.'

'Don't hijack my life, Raisin.'

'Let me do it. She mustn't get away with it.'

'She did it to *me*, not to you.'

'I never helped when you needed me then... let me at least do something now that I can.'

'You're not listening, God damn it. I don't want your fucking help.'

'Why the hell not? She ruined your life!'

'Why don't you look at your own fucked-up life before interfering in mine?'

'My life's fine.'

'Yeah right. You had yourself sterilised like a dog. You call that *fine*?'

She gasped in shock.

'Shit, Raisin. I'm sorry. I didn't...'

'You told me what happened to save me from my fucked-up life?'

'No, of course not. I told you for *me*. But Paula thought...'

'So Paula's got an opinion about *my* life?'

'Look Raisin, Mum may have fiddled with me but...'

'She didn't goddamn *fiddle* with you... she *molested* you.'

He flinched, touched the side of his nose, as if checking that it still hurt. The blank expression of the boy in the bathroom blanketed his face.

'You're affected because you knew,' he said quietly. 'That's the point Paula's making. She thought it would help us *both* if we talked about it.'

Guilt overwhelmed her. She should have stopped Mum or at least *told* someone. She stared into the darkness.

'I can't think straight,' she mumbled.

'What I'm trying to say to you is that we were both affected by it.'

'How can something I didn't remember affect me?'

'I made up Craigy, and you... you had your own way of dealing with it. But the damage was done.'

'What damage? I'm fine.'

'Have you heard *anything* I said?'

'I'm going to sleep.'

She flattened the cardboard he had prepared for her, stretched out on it and burrowed under the second piece of board. She heard him rustle about on his board and kept still. Anger twisted inside her like barbed wire. She would call the police the minute she was free again. Mum should rot in prison. And Dad? He must have known. She always thought he had left Mum for another woman, but maybe he had left because he had known.

She would fly to Cape Town and confront them both. If Geoffrey didn't have the balls to do it, she did. She would show him *damaged*.

The candle flickered shadows around them. Her thoughts drifted to Matt. She dug her fists into her stomach. Was he still looking for her?

17

THE SCREECH OF wood over stone jerked Raisin awake. Someone was coming inside. She rubbed her eyes, alert, terrified. The light in the stairwell was on. Geoffrey had blown out the candles and was pushing the food cans out of the way. He hushed her, finger on his lips.

'*Daddy! Daddy!*' a child screamed.

'Nicolas…' Geoffrey whispered grimly.

She broke out in cold sweat. Why was he being brought here? She jolted upright as the door slammed shut and the bolts clunked into place.

'Let me go! Where's my daddy?' Nicolas yelled.

'Shut up, you stupid pain-in-the-arse brat!'

'Eric…?' Raisin mouthed.

Geoffrey's nod chilled her. The cellar door could only be bolted from the outside. That meant Eric was locked *inside* with them. She inched closer to Geoffrey just as Eric staggered into sight, dragging Nicolas behind him. His face was red and swollen, and his eyes darted about in terror. When he saw Geoffrey, his arms flailed in the air towards him. Geoffrey gave an angry shout and bolted forward. Eric grabbed the child in a chokehold.

'Get back!' he yelled.

Nicolas jostled his head free and sank his teeth into Eric's hand.

'What the *fuck*!'

Eric slapped him away and Nicolas fell face down on the ground, short spiky hair bristled on the back of his head. Raisin paled. They had also taken his hair.

'Leave him alone. He's just a child,' Geoffrey pleaded.

'A full of shit one.' Eric pulled Nicolas up by his collar and shook him. 'Try that again and you'll *never* see anyone again.'

Nicolas burst into panicked sobs, shoulders heaving.

Eric shook him angrily. 'Shut up!'

'He's bleeding. Let me look at him,' Raisin said.

'Daddy,' Nicolas whimpered between his fingers.

'He's petrified. Let him go,' Raisin begged.

'You fucking women are all the same. How much of a woman are you anyway? Take off your shirt... show me your tits.'

Her hands sprang to her chest. 'No!'

He jabbed the rifle at her. 'Off!'

'Put that down,' Geoffrey said calmly.

'Who the hell asked *you*? Get the shirt off, bitch.'

Eric licked his lips and leered at Raisin's breasts. Nicolas stood paralysed between them, mouth clenched shut to stifle his sobs.

'Let's see if I remember how this works: undress or I shoot the brat.'

She fumbled nervously with a button. Eric looped a finger over the trigger. Nicolas let out a frightened yelp.

'Let him go!' Geoffrey yelled.

'Geoffrey, don't. I'll take it off. It's nothing.'

He ignored her and pointed at Eric's gun.

'Isn't that the tranquiliser gun you used on the wolves?'

'So what? Is your bitch sister deaf? Take... it... off!'

Raisin undid another button. Her fingers hovered uncertainly over the next one.

'Not enough. Show me *skin*,' Eric shouted.

'The dead wolf weighed twice as much as the kid does. Shoot him with that thing and he'll die,' Geoffrey continued coldly.

Confusion flashed across Eric's face. He looked at Nicolas then back at Raisin. Nicolas flinched every time the gun moved. Raisin longed to snatch him into her arms.

'I don't give a shit. Give me those beautiful big titties,' Eric blustered.

'Do the maths, moron,' Geoffrey snapped.

'Geoffrey, *don't*,' Raisin begged.

'It's okay. Our young friend needs a quick science lesson. Small kid. Big dose of tranquiliser. You shoot. Kid dies.'

'Crap,' Eric snorted, stamping his boot on Nicolas' foot.

Nicolas screamed. Eric clapped his hand over his mouth then pulled it away in disgust and flung Nicolas to the ground, furiously wiping his bloodied fingers on his jeans.

'Fuck it!'

Nicolas crawled frantically to Raisin. Geoffrey lunged for Eric's gun. A deafening crack exploded through the air. She clasped Nicolas to her and ran to the other side of the cellar and watched in horror as the gun zigzagged wildly between the two men.

'They'll kill you if you piss them off any more than you have already,' Eric shouted.

'From what I saw up there, you're confused about who's pissing who off,' Geoffrey said, gripping the gun towards him.

'Nicolas says he saw his dad in the garden,' Raisin shouted.

'So *that's* why the kid's in here. The police are knocking,' Geoffrey smirked.

'They didn't come in. We told them they needed a warrant.'

'Them? Well, *they'll* be back then, won't they?' Geoffrey snorted.

'And you'll be long gone.' With a violent yank, Eric twisted the gun free then slammed it in Geoffrey's direction. 'Get the fuck away from me.'

Geoffrey retreated slowly towards Raisin and Nicolas. Eric backtracked just as carefully, gun held high. They both jumped when the cellar door opened.

'Get up here! Leave the kid. They've gone,' Thomas called from the top.

'What did I tell you?' Eric sneered.

Their circumstances changed so swiftly that Geoffrey and Raisin gaped at each other as Eric ran up the stairs. Nicolas clung to her, chest heaving as he sobbed.

'Jesus, that was close. I wasn't joking about that gun being able to kill...'

Geoffrey's voice trailed off. She cleaned the blood off Nicolas' face with her shirt and held him close. The short spikes on his head scratched her chin.

'You're safe with us,' she murmured.

'Is this a jail?' he whispered.

'No, it's a pantry with lots of food,' she smiled.

He looked around curiously but didn't get up. She fought back tears. He felt unbearably small and vulnerable in her arms.

'Are you hungry?' Geoffrey asked.

Nicolas shook his head.

'Why were you in that cage?' he asked.

'Because they hadn't cleaned out the cellar for us yet. But we like it here because it's not as hot as up there, and look how much food we've got,' Raisin said.

His thumb crept into his mouth and his body relaxed. She pulled his shirt over his legs to keep him warm. It was a clean shirt and she wondered who had given it to him. Probably Maria. Tiredness overwhelmed her.

The cellar light flickered. Her head shot up. No, not now. It flickered again; once, twice, then darkness blanketed them. Nicolas crouched against her.

'Light a candle, Geoffrey.'

'Is he coming back?' Nicolas whimpered.

Matches rattled as Geoffrey fumbled with the box, then a flame flared high. He quickly lit a candle, hand trembling.

'Why don't you light another one for our special guest?' Raisin said.

'Is it a *party*?' Nicolas squealed.

She hugged him to her. *If only.* A pang shot through her. Her birthday was just five weeks away. Would they be free by then?

'No sweetheart, it isn't. How old are you?'

He splayed his fingers. 'Five! Can I blow them out?'

'No. Not yet!' Geoffrey said quickly. 'Only when the light comes on again.'

Nicolas glanced anxiously at the stairwell.

'If the man comes back to fetch me... I want to stay here with you...'

'We also want you to stay,' Raisin soothed.

'Where were you when you saw your daddy, Nicolas?' Geoffrey asked.

'Upstairs in a bedroom. But there were no sheets.'

'Did they hurt you?'

The child nodded.

Geoffrey's jaw tightened. 'What did they do?'

'He hurt my arm.'

'Did they… do anything else?'

'Geoffrey, he looks fine,' Raisin said softly.

He scowled at her but kept quiet.

'Who else was with your daddy?' she asked.

'A lady… and a man with a shiny head.'

'Matt!' she gasped.

'Was the lady tall or short?' Geoffrey asked.

'She was like my teacher at school.'

'What does your teacher look like?'

'She's short but she isn't pretty.'

'What colour hair did the lady have?'

'I don't know, but not red like you.'

'Was it dark or light?' she prodded.

'Black,' he said with sudden confidence.

'Could be Michelle,' Geoffrey murmured.

'Did the man with the shiny head have a tummy like my brother, or one like mine?' Raisin asked.

He inspected Geoffrey's stomach then pointed to her.

'It's Matt! He found me,' she grinned.

'What were they doing?' Geoffrey asked.

'Looking at the house, but Daddy didn't hear me when I banged on the window.' His bottom lip trembled. 'Then they took me away.'

'Your daddy must be proud that he has such a brave son,' Geoffrey said, giving him a gentle squeeze.

Nicolas recoiled from him.

'That's the bad lady's ring!' he shouted.

'Damn it, Geoffrey! You're still wearing the goddamn ring. What if

160

Eric saw it?'

'Eric's an idiot.' He took the ring off. 'It's okay, Nicolas. It's not mine. My sister found it in that box over there. Tell him, Raisin.'

'Geoffrey's my brother and definitely not a bad man. You remember how he tried to help you outside, don't you?'

Nicolas nodded dubiously then looked up at her.

'What's your name?'

'Raisin.'

'That's not a real name,' he giggled.

'You're right. It's a nickname. My real name is Sarah. You can call me Sarah if you want.'

'I have *three* names.'

'You do? What are they?'

'Nicolas Pascal Fabrice. My daddy also has three names.' He glanced at the ring. 'And he has a ring like that but he's not a bad man and sometimes we put it in red wax and make small pictures.' He pressed his thumb into his palm. 'Like this.'

'Why don't we do that with this one?' Geoffrey asked.

He eyed the ring but didn't move.

'Can a ring *really* make pictures?' Raisin asked innocently.

He gave a half-nod and Geoffrey held the ring out to him.

'Let's turn it into a good ring and make pictures with it. We don't have any wax here but we've got lots of tomato sauce we can play with.'

The child hesitated for a moment then untangled himself from Raisin and stepped forward awkwardly, avoiding Geoffrey's outstretched hand.

Geoffrey opened a spaghetti tin and helped Nicolas dip the ring into the sauce. Together they made prints onto the carton they were sitting on. Sadness swept over her. Nicolas was the same age as Geoffrey had been when it had started. She felt nauseous at the thought. How could she have forgotten everything when the memories were so brutally vivid now?

Geoffrey's been a good boy today.

How quickly she had adapted and learned to recognise the lilt in

Mum's voice, see the mask drop over Geoffrey's face, and know *treat time* was close. Within seconds, she would bolt into the tool shed to hide from her mother's confusing favouritism.

Raisin dug her nails into her palms. Her cowardice revolted her. How could she have abandoned Geoffrey again and again? Abuse happened to *other* people. Poor families. Girls. Choir boys. Not to her brother. Not by Mum. She never knew such a thing existed.

But it *had* happened. Right in front of her. And what had she done? Nothing. Geoffrey had escaped behind Craigy, and she had escaped to the tool shed. Never helping him, not even once.

She took Matt's feather out of her pocket and rocked it on her palm. Would he still love her when he knew her family's shame? A tear slid down her cheek. The feather was supposed to replace the ring, but for the life of her, she didn't know why... or what he meant by it. She ran her fingers over its bedraggled fibres.

Was it something as simple as freedom? Had he understood, long before she had, that *marriage* petrified her, not *him*? Had he accepted they could be together without a ring on her finger? She groaned in despair.

Geoffrey looked up. 'What's wrong?'

'Nothing... I'm hungry,' she stammered. Her hand closed over the feather. 'How are you boys doing over there?'

'The sauce is too runny and we can't get a clear print.' He studied the ring. 'This is a mirror image of something.'

'A mirror image?'

'Daddy uses red wax,' Nicolas said impatiently.

'What about using candle wax?' she suggested.

Geoffrey's eyes gleamed. 'Brilliant.'

He blew out a candle, broke off the soft wax near the top and moulded it into a block, then he helped Nicolas press the ring into it.

Raisin envied them. Geoffrey's head was bowed, brow furrowed, as he guided the child's hand. Fear forgotten, Nicolas shifter closer, their bodies touched with easy trust as they chatted in low murmurs.

How far had the abuse gone? Geoffrey said it had stopped when he was twelve. Old enough for *sex*? The questions crushed her and made her want to throw her head back and howl like an injured animal.

'Raisin! Look at this,' Geoffrey said.

Nicolas was pressing tomato sauce-covered palms into every surface he could find. The red prints shimmered hazily. She looked more closely. A flash in the shadows caught her eye. She blinked, looked again.

The slope-browed cavewoman flitted towards her, green eyes glittering. The hair on Raisin's neck prickled. The woman beckoned to her. Raisin frowned in confusion. Go where? Do what?

'Look at this,' Geoffrey said excitedly.

She took the wax print from him and angled it to the light, eyes flitting about for the tribeswoman. Had she really seen her or was being locked up making her crazy?

'Read what it says,' he said impatiently.

She stared up at him.

'Assembly of… *Jupiter*? What the hell?'

'It must be what they call themselves. What exactly did they say about Jupiter on Sunday night?'

'Something about it being at its highest at midnight.'

'*Seal* of Jupiter… *Assembly* of Jupiter… the fucking *planet* of Jupiter. I don't get it.'

A frightening thought struck her.

'At the police station you said the seal comes from a magic square. What if it's *black* magic?' She gave Nicolas a worried look. 'Or satanic?'

18

'You're reading too much into the word magic. It's maths not magic. There's a logical way to figure this out. Think. *Think*,' Geoffrey grunted.

'What did people use these magic squares for?'

'Nothing really. Mathematicians loved them because the numbers are perfect, and the mystical properties only came in the middle ages. But even then, they weren't anything more than good luck charms.'

'So what's the Jupiter Seal supposed to be good for?'

'I haven't a clue. I was only ever interested in the numbers.'

'What about mythology? Isn't Jupiter the god of thunder?'

'He is, but that doesn't explain why they would brand *wolves* with an ancient talisman.'

'Romul and Rema are clearly the leaders but where has everyone else disappeared to? There were so many of them at the protest in the village.'

'Romul and Rema,' he repeated slowly. 'Romulus and Remus…'

She looked at him blankly.

'*Romulus* and *Remus* were babies saved by a wolf in Roman mythology.' His eyes shone. 'They were the founders of Rome.'

'You're saying Romul and Rema took their names from them?'

'And founded the Assembly of Jupiter.'

'But *why*? To worship Jupiter? Or wolves? That's just ridiculous!'

Her voice rose in frustration and Nicolas looked up. She gave him a reassuring smile and bent over him.

'Have you finished painting? Shall we try clean that tomato sauce off you?' she said.

He wiped his hands on his shirt.

'Can I go home now?' he asked unsteadily.

She bundled him in her arms.

'Let's use something other than your shirt to get you clean.'

'But we don't have soap,' he protested.

'You're right, but we do have water.' She glanced over his head to Geoffrey. 'The more jigsaw puzzle pieces we find, the more confusing it gets.'

'There's got to be an explanation,' he sighed.

She opened a bottle of water, wet Nicolas' hands and rubbed them between her palms. He twisted away when she wiped his face.

'Your mummy won't recognise you with such a dirty face,' she coaxed.

'*Yours* won't either,' he said crossly.

The image of her mother bathing Geoffrey flashed before her. Her cheeks burned and she snatched her hands away, feeling like a criminal. Nicolas stared at her in confusion. Her body sagged and she pulled him into a tight embrace.

Geoffrey, I'm sorry. I should have protected you.

Nicolas wriggled indignantly. 'You're *hurting* me!'

'I'm sorry, sweetheart. I didn't mean to.' She curled his fingers around the water bottle. 'Why don't you wash your arms and legs with this while I wash mine?'

She took off her shoes and massaged her feet clean. Could abuse be inherited? *Stop.* She cradled her foot in her palm. *No more memories. No more questions.* She wasn't her mother. Nicolas gave her the bottle back.

'Your face is still dirty.'

'You're a little darling,' she sighed.

He smiled shyly then leaned right up to her, frowning in concentration, and rubbed the dirt from her cheek. She shut her eyes. His movements were timid and unsure but full of trust. *She wasn't her mother.*

Having Nicolas with them changed life in the cellar. They did their best to create a routine of meals, play and sleep for him, and without specifically talking about it, they dropped the subject of the abuse and the Assembly. Two days slipped by before the cellar door opened again. Nicolas crept onto Geoffrey's lap and she flashed Geoffrey a warning glance. The last thing she needed was another run-in between him and Thomas. Seconds later Rema appeared.

'Good afternoon,' she said pleasantly.

A tall man stooped through the stairwell arch behind her. He brushed aside wispy blond hair and coldly surveyed the room. An elderly woman with shrunken cheeks and watery blue eyes followed him. Raisin didn't move. The man looked cruel, the woman grandmotherly, and she didn't trust either. Rema held out her hand to Nicolas.

'Come, child,' she said brightly.

Geoffrey's arms tightened around him.

'Let him stay,' he pleaded.

'You're coming too.'

'And my sister?'

'Ah… your sister. She has beautiful hair, doesn't she, Alana?'

'Lovely, Mistress,' the older woman murmured.

'Just you and the boy,' Rema said to Geoffrey.

Raisin's stomach churned.

'I'm not leaving without my sister.'

'You'll be back in an hour.'

'Why? Where are you taking us?'

The blond man spun a bundle of black cable ties between his fingers. 'Stand up.'

'Put those away, Daniel. The boys will behave. Won't they?' she said to Geoffrey. 'Your sister stays. Any trouble and Daniel will pay her a little visit.'

Raisin paled. Geoffrey looked at her in despair.

'Go. I'll be fine,' she lied.

Geoffrey hoisted Nicolas onto his hip and spread his hand protectively over his back, eyes gripping Raisin. She acknowledged his concern with a nervous grimace.

The blond man pushed Geoffrey and Nicolas up the stairs, and Rema and the older woman disappeared after them, then the door crashed shut and Raisin was alone.

It took a few minutes for it to sink in that the stairwell light hadn't been switched off, and that she hadn't heard the bolts clunk shut. Rough stone chafed her soles as she crept up the steps. Near the top, she paused and dropped to her knees. Silence and black shadows curved around her. Would she dare escape if the door wasn't locked? She crawled the rest of the way and tentatively tested the door. Locked. She dug her fingers in the grooves between the panels to lever it open. Not even a creak. She ran her hands along the sides in search of something to grip onto. Nothing. She slapped her palms helplessly against the wood and crumpled to the floor.

Time stood still. No-one came. She huddled in the corner and waited. Tiny splinters of light pierced between the warped panels; her only link to Geoffrey and the outside world.

She heard voices and braced herself against the door. A key jangled inside the lock and she flew back down the stairs. The door opened and a man cursed loudly. She heard the thump-thump of something being dragged down the stairwell and hid behind the trolley.

'Girl, your brother's here,' Rema announced.

Raisin slowly came out of hiding and froze. Geoffrey was spread-eagled on the cellar floor wearing a long white robe. She ran to him and cradled his head then cried out in horror. His hair was gone. Even his eyebrows. There wasn't a single hair left on his head. His eyes fluttered open.

'Nicolas…?' he mumbled.

'Crying upstairs,' Rema said coldly.

'Bring him back to us,' Raisin begged.

Daniel yanked her to her feet.

'Careful Daniel. No more bruises,' Rema said.

Geoffrey groaned and rolled onto his side. Raisin screamed into her hands. The Jupiter Seal blazed on the back of his head. She tried to wrest away from Daniel, but he laughed and tightened his grip.

'Geoffrey! Help me! Wake up!'

'Alana…?' Rema said.

The older woman unscrewed a small flask, poured steaming liquid into the lid and gave it to Raisin. She knocked it to the ground. Daniel shook her angrily. Alana stopped him with a gentle touch, picked up the cup and refilled it.

'It's tea... it'll calm you. The boy needs you.'

'I can't leave my brother like this.'

'He'll be fine. Nicolas needs you more.'

Alana pushed the cup into her hand.

'No,' Raisin said shakily.

'Oh, but you must,' Rema said and signalled to Daniel.

He immobilised her while Alana held the tea to her mouth. Rema pinched her chin.

'Drink or your brother gets hurt.'

'I'll come with you... but I don't want to drink it.'

'Break his hand,' Rema ordered.

Raisin sipped the bitter liquid.

'All of it,' Rema snapped.

It sandpapered her throat and burned her chest then her legs buckled and she collapsed.

One, two, three slaps. Raisin's cheeks stung as she fought to focus. Blurred shadows shifted in front of her. Someone hit her again. She tried to protect herself but her hands were tied. Something acrid seared her nose and lungs. She gasped for air.

'She's back,' Alana murmured.

Soft fingers wiped her brow and a glass was pressed against her lips.

'Drink... you're thirsty,' Alana said.

Raisin blinked and shook her head. Her mouth was parched, her tongue thick and dry, but she didn't trust anyone.

'Where am I?' she croaked.

'Drink,' Alana urged.

'Where's my brother?'

'Right next to you.'

'Raisin,' Geoffrey whispered.

She turned towards his voice. He was right next to her in a heavy wooden throne-like chair that dwarfed him; his face was gaunt with fear. Her pulse pounded. She leant forward to get up but heavy ropes bound her wrists to an identical mahogany chair. She writhed against the restraints.

'Where am I?' she sobbed.

'Tell her you're not hurt,' Alana said to Geoffrey.

'Raisin, I'm fine.'

He didn't sound fine. Why was he lying?

'Let me go!' she shouted.

'Rema will hear you. Shhhh,' Alana begged.

'Raisin, *look* at me! Calm down. *Please*. You're making it worse.'

His voice was a vague mumble. She looked right, left, up, down. They were underground.

'Help! Someone help! *Help!*'

'Raisin! For fuck's sake… *shut up*! Think of Nicolas.'

She turned to him, stunned. 'Where is he?'

'You have to calm down,' he said desperately.

'Where's Nicolas? Why are we here?'

'Keep your voice down, for God's sake. They drugged you to get you here. They'll knock you out again if you don't shut up.'

She gripped the chair. Alana nudged the glass against her lips.

'It's water… look,' she said and drank some.

Raisin reluctantly tested the liquid with a tentative sip. Reassured, she drank the tumbler dry. Alana gave a satisfied smile.

'Please free me. *Please*,' she begged Alana.

'You are free,' she said softly and walked away.

'Where *are* we?' Raisin whimpered.

'*Grotte des Loups*. The cave with the wolf paintings. We've been here for hours,' Geoffrey said.

'But *why*?' she stammered.

He didn't reply. The cave was much bigger than she remembered. Stalagmite trunks soared on either side of their thrones, casting long shadows that grasped the ground like talons. Gnarled cave walls twisted in uneven furrows around her. Not even twenty metres away, the wolf paintings swarmed over the rockface behind a high altar structure that was covered in folds of red velvet. Robed figures circled it in slow even steps. She felt like she had landed in Hell.

Someone lit six tall candles on the altar and a second robed person lit a wide ring of candles on the ground. Soft light halos billowed out through the cave. Raisin counted seventeen people, not even a third of those at the protest. Some sat, some stood, no-one spoke. She heard agitated snuffles and frowned at Geoffrey.

'What's that?'

'Wolves,' Geoffrey muttered.

'*Here?*'

'We're in big shit, Raisin.'

His voice cracked. Without hair, he looked shrunken, his eyes too dark and too big. A sharp pain shot across the back of her head. She twisted her head sideways.

'My hair…?' she whispered.

'Shaved,' he winced.

'Did they put a…?'

'Yes.'

She stared at him. Branded for life with the Jupiter tattoo. What if her hair didn't grow back? Hot tears burned her cheeks. She looked down at her white dress. It barely covered her shoulders and tumbled in deep folds to her ankles. Red braid looped below her breasts and around her waist.

'It's like the one in the cellar,' she said hoarsely.

He nodded grimly. A gilded staff in the shape of a long-stemmed flower lay at her feet. Its slender stalk ended in petals that were peeled open into a receptacle.

'What is it?' she asked.

'A Roman-style torch. These robes are also Roman.'

'And the things in front of you?'

Three long metal zigzags were bundled together with coils of barbed wire.

'I wish I knew,' he said bleakly.

'Where's Nicolas?'

He wouldn't look at her.

'Tell me he's okay.'

He gestured to the front with his head. She leant forward, squinting in the shadowy light and stifled a cry.

'Oh God, *no!*'

Underneath the red velvet on the altar, she could just make out the outline of a small body.

'Nicolas?' she asked in a strangled voice.

'Who else?'

19

TIME STOOD STILL, even the cave seemed to fall silent. Nicolas. On the altar.

'Is he dead?' she whispered.

'He must be. He hasn't moved since we got here.'

Pain shot through her as she yanked and twisted her arms against the rope. She didn't care how much it hurt. Anything was better than the numbing horror of the small form on the altar. It was happening again. Another child she couldn't save. She wrenched at the ropes. No give. No escape. She was as powerless to help Nicolas as she had been for Geoffrey. She dropped her head against the chair and stared up into the dark heights of the cave. How could this be happening?

Angry snarls suddenly savaged the cathedral quiet. She jerked upright and scanned the cave. The wolves.

'Where are they?' she asked Geoffrey

'Somewhere near the altar. Someone's coming. Pretend you've blacked out.'

She slumped into the chair but kept her eyes open a crack. Romul. His stride long and purposeful. The little courage she had left shrivelled into nothing. Rema, Alana and Thomas followed him, wearing identical floor length robes. Only Romul had hair; its white wildness obscene next to everyone's baldness.

'My sister needs a doctor,' Geoffrey said.

'Nonsense. She'll come round sooner or later,' Rema shrugged.

'Alana? You said she was fine,' Thomas snapped.

'She's not. You can see she isn't,' Geoffrey said.

'No more mistakes, Rema,' Romul said coldly.

Impatience flashed across her face as she withdrew a blue phial from the folds of her robe, unplugged the glass stopper, and held it under Raisin's nose. Her eyes flew open. She spluttered and coughed, cringing back against the chair. Rema's face was inches from hers. So close that her freckles bled into one another and became bruise-like smudges on her flawless skin. Rema stroked her cheek.

'Like Alana said, you're fine. Aren't you, girl?'

Raisin tugged violently at the rope, ignoring the pain shooting through her arm.

'Help! Someone help me!' she screamed.

Two robed figures near the altar turned and looked at her.

'Help me!' she yelled at them, kicking her feet wildly against the chair.

'Sedate her,' Rema ordered.

'Raisin, for God's sake! *Stop it…* she means it!'

'I don't care. Someone *help!*'

Rema struck her twice across the face. Her head slammed into the chair, her vision blurred and her mind went blank.

'Rema!' Romul warned.

'I've never let you down. I won't today,' Rema snapped.

'Just knock her out. We only need her for five minutes,' Thomas grumbled.

Romul's mouth tightened.

'No. I want them aware, and involved. They must know what greatness they're participating in.'

Rema dipped her head.

'You're right, but she's ignorant of all this and unlikely to understand.'

'Please let us go. We won't say anything to anyone. We didn't mean to come to your house. I'm sorry we did. I'm sorry I shouted. I'll do anything you want. Just let us go. I'm so sorry,' Raisin sobbed.

'Do as you're told and you won't get hurt,' Rema said.

'I said no more mistakes, Rema. Not even one.'

'Wait! Is Nicolas dead?' Geoffrey blurted out.

Rema narrowed her eyes, gave a small smile and brought her mouth close to his face.

'No, but his life is in your hands,' she purred.

'Okay. That's good. That's wonderful. We'll do anything, just don't hurt him. He's just a child. What do you want us to do?'

'Exactly as the master asks.'

'I want more than mute compliance. You must declare your willingness for all to hear,' Romul said. He motioned to Rema. 'We begin in nineteen minutes.'

'We'll be ready.'

'As you should be. The alignment is approaching and this is our only chance.'

Romul's bullet eyes bored into Raisin. She squirmed. *Willingness for what?* She glanced at Nicolas' body. Was he really alive or were they lying just to control them? Romul followed her look and smiled. She glanced anxiously at his smug face. Dread gripped her. Something was about to happen. Romul beckoned to Thomas.

'Help me with the wolves,' he said.

Thomas followed him obediently, leering lazily at Raisin over his shoulder. She watched them walk away, master and slave. Why were they going to the wolves? She tested the ropes again. They ground into her wrists but had no give. She gulped back tears. A hand brushed her naked head.

'No more antics, girl. This is the most important day of your life,' Rema said.

'I don't... feel good.'

'Really? I have just the thing for you.'

Rema thrust the open phial in her face. She convulsed forward, her throat closed, her lungs burned.

'Please... *no more*,' she rasped.

Rema swirled the phial closer. Black dots swum before her eyes and she began to choke. She couldn't speak. Was this how dying felt?

'For God's sake, stop torturing her!' Geoffrey cried.

'Then honour your responsibilities. Powers far greater than you demand it,' Rema spat. She plugged the phial and waved Alana closer. 'Purify them.'

Raisin took deep gulps of air. The dizziness eased and the cave pulled back into focus. Alana bobbed up and down in front of her like a bird. White steam shivered from a bowl balanced on her hip. Rema came up behind her and stabbed her nails into Raisin's head.

'Juno claims you!' she hissed.

Raisin tried to pull away but Rema dug deeper. She jostled backwards and forwards in the chair like a trapped animal. The woman was mad. Rema chuckled dryly and drifted to Geoffrey, tracing her fingers over his tattoo.

'And Jupiter claims *you*...'

A spine-chilling howl sliced through her words. Raisin screamed; her eyes scanned the cave. It sounded like a death cry. Were the wolves being slaughtered? Why was nobody reacting? Rema raised her arms in the air as if in prayer.

'Soon, my wild ones, soon,' she called.

Another howl tore across the cave. Then a third. The wolves' chains crashed and clattered against the rock. Raisin craned her neck to see. Had they been let loose? Why was everyone so calm? Rema twisted her hair around her hand and walked slowly towards the howling, as if reeled in by invisible coils. Alana lowered the dish to the ground in front of Raisin and smiled.

'What's going to... happen to us?' Raisin stammered.

Alana dipped the cloth into the hot water without replying. Raisin searched the cave for hints of what was in store. Romul and Rema were out of sight and the robed figures were still padding around the altar. Puppets, all of them, she thought bitterly. Some had to be parents, so what dreadful hold did Romul and Rema have over them that they wouldn't fight to save the child on the altar? Her eyes narrowed. The followers had stopped and turned to face the altar then began to sit cross-legged on the cave floor.

Raisin jumped when the hot cloth touched her. Alana tutted and wiped her feet with long steady strokes. Sick to her stomach, Raisin stared blankly over Alana's head. She bit her lip. It felt good. Too good. Comforting as a mother's caress. She was desperate to jerk her feet away. Alana bowed low and pressed her forehead against Raisin's feet.

'Bless this vessel of Juno,' she prayed.

Raisin trembled. It sounded like a curse. Alana carried the bowl to Geoffrey and wrapped the steaming cloth around his feet.

'Tell us why we're here,' he begged.

'Ask your sister. She knows… she senses their presence.'

'But I *don't*! *Whose* presence?'

'Jupiter and Juno. Grandparents of the great twins of Rome.' She lowered her forehead to Geoffrey's feet. 'Bless this vessel of Jupiter.'

'Why isn't Nicolas moving? Is he already dead? Are we also going to die?' Raisin cried.

Alana's eyes widened in shock.

'No, of course not. Just don't anger them. *Please* don't anger them.'

'But why us?' Geoffrey asked.

'Shhhh… don't speak. They'll hear.' She inclined her head. 'Thank you. This was my greatest honour.'

'Wait! Is he alive? *Please*, just tell me!'

'Shhh. Don't attract attention. I must go… it is time.'

'Wait! *Tell me*…! Is he alive?' Geoffrey shouted angrily.

'Be careful,' Alana pleaded, glancing nervously at the figure walking towards them.

Raisin's heart sank. Thomas. Alana snatched up the bowl but didn't leave. He stopped in front of Raisin, legs spread, crotch thrust forward. She fought not to show her terror. Men like him thrived on the fear of others. He slid a finger under her neckline, nudged the white gown aside and exposed her breast. She flushed and glared at him.

'Thomas, *no*!' Alana gasped.

'Just saying goodbye to my princess,' he said thickly.

Raisin stared at Alana, eyes pleading for help. The older woman shrugged feebly. Thomas sniggered and lifted Raisin's chin. His lips twisted into a wet sneer.

'You're lucky you're Romul's.'

Low drumbeats rumbled from the seated congregation, and with great poise, Romul and Rema took up position on either side of the altar. Thomas sighed, squeezed her breast hard then yanked the robe

176

closed and walked quickly to the front. Alana's hand shook as she adjusted the dress over Raisin's shoulder.

'I'm so sorry,' she mumbled.

'What did he mean that *I'm Romul's?*'

'Just be still... don't provoke them. It is time, I must go.'

She shuffled away, head low. Raisin watched her take her place on the ground with the others. Their last hope of help was gone. The cave throbbed with anticipation then fell silent. Raisin's skin prickled. Even the wolves were quiet.

Romul and Rema circled the altar. The followers swayed back and forth, and subdued humming sandpapered the air.

The animals on the cave wall shimmered in suspended vigour. Raisin stared at the striding wolf in the middle of the fresco. Its legs were extended in full running gait as if vaulting over the deep break in the rockface. There were handprints everywhere; between the animals, over the animals, alone, interlinked. Did they belong to the tribeswoman and her clan? Had a similar ceremony happened here all those lifetimes ago? No. Evil pumped in the cave today, nothing like the serene sacredness that had surrounded the tribeswoman and her gentle adviser.

The drums exploded, louder, faster. Heavy thuds filled Raisin's chest, convulsing in waves, thundering high. She became drowsy, disorientated. The wolf on the rockface began to vibrate. The handprints quivered; crazed palms pushed out of the mountain. Romul and Rema turned to the congregation, arms raised, faces euphoric. Raisin leant towards Geoffrey.

'We're going to die, aren't we?' she said hoarsely.

He didn't reply but his eyes screamed *yes*. Her insides cramped in despair. She would never see Matt again.

Four women approached the altar and lit the flower-shaped heads of their golden torches from the candles. Fire erupted from the graceful ends and the women stabbed the flaming lights high in the air.

Unseen, the wolves snarled and wrestled against their chains.

Raisin gripped the chair. *Let the chains be strong enough.* The drumbeats turned erratic, wild. The ropes tore her skin open. She was trapped. Wolves, lunatics, sacrifice. This was the end.

Alana led the lightbearers away from the altar with a gentle smile on her lips. She clasped her torch in white-gloved hands, arms deathly pale against the orange flames. Four men followed; Thomas loomed tall in the rear. Raisin and Geoffrey exchanged terrified looks. They were walking their way.

Drumbeats ricocheted off the gnarled walls, ripping between the soaring stalagmites. The chaos was crushing. The women knelt before Raisin and Geoffrey, expressions grave. Two men halted like sentries on either side of them. Raisin felt Thomas undress her with his eyes. Alana signalled to the man on Raisin's left.

'Go ahead, Victor.'

A Jupiter Seal ring flashed past Raisin as he removed the ropes from her wrists. Free. She clamped cool palms over her raw wounds and scanned the cave for somewhere to run to.

'Oh no you don't, Princess,' Thomas drawled, dangling a rope end between her breasts.

She shrank against the chair.

'Thomas, *no!*' Alana panicked.

He ignored her and stroked Raisin's nipples through her dress with the rope. Victor snatched it away.

'You dare violate the vessel of Juno?' he rebuked.

'The Master is watching,' Alana whispered.

Victor took Raisin's right hand and dipped his head in apology. She frowned, confused by his courtesy. He drew a slender gold cord from his robe, tied one end around her wrist and the other around the chair. The cord was long enough for her hand to move freely. She watched in bewilderment as he did the same to Geoffrey's left wrist. Their tethered hands were just inches apart. Victor bowed and moved back into position next to their chairs.

Raisin stared longingly at Geoffrey's hand, hungering for comfort. Her heart raced. The new cord was long. Could she reach him? She raised her hand a fraction. No-one noticed. She floated it over, not daring to breathe, then gently covered his hand. Their fingers linked.

'Now!' Alana instructed.

Their chairs flew into the air, their hands were wrenched apart, and the men carried them slowly towards the altar. The congregation rose and began to chant. Drums battered Raisin's senses. Geoffrey swayed ahead of her, the Jupiter Seal floating like a malignant eye on the back of his head. Her chair tilted dangerously as the men stepped onto the altar's platform. Her heart stopped.

Five wolves were shackled to thick metal rings in the rockface. They whipped their bodies from side to side in rage. She crumpled against the back of the chair. It was over. They would never get out alive. Tears slid down her cheeks. She wished she had Geoffrey's forgiveness for not saving him from their mother. She had hurt everyone she loved and felt shrivelled and unworthy.

They were lowered to the ground, within touching distance of Nicolas. Heart in her throat, she refused to look. The chanting throbbed. The candles on the ground lassoed the altar and fires flared high on either side. The worshippers curved closer like pincers. The wolves raged, yellow incisors gleaming.

Quirinus, Quirinus, Quirinus.

Wave after wave of drumbeats crushed her senses. The cacophony careened into anarchy.

Blackness danced before her. The animal fresco burned with life. Her eyes stung. The large striding wolf quivered as if leaping free. Flames danced from a golden torch that was thrust in her hand.

'Raise fire to heaven,' Rema commanded.

Raisin lifted the torch uncertainly.

'Stand!' Rema snapped.

Raisin wobbled to her feet, the cord around her wrist tightened. She couldn't bring herself to look at Geoffrey.

'Reach for Juno!' Rema ordered.

Raisin held the torch higher, shaking under the weight. Rema pointed to the jagged rods in Geoffrey's hand.

'Raise the thunder!'

Cold air gusted over Raisin's face. The flames jittered. Geoffrey's tethered hand sought hers. She clung to him, drenched in sweat. Rema wafted towards them; her white gloves danced phantom-like in front of her. Romul waved in Geoffrey's direction.

'Do you, stranger sent by the powers, accept to be the vessel of Jupiter?' he thundered.

Rema pushed Geoffrey into a low bow.

'I do,' he mumbled dully.

'And do you, unknown maiden, accept to be the vessel of Juno?' Romul directed at Raisin.

Cool leather grazed her skin as Rema also forced her into a bow. Geoffrey squeezed her hand.

'I… I do…' she whimpered.

Rema released her hold and they straightened up warily, still clinging to each other. Romul drew a gleaming dagger from a silver sheath and raised it above the altar. Feet stamped. Hands clapped. Palms slammed drums.

A single howl rose from the wolves then one by one, they raised their heads and blood-curdling howls tore from their gaping jaws. Raisin shook uncontrollably, too terrified to look, too terrified not to. The stiletto blade glinted in Romul's hand.

'Do you, vessels of Jupiter and Juno, demand this sacrifice?' he shouted.

'*No!*' Raisin screamed.

'No!' Geoffrey roared.

'Do you sanction it?' Romul boomed, swaying his arm backwards and forwards. 'Do you? Do you?'

Rema threw her hands in the air in frenzied abandon.

'They do! They do!' she cried.

20

WOLF HOWLS WHIPPED around them like angry tornados. Romul hoisted the dagger higher. The drums thundered into a crescendo. A robed figure ripped the red velvet off the altar. Raisin dropped her head, petrified. The torch shook dangerously in her hand.

'Raisin… it's not Nicolas,' Geoffrey gasped.

She looked up, gagged. The knife was buried to the hilt in the proud curved chest of a wolf. A *wolf*? Then where the hell was Nicolas? She watched in open-mouthed horror as Romul ripped the animal from throat to pelvis, its pelt splitting wide with each slash.

She groped for Geoffrey's hand, stomach heaving. Even after years of farm life, she hated the violent stench of slaughter. Romul threw the knife down. It clattered across the altar, splattering them with blood. Rema moaned and gripped the back of Raisin's chair. Raisin cringed and twisted away from the hot breath gusting over her head. Her torch careened forward and a stream of flax oil and fire shot to the ground, skittering flames around the foot of the altar. She corrected her arm in panic. Romul froze, hands mid-air. Blood hung like glistening beetles on the coarse white hair of his arm. Rema stabbed her nails into her shoulder.

'Be careful…' she breathed.

Raisin shrank back. 'I'm sorry.'

Geoffrey tightened his hold on her hand. She bit her lip to stop the tears. The wolves bucked and twisted, saliva flew from their raging jaws. Rema's ragged moans became louder. How many others had died here? Would she and Geoffrey be next on the altar? She couldn't bear that Matt would never know how sorry she was. How much she loved him. She glanced at Geoffrey. Did he regret that he had told her about Mum? She hoped not. He turned to her, face taut with fear. She blinked rapidly and squeezed his hand, love welling up inside her. He nodded, as if he understood. They both stiffened as someone shuffled past.

Victor, his biceps bulging, hoisted something heavy onto the altar. She went cold. A massive stone skull glared blindly at them. She looked around frantically. A sea of faces gazed adoringly at her. Rema slapped her head forward.

'Pay attention,' she snapped then drifted to Romul.

The two leaders faced their followers, then Rema waved Alana to the altar. The old woman approached holding high a tall silver goblet. A young girl followed closely behind her and placed a wooden bowl filled with honey-coloured mushrooms in front of Rema. Raisin's eyes glazed over. Identical mushrooms had spiralled the tattooed man into madness. Romul and Rema's crazed faces swum before her. Drugged, they were capable of anything. She twisted her arm against the gold cord. It slackened a little. She pulled harder. Could she wriggle it loose enough to unknot?

Rema reached over the wolf's body to take the goblet from Alana. For a moment it hung motionless between the two women. Hope flickered. Was Alana a reluctant participant? Rema's face tightened with menace and Alana's hands dropped away. Was that defeat Raisin saw in her wilted shoulders? Rema locked eyes with Romul over the gleaming goblet.

The chanting quietened to a hush and the drumbeats stilled to a steady thud. The wolves howled in tortured unison. The robed figures closed in.

Romul plunged his hands into the wolf's gaping chest and brought out its slippery, dripping heart. Raisin screamed and collapsed into the chair. Unseen bodies pulled her upright. Tears streamed down her face as Romul slashed the tangle of arteries and veins then raised the heart above his head. Blood rained on his upturned face.

'Planet of Jupiter, red as blood, welcome to our skies,' Romul cried. 'Open the path to Quirinus.'

'*Quirinus, Quirinus, Quirinus.*'

Rema pushed herself against Romul and held the goblet under the oozing organ, grinning manically as it filled with the wolf's blood. Excited whispers rippled through the congregation, then Romul nestled the heart back into the wolf.

'*Quirinus, Quirinus, Quirinus,*' Rema sang with angel purity.

'*Quirinus, Quirinus, Quirinus,*' the followers echoed.

Drumbeats rumbled, dropped to a murmur, rose again and fell back. The wolves howled as if dying. Movement on the rockface caught Raisin's eye. She blinked, tried to focus. Her torch arm hurt and began to sway. Red handprints shimmered behind the burning flames as if beckoning her. She stared in disbelief.

Deep in the fresco's alcove crouched the cavewoman, her arms around a powerful savannah wolf. Raisin tugged Geoffrey's hand. *Look up!* she signalled. He followed her eyes, frowning in confusion. *Look harder!* she implored.

The woman rubbed her cheek against the wolf, as if consoling him, and together they surveyed the brutal sacrifice below, then the savannah wolf raised his head and howled. And as one, the chained wolves looked up, and fell silent.

Romul's head cocked to the side. The tribeswoman's wolf hunkered down and dropped his head on his paws, eyes never leaving the chained wolves. They did the same, calm, mute, riveted on the wolf in the alcove.

'Quirinus, Quirinus,' Rema sang.

'Quirinus, Quirinus,' Romul roared.

Help us, Raisin begged.

The savannah wolf turned his elegant head towards her and pierced her with a steady gaze. She stared back. Wisdom and knowledge burned in his amber eyes. She trembled but didn't look away. He knew her dreams, her fears, her family shame. And he and the cavewoman would help. Her terror eased. Maybe, just maybe, they would get out alive.

The tribeswoman lifted something over her head and twirled it in front of her. Raisin screwed up her eyes, looked harder. A necklace? She leant forward in astonishment. Wisps of candle smoke were curling up from the altar to the necklace, past the wolf, past the tribeswoman, and into the darkness behind them. Raisin's pulse quickened. Air flow? She could hardly believe her eyes, but loop after loop of smoke drifted upwards and into the mountain. Could that be a way out?

The tribeswoman gave a small satisfied smile then let the necklace drop. Raisin watched it swirl slowly over the ledge and into the cave. When she looked up again, the cavewoman and wolf were gone. She squared her shoulders, sat taller. They weren't alone.

Rema scooped handfuls of mushrooms into the skull receptacle then crushed leaves and berries between her fingers and scattered them on top. Romul poured in some of wolf's blood. They took turns to pulverise the contents with a pestle the size of a fist. Rema sprinkled in more mushrooms. Romul emptied the goblet of blood into the skull. They grounded and pounded.

Smoke from the candles still wafted in white curls to the alcove. Raisin watched, mesmerised, hopeful. So close, so out of reach.

Romul held out his hand to Rema. She gently dropped her hand, palm up, onto it. He brought it to his lips, kissed it, then lowered it again and sliced it quickly with the dagger. She groaned in delight, face rapturous. He gashed his own hand and pressed it against hers. Their blood spiralled together into the stone skull. Drumbeats hammered like gunfire. The followers heaved forward like a tidal wave.

Romul signalled to Victor to come forward and together they lifted the stone skull and filled the silver goblet to the brim. Victor bowed and moved away. Romul raised his eyes skyward. Rema spread out her arms, threw back her head and let out a blood-curdling cry. He held the goblet to her lips. She convulsed and shuddered as she drank in frenzied gulps.

'Jupiter! Juno! Approach!' Romul commanded.

Alana untied Raisin and Geoffrey, and Victor took the torch and metal rods from them. Raisin rubbed her wrists and glanced over her shoulder. Dare she run? She would rather die trying to escape than die with a dagger in her heart. Geoffrey took her hand and squeezed.

'Don't,' he begged hoarsely.

'Approach!' Romul shouted.

Alana led Raisin and Geoffrey to the altar. Raisin stopped breathing when she saw the massacred chest of the wolf. It stank of filthy copper coins and the heart glistened inside like putrid fruit.

Something soft drifted around them. Fine strands of hair. Black, brown, blonde... red hair. Geoffrey looked behind them and yanked her hand. Two young girls were showering them with hair from woven baskets.

'Jupiter... Juno,' the congregation chanted.

'What's happening?' she sobbed.

'They're *worshipping* us.'

'Jupiter... Juno... Jupiter... Juno.'

The fervent faces sickened her. Even Thomas' sardonic mockery was gone. The drums slowed to a steady heartbeat.

'Welcome Jupiter, God of Sky and Thunder, and Juno, Queen of Heaven, guides to our last incarnation,' Romul intoned. 'We have waited seven years, but here you are to lead us through the last steps to Quirinus. We are ready!'

Raisin squirmed. Ready for *what*? Alana's veined feet shuffled closer. Hair rained over them like confetti. Anguished howls tore from the wolves. Raisin searched the cave in despair. Why had the tribeswoman abandoned them?

'Your hand,' Alana said softly.

Victor stood next to her with the dagger.

'No... please *no*,' Raisin begged.

'Yes,' Victor said.

Geoffrey's hand shot forward. 'Use mine.'

Strong arms yanked him away. Victor prised open Raisin's fist and sliced her hand. She screamed in pain, blood bulged across her palm and into the goblet. Matt's beautiful smile flashed before her. She looked desperately at the dark hole in the fresco and willed the tribeswoman to appear. The goblet was pressed into her hands; its warmth repulsed her.

'Drink,' Alana urged.

Raisin panted for air. It stank of rotting carcass. The wolf howls melted into a lament and the drumbeats stilled into a quiet pitter-patter.

'I can't,' she whispered.

'Oh but you must.'

'Drink!' Romul called.

'Drink! Drink!' the congregation echoed.

The pulpy liquid stung her lips. She pretended to sip and lowered the cup. Alana frowned. Raisin begged her to accept the charade with desperate eyes.

'You are Juno… we need your guidance,' Alana murmured.

'I don't… know anything,' Raisin protested tearfully.

Victor held the warm cup against her mouth. 'Drink.'

She forced down a few drops. Her tongue swelled. They made her drink more. Her head spun.

'Raisin…?' Geoffrey shouted.

Her legs wobbled, sweat flowed from her pores. Someone helped her to sit. She gagged. Strong fingers massaged her neck.

Red circles, pink squares careened in front of her. Her vision blurred. Giant bees whizzed around her head then morphed into purple planets.

'What do you see? What do you see?' Romul called.

Wolf howls took form and spiralled between the racing planets. Sounds transformed into rope then the ropes became snakes that coiled around her neck. She gasped for air. Something dislodged from her throat and she vomited black fire onto the ground. Then the soaring onyx flames parted and revealed a trapdoor.

'Tell us what you see… *tell us*,' Rema shrieked.

'A trapdoor…'

'Open it,' Romul instructed.

Her head became a strobe light pulsing to the rhythm of drumbeats. She pulled at the trapdoor's brass ring.

'I can't,' she wheezed.

'You *must*,' he insisted.

'Raisin… Raisin… Raisin.' Geoffrey's voice was muted and otherworldly.

Yellow and green ladders pitched in mad circles over the trapdoor. She caught one with both hands. It grew longer and longer until its legs smashed open the trapdoor. She peered into the gaping pit underneath.

'Mum? Dad?' she cried in horror.

Her parents were spread-eagled against a gnarled baobab tree, held by fluorescent vines that writhed like laser beams.

'Ask for instructions,' Romul called.

A gaggle of clacking skulls closed in on her. Manic guffaws gurgled from their yawping jaws.

'Raisin!' Geoffrey shouted.

She frowned and tried to focus on him. He grew a long orange beak that snapped soundlessly within inches of her.

'I have to save Mum and Dad,' she screamed.

The vines torturing her parents fused into a candy-striped cobra whose golden forked-tongue zapped lightning bolts at her.

'So beautiful,' she sighed.

Romul shook her violently. 'Give us instructions.'

The cobra rose out of the pit and floated towards her. Its eyes were amethysts and peacock feathers lolled from its back.

'I love you,' she giggled.

'Ask what we must do!' Rema screamed.

Raisin gently caressed the serpent.

'Why did you call me?' it hissed.

'To understand,' she mumbled.

The cobra swayed closer. Its flicking tongue caressed her cheeks. She closed her eyes. The snake knew her.

'The answer is in your heart,' it whispered then twisted into a gigantic loop and slithered back into the pit.

She ran screaming to the edge. 'I love you! Come back!'

'What must we do?' Rema wailed.

Raisin grinned and stretched out her arms. She was a sunflower in the wind.

'*Look in your heart*,' she laughed and fell back onto a sea of purple peonies.

21

THE BURN OF ammonia razored Raisin awake. Her eyes watered. Her tongue felt dry and too big for her mouth. Where the hell was she? A blurred shape moved towards her.

'Raisin!'

Pain shot through her skull. 'Geoffrey…?'

'Get up… we don't have long.'

Shocking images bulldozed her. A wolf. Candles. Nicolas. A chalice. She groaned and held her head. Mum. Dad. *Where* were they?

'My head hurts,' she wheezed.

Geoffrey held Rema's phial under her nose.

'Smell this…'

Her lungs squeezed shut. She pushed his hand away and gulped for air. He threw the phial to the ground and slid his hands under her arms.

'Get up,' he begged.

She stumbled against him, saw the butchered wolf in front of her and screamed, staggered back. Romul lay at her feet, the wolf's mutilated heart on his chest.

'Is he dead?' she stammered.

'Unconscious. They all are.'

She glanced around unsteadily. 'Even Thomas?'

'Yes.'

'What happened?'

'They believed you had a vision that told them the blood potion would free them. Fucking lunatics.'

'And you? Are you okay?'

'They were in such a frenzy to drink the stuff, they forgot I existed.'

'Is that Alana over there?' she mumbled.

A woman lay sprawled on her back between the altar and the

wolves. Her robe was twisted low around her waist, exposing her withered breasts. Raisin wobbled through the tangle of bodies towards her and carefully covered her up.

'Raisin, we need to get going!'

She nodded but didn't turn back. It looked as if Armageddon had pounded the cave. Had good or evil won? She stood still, senses bristling. Lifetimes ago, shamans had communed with gods here. She felt their presence. Had good won after all? The wolves watched her, still as statues. *They feel it too.* Her anxiety eased.

'Raisin!'

She shuffled back to him but stopped next to Thomas, hesitated for a second, then kicked him with all her might. A glimmer of power fluttered inside her. Escape was close.

She led Geoffrey behind the altar and pointed to the dark alcove in the middle of the fresco.

'That's our way out,' she said.

'Nonsense. We'll leave the way we came in.'

'No, Geoffrey. If they wake up, they'll come after us. I saw the cavewoman again. She wanted me to know this was…'

'You're still hallucinating. Come…'

Was he right? Had she imagined the woman and her wolf? She dropped to her haunches and searched the ground under the ledge. Something glistened in the crease between the rockface and the ground. Heart racing, she leant forward and hooked the tribeswoman's necklace up with her finger. No hallucination here. The necklace was real.

'Pass me a candle!' she said desperately.

'We're wasting time…'

'*Please*, Geoffrey. If this doesn't convince you, I'll do it your way.'

She took the candle from him and held it high. The smoke swooped upwards in lazy loops. She grinned triumphantly. He shook his head.

'It can't be that easy,' he murmured.

'Please can we try? I know I'm right. The alcove isn't much higher than your head. We should be able to get to it.'

He frowned, moved back and studied it. She lifted the candle higher, desperate for him to believe her. He took the candle, stretched up and carefully balanced it on a flat ridge then dropped to his hands and knees.

'Okay, climb up,' he said.

She kissed the necklace, slipped it over her head and climbed uncertainly onto his back. He wobbled as she perched onto her toes to look into the alcove. Candlelight licked long shadows over the dark walls of a small cave that didn't look much more than a metre high, and that seemed to curve into an L-shape at the back. Green moss freckled the walls and the dank smell of wet stone drifted towards her. There was no sign of a tunnel. The candle flickered. She quickly cupped her palms around it. Geoffrey shifted under her weight.

'What can you see?' he grunted.

'Not sure.'

She caterpillared her fingers over the rocks in front of her, found two sturdy outcrops and clamped onto them, wincing at the pain that shot through her cut palm, then she took a few anxious breaths and sprang as high as she could. Her stomach slammed into the sharp rock. She teetered precariously, writhed forward, scraping her shins, then lost her balance and crashed on top of Geoffrey.

'I don't think I'm strong enough,' she moaned.

He helped her up.

'Try again. Lever your foot on the wall and focus on getting your upper body as far over the ledge as you can.'

She reluctantly got onto his back again and tested a craggy bulge in the rockface with her toes. It felt solid. She looked up and hooked her fingers over the ledge. The fresco shimmered around her as if urging her on. She tightened her grip. Now or never. She took a deep breath and jumped. Her robe ripped apart, her legs shredded against the rockface, but she was up, seesawing alarmingly, legs pummelling the air. Her arms shook under her weight. She fixed her eyes on the back of the cave and lurched forward, but her arms collapsed and she plunged back to the ground.

'Damn it! I'm too damn fat,' she sobbed, covering herself with the torn fabric.

'Try again. You got close then, really close. Get back on, Raisin. Think about Matt.'

Yes. Matt. She scrambled to her feet, jaw clenched, and looked longingly at the ledge. Damn it to hell, she couldn't let it beat her. Shadows fluttered on the alcove wall and her heart missed a beat. Was her cavewoman back?

Trust, a voice murmured.

Determination surged through her. She had to get to Matt. There were things she had to tell him. She knotted her robe together and jumped onto Geoffrey's back.

'Last time,' she said angrily and launched herself upwards.

Her hands scrambled for grip; her hips tore over the rock; her robe came loose. She swivelled her leg high and hooked her knee over the alcove shelf. Inch by inch, she clawed forward into the safety of the small cave. Once in, she twisted onto her back, panting like a woman in labour. Her vision fragmented, dots and colours careened in front of her. She gasped for breath. The flame twitched nervously. She felt like a beached whale. As a child, she had so easily flown over walls and scrambled up trees. She flipped onto her stomach and crawled to the edge to help Geoffrey up.

He clamped his hands over her outstretched hand, propped his foot on a gnarled rock and yanked himself up. She flew forward, dangerously close to the drop. He yelled, lost his grip and fell. He waved her away.

'Go! Get help!' he shouted.

'No… I'm not leaving you.'

'Raisin, get help! *Go* damn it!'

She swung her legs over the ledge. It wasn't far but it felt like a precipice.

'Help me down,' she begged.

He refused and waved her away, but she manoeuvred around his arms and slithered to the ground, gashing open the knife wound on her hand.

'You should have gone!' he said angrily.

She pressed her bleeding palm against her thigh.

'I let you down once, I won't do it again.'

'That's ridiculous. You were a *kid*. This is just plain *stupid* of you.'

'I'm not going without you,' she insisted tiredly. 'What if we use one of the chairs?'

'You saw how heavy they were. We'll never get it over here.'

Low growls rumbled behind them. Raisin and Geoffrey spun around. The wolves were up, backs humped, ears flattened.

'I hope those chains hold,' she muttered.

'It's not *us* they're growling at.'

She followed his gaze. Thomas was awake and staggering to his feet. Geoffrey snatched Romul's dagger off the altar.

'Stop right there, you bastard!'

'What do you think you're doing?' Thomas slurred.

He dived over the altar for Geoffrey but tripped and fell face down on the dead wolf. Geoffrey dropped the knife and pushed him into the bloody torso.

'Now who's the big boy?' he mocked.

Thomas' arms and legs jerked frantically.

'Speak up,' Geoffrey taunted.

'He's suffocating, Geoffrey,' Raisin said nervously.

'Like I give a shit.'

But he pulled him backwards and pushed off the altar. Thomas crumpled onto the ground, spluttering and coughing.

'Get the ropes,' Geoffrey said tersely.

She sped to the mahogany chairs and picked up the restraints. The shells around her neck clattered as she ran back. She caressed their ribbed surface. The tribeswoman was with them.

They left Thomas trussed like a heretic next to the altar and began to drag one of the chairs towards the alcove.

'This weighs a blasted ton. How did they get these damn things down here?' she grunted.

'Don't think... just pull.'

The chair lurched and screeched over the rocks. Raisin looked worriedly at the bodies sprawled around them. What if someone else woke up? She could barely breathe by the time they settled the chair under the fresco.

'You first,' she muttered.

He climbed up but his robe caught on the armrest and hooked him back. He bent down, angrily slashed the bottom of the fabric with the knife then reached up, gripped the ledge and with an explosive grunt, hoisted himself up. She laughed in nervous relief. He had done it! She turned for one last look at the cave.

The stalagmites stood tall and proud like ancient totem poles. She was sure the tribeswoman and the wolf were nearby, silently applauding their escape. Most of the candles had died and the fires were beginning to fade; their smouldering coals reminded her of winters with Matt in London.

'Raisin!'

She stretched her arms towards him and he grasped her hands. If she didn't get up, he would have to go find help without her. She gritted her teeth. That was the last thing she wanted. He counted to three and pulled hard. She clamped her elbows over the ledge. He rolled onto his side and dragged her with him. Her body tore over the rocks. Her limbs flailed, searching for foothold.

'I'm slipping,' she cried.

He hooked his hands under her arms and heaved her towards him. She slammed her feet against an outcrop and pushed violently. Her body jolted forward and she landed on top of him. They lay still, out of breath, stunned. She rolled off him.

'We fucking did it,' he mumbled.

They crawled to the back of the alcove. In the far corner, at the end of the L-shape, was a narrow opening. Geoffrey held up the candle.

'It's still flickering,' he said.

They clambered through the gap and hugged each other fiercely on the other side. One more step away from the Assembly and closer to trying to help Nicolas. A tunnel snaked ahead into a steady climb. They crept up it; their shadows trailing them like watchful guardians.

'I'm starving. What's the first thing you're going to eat when you get out?' she said.

'To hell with food. I'm phoning Chris.' He gave her a wistful smile. 'You're lucky Matt's here.'

'I know.'

'You still love him, don't you?'

She didn't reply, not ready to admit that he was almost constantly on her mind. Geoffrey stopped and held the candle up. The tunnel forked just ahead.

'Fuck it,' he snorted.

'Just relax... the candle will guide us. Go into both of them and see what happens to the flame,' she said confidently.

It shuddered wildly as he walked into the first tunnel. He paused. The flame leapt and swirled then burned without moving, still as a nun in prayer.

'No air flow here,' he murmured.

'Try the other one.'

He walked three metres into the second tunnel but the candle burned serenely. He held it higher. The flame barely moved.

'Check the first tunnel again,' she urged.

He kicked a small object on his way out. It ricocheted off the wall and against her shin. Her eyes widened. A heart-shaped clamshell lay at her feet. Fine ribs rolled from its centre in slender ripples. She picked it up and pointed with a smile to the tunnel he had just come out of.

'That's the way we should go.'

'From a *shell*...?'

She took off the tribeswoman's necklace and draped it over her palm. The shells were identical.

'This shell is from her. She's showing us the way.'

'I'm not listening to a ghost.'

'Trust me, Geoffrey.'

'You're losing your mind. We're taking the first tunnel. At least the flame showed some sign of life.'

She showed him the tiny hole at the top of the clamshell.

'She *wore* it, Geoffrey. This is a sign.'

'Signs are for pixies. Logic tells me it's the tunnel on the right.'

'Logic isn't always the answer.'

'I'm a mathematician, it's all I know.'

She walked into the left fork and held out her hand to him.

'Please...'

'Raisin, this is crazy. It's a dangerous maze down here.'

'Let's just try,' she begged.

'Okay, fine. Fifteen minutes and if the flame isn't doing a tango by then, we turn back. Deal?'

Was a quarter of an hour enough?

'Deal,' she agreed carelessly.

22

'WE'RE STILL GOING uphill. Surely the surface isn't far,' Raisin said.

Geoffrey took his cupped hand away from the flame. It burned without moving. He raised his eyebrows.

'That doesn't mean anything,' she protested.

'Not even a flicker. No air flow means this isn't the way out.'

'We're in the right tunnel. I *know* we are. Just a bit further,' she pleaded.

'We're wasting time. We should've taken the other one.'

'What difference will a few more minutes make?'

She continued to walk. The ground gleamed like the night sea. He grunted irritably but trailed after her. She sped up, thinking of ways to distract him.

'I never realised how much existed under the earth's surface. Bit like you,' she said lightly.

'It was always there.'

'So lead the way. Start with Chris.'

'Now?'

'You see! It's you. You don't *want* anyone digging around in your life.'

'He lives in London.'

'That's old news. What does he do?'

'He's a builder... fixes people's homes.'

'I thought you met him at a maths conference?'

'I didn't say he was *at* it. There was a bad storm the week before and he was fixing the hotel's roof.'

'Brawn over brain? Now that's a surprise. So what should I expect? Oxen shoulders and biceps like melons...?'

'A great big bear of a man,' he nodded wistfully. 'And gentle, like your Matt.'

The tunnel twisted into a tight s-bend and she paused to let him take the lead. His hand sheltered the flame as he brushed past her. She eyed the candle anxiously. If it went out, the darkness would be total. She pushed the thought away.

'Isn't it hard living so far apart from each other?' she asked.

'Not really. We Skype almost every day and we see each other a few times a year.'

'I'd hate that.'

'Nonsense, you'd love it. Not wanting to marry Matt is no different to being happy ten thousand kilometres apart... textbook commitment issues.'

'That's crap, Geoffrey.'

'You love him but you don't want marriage. I'll say it again... commitment issues.'

'Please don't use Paula-speak on me. Besides, if Chris is so much like Matt, why is *he* happy about the distance? Matt would never be.'

'He doesn't like it one bit and wants me to move to London.'

'What a cheek. He can be Mr Fixit anywhere. Why doesn't *he* move to you?'

'It's not that easy. He's got kids.'

'Kids?'

'We don't just have pets, Raisin.'

She winced at his tone and didn't reply.

'Sorry, that was unnecessary,' he sighed. 'He has two. A fifteen year old girl and a ten year old boy.'

'And they live with him?'

'Joint custody... but enough about me.' His voice softened. 'Do you regret that you can't have any?'

'Not really.'

Her real regret was that she had never told Matt. Would he give up being a father to be with her? Did she want him to? The ceiling rose and the tunnel narrowed. They continued along the shrinking passage until the walls scraped against them. She bit her lip. Had she done the right thing making them go this way? She imagined Matt's face and swallowed hard. She couldn't wait to see him. Geoffrey stopped.

'This is ridiculous. Your fifteen minutes are up. We're going back,' he snapped.

'It can't be fifteen minutes already.'

'We'll never know without a watch, will we? But *this* is madness. What if we get stuck?'

He was right but she turned sideways to squeeze past him, palms skidding along the slimy rockface. He didn't follow.

'Raisin… don't go any further.'

She ignored him and shuffled further. But then the mountain defied her and a large rock bulged in front of her and blocked her way. She stretched onto her toes and tried to look over it.

'Romul and his lunatics will have seen the chair, and they'll be after us. We need to get to the other tunnel.'

'We can probably crawl underneath this rock. Maybe the tunnel widens after it.'

'We're going back.'

'At least tell me what you can see on the other side. I'm too short. Just *look*,' she wheedled.

'Damn it, Raisin,' he sighed.

They retraced their way to a wider section and swopped places. He jostled his lanky frame back to the blockage.

'Yes, it gets wider, but so what? It's not the right tunnel.'

'Except I'm very sure it is,' she said confidently. 'What else can you see?'

He gave a resigned shrug. 'Palm prints.'

'*What*?'

'Here on the wall.'

'I knew it! It means it's the right way.'

'Yeah right. Like a map.'

'Mr Cynic, you're a pain in the arse. Come on, Geoffrey. Jean-Philippe *told* us shamans used to come down into the mountains to communicate with their gods. They've been here.'

Dull thuds vibrated through the air. They exchanged shocked looks.

Geoffrey dropped to the ground, rolled onto his side, and scrambled under the outcrop. She hiked up her dress and clawed after him. Her hips jammed. The thuds grew louder.

'Give me a hand!' she shouted.

He pulled her arm but she barely moved. She pushed furiously, ignoring the pain, but her body stayed lodged. He hooked his hands under her arms and heaved. Men's voices hammered closer. He yanked harder. She slammed her feet into the tunnel walls. Her hips crunched into the rock. She was trapped in a stone manacle.

'Give me your other hand!'

'It's stuck under me,' she whimpered.

'Bend your elbow and move it backwards.'

She obeyed and her arm slid free.

'Keep it bent and wriggle your hand towards me.'

His solid grasp filled her with tears.

'Count to ten,' he said.

'Why?'

'Just do it, for Christ's sake! Count!'

'One, two, three… four…'

He gave a hard tug and she shot free.

'You relaxed…' he grimaced.

He helped her up and they ran down the passageway. The Jupiter tattoo gleamed like a bad omen on the back of his head. Her laboured breathing sounded louder than a chainsaw. She might as well be yelling directions to the men tracking them. She felt sick at the thought of what Thomas would do if they were caught. They raced around a corner and she skidded on loose rocks. Her foot shot forward and she crashed onto her back. She shut her eyes, panting, ready to give up. Had she imagined the cavewoman's message? She raised herself painfully onto her elbows. Geoffrey stood next to her, arm outstretched. She frowned. Why were her feet lower than her body? She tossed a handful of stones in front of her; they tumbled downhill.

'We're moving *away* from the goddamn surface,' she said hoarsely.

He propped the candle between them and sat down in a daze. She dropped her head back and waited for him to explode with anger.

'Our only option is to keep moving,' he said tiredly.

She shot him a grateful look then noticed the candle. The flame bounced wildly.

'Look,' she said.

'Whatever. Let's go,' he snapped.

'Maybe they'll turn back when they see the tunnel is blocked.'

'Yeah right, and maybe they'll offer us something to drink and apologise.'

She bit her tongue and followed him. Her ankle hurt but she kept quiet. When Geoffrey broke into a slow trot, she blanked out the pain and hobbled after him, concentrating on the back of his legs as she struggled robot-like to keep up. The tunnel curved to the left and became wider.

'What the hell?' he gasped.

The tunnel exploded open into a cave the size of a stadium. Geoffrey held up the candle. Long shadows licked the cliff-high walls. She staggered inside. Was this a dead end?

Great hunks of rock were scattered everywhere, as if God had lifted the cap off the mountain and tumbled off-cuts inside. The walls veered at jagged angles, serrated stalactites hung over their heads, and deep hollows pitted the surface like leering eyes.

'It's *huge*,' Geoffrey murmured.

His voice bounced off the rock. *Huge, huge, huge.*

They walked into the middle and stared. It didn't seem possible that a mountain could have so much space inside it. Geoffrey pointed to a dark opening on the left wall. She followed him to it, but wouldn't go in, not daring to hope. He took a few steps inside then turned and came straight out, shaking his head. Tears welled in her eyes.

'I think we should go back,' she mumbled.

'This goddamn flame is still jumping about,' he said angrily. He waved his arms in the air. 'We need to be more methodical. We'll walk once around the entire perimeter and then decide what to do.'

She nodded helplessly and studied the candle. They didn't have more than an hour or two of light left. The flame swirled jauntily. *Show us where to go*, she begged. They walked slowly along the wall. It buckled in and out without a single cavity or tunnel. She trudged after him, hungry, cold and despairing. He stopped, put his arm around her and manoeuvred her sideways to face a massive protrusion that bulged out of the back wall like a paunch. She shrugged.

'Look closer,' he said.

She blinked, took a step closer. Three bison with oversized upper bodies, puny hindquarters, and peg-thin legs ran across its extensive girth; two wolves leapt skywards as though vaulting the rock, front legs disappearing over the top. Red handprints collided with the animals in a chaotic tangle of spread fingers. She walked up to the painting and laid her palms against the rock. Was it her imagination or did it feel warm? A flicker of hope twitched inside her.

'All the fingers point up, except those near the wolves,' she said. 'I wonder how anyone got that high?'

She gave him the candle and explored the pregnant curve of the rock, fingers trailing its textured surface. A soft breeze tickled her skin. She shot Geoffrey a startled glance.

'Did you feel that?'

'Yes...'

They walked around it and stopped. Boulders as big as cannonballs formed an avalanche against it. The candle shivered restlessly.

'Airflow,' Geoffrey nodded.

She bit back an I-told-you-so, then struggled up the boulders to the flat crest of the massive rock and slithered on her stomach towards the side with the rock paintings. The rock *was* warm. She fought down her excitement. Two sets of black lines pointed up to her. Front paws. She scrambled closer to the curved edge, draped her arms over, and covered the handprints with her palms. A perfect match.

'So this is how you did it,' she whispered.

She scanned the surface, the rockface, the walls. Her spine tingled. The cave wall buckled *behind* the rock. She wriggled towards it and stared into a gaping mouth of blackness.

'What's there?' Geoffrey shouted.

'Some kind of cave! Bring the candle!'

The flame leapt with dancer's abandon when he dropped down next to her. They leant under the overhang with the candle in front of them. A cylindrical shaft shot up into the mountain over their heads, and disappeared so far below, they couldn't see the bottom. Wide shelves staggered up the side of the wall, swooped past them into the darkness above.

'Are those *steps*?' she murmured.

She slid her legs over the edge, found foothold, and slithered inside. The cave was at least three metres wide and corkscrewed skyward like the inside of a spire. Well-placed outcrops and rock strata had been incorporated into a stairway that spiralled along the wall. Where nature hadn't provided, wide ledges had been hacked straight out of the rockface. Geoffrey manoeuvred himself next to her. Raisin shuddered.

'Where the hell does it go?'

'Who cares? It goes up and Romul will never find us here.'

Nor will anyone else, she thought.

They started to climb. She stopped counting after eighty-four steps. Only the rattle of crumbling rocks plummeting into the pit beneath them broke the stillness. Who would have built a stairway in the bowels of a mountain? She paused. The next step was too far away. Her head spun, her legs wobbled. *Get a grip.*

She eyed it nervously. The wide rocky ledge flared out of the wall like a fan. Big enough for two people but too far for her short legs to reach. She looked down. Blackness squatted there like a monstrous toad, devouring the feeble candlelight and drawing her down. She reeled back and forced herself to concentrate on the next step, stretching her leg desperately towards it. Her robe fluttered in ragged tentacles around her thighs.

'Geoffrey, please help me.'

He climbed back down to her and she saw the wound on his

forehead was bleeding again. He looked exhausted. She eyed the diminishing candle. Time was running out. He propped it in a crevice next to him and pulled her up with both hands. She clung to him. He hugged her fiercely. She brushed away frustrated tears.

'We've been climbing for ages and still nothing.'

'It isn't nothing… we can't go up forever without reaching the surface.'

'What if it's another dead end?'

'It won't be. It can't be.'

'Geoffrey, if we… if I don't get out…'

'We will.'

'Tell Matt…'

'Stop it. Why would *I* get out and not you?'

'Tell him I'm sorry.'

'That's the last thing he wants to hear. Tell him you love him. And tell him yourself.'

'You think we'll make it?'

'We have to. Focus forward and don't look down.'

Her breath tore out of her as they laboured higher. When the shaft curved to the left, Geoffrey stopped to check on her. She smiled gratefully. He gave her a thumbs up and continued to climb but his foot shot forward and he lost his balance. Candle wax spewed past her and everything went black.

'Geoffrey!' she screamed.

The flame flared once, twice, but blinked back to life.

'Are you okay? What *happened*?' she shouted.

He pointed to the wall. Mercury-thick rivulets of water glistened down the rockface.

'It's wet here. Jesus, I thought I was…'

She wet her fingers on the wall and stuck them in her mouth. It wasn't enough. She pressed her lips against the rock and lapped water straight off the wall. Sweet, sweet water. Geoffrey did the same. She wet her hands and wiped her face.

'Are you okay?' he asked.

'If we get out, I'll damn well tell him I love him.'

'When we get out, Raisin. When.'

He picked up the candle. A flash of white caught her eye. She grasped his wrist and manoeuvred it higher. A robed statue stood sideways in a deep crack with its hand extended to them as if giving them the delicate bird perched on its fingers. They exchanged stunned glances.

'St Francis again,' Geoffrey said.

'Why *here*?' She glanced around anxiously. 'Protecting *what*?'

He patted the ground at the statue's base and pulled a face.

'Wet,' he grimaced.

'What are you doing?'

'Checking if anything was left here.' He held up a curved yellow tooth. 'Another tooth. Here, take it. We need all the help we can get.'

'Protect the vulnerable,' she whispered.

She was tempted to keep it but didn't dare. The last time she had stolen something, he had almost drowned. She reluctantly put it back and gazed longingly up into the shaft. Would she feel Matt's arms around her soon? She rubbed her eyes. A long way above, a needle of light punctured the darkness.

'Geoffrey!'

He stared up at the wisp thin beam. 'Daylight…?'

They struggled up the steps. Almost free. Blackness melted into indigo. The climb became less sheer, the steps easier to reach, and the air lost its chill. He paused and touched the rockface next to him. She stopped and looked up. Now what?

'Goddamn… it's a *wall!*'

'Of course it is,' she said impatiently.

'Look closely.'

Her heart lurched. Manmade chiselled stones had been positioned around the rocks to form a manmade wall. She frowned in confusion. Where the hell were they? He scrambled up to the shaft of light and held his palm in front of it. A perfect circle bored into his skin. He pulled his hand away. The light sprang across the chamber.

'We're above ground. That's all that matters,' she grinned.

The shaft narrowed and within a few metres, they reached a wide ledge that swept around the wall like a shelf. A rusted ladder was the only way up. Wooden beams, thick as railway sleepers, plugged the shaft.

'Doesn't look good,' he said.

'Go,' she urged.

He mounted the rungs, testing each one before he went higher. She followed in slow lurches. He slammed the side of his fist into the wood. Sand and grit drizzled over them. He positioned his shoulders against a beam and heaved.

It jerked up and light poured in.

23

GEOFFREY INCHED THE heavy timber higher. Wind gusted inside, exploding sand and leaves in Raisin's face. She coughed violently and covered her eyes.

'What do you see… is it safe?' she wheezed.

'A lot of rubble and… it looks like we're in some kind of building.'

'*Building?*'

He dropped the beam and furiously punched the ladder.

'We're trapped. Fucking trapped!'

The draft killed the flame and the sudden darkness blinded her. She groped for his leg.

'But that's impossible!'

'How much more unlucky can we get? We've come up inside some goddamn stone building,' he seethed.

She dropped the dead candle, grimacing when she didn't hear a reassuring thud. Her eyes began to adjust to the indigo darkness. She climbed higher until her head was next to his knees. Tiny diamonds of light glinted in the cracks of the wooden platform above him. Anything was better than being underground.

'How can we be *inside* with all that wind? Just lift the beams so we can get the hell out of here.'

He repositioned his shoulders against the wood and heaved. Light shot inside like gunfire. She winced and looked away. He paused. She pushed him impatiently. He grimaced under the weight.

'What else can you see?' she asked.

'Buckets… and what looks like blocks of stone.'

'But are we alone?'

He climbed up another rung. 'I think so.'

She felt him steady his feet next to her then he pitched his body sideways and the beam crashed off his shoulders onto the wooden platform. *Don't break,* she prayed. They waited for the dust to settle and clambered out. Her heart leapt. It looked more like a ruin than a building, and certainly didn't seem hard to get out of.

She craned her head back. The structure was round and soared high above them. Shafts of light sliced through deep-set arrow slits and age-black beams criss-crossed the void to the top. Her shoulders sank. They had come up in some kind of tower. A ramshackle stairway slunk along the wall to floors long gone. She hugged herself against the cold, teeth chattering, and searched desperately for a way out. Nothing. The only exit was an arched opening through the metre thick wall that was blocked by a latticed steel gate. They stumbled towards it.

The gate's hinges disappeared deep into one wall of the opening, and a modern brass padlock locked it to a ring on the opposite side. So much for an easy escape, the place was like Fort Knox. The tower had been built to withstand an onslaught far greater than two tired human beings. Vestiges of a second gate protruded from the exterior perimeter.

They leant against the ice cold grid, silent and despairing. Outside, mountains hunched like hooded monks and fierce clouds boiled around their peaks.

'That's all we need… a damn storm,' she said bleakly.

'Raisin, I know where we are.' His voice rose. 'We're inside the fucking Massane tower.'

'It can't be,' she stammered.

'Look outside. Recognise those steps? We stood right there! The wolf left the cubs at the bottom of them.'

'And Romul was here,' she whispered.

He laughed crazily.

'If we can't get out, he can't get in. It doesn't matter. We're in the Massane Tower. Someone's bound to find us!'

Her eyes flew to the hole they had left in the tower floor.

'Except if he gets to us first.'

'I'll close it up again. Smile, Raisin. This is the first thing that's gone our way in days.'

'I'll smile when I see Matt,' she said grimly.

The wind turned violent, whipping grit and sand through the grid. Rain started to fall in thick grey sheets. She pressed her face between the bars.

'Help! *Help!*'

'No-one will hear you in this wind.'

'*Help!*'

'Save your energy, Raisin. Sooner or later, someone will pass. This is tourist heaven.'

'In *this* weather?'

'Help me put the beam back.'

She shook her head, dazed.

'Matt's forestry station is so close by.'

'Come… let's put the beam back.'

She froze, held up her hand. 'I can hear a dog!'

'Stop torturing yourself and help me.'

'I heard a dog,' she insisted, kicking the gate in frustration.

He tried to pull her away but she shrugged him off.

'Help! Over *here*! In the *tower*!'

'For God's sake, *shut up!*' he snapped.

She collapsed against him in sobs.

'No-one will find us here. This weather could last days.'

Water gushed inside across the gateway's stone paving. Her feet were so cold she couldn't feel them. Lightning flared, blazing the tower in blue light. Thunder pounded the walls.

'That was right above us! If the tower catches fire…'

'It's been around for centuries. One more storm's not going to kill it.'

Thunderclap after thunderclap crashed overhead. She looked up nervously. The tower was terribly exposed on the highest point on the mountain. An explosion of light blinded her. She huddled against him, waiting for the thunder to follow but it never came, just a faint rumble rolled in the distance. She didn't dare hope the storm had passed. Minutes flew by, no thunder, even the rain eased into a drizzle. Still she couldn't relax. He hugged her.

'Jesus, that was worse than the Karoo storms. Are you okay?'

'Glad it's over, if it really is.'

He stood next to the loose beam.

'Let's get this back where it belongs.'

Together they repositioned the platform then heaved stone blocks on top of it.

'Nobody will get through that lot,' he said.

A loud staccato noise clattered close by. She stiffened. He walked to the steel gird and peered outside. She pointed nervously to the wooden platform.

'Do you think it came from down there?' she whispered.

He stood still, listening. The noise started again. An uneven jangling sound.

'What is it?' she said hoarsely.

'Sounds like something metal hitting stone.'

She stared at him, heart pounding. Were Romul and his men coming up from the cave? Or were they outside trying to get in? She hung her arms limply over the bars. The storm had swallowed the sky and the horizon was pewter grey. Matt felt worlds away.

'The noise has stopped,' Geoffrey said.

She cocked her head. The storm still belched in the distance but he was right, the metallic clatter was gone.

'I don't like this... something's not right,' she said.

Geoffrey climbed on top of the platform.

'Anyone coming through here will have to get past my dead body first,' he grunted.

She sat next to him, covering her legs with what was left of her robe. Her palm stung and her body ached.

'I've been thinking,' she murmured. 'When we get out, I'm going home to speak to Mum.' She glanced at him. 'You should come with me.'

'Not now, Raisin.'

'We should speak to her.'

'There's no point, and you know it.'

'I don't agree. We have to face what she did.'

He looked at her with hollow eyes.

'Maybe it'll help *you*, but not me. A long time ago I was obsessed with getting an apology from her but…'

'So come with me and get one.'

'I don't need it anymore.'

'I want her to know I remember the revolting things she did. We can't let her get away with it, Geoffrey.'

'She already has. And getting back at her does nothing. Because that's what this is all about for you, Raisin. You should see your face. You're kidding yourself if you say it's an apology you want. I've been down that road.' He took a deep painful breath and stood up. 'What I want is to be free of her, and that means having nothing more to do with her. She was poison then, she's poison now.'

'*Allô…? Il y a quelqu'un…?*' Hello? Anyone there?

Geoffrey got to the gate first. 'We're in *here*!'

'…in the tower!' Raisin screamed.

The grizzled face of Henri appeared in front of them. A drenched Border Collie panted at his side.

'*Mon Dieu! Qu'est-ce qui se passe ici?*'

'Henri! Oh, thank God, it's you.'

'We're trapped,' Geoffrey shouted.

Henri jostled the gate's padlock. 'How did you get in there?'

Geoffrey pointed to the wooden platform.

'Through there. There are caves under it that connect to the *Grotte des Loups*.'

'That new cave?' he frowned.

'That's where they held us. They murdered a wolf and we're worried about Nicolas,' Raisin cried.

'Slow down, *jeune fille*. Who is Nicolas and who are *they*?'

'They kidnapped him… he's the mayor's son, and they're following us. I think we just heard them. Please get us out!'

The old man scrutinised them, twisting his beard into a spiral.

'Are you in trouble with the police?'

'No! *Call* them! They need to know we've seen the boy and he's still alive,' Geoffrey said.

'*Bon d'accord.* I'll go and get René from the forestry station. He'll know what to do. Right now the safest place for you is right where you are.' He rattled the padlock. 'Nobody can get to you without a hacksaw.'

'We heard metallic noises. What if it's them?'

He shrugged helplessly.

'There's nothing more I can do but get René.' He chivvied his dog. '*Allez, Pastis!* Get to work!'

Pastis trotted obediently into the rain. Seconds later, the clattering started again. Raisin shot her hand between the bars.

'Henri, wait! Please don't go! The noise… it's started again.'

'*Ma fille*, don't panic… that's just Pastis chasing my goats off the rocks next to the tower,' he laughed.

Goats? The hammering stopped. Geoffrey grinned tiredly.

'The clang of bloody goat hooves. Look…'

She gaped as Pastis herded seven sopping wet goats into a tight bundle near the tower.

'They escaped and believe me, that's the only reason I'd be out in this storm.' He unzipped his jacket and passed it to her. 'You're cold. Put this on.'

She draped it over her shoulders and pulled it tight. It was warm as an embrace.

'Thank you,' she murmured.

He gave them a broad smile.

'Someone was watching over you. The Marin wind always brings rain but today it also brought me your voices. Any other wind and I wouldn't have heard you.'

He unbuttoned his plaid shirt and gave it to Geoffrey. A thin white vest drooped from his still sturdy shoulders.

'No, I'm fine,' Geoffrey protested.

He crammed the shirt through the steel gate.

'René will have something for me to wear. I'll be back in an hour.'

'Wait! My boyfriend works with him, please tell him I'm okay. His name's Matt…'

Geoffrey squeezed her arm. 'Let him go, Raisin.'

The old man waved goodbye and disappeared down the steps. He returned seconds later and dangled his watch between the bars.

'So you'll know when to expect me back,' he said kindly.

She looked at the time. 10.40 am.

'Please ask Matt to come back with you,' she pleaded.

24

TIME CRAWLED. IT was still raining and ghostly lightning flared over the horizon. Raisin wondered bleakly what day of the week it was. Henri's promised hour bled into two.

'What if something's happened to him?' she fretted.

'He's a shepherd… he's used to storms.'

'What if Romul found him? He's an old man.'

'He's a *wily* old man.'

She fastened the watch on her arm. The leather strap was too big and it slipped around her wrist; the yellow face and cracked glass were a comforting link to normal life. Hunger pangs cramped her stomach. She would never eat another meal without appreciating it. She hooked her arms through the grid, pressed her face between the bars and watched the hands of the watch move.

'*Where* is he?' she groaned.

Pastis flew into the entrance, yapping furiously.

'It's Pastis! Something's happened to Henri!'

'*Mais non, ma fille. Me voilà!*' Henri's gravelly voice called. *Here I am.*

He wore a yellow oilskin jacket that swamped him. René appeared behind him, grey hair in wet strands. He wiped his face and shooed Pastis out of the narrow passageway.

'*Va-t-en!* There isn't room for all of us in here.'

Raisin stood on her toes and peered over the men's shoulders. Where was Matt? René waved a gleaming hacksaw in the air.

'Sorry we took so long. I couldn't find my saw. Are you alright? What happened to you? Matt's been frantic, and the police have been looking everywhere for you.'

Henri passed them two cokes, a Mars Bar and a Kit Kat.

'I'm sorry, it's all I could find.'

'Did you tell the police we're here?' Geoffrey asked tersely.

'*Oui*. They're on their way. Henri tells me you saw the boy.' He paused. 'Please say he's okay.'

'We don't really know,' he said bleakly. 'He was fine when we saw him at the house but…'

René ran his finger over the saw blade.

'They better keep those bastards away from me when they catch them.'

Raisin held the two chocolate bars in front of Geoffrey. He chose the Kit Kat but barely looked at it.

'René…? Is Matt not with you?' Raisin asked.

'He went to fetch his mother from the airport, but don't worry he knows you're safe. I phoned him straight after I spoke to the police.'

'Did he… have a message for me?' she asked, embarrassed at how needy she sounded.

René shook his head and positioned the saw on the padlock.

'When will he be back?'

'He said around four. Not long to go,' he smiled.

Her heart sank. Three hours was a lifetime away. And he wouldn't be alone. She buried herself deeper into Henri's jacket and tore open the Mars Bar. It was her own fault that she didn't know about his mother. She hadn't exactly welcomed him, had she? She swallowed back tears. So much for falling into his arms and telling him she loved him.

'At least he's in France,' Geoffrey said.

She nodded and gave him a hug, half expecting him to clear his throat and move away, but he clung to her, and for a wistful moment, they were children again, free to show love and need.

'I'm starting… cover your ears,' René warned.

Metal shrieked over metal, shredding her nerves. She paced restlessly. Geoffrey leant quietly against the wall, eating the Kit Kat. She was sure he was thinking about Chris.

'Ça *y est!*' René grunted. *It's done.*

The gate grated open over the stones and Raisin ran into the downpour. The raindrops bit like spinning grit but she didn't care. They were free and she couldn't wait to see Matt. Henri came up behind her and grasped the back of her head between leathery palms.

'*Mon Dieu… w*here did you get this?' he rasped.

'The kidnappers tattooed us. Geoffrey's also got one.'

He paled as he inspected Geoffrey.

'What's the matter, *mon vieux*?' René asked.

Henri shook his head. '*Ai ai ai.*'

Raisin glanced worriedly at Geoffrey. What did the old man know about the Jupiter Seal? Henri lifted something over his head and gave it to her.

'Take this. We'll talk about it later,' he said heavily.

She stared at his wolf tooth amulet in dismay.

'I can't take that!'

'Give it back when you don't need it anymore.'

'But why do we need it?'

His dark eyes bored into her as he carefully looped it over her head. Her fingers curled around the tooth. Warmth flooded her body, but her heart raced. He hadn't answered her question.

'Henri, what's happening…? You're scaring me,' she said.

'Please… just humour an old man,' he murmured.

The amulet had been in his family for generations. What if she lost it? She raised her eyebrows at René for guidance but he threw his palms in the air. She held the tooth to her lips. The old man nodded approvingly then whistled for his dog.

'Pastis, *heel*! Time for us to get out of the rain.'

René and Henri walked slowly but she and Geoffrey struggled to keep up. She concentrated on the faded Nike logo on Henri's shoes, forcing herself to match him step for step. His amulet tangled with the tribeswoman's necklace against her skin. Pastis trotted next to her, nudging her with his wet nose every time she stopped.

At last the research station was visible between the trees. She could see Chilli sleeping on the front doormat. Pastis jumped onto the deck and nuzzled the ginger cat awake. She stretched, uncoiled onto her back and meowed hello. René took his pipe from the banister and scratched her belly.

'*Salut,* Chilli.'

The simple homeliness engulfed Raisin like a warm shawl. No matter how worried Henri was about them, she felt safe.

'The police are on their way. In the meantime, food or shower first?' René asked.

'A phone for me, please,' Geoffrey said.

'A shower sounds heavenly,' Raisin sighed.

René pointed to the corridor leading off the living area.

'Matt's room is second on the left and the bathroom is opposite. I'm afraid things are a bit basic here, but we have nice soap.'

He gave her a blue towel and a block of Marseille soap so big, it barely fitted in her hand, then he escorted Geoffrey outside to the office so he could make his call.

She entered Matt's room nervously. The bed was unmade and his leather satchel lay open on the crumpled sheets. A torn world map hung on the wall next to a poster advertising a safari to Kenya. Plastic containers with plant samples stood on every available surface and tree cuttings stapled onto white boards were spread out over the table under the window. She smiled. It looked like he had been there a lot longer than a week.

A close-up of the two of them, heads together and laughing, danced on his laptop. The photo had been taken just weeks before she had run away. She dropped the towel and soap on the bed and pushed open the French doors. Fresh air was another thing she would never take for granted again.

Outside, the beech trees floated like emerald mist in the gentle rain. No wonder Matt loved it here. Beech trees were his favourite trees. Goddesses of the forests, he called them.

She took off Henri's watch. 3.10pm. An hour and Matt would be home. What would she say to him? How would he react when he saw her? What had he told his mother about them?

Chilli ambled inside and rubbed her body against her leg. She scooped her into her arms, nuzzled her then yawned and put her on the bed. If she didn't have a shower soon, she would fall asleep on her feet.

The bathroom was tiny but clean. She stood in front of the mirror and stared in horror at her reflection. Nausea rose like a tidal wave. Without her hair, she looked exactly like her mother. She touched her cheek, fear thudding. Was evil hereditary? Would Matt still want her when he knew what Mum had done? She ran her fingers over her head; down soft bristles were just beginning to grow back. She couldn't bear how vulnerable she looked and angrily ripped off the Jupiter robe. It landed on the floor with a faint clunk.

She fell to her knees and scrambled through the ragged cloth, carefully undoing a knot in the hem. The ribbed cockleshell rolled into her palm. She clutched it to her chest.

I'm glad I listened, she whispered to the tribeswoman and her wolf companion.

Steam heaved around her in the shower. She had to find a way to persuade Geoffrey to go with her to confront Mum. She turned the hot tap higher, welcoming the water's fierce heat. Even if he didn't come with her, she would drag an apology out of her. Dad was also on her hit list. Why hadn't *he* done anything to protect Geoffrey? She was desperate to hear him say that he hadn't known. Tears poured down her cheeks. *Damn them both to hell.*

The towel was scratchy but she rubbed and rubbed until her skin turned bright red, then she wrapped it around her and slipped back across the passageway, leaving the Assembly's robe in a heap on the floor.

She picked up a creased khaki shirt from the floor, her last Christmas gift to Matt. The pocket was torn and she smiled at the way he had stapled one side to keep it in place. She buried her face in it and breathed in his smell. She could just picture him crawling into the undergrowth in it. She pulled it on, choking on furious tears. She wanted *him*, not his goddamn shirt.

A dreamcatcher swayed from a curtainless rod at the window.

Pale feathers pirouetted on fine leather cords. She frowned and went up to it. There were four cords but only three feathers. She brushed them with her fingers. So this was where Matt's mysterious feather had come from. She tapped the intricate spider web hoop and made a wish. *Let him still love me after he knows.* The feathers swirled lazily.

She checked the time. 3.40 pm. Twenty minutes and he would be home. She curled around Chilli on the bed to wait. The quiet murmur of men's voices floated in from outside and within minutes she was fast asleep.

She rolled over and groaned. Muted light caressed the room.

'Sarah sweetheart…'

Her heart lurched, her eyes flew open. Matt stroked her cheek.

'Matt…?'

He leant close and kissed her, his breath soft and warm.

'Morning, sleepyhead.'

She touched his cheek. 'You're here…'

'I've been home for ages.' He held her hand against his cheek. 'Sarah… Sarah… I thought I'd never see you again.'

She bit her lip and struggled to keep his gaze. Words disappeared. She felt shy and anxious.

'Matt, I'm sorry I was so…'

He shushed her with a fingertip. She shifted back so he could join her on the narrow bed. He lay next to her, face inches from hers.

'I didn't mean to leave London without seeing you,' she mumbled huskily.

'I know.'

'It's just…'

'Shhhh… not now, sweetheart.'

'There's stuff… I have to tell you.'

'Later. Right now I just want to look at you.'

His breath was ragged as he traced the outline of her face; his thumb wiped her tears away. She buried herself in his arms, sheltered and safe for the first time in days. His hand slipped under her shirt and rubbed her back. She gave a small moan and kissed him; their lips soft and hesitant. She stretched sleepily.

'What time is it?' she whispered.

'Early… about five I think. You slept through the night.'

'Why didn't you wake me when you came home?'

'Would *you* have woken me?'

'No,' she grinned. 'Is anyone else up? Where's Geoffrey?'

'He left with the police just after I got here. When they heard about the cellar in the house, they went straight away hoping the boy would still be there.'

'Have you heard from them? Did they find him?'

'They only found an old woman.'

'Matt, listen to me…'

This time he didn't stop her. A bird trilled jauntily in the garden. She twisted onto her stomach and looked outside. The beech trees shimmered like coral candyfloss in the breaking dawn.

'I don't know where to begin,' she sighed.

'Is it about us?'

'No, it's about Geoffrey… and me.'

There was a quiet tap on the bedroom door.

'Is that my daughter I hear?'

Raisin froze. A small woman with long white gypsy hair smiled at her from the foot of the bed.

'Hello darling, you're awake!'

'*Mum…*?' Raisin stammered.

25

MATT SPRANG OFF the bed like a guilty teenager.

'Mrs Radcliffe…!'

'Dear boy, call me Jane. Mrs Radcliffe makes me sound like a headmistress.'

Raisin didn't move. What the hell was Mum doing here? The room distorted into blurred shadows. Her mother walked closer, arms outstretched, blue kimono sleeves undulating. She looked like a swooping hawk. Matt grinned broadly at her.

'When you and Geoffrey went missing, the police insisted I contact next-of-kin,' he said.

'But René said you'd gone to fetch *your* mother,' she stammered, betrayed by the one person she trusted.

'*Yours*,' he beamed.

'I came as soon as I could,' her mother smiled.

Raisin shrank against the wall. *Let me wake up*. Elegant fingers curled around her hand; the vermillion nails looked dipped in blood. A tiny diamond glinted on her pinkie finger.

'I've been so worried,' her mother said.

Raisin's hand drifted to her head, hating how exposed she felt without hair. She glanced desperately at Matt. He gave her a bewildered frown. Her mother drowned her in a ferocious hug and she was catapulted back her to her childhood when the smell of *Opium* had cloyed to every surface of their home. It welcomed her from school more often than Mum had. Even the dogs had smelled of it.

How she had loved the exotic bottles that lined her mother's dressing table, looking like Chinese royalty with their magnificent red lacquer and luxurious black tassels. But no matter how hard she begged for one, Mum never relented, not even on her thirteenth birthday.

For a split second, she surrendered to the embrace. Then reality jolted. Mum was a monster. She pulled away. A cool hand stroked her face. Another whiff of *Opium*. The smell and memories suffocated her.

'Goodness child, you look *terrible*. Your beautiful hair... your *best* feature.'

'It gets worse,' she mumbled and turned her head.

Her mother's hands jerked back in fright.

'It's just a tattoo. You can't catch anything from it,' Raisin snapped.

Matt stood at the foot of the bed, looking wretched.

'We found your clothes and bits of red hair when we went back to the house with the search warrant,' he said.

His eyes were dark with love and confusion. Raisin softened. He couldn't have known Mum was the last person on earth she wanted to see.

'I knew from Nicolas' description that it was you. How did you know to come back?' she said softly.

'We snooped around outside and found Pi's body and saw he'd been shot. That was the first sign there had been trouble there. When we came back with the paperwork, you were gone.'

'*Whose* body?' her mother bristled.

'Pi... Geoffrey's dog. They shot him... right in front of us,' Raisin whispered.

'Why isn't Geoffrey back yet?'

Raisin shot upright. He didn't know Mum was here.

'The police should never have asked him to go with them. It's far too dangerous,' her mother complained.

'He won't stop until Nicolas has been found,' Raisin said.

'Well, I'll tell you right now... if anything happens to *my* son while he's looking for someone else's son, I'll sue the entire French government.'

But this is all your fault! Raisin wanted to scream. She swung her legs off the bed.

'What's for breakfast?' she said with forced lightness.

René was already up and sipping espresso on the deck. A grey-streaked wolf cub straddled his forearm.

'*Bonjour*, René,' Raisin greeted. 'How are the cubs?'

'*Tiens* Merguez, look who's here!'

The knot in her stomach loosened a little.

'Merguez? Is that really his name?' she smiled.

'I had to call him something worthy of his courage.' He held the cub out to her. 'You should see him take on Chilli.'

She cradled the tiny wolf against her. He yawned and studied her with shy curiosity. She showed him to Matt.

'Isn't he cute?'

He tickled it under its snout.

'René told me what happened,' he nodded.

'Where is the other one?' she asked worriedly.

'She's still asleep,' René said.

'He named her Cava, after Spanish champagne,' Matt laughed.

'Is that animal *wild*?' her mother asked.

'We're not sure what they are. They were rescued by a shepherd,' Matt said.

'There were seven wolves in the cage next to us that had been branded like the cubs' mother.' Raisin's voice broke. 'They sacrificed one of them in the cave... cut its heart out... made me... drink its blood.'

Matt was instantly at her side. He coaxed her into a chair and kissed the top of her head.

'Sit. I'll make us some breakfast. There's lots of time for you to tell us what happened,' he said.

'You drank wolf blood? Surely we need to get a doctor? Did *Geoffrey* also drink it?'

'Mrs Radcliffe, I don't think...' Matt said.

'It's Jane.' She waved at René. 'Kindly take that *thing* away from my daughter. She's not to touch them.'

René's eyebrows twitched. Raisin buried her face in Merguez's fur. Matt slid his hand over her shoulder. René's espresso cup clattered in the kitchen sink. Raisin looked up nervously, caught the tight glint in his eyes as he bent down and stroked the dozing cub.

'I assure you, Madame Radcliffe, our little miracle here will heal more than he will harm. I wouldn't dream of taking him away from her.' He gave Raisin a soft smile. 'I need to check on the reserve fences. Will you feed Cava when she wakes, *s'il te plaît*? And Matt... I'll manage the station on my own the next few days. Do what you need to do. Family comes first.'

'What an *extraordinary* man,' her mother fumed when he left.

Raisin said nothing, mind racing. She had to warn Geoffrey. Cava chose that moment to scramble up the side of the box and topple it over. Matt caught her as she charged under the table.

'Good timing, Cava,' Raisin muttered.

Out of the corner of her eye, she saw her mother's blue sandals approach. She pitter-pattered her finger over Merguez' snout. He snapped his baby teeth at her.

'I wish you wouldn't do that. It's unhygienic.'

Raisin studied her mother's toes. Perfectly groomed vivid red. Who would guess the blackness of her soul from those perfect feet? How could she expect anyone to believe what Mum had done to Geoffrey when she could barely believe it herself? The sandals didn't move. Raisin was aware of Matt emptying a sachet of puppy food into a metal bowl. She took a deep breath and looked up.

Her mother was studying her with a puzzled expression. Her thick white hair was curled like rope around her hand and she was brushing her cheek with its wispy end. Her face was lifeless without the usual mascara-thick lashes and blue liner, and Raisin was shocked how withered she looked. She lowered her eyes, unsettled. She had yearned for Mum's love her whole life but now it repelled her.

Cava's bowl clanked on the ground and excited yaps skittered through the kitchen. Merguez wriggled wildly and tried to squirm off Raisin's knees. She tucked him under her chin.

'Let your sister eat first,' she said.

'I think I'll take a shower and change,' her mother murmured.

Raisin waited until she heard the bathroom door click shut.

'Matt, we have to find Geoffrey.'

'What's going on, Sarah?'

'I have to warn him she's here.'

'Why? She's not an axe murderer,' he smiled. 'And she's come a long way.'

'Trust me… he won't want to see her.'

Matt took the restless cub from her and put it on the ground next to Cava then he cupped her chin.

'Talk to me.'

She turned away. He made her look at him.

'Sarah, what's going on?'

'She… she used to… touch him…'

'What do you mean… did she hit him?'

'No, Matt. *Touched* him… sexually.'

She whispered *sexually*, as if by half-saying it, it would be less grotesque, but it came out like a hiss. He went white and enveloped her in his arms. She broke into sobs.

'She did it for years, Matt. *Years.*'

A door slammed in the corridor. She jerked upright and wiped her eyes. Matt picked up the cubs.

'René built them an area outside where they can play. Let's get out of here.'

Morning light tempered the world in a tender haze as they walked through the willow trees. Matt stepped over a low wooden fence and set Merguez and Cava free in their enclosure then he led Raisin to a fallen tree and spooned behind her as they straddled it.

'What about *you*? Did she…?'

'No, not to me, but I…'

He hugged her without interrupting.

'She did it… she did it in front of me.'

'I don't understand… did what, sweetheart?'

Her chest tightened. 'Masturbated him.'

'Oh *Sarah*…'

'She *wanted* me to see. And Geoffrey, poor Geoffrey. He'd disappear from his body, escape to some safe place. God knows how. She kept doing it. Called it his *treat*, but he *hated* it, Matt. He *hated* it.'

Her shoulders sagged. The secret was out. She turned and searched his face. What was he thinking? He stroked her cheek.

'Was there no-one you could tell?' he asked.

Tears rolled down her cheeks.

'I can't forgive myself that I never did. It's all such a jumble but I *should've*.'

'Shhh… it wasn't your fault. You must have been terrified. But Sarah, why didn't you tell me? Why carry this all on your own?'

She watched Merguez chase Cava under a purple flowered bush. A whiff of wild lavender floated to her. How could she explain that until Geoffrey's arrival, she had forgotten every awful moment? She chewed her lip. Was this the right time to tell him she couldn't have children? He kissed her lightly.

'Don't say anything else. I'm glad you told me,' he whispered.

She sighed. No, she couldn't risk making him love her less.

'Matt… you've got to help me warn Geoffrey.'

'We'll take my scooter and go look for him.' He stared up at the house. 'I can't believe what she did.'

She cocked her head. 'Listen. A car…'

A dark blue Suzuki 4x4 bounced up the dirt track and shuddered to a stop. Michelle and Vincent sprang out.

'*Bonjour*, Raisin,' she said tersely.

Vincent waved hello and lowered his head to light his cigarette. Raisin introduced Matt.

'Did you find Nicolas?' she asked.

'*Non*. Just an old woman. If your brother hadn't told us about the cellar, she would be dead. Romul had stabbed her then left her down there.'

'What bastard leaves his own mother to die?' Vincent muttered.

'Maria is Romul's *mother*?' Raisin gasped.

'That's what she said. It seems that after you and Geoffrey got away in the caves, Romul came to the house for Nicolas but his mother wouldn't let him take him. So he stabbed her,' Michelle said.

'She was the only nice person there. Will she be okay?' Raisin asked.

'She's in ICU at Rivesaltes General but it's touch and go.'

'And Nicolas?'

'Gone. Romul took him.'

'Did Maria say *why*?'

'It seems you ruined some transition ceremony and he needed a new… sacrifice.'

Vincent stomped on his cigarette.

'Come. We're wasting time. We need to run over some details with you,' he said to Raisin.

Matt slipped his arm over her shoulders. 'Now?'

'I'm fine, Matt. Romul will kill Nicolas if we don't get to him first.'

'Is there some way we can contact Geoffrey?' Matt asked.

Raisin shot him a grateful look. Michelle checked her watch.

'I'm afraid it's too late. They were meeting the Special Services unit from Collioure at 6 am to go into the *Grotte des Loups*. They'll be down there already, and there's no signal.'

'Is he safe? Who's with him?'

'Jean-Philippe the guide, and Brigadier Guillaume.'

'The media went wild with the kidnapping story and *suddenly* the esteemed brigadier shows interest,' Vincent snorted.

'Vincent, he's our colleague, and we need him on our side,' Michelle cautioned.

'Geoffrey won't be happy about going into the cave with him. We thought he was an idiot.'

Vincent shot her a surprised look. She shrugged. Too bad if he found her rude. The brigadier had been less than helpful. She hoped Geoffrey kept his cool around the man.

'Shall we go inside?' Matt suggested.

Raisin walked into the kitchen, relieved her mother wasn't there. They clustered around the table and Vincent snapped out a notebook.

'What do you need to know?' she asked.

'Start with what happened in the cave then tell us how you got to the Massane Tower.'

'We're trying to understand how the Assembly managed to get in and out of the cave without being seen,' Michelle explained.

'Let me get the girl some coffee first. Any other takers?' Matt asked.

Raisin glanced nervously towards the bathroom. Matt saw and popped his head in the corridor.

'The door's still shut,' he nodded.

'Tell us how they took you into the cave,' Vincent said.

'I don't know how. They drugged me while I was still in the house and I woke up down there. Geoffrey will be able to answer that better than me.'

For the next fifteen minutes she described what she remembered about the cave, explaining how they had climbed up to the tunnel using the chair. She didn't mention the tribeswoman. When she got to the fork in the tunnel, Vincent stopped her.

'How did you know which way to go?'

She hesitated. Would they believe her if she told them?

'I found a cockleshell on the ground and decided it was a sign,' she said lamely.

'From…?'

'Just a sign,' she shrugged. 'And as it turned out… I was right.'

There were footsteps on the deck and for a panicked moment, she thought it was Geoffrey. She groaned in relief when she saw Henri at the door, walking stick raised in greeting. Pastis trotted behind him, panting loudly. Vincent jumped up.

'*Monsieur*, we're in a meeting!'

'It's okay, Vincent. It's Henri. He knows the mountains better than God,' Michelle smiled, waving the old man in.

'It's *under* the mountains where we need God,' Vincent grunted.

'You came at the right moment, Henri. We'll finish off with Raisin then maybe you can help us.'

Henri stood to one side with quiet patience. His leathered fingers toyed with the long welts patterned into the wooden shaft of his hiking stick.

'*Assis*, Pastis,' he murmured to his dog. *Sit.*

Vincent scanned his notes.

'So how did you find the stairway to Massane?'

Raisin squirmed. 'I followed the cave paintings…'

'Cave paintings…?'

'There were animals and handprints painted on a rock… like in the *Grotte de Loups*. But they were really high and I was curious how someone could have reached that far up so we climbed up to see and…'

'Was there a wolf amongst the paintings?' Henri interrupted.

Vincent shot him an irritated look. Michelle laid a restraining palm on his arm.

'Was there?' Michelle prompted Raisin.

'Yes. There were two facing the opening we found. Why do you ask Henri?'

His hands tightened around his walking stick.

'You said there was a manmade stairway going up along the cave wall?' Vincent asked impatiently.

'That's right. We climbed along it until we got to a wooden platform that blocked our way.' She grimaced at the memory. 'We thought we'd come to a dead-end but Geoffrey managed to move one of the beams and the next thing we were inside the Massane Tower.'

Henri coughed, and carefully pushed the coffee cups aside with his hiking staff then pointed a blackened nail to the carvings below the top of his stick. Three symbols were engraved into the dark wood:

26

NOBODY SPOKE. HENRI'S amulet burned her skin. Raisin laced her fingers around the necklaces. Why was the Jupiter Seal on the old man's walking stick? She couldn't bear it if he was part of the Assembly. Was there no-one left to trust? Vincent's hand slid to his gun. Michelle gestured irritably to him.

'Let him explain,' she snapped.

Henri tapped the walking stick.

'This *makila* belonged to my great-great-grandfather, Stéphane Arana. He was from a Basque mountain hamlet called Itxassou, and at the age of eight, he saved the village sheep by breaking the padlock of their enclosure as the waters mounted during the floods of 1798. The villagers thanked him with this *makila*, an unheard of honour for a child.'

'Tell us about the symbols on it,' Vincent interrupted.

'Vincent...' Michelle warned.

'For the Basques, a *makila* is both a practical shepherd's staff and a weapon,' Henri explained.

He unscrewed the stick's handle, exposing a stiletto-sharp dagger. Click. Vincent unclipped his holster. Raisin glanced uneasily at Matt. He moved behind her, hands dropping protectively onto her shoulders.

Henri swung the stick upside down, rubbed the wide silver band at the bottom and pointed to the names and dates engraved in elaborate swirls.

'*Makilas* are traditionally bequeathed from firstborn to firstborn, so when my son becomes its keeper, his name will be added to this list.'

'You know something about Raisin and Geoffrey's tattoo, don't you?' Michelle asked.

He nodded gravely. Vincent twirled a cigarette between his fingers. Raisin rested her head against Matt's stomach. Michelle circled the Jupiter Seal on the stick with her forefinger.

'We know the symbol has been around across different ages… but what is the story behind this one?'

'On his deathbed, my father told me that it represents two ancient buildings. One of them is right here in our village… the *Torre de Pérabona*.'

'That's Catalan for *Tower of Good Stone*,' Michelle mused. 'I've never heard of it.'

'You know it as the Massane Tower.'

'No!' Raisin gasped.

'How can a stick from a Basque village five hundred kilometres away have anything to do with a medieval watchtower in *our* village?' Vincent snorted.

'Stéphane Arana is the link. He came from a family of Basque mystics and moved here after marrying a Catalan healer. Before he died, he engraved the symbols as a warning to future generations. Each father passes both the *makila* and the warning on to his son, but…' He faltered for the first time. 'I never took it seriously until I saw…'

His eyes fell on Raisin. She went cold. Could Henri's knowledge have *prevented* what had happened in the cave? She nervously touched the back of her head. Could they trust him? Henri watched her closely. She looked down, unnerved.

'What about the other building?' Michelle asked.

'Patience, *ma chère*,' he murmured, polishing the middle engraving with his thumb.

'This represents a wolf tooth and it is symbolic of the shepherd's *métier*. A constant reminder to be vigilant over his sheep. The only thing standing between life and death for the sheep is their shepherd.'

Raisin fingered the amulet, desperate to believe him.

'And although this last symbol looks like a simple line, it's the most important one. It represents the *Linía de Llop* and is what links our tower to the second building, the Colosseum in Rome. But it also...'

'Enough! We're wasting time with this mumbo jumbo. *Colosseum...* that's just ridiculous!' Vincent exploded.

'Calm down,' Michelle said sharply. '*Linía de Llop* means *Line of the Wolf*. Doesn't it, Henri?'

'That's right. The *Linía de Llop* is like a sacred ribbon that embraces the earth... a broad band that connects places of great spiritual importance. From Itxassou, where Stéphane Arana was born, to Lourdes to Collioure to Rome to Assisi... and that's just Europe. It extends all the way to sacred territories across America and Asia.'

'So...?' Vincent said irritably.

'The *Linía de Llop* has great power... for those who need healing and for those who are healers.'

'Did you say... *Assisi*?' Raisin stammered.

'*Oui...*' he nodded.

'But that's *north* of Rome. How can they be connected?' Vincent said.

'In terms of the Earth, the distance between Rome and Assisi is almost nothing,' Henri replied.

'We saw two statues of St Francis of Assisi,' Raisin whispered. 'Not one, *two...*'

'Where?' Michelle asked.

'One was at the entrance to the dolmen, and the other near the top of the stairway in the cave that took us into the Massane Tower.'

Henri stared out the kitchen door, leathery hands wrapped around his shepherd's stick.

'Guardians watch over what is sacred in the world and most of the time, we aren't even aware of them, or recognise the form they appear in, but they're there. Always. Stéphane Arana was one of them. Almost two hundred years ago, he predicted that the power of the *Linía de Llop* would be abused. Someone else must have known about the threat and placed the Assisi statues to protect the site. I believe your Assembly of Jupiter people also know about the *Linía de Llop*, but they do not seek to be healers or to protect the sacred.'

'How could Arana have known anything about *our* tower when he was from the other end of the Pyrenees?' Vincent said sceptically.

'Not just any end, *jeune homme*. Itxassou has a history of mystic healers going back to ancient times. By the time Stéphane Arana recorded this warning, he had lived here with his Catalan wife for years. Both were healers who drew on the *Linía de Llop* for their work. Ask the old people, they remember the stories.'

'Colosseum, huh?' Vincent sniffed.

Henri stamped his stick angrily on the floor.

'Don't mock what you don't know. Long before modern medicine, healers cared for the sick with knowledge passed down through their forbearers.'

Relief washed over Raisin. His words rang true. Hadn't *she* experienced the power and protection herself? She longed to tell him how the tribeswoman had guided them out of the cave.

'What was the warning your father gave you?' Michelle asked.

'He told me that the circle represents both the Colosseum *and* the Massane Tower. As for the two diagonal lines across it, one is the *Linía de Llop,* and the other is symbolic of the passage of time into the future... to when the sacred power would be abused once again. No-one knew when it would happen but he warned me to always be vigilant for signs of it.'

'No, *mon vieux*. Not possible. The Jupiter Seal dates back to King Solomon's time... that's 1000 years BC,' Vincent said.

'The symbol transcends time and has powerful meanings across cultures and histories,' Henri shrugged.

'I wish Geoffrey was here,' Raisin grumbled. 'He knows more about the Jupiter Seal than any of us. I'm sure he told me that in King Solomon's time, it was a thing for maths purists, and it was only later, around the 15th century I think he said, that the magic squares were turned into talismans.'

'And that's long *after* the Colosseum and the Massane Tower were built on top of ancient burial sites,' Henri agreed.

'It's well known that cave paintings and prehistoric burial sites are concentrated in areas of spiritual importance. Perhaps Stéphane Arana discovered that the Massane Tower led to the *Grotte des Loups*?' Matt said.

'He may even have helped build the stairway! But Henri, how did the Romans abuse the *Linía de Llop*?' she asked.

'They massacred innocent people and animals in the guise of games to honour the dead, and to appease the gods, but in doing so, they broke the covenant of the *Linía de Llop* to heal,' Henri said.

'Why are wolves so important?' Michelle asked.

'This is where I failed my father. The dead wolf with the terrible brand on her hip was a sign, but I didn't realise it at the time.' He glanced at Raisin, eyes burning with regret. 'It was only later, when I saw it on you that...'

Raisin felt a twinge of guilt that she had doubted him.

'Henri, you couldn't have prevented any of this,' Michelle reassured him.

'A child might die because I wasn't vigilant. The sign was given to me on a wolf and I didn't see it. For those who work with the *Linía de Llop*, wolves are revered and magnify its power. Rome wouldn't exist today if a female wolf hadn't rescued its infant founders.'

'And it's from them that we believe Romul and Rema took their names,' Michelle explained.

'Nothing surprises me anymore about the Assembly,' Raisin said. 'But why *us*? Why did they need Geoffrey and me?'

Vincent scribbled impatient circles on his notepad.

'Thank goodness, we're back in the real world again. I need more information about the ceremony,' he said.

'I've already told you everything I remember,' Raisin groaned.

'Run through it again, please. You never know what else you might remember.'

'He has a point, Sarah,' Matt said.

She winced, longing for everyone to leave so she could be alone with him. The kitchen fell silent. Matt filled her cup with more coffee. She scooped in sugar and stirred, not sure where to begin.

'Why don't you start with what you told me about the wolf sacrifice,' Matt suggested. 'Don't rush... maybe more details will come back as you go along.'

In a small voice she described the horror of Romul cutting the heart out of the animal.

'He held it over a stone container shaped like a skull, and let its blood run into it... then they added other stuff...'

'What kind of stuff?' Vincent prodded.

'Leaves, berries... mushrooms... like the ones from the cave where we found the Omega man.'

'Psilocybin mushrooms... it was in Cardona's report,' Michelle said to Vincent. 'Go on.'

'Then they sliced their palms with a knife... and let blood run into the skull. They cut me too.'

She showed them her hand. Matt crouched next to her and cradled it.

'I'm... fine,' she mumbled.

'I know. You're doing well.'

'They poured the concoction into a silver chalice then... Romul and Rema drank from it... and they forced me to drink it too.' She shook her head. 'After that, everything's a blur.'

'It doesn't matter... describe the blur,' Matt said.

She frowned at the urgency in his voice.

'I... I saw geometric shapes, patterns... ladders, skulls, snakes... then a trapdoor and underneath it... I saw Mum and...'

'Raisin darling, you saw *me*? *Where*?'

Her mother swanned into the kitchen, arms spread in welcome. A floral skirt swished around her ankles, and her white bohemian blouse showed off more than a glimpse of cleavage. Russet lipstick burnished her lips. The mask was back.

'Good morning, everyone. I'm Raisin's mother, Jane. Why did you tell them you saw me? I've only just arrived!'

'It was just… a *dream*, Mum.'

'*Bonjour, Madame*. I'm Captain Michelle Valette and this is my colleague, Detective Vincent Dupont. The gentleman on my right here is Henri Arana.'

'Where is my son? Is he safe?'

'He's helping us find the people who kidnapped your children.'

'You're not even close to catching them, are you?'

'That's why they're here, Mum,' Raisin said dully.

'Mrs Radcliffe, may I suggest you wait for us on the deck while we finish with the police? I'll bring you a cup of coffee,' Matt said.

Her lips tightened briefly then unfurled into a poised smile.

'It's Jane, dear boy. Do you have herbal tea?'

'I'm sure I can find some.'

Raisin caught Vincent's curious stare. She blushed. Their family shame lodged like tar in her chest. The crabby gendarme was too observant. Would he know a child molester if he saw one?

Within five minutes the kettle lid was clattering and steam pumped into the kitchen. Matt made tea and took it outside, returning with a wry look.

'I suspect we have about ten minutes,' he said.

'Do you know *why* they wanted you to drink the mixture?' Michelle asked Raisin.

'No, but according to Geoffrey, everyone drank it.'

'Can you try and tell us more about what happened after you began to hallucinate?' Matt pressed.

'My mind was a mess. Romul kept asking me what I was seeing and when I told him about the snake, he said I had to ask it for

237

instructions. I didn't know what he meant.'

Matt warmed her clammy hands between his.

'I'll tell you what I think he wanted. Shamans around the world induce trance by eating or drinking plant concoctions in exactly the same way. They do it to open communication with the spirit world. For some reason Romul and Rema were trying to duplicate this procedure,' he said.

'And you're an expert on this because...?' Vincent drawled.

'I study plants,' Matt replied evenly. 'It sounds to me like Romul believed he needed guidance of some sort.'

'So we should be asking *what* they hoped she would see,' Michelle said.

'I agree with Matt's theory, but right now the whys and wherefores aren't important,' Henri murmured. 'These people expect much from the *Linía de Llop* and that makes them dangerous. My fear is that sacrificing the boy represents their only hope of reaching the other side.'

Raisin gripped Matt in panic.

'If they're still down in the cave then I think I have an idea how we can rescue Nicolas, but it'll mean I have to go there myself,' she said.

'No, Sarah. It's too dangerous.'

'I agree,' Michelle said.

Raisin rubbed Henri's amulet between her fingers. *Protect the vulnerable.*

'It's our only hope of getting Nicolas out alive. During the ceremony, they treated Geoffrey and me like gods. In their eyes, we *became* Jupiter and Juno. We can use that.'

'She's right. Let's do it,' Vincent said, throwing his unsmoked cigarette into the sink.

'No, it isn't safe,' Matt said firmly.

'What do *you* think I should do, Henri?' Raisin asked.

'You already know. Let the *Linía de Llop* guide you. Trust your instincts.'

She looked at Matt. 'Will you come with me?'

'Are you *sure* you want to do this?'

'I have to.' She turned to Michelle. 'Can we go back to the house first? I need something from the cellar.'

Raisin's skin crawled as the 4x4 jostled over the potholed driveway. Shutters covered the house's windows and yellow crime scene tape criss-crossed the front door. Birdsong wreathed the building in solitary bleakness. They walked to the back in a tight group.

'Shouldn't we be doing this with a warrant?' Matt asked.

'We'll be discreet,' Vincent said.

Raisin pointed to the cages at the end of the garden. The doors were wide open and the fig tree over the enclosure shivered in the wind as if afraid.

'That's where they put us when we arrived,' she mumbled.

Matt wrapped his arm around her. A deafening crash exploded behind her. She yelped and buried her face against him.

'*Voilà,*' Vincent said, jumping over the shattered kitchen door.

'That was *discreet*?' Matt said.

'Vincent is Vincent,' Michelle shrugged.

Fear gripped Raisin. What if Romul was here, watching them? Vincent and Michelle cocked their guns, then hands low they edged towards the cellar. Raisin paused at the top of the stairs, heart racing.

'I'm right behind you,' Matt whispered.

She nodded and went down, fingers clutching the cold stone wall. Blue plastic police markers outlined a pool of dry blood on the cellar floor. What madness had led Romul to leave his mother here for dead? Just thinking of him made her feel dirty.

'What are you looking for?' Michelle asked.

'This,' Raisin said, opening the container with the Assembly of Jupiter items.

'I need a robe and this...' She grimaced as she slid the Jupiter Seal ring on her finger. 'Did you find the clothes we were wearing when they captured us?'

'They're upstairs. Why?' Michelle frowned.

'I'd like to see them, if that's possible?'

Raisin ran back up the stairs. If she never went underground again in her life, she wouldn't care.

'I'll go and get the clothes,' Vincent said.

He ducked under the yellow tape barring the way to the first floor and loped up. His footsteps pummelled the floorboards overhead.

'They kept Nicolas upstairs at first but brought him to the cellar after he banged on the window to get his father's attention in the garden,' Raisin said. 'Poor thing, he was terrified.'

She didn't add what a godsend he had been, taking their minds off Geoffrey's shocking disclosure. She shuffled her feet. Geoffrey still didn't know Mum was here.

Vincent returned and handed her a bundle of clothes. She carried them to the kitchen, turning her back so no-one could see. Inside the left pocket of her shirt, she found Matt's feather. Bedraggled and grey, but still there.

'*Alors?*' Vincent asked.

She closed her hand.

'It doesn't matter. It's not here,' she lied.

'Then let's go and get this thing over and done with.'

27

THE TRAMONTANE WIND roared around the *Grotte des Loups'* cavernous opening and whipped the Assembly robe against Raisin's legs. She felt tainted just wearing it and pulled Matt's jacket tightly around her. Why was it so damn cold in the middle of summer? A lone gendarme stood at the cave's heavy duty security door.

'What time did the Special Forces team arrive?' Michelle asked.

The gendarme shuffled his feet. 'They haven't.'

'*Comment* ça? What do you mean... *haven't?*'

'Brigadier Guillaume said it wasn't necessary so I cancelled them... on his specific orders.'

'And Jean-Philippe?' Vincent asked.

'He went home.'

Raisin paled. 'So *who* is with my brother?'

'Just the brigadier.'

'That's *madness!*' Vincent snapped.

Face grim, Michelle stabbed her mobile.

'I'll get them back here.'

'Who's the man with Geoffrey?' Matt asked.

'An obnoxious bureaucrat more interested in his dinner than finding Nicolas,' Raisin said.

'A civil servant looking for glory before he retires,' Vincent muttered.

Michelle held up her phone. 'Half an hour.'

'That's too long to wait. I'm going in,' Vincent said.

'I'm going too,' Raisin said.

'Oh no you're not. Stay here, I'll go with Vincent,' Matt said.

Raisin held up her ring finger.

'I'm the only one they might listen to.'

'You should all go. Given what's happened, I prefer everyone to stay together. I'll come down with the men as soon as they arrive. When you find the brigadier, ask him to wait for us in the *Galerie des Mains*,' Michelle said.

'Tell a man who told Special Services to fuck off to *wait*…?' Vincent scoffed.

'He doesn't know who he's dealing with,' Michelle said.

'I think he knows *exactly* who he's dealing with.'

'You'll be polite to him, Vincent. Now go.' She gave Raisin her torch. 'Don't worry, I'll get another one.'

Vincent motioned the young gendarme aside and entered the steel passageway, waving at Raisin and Matt to follow.

'Stay behind me. How far is the *Galerie des Mains* from here?'

'About fifteen minutes,' Raisin said nervously.

The men checked their watches.

'It's twenty to eight,' Matt said.

Geoffrey had been in the cave for more than an hour and a half. Raisin curled her fingers around her necklaces. *Keep him safe.* They went through the second door at the end of the passage and stepped into the first cave. The long thin stalactites hanging from the roof made her shudder. It looked like it was raining sabres. Before they entered the tunnel, on the opposite side of the cave, she stopped and showed the men the frenzied handprint splatter on the rockface. She glanced at Matt, longing to tell him about her tribeswoman. Another time. She wasn't in the mood for Vincent's scorn. She hovered her hands over the prints. A hot glow warmed her palms. Why were they here? What did it mean? A flash caught her eye. She swivelled the torch towards it.

A wolf, deep in the tunnel, amber eyes searching hers. She kept still. *What do you want?* It blinked, twisted around and ran, savannah tail swishing. She cautiously went after it. It stopped and faced her again, as if waiting for her. What did it want?

Protect the vulnerable. She gasped. It was warning her. Geoffrey? Nicolas? Both of them? She didn't know. But someone was in terrible danger. It broke eye contact and disappeared into the darkness. She clutched Vincent's arm.

'Something's wrong. I just saw...'

'I'd say quite a lot is wrong,' he snapped.

She fell silent. He wouldn't believe her anyway.

'Please, we must hurry,' she begged, breaking into a run.

They jogged steadily for ten minutes. Her lungs hurt and her chest ached but she kept up with the men. *Where* was the wolf? She heard voices and stopped. Tense male voices.

'Geoffrey?' Matt mouthed.

She nodded. Vincent dimmed his torch and signalled for her to switch hers off. Her eyes struggled to adjust. The voices seemed horribly close in the darkened light. And loud. She heard two men. Geoffrey and the brigadier. But she couldn't make out what they were saying.

They crept along at snail's pace, her shoulder against the wall for guidance, her back burning under Matt's protective hand. The rest of her was ice cold. Fiery snippets floated towards them.

'You and your sister fucked up... and you're going to pay,' the brigadier shouted.

Geoffrey's reply was inaudible. Raisin saw shadows shimmer at the end of the tunnel and cupped her hand close to Vincent's ear.

'*Galerie des Mains*,' she whispered.

He held up his palm. *Wait.* She stopped grudgingly, desperate to be with Geoffrey. Vincent approached the cave like a stalking animal. A stone skittered across the ground. They froze. Raisin held her breath.

'You fucking *ruined* the ceremony once. But not a second time. *Get up!*' the brigadier yelled.

Raisin's shoulders sagged with relief. He hadn't heard them. She ignored Matt's warning squeeze and edged after Vincent, who glowered at her and waved her back.

'Get the fuck up and *jump!*' the brigadier snarled.

Raisin clamped her hand over her mouth. Jump? Not from the platform, surely not. No-one would survive that. Matt manoeuvred in front of her, eyes ablaze. *Don't do anything stupid.*

'You want me to jump? So make me, arsehole,' Geoffrey goaded.

Panic seized her. She recognised that tone. He was beyond caring. She shot past Matt but he yanked her back.

'See those spanking new steps? *Climb!*' the brigadier ordered.

'Go to hell!'

The brigadier's voice became dreamy.

'I'm *leaving* hell, moron. I'm ready for Quirinus at last. When they know what I've done, they won't say no. Not this time.'

Vincent turned to Raisin and raised his eyebrows in question. She shrugged. The words meant nothing. She took another step forward.

'First tell me about the boy. Why a child, for God's sake?' Geoffrey asked.

'Innocence and blood are essential for the incarnation,' the brigadier sighed.

Raisin went cold. Innocence? Henri had been right. Romul wanted Nicolas as a sacrifice. They had to get to him and stop him before it was too late. Why wasn't Vincent *doing* anything? She sidled closer. Matt chased after her, doing his best to restrain her.

'*Enough!* Get up the stairs!' the brigadier ranted.

Vincent peered around the corner into the cave then jerked back and pointed to his gun. The brigadier was armed. Raisin crumpled against Matt. Geoffrey didn't stand a chance.

'*Do* something,' she blurted furiously at Vincent.

He pressed the gun barrel against his lips, eyes flashing her into silence.

'Get up or I shoot!' the brigadier shouted.

'Fuck you.'

'Hurry... *please*,' Raisin whispered.

There was a scuffle and a stifled shout. Raisin jerked out of Matt's hold, shot past Vincent, and ran into the cave, hands flailing.

'Stop!' she yelled.

The brigadier whipped his gun towards her. Geoffrey lunged for his arm.

'*No!*' he screamed.

Matt threw Raisin to the ground. A gunshot cracked. Then another.

And another.

'Geoffrey!' she howled.

She couldn't move with Matt on top of her. His breath seared her neck. Two more shots exploded in quick succession. Her head rang. Her body shook.

'Get off me,' she wheezed.

Geoffrey ran to her and crouched down beside her.

'For God's sake! What are you *doing* here? Are you hurt?'

She didn't know; she couldn't feel her body.

'The brigadier's dead,' Vincent shouted. He waved his pistol at them. 'You're too exposed out there! Get against the wall. Someone may have heard the shots!'

Matt stirred and rolled off her.

'Jesus! They've been shot!' Geoffrey cried.

Shot? She twisted onto her back. Why couldn't she feel anything? Vincent's fingers were cold against her neck.

'Matt... your arm!' Geoffrey shouted.

'I'm fine,' Matt groaned.

Raisin's heart thundered. She crawled towards him. *Don't let him die.* Vincent ripped Matt's sleeve apart.

'You're not fine... you've been shot. Geoffrey, use your shirt... against the wound. Quick.'

Geoffrey took it off, bundled it into a tight pad and pressed it against Matt's arm. He grunted in pain. Raisin grappled for his hand. How often hadn't Mum warned her that she would live to regret her impetuousness?

'Is it bad?' she asked Vincent.

'What do you expect... he's been shot.'

She cringed. He blamed her.

'Are you dizzy?' Vincent asked Matt.

'Just thirsty...'

'Hold his arm up,' Vincent instructed Raisin. 'I'm going for the boy.'

'I'm going with you,' Geoffrey said.

'No. One dead body is enough.'

'I don't like the sound of that,' Michelle snapped from the tunnel entrance.

She stood feet apart, steeled for an attack. A small band of booted, padded, weaponed men sidestepped cautiously around her. They paused for a brief second then approached steadily, balaclava-black faces unreadable.

'Situation's under control. No thanks to the redhead,' Vincent snapped.

The six commandos formed a silent circle around them. Michelle nodded to the man next to her.

'Captain Auberger's in charge.'

A short robust man scrutinised them. His masked eyes flicked from person to person, resting a fraction longer on Raisin. She flushed. He knew it was her fault. He jerked his head at Michelle and Vincent.

'We need to talk,' he said.

A heated exchange took place at the tunnel entrance. Geoffrey tried to listen then scowled in frustration and began to pace.

'Nicolas is in danger, and they're having a fucking power struggle,' he complained angrily.

Raisin watched him storm up to the brigadier's body, half expecting him to give it a violent kick. If only she hadn't rushed into the cave. Matt tapped her head.

'What's going on in there?'

'Guilt… lots of it. Are you sore?'

'I'm fine, Sarah. Relieved you're okay.'

'Matt, I'm so sorry…'

'He's your brother. I would've done the same if it'd been you.'

'No, not about that. I'm sorry about running away from you.'

'You weren't running from *me*, Sarah.'

She searched his face. How could he say that with such confidence? He looked straight back at her, eyes burning into her.

'You were running from… all that other stuff.'

'I love you,' she said, throat dry.

'I know, sweetheart.'

She fumbled through her jacket pocket and showed him the bedraggled feather.

'What does this mean?'

He closed her hand. 'Not now.'

'But…'

Geoffrey strode back towards them.

'Looks like the debating society's disbanded at last,' he muttered.

Michelle and a man lugging a backpack the size of his torso joined them. He squatted next to Matt, sparking adrenaline.

'This is Lieutenant Leroux, the medic,' Michelle said. 'If he says you're fit to move, you're coming with us.'

'Don't waste time on me. Nicolas needs…'

'We're not separating. Once Leroux's given you the okay, Auberger and his men will lead, and we'll follow at a safe distance.' She gave Raisin a withering look. 'Please remember, it's *their* show.'

Raisin gripped the feather. 'It won't happen again.'

'I hope not.' She motioned to Raisin and Geoffrey. 'Come with me. The men need to be briefed. They want a description of the cave and everything in it. Layout, number of people… whether they're armed… don't leave anything out.'

'Geoffrey can do it. I'm staying with Matt.'

Matt shook his head.

'Tell the men what you know. It could save Nicolas' life.'

She left him reluctantly, looking back twice for reassurance. He waved her on. At the tunnel entrance, a lean man with a barbed wire tattoo around his neck led the questioning.

'How big is the cave?' he asked.

'About three times the size of this one,' Geoffrey said.

'How many people?'

'About twenty,' Raisin said.

'Who are the leaders?'

'A man called Romul and a woman called Rema.'

'Romul is Jean-Luc de Marigny in the real world, and in the criminal database,' Vincent interjected.

'Known usage of weapons?'

'No, white collar crime as far as I know.'

'See any weapons in the cave?' Captain Auberger asked.

'Romul has a knife,' Geoffrey said. 'But he could've brought back weapons when he went to get Nicolas.'

'There are wolves,' Raisin said.

'*Wolves*?'

Geoffrey explained the cages at the house and what they had seen in the cave.

'We believe we're dealing with a dangerous cult,' Michelle said.

The interrogation continued another fifteen minutes.

'So let's run through this one more time. From where the tunnel opens into the cave, we'll see an altar opposite us, about twenty two metres away. Correct?' Auberger stated.

'Yes,' Raisin and Geoffrey nodded.

'No other way out?' Barbwire asked.

'We don't know how Romul got to the house,' Vincent said.

'There's a tunnel above the altar,' Raisin said.

'Do they know about it?' another man asked.

'We left a chair under it,' she admitted grimly.

'Too many unknowns here,' Auberger announced. 'Vincent, come with us and secure the tunnel where it hits the cave. Michelle, follow with the civilians. We'll recce the situation and come back for Geoffrey if we can't identify the leaders. Our priority is to chop off the head.'

The men melted out of the cave. The air turned cold without their white-hot presence.

'Leroux said move slowly,' Michelle cautioned Matt. 'I'll go first; Raisin and Geoffrey will come behind you. Questions?'

Raisin shook her head. Even if she did, she wouldn't dare ask. She looked worriedly over her shoulder at Geoffrey and hoped he would be okay in the bad light. Thank God Michelle had extra torches. She fell in step with Matt.

'What did the medic say about your arm?'

'The bullet grazed me, that's all. Stop fretting. They wouldn't have let me come with you if it was serious.'

She winced at the strain in his voice. First Geoffrey, now Matt. When would it end? They left the *Galerie des Mains* in single file and walked in silence until they reached the metal ladder to the last tunnel.

'I'll help Matt from the top. Geoffrey, support him from behind,' Michelle instructed.

Matt hauled himself up with one arm while Geoffrey buttressed his legs with his chest. Matt's pained grunts spluttered through the cave. The group paused at the top so he could catch his breath. Raisin stamped her feet against the cold. Water trickled down the walls and slime smeared the ground.

'It's slippery, be careful,' Michelle warned when they set off again.

Raisin's mind drifted to the shamans that had walked the tunnels lifetimes ago. Men and women so in harmony with the earth, they had known exactly where the holiest places were. What had they believed in? God? Gods? Nature? Spirits? Whatever it was, she felt it. The mountain vibrated holiness. Or was it Henri's *Linía de Llop* she felt? The back of her neck prickled. She scanned the tunnel. The tribeswoman was close by. She sent out a fervent plea. *Let it end without more death.*

The dull thud of drums and chanting shook her back to reality. The *Grotte des Loups* was close. A dark figure appeared and Barbwire ran up to them.

'They all look the same. We need Geoffrey.'

Raisin stomach lurched. Was it safe?

'Go with them Geoffrey,' Michelle said.

'Is Nicolas in there?' he asked the commando.

'We don't know, but there's been another sacrifice… not the kid.'

'Another wolf?' Raisin grimaced.

'Negative.' He signalled to Geoffrey with his weapon. 'Hope you're fit, we're running.'

There was no time to say goodbye. Raisin watched Geoffrey disappear. *Who* had been killed?

28

PANDEMONIUM FROM THE *Grotte des Loups* slammed into them as they approached. Raisin stopped dead. The Assembly sounded out-of-control wild. Had more followers joined? Had she been crazy to suggest this? Matt hugged her with his good arm.

'The commandos know what they're doing, and we've got Michelle and Vincent with us. Romul is a nutcase, but you said yourself they weren't armed. We'll make it. Stay focussed on why you're here.'

Nicolas. He was right, but how the hell could eight people take on a stark-raving mad cult? She squared her shoulders. They were here for Nicolas and she would see it through. Geoffrey would never forgive her if she backed out. She gave him an anxious smile.

'Let's hope he's still alive,' he murmured.

With Michelle in the lead, palm dimming her torch, they crept closer. Long shadows danced alongside them in the amber light. Raisin hoped Geoffrey was coping. The noise was ear-splitting. What if there were too many, even for specially trained men? Despite the cold, sweat soaked her clothes. Romul and Rema were probably in the midst of another sacrifice. She swallowed hard. The taste of the blood mixture still lingered on her tongue. She rubbed the Jupiter Seal ring, all bravado gone. If push came to shove, could she convince these madmen to listen to her? Now she was here, she doubted it. Romul was more likely to kill than to listen. Or give her over to Thomas. And the Neanderthal thug wouldn't kill her, not immediately. Her chest constricted. She had dragged everyone right to the heart of the storm. If something happened to Matt or Geoffrey, she would never forgive herself.

Two figures loomed ahead.

Michelle tensed and unlatched her holster then carefully allowed light to bleed from the torch. Matt moved in front of Raisin. She hunched her shoulders and lowered her head to make herself less noticeable. *Don't let it be Romul and Thomas.*

The figures moved closer. Then Raisin saw unruly hair and breathed again. Vincent, with a Special Services man who towered over him. He beckoned to Michelle.

'Wait here,' she said to them, then glared at Raisin. 'That means *don't move.*'

Raisin nodded meekly.

'Why isn't Geoffrey with them?' she whispered to Matt.

'He'll be fine, Sarah.'

Her voice rose in panic. 'I don't like it. Where is he?'

A third person shifted in the shadows behind Vincent and she bit her lip to stop herself crying out. She recognised Geoffrey's slouch, but even from far, she could see he was in a bad way. The pressure to save Nicolas was destroying him. And he still didn't know about Mum. The thought of telling him nauseated her. She glanced at Matt. Maybe he would do it for her. Michelle darted back.

'Vincent wants you in a recess to the left of the *Grotte des Loups* entrance immediately. Hurry! The raid starts in five minutes.'

The tall commando acknowledged them with a brusque dip of his head. Raisin did a double take and realised she was a woman. Just eight people against Romul and his crackpots, and two weren't even men. The woman scowled at her as if reading her doubts. Raisin gave an embarrassed shrug and went to Geoffrey. He looked ashen. Rock hard fists punched her heart. Did he know who had been killed? She grabbed his arm.

'It's not Nicolas… please say it isn't.'

He shook his head. 'They… ripped him open.'

'*Who?*'

'Eric.'

'*Eric?* Their *son?*'

'They dug his heart out.'

She stared, aghast. 'And Nicolas?'

The Special Services woman held up a pair of khaki night vision binoculars.

'I've scanned the cave… the boy's gone, and so has the woman.'

'She means Rema,' Geoffrey said. 'The fucking bitch has disappeared into thin air.'

Vincent herded them into a damp cavity no deeper than a cramped bus shelter. The *Grotte des Loups* was less than five metres away. They could hear everything but see nothing. She huddled against Matt, careful not to bump his arm.

'Don't move unless told to,' Vincent snapped.

'I'll make sure they don't,' Michelle said.

The chanting and drumming turned frantic. Raisin kneaded her temples then gripped Geoffrey's arm.

'The wolves. Where are the wolves?' she said abruptly.

'What do you mean?' Michelle frowned.

'She's right. They're too quiet,' Geoffrey said.

Raisin pushed back against the rock. The animals probably hadn't eaten in days. Deranged by hunger and the smell of blood, they would be killing machines.

'We don't stand a chance if they're not chained up,' she said.

'I'll warn the men,' Michelle said tersely.

The drumbeats hammered faster, stronger; the chanting feverish and high-pitched. Raisin hunkered low on the ground, knees up against her chest, senses burning. Everything was too loud, too close, too dangerous. And somewhere in the chaos slunk the wolves. She looked around in a panic. If the animals came in here, they would be trapped. She clung to Matt.

'Where the *hell* is Nicolas?' Geoffrey breathed.

She didn't trust herself to speak, and leant against Matt and closed her eyes. At least they were together. Michelle reappeared.

'The wolves are next to the altar, and they're still chained up.'

'Are they dead or alive?' Geoffrey asked.

'Alive. Bunched together… just watching… it's so bizarre.'

'Something's not right,' Raisin fretted.

Gunshots exploded; anguished cries ripped through the air. Raisin screamed and covered her head with her arms. Michelle spun around in combat stance. Auberger's voice thundered across the uproar.

'Police! Everyone on the ground! *Police!* Get down! *Down!*'

Light flooded the *Grotte des Loups*, so violently white it exposed their hiding place. They heard people stampeding. Bodies crashing against bodies. The drumbeats slowed, stopped. Lone voices chanted on. They listened to the chilling sound of people fighting one another to escape; a panic-stricken snarl of arms, legs, flailing bodies. Raisin blocked out the image of Nicolas' tiny body being pummelled by stamping feet. More shots cracked. Women shrieked. Raisin buried herself against Matt, sure she could smell death.

'*Police*! *Get down!*' they heard Auberger yell.

Shrill hysteria pierced the air. Men yelled commands. The chanting started again. *Quirinus. Quirinus.* The hollow boom-boom of drums rattled over the chaos. Steady. Faster. Crazed chanting reached them. *Quirinus. Quirinus.*

'Police! *Get the fuck down!*'

'*Quirinus! Quirinus!*'

'Hey you! Stop right there! Get back!' Vincent yelled, just metres away.

Raisin exchanged terrified looks with Matt. Were the mob rushing the tunnel? Vincent would never stop them alone. Where were those goddamn commandos? Where was that whippet thin Special Services woman with her angry glare? Raisin hated not knowing, not seeing. Michelle sprang out of the recess to help Vincent. Raisin balled her fists, nails digging into her palms. Now nobody was protecting them in the alcove.

'Stop or I'll shoot!' Michelle shouted.

Vincent came into view, gun high, face grim. Raisin struggled to breathe. This was it. Whoever was coming would find them and kill them.

'One more step and I'll shoot!' Vincent threatened.

He backed further into the tunnel, arms and legs spread like a goalkeeper. Two robed figures, one tall, one small, rushed at him.

Michelle hooked the shorter one's ankle and brought him crashing down. Thin arms shot forward to break his fall. A giant of a man flew past Vincent and disappeared into the tunnel. Michelle bolted after him, gun arm erect. Raisin's world shifted into slow motion. Thomas. She twisted onto her knees, groping for a rock, stone, anything to fight him off. She didn't feel the wound on her palm tear open; she didn't hear Matt's voice. He shook her shoulders.

'Sarah, look at me. He's gone. Michelle will get him.'

'What if she doesn't?' she sobbed.

Over his shoulder, she saw Vincent kick the second escapee.

'You're under arrest, *imbécile*,' he yelled.

A trembling hand stretched up towards him.

'Don't shoot… please don't shoot,' a woman pleaded.

'Alana…?' Raisin cried.

'Head down! Hands behind your back!' Vincent shouted.

'No! Don't hurt her!' Raisin begged, pushing Matt aside.

He caught her wrist.

'Don't even *think* about it!' he said angrily. 'No more knight-in-shining-armour moves. You're staying right here.'

She recoiled in shock at his voice. 'It's Alana…'

'Nothing will happen to her if she does as she's told.'

She sagged into him and watched helplessly as Vincent looped an orange band around Alana's wrists. The old woman groaned in pain as he tightened it with a violent tug.

Michelle returned with a stumbling, cuffed Thomas. His robe was ripped, his left eye swollen shut, and a large red stain bled through the white fabric at his knee. His eyes burned like coals. Even handcuffed and crippled, he was full of bluster. She hid behind Matt, wheezing for air. If he escaped, he would tear them apart. Michelle kicked the back of Thomas' legs and forced him to the ground next to Alana.

'Stupid bitch whore. You'd be fucking mincemeat without your gun,' he snarled.

'Shut up or I'll show you what a shot to the knee feels like.'

Raisin hid behind Matt, felt the rigidity in his body, his fear. She pressed her bleeding palm into her leg. The bedlam in the *Grotte des Loups* hadn't subsided. Why was it taking the men so long to get the Assembly under control? Vincent and Michelle stood braced for another escape attempt. Thomas seethed with his back against the rockface. She hoped to God he hadn't seen her. Alana's head drooped on her chest in defeat.

'*Quirinus! Quirinus!*' a voice bellowed.

Romul. Alana rolled onto her knees. Thomas struggled to his feet, mouth deformed in pain, blood crusting his lips.

'*Quirinus! Quirinus!*' Romul screamed.

Alana tried to crawl towards her leader's voice.

'Alana, *don't!*' Raisin shouted.

Vincent kicked Thomas and then Alana to the ground, and cocked his gun. The ominous clunk of metal on metal sickened Raisin. She was desperate for the violence to end.

'One more move like that and you'll never walk again,' Vincent growled.

'Please don't hurt her,' Raisin begged.

Michelle circled Thomas. He glared belligerently at her. She skewered him with her eyes, a fearless hunter. Vincent circled behind Thomas, yanked his handcuffs into the air then rammed a knee into his back. His face smashed against the rocks. Raisin gagged at the stomach-churning crunch of splintering bone. Matt covered her eyes with his hand.

'Don't look,' he murmured.

Barbwire bounded in from the *Grotte des Loups*. She pulled Matt's hand away.

'Cave's secure. Got the man, no sign of the woman,' he announced. 'What the *fuck* happened here?'

'He tried to escape. I had to shoot. He needs Leroux,' Michelle stated.

'He needs a prison not a medic,' Vincent snapped.

'What about Nicolas?' Geoffrey asked hoarsely.

'Gone.'

'Where can he be?' Raisin panicked.

'Captain wants everyone in front,' Barbwire snapped. He gesticulated at Raisin, Geoffrey and Matt. 'That includes you.'

Despite the gruesome circumstances, the *Grotte des Loups* took Raisin's breath away for the second time. The police lights intensified the colours, breathing life into the shapes and forms that contorted the rockface. Folds of ancient calcium tumbled to the floor like gold velvet. The cave glowed with the same caramel hue of the grand old cathedrals of Paris, and revealed as many mysterious corners and shadows.

The stalagmites on her right were even more awe-inspiring than she remembered. Knots and ruffles circled their baobab-girths, swirling around their gracious spires. Man may have built cathedrals to honour God, but nature with its glorious mountains had honoured him long before. How dare the Assembly desecrate it?

The followers lay in a long row, face down, wrists cinched behind their backs; their legs alabaster white in the violent light. Four of Auberger's men prowled between them. Thank God someone had thrown a jacket over Eric's body. The sharp bite of sulphur stung her nose as a commando killed the candles. White smoke looped up to their escape tunnel in the rockface. Raisin wondered if the tribeswoman was watching.

'*Quirinus! Quirinus!*' Romul blared from behind the stalagmite forest.

'Why don't they shut him up?' Geoffrey snapped.

Two followers feebly raised their heads.

'Quirinus! Quirinus!' they echoed.

'*Quirinus!*' Romul howled.

'He sounds desperate,' Matt remarked.

'He should be… he killed his son for nothing,' Vincent snorted.

'Still no sign of Rema?' Geoffrey said.

'Nope. And no sign of Nicolas either. She must've taken him.'

'Fuck it! If that bitch harms a single hair on his head, I'll fucking kill her with my own bare hands,' Geoffrey exploded.

'Then we'll make sure we get to her before you do,' Michelle said dryly.

'What'll happen to the wolves?' Raisin asked.

The animals were sitting in a tight cluster, alert, ears quivering at every sound.

'That's for the police vet and SPCA to deal with.'

Auberger and Barbwire marched towards them through the stalagmites, stony-faced.

'The sooner that lunatic's in custody, the better,' Barbwire muttered.

'Michelle, Vincent, take the civilians back to the surface,' Auberger ordered. He motioned to Barbwire with his head. 'Go with them and radio for vans.'

'And a vet for the wolves? Please…?' Raisin asked.

Auberger glared at her and didn't bother to reply.

'*Quirinus! Quirinus!*' Romul roared.

A breath of air stroked Raisin's skin. Goosebumps tingled. The tribeswoman was near. But where? Movement near the altar caught her eye. She turned excitedly then recoiled.

The chained wolves were watching her, jaws parted, teeth glistening in the light. The biggest one lowered its front paws and sank slowly to the ground, its eyes never leaving her. She nudged Matt with her elbow. Another wolf lay down.

'What is it?' he said tensely.

A third wolf dropped to its belly. Then another. She gasped. Blinked. Looked again.

'Sarah?'

Her chest tightened. She couldn't breathe.

'Nicolas…' she said in a strangled voice.

Deep inside the cocoon of wolf bodies, sat Nicolas.

29

No-one spoke. Auberger signalled to his men to drop back then began to inch towards Nicolas and the wolves. Nicolas stood up shakily, hands cupped over his eyes against the glaring light. Geoffrey lurched for him but Vincent pushed him back.

'Don't move,' he snapped.

Geoffrey stumbled against the back wall.

'I can't believe we found him.'

'I can't believe he's alive,' Raisin said hoarsely.

Auberger edged closer, finger looped over the trigger of his Berretta, thumb hovering over the hammer. The alpha male rose, arrogant and unafraid, mahogany coat gleaming like a coffin. Raisin stiffened. Geoffrey cracked his knuckles. The wolf pushed forward, tail flicking angrily.

'He's establishing power over Auberger,' Matt explained in a low voice. 'Let's hope Auberger gives it to him.'

With his body firmly facing the wolves, chest set in steely readiness, Auberger closed in on the wolves. Nicolas balled his fists in his shirt and shuffled back, eyes darting about like a cornered animal. He reminded Raisin of Geoffrey as a child, desperate to hide his phobia of the dark and failing. As if sensing her thoughts, Geoffrey looked up. She winced at the fear she saw in him.

'He'll be okay,' she promised, not believing her own words.

He nodded bleakly. She pressed the gash on her palm against her mouth and tasted blood, dreading having to break the news to him about Mum. It wasn't right that after all this, he still had to deal with her. Damn her a thousand times over for coming to France.

Auberger was less than five arm lengths from Nicolas. The alpha male snarled. Auberger ignored it and maintained his approach.

'He's turning this into a stand-off,' Matt groaned. 'Someone tell him he has to give the wolf control.'

Nicolas cowered behind the alpha male. The rest of the pack closed ranks around him, chains clattering on the ground.

'*Putain*, they're protecting him,' Vincent whistled.

Auberger jabbed a finger at three commandos. They approached swiftly, leaving the tall woman and Lieutenant Leroux with the prisoners. Auberger darted forward, elbow straight and rigid, Berretta still. The three men trained their assault rifles on the animals. Raisin held her breath. *Don't shoot. Please don't shoot.* Nicolas peered out from between the brown bodies, white with fear. He slid his arm over the sturdy neck of the alpha male and dropped his head against it. It nestled closer, as if comforting him.

'*Quirinus! Quirinus!*' Romul roared from behind the stalagmites.

'*Quirinus*,' a lone voice bleated from the prisoners.

Two wolves snapped their heads towards the noise. Nicolas ducked out of sight. The commandos slunk closer. Raisin rubbed Henri's wolf tooth and wondered what the old man would do. Probably risk his life to protect the animals. She felt powerless and angry. They didn't deserve to die, but she wasn't Henri and didn't know how the hell she could prevent their deaths.

'He's getting too close,' Matt fretted.

The wolves rose in unison, bodies flexed to attack, jaws wide and panting. Nicolas stayed behind the alpha male, clutching its fur with both hands. Auberger motioned to the men to hold back, then took a measured step forward. He was near enough to lunge forward and snatch Nicolas away. The wolves growled viciously. Auberger paused, lowered the Berretta, and beckoned to Nicolas.

'Boy, I want you to walk towards me. Slowly.'

Nicolas blinked then shook his head. Auberger edged up another pace. The alpha wolf snarled, saliva swinging from its fangs. The captain stopped. The commandos slid in behind him.

'They're going to shoot the wolves!' Raisin cried.

'Michelle, let me talk to Nicolas,' Geoffrey pleaded.

'No, out of the question.'

'Let him try. I'll go with him. Nicolas *knows* us,' Raisin said.

'Sarah, don't. Please don't,' Matt said. 'The situation's changed. The wolves will do anything to protect Nicolas.'

'But they might recognise us. It's worth trying to save their lives, damn it. Someone ask that bloody captain if we can try.'

'Auberger knows what he's doing,' Michelle said.

'*Auberger* doesn't give a damn about the wolves.'

'*And* Nicolas doesn't trust him,' Geoffrey said furiously.

'Just let him handle it,' Matt urged.

Raisin watched apprehensively as the captain backtracked and conferred with his men. Her sodden robe clung to her back. A deep chill filled her heart. She tugged Michelle's arm.

'Can you at least *suggest* it to him?'

Michelle gave an exasperated sigh.

'I warned you, it's *his* show. We're bystanders and we're going to keep it that way.'

Matt drew her aside. 'Listen to her, sweetheart.'

'But...'

She fell silent as Auberger and his men broke into two groups and began a pincer movement on either side of the wolves. Auberger must have decided to attack. The animals sensed it and charged forward, jaws spread like unsprung traps, but their chains yanked them back mid-air. Raisin forced herself to watch. Surely they wouldn't shoot if they couldn't see Nicolas? Auberger raised his index finger in the air. The commandos stopped. He raised a second finger. The men slotted rifles against their shoulders.

'No!' Raisin screeched.

A flash of savannah shot over the altar and streaked towards the wolves. Raisin saw the tribeswoman crouched in the tunnel opening, face stricken. Their eyes locked. Raisin pushed Michelle aside and ran towards Auberger.

'Don't shoot!' she screamed.

Michelle raced after her and grappled her to the ground. Geoffrey sprinted past the two women.

'Hold fire! *Fuck it!*' Auberger yelled.

The alpha male raised its head and howled. The others joined in. Nicolas stayed hidden. Auberger gesticulated to the men to fall back. They padded backwards in slow retreat, guns still levered against their shoulders. Howls ripped across the cave. Auberger stormed over to Raisin.

'What the *fuck* do you think you're doing?'

'Sir…!' Barbwire shouted.

Geoffrey had reached the wolves. The alpha wolf lowered its head and gave a warning snarl. Geoffrey calmly raised his palms and stood still. Silence blanketed the cave. Geoffrey lowered his body until his head was the same level as the wolf. It jerked forward, growling. Geoffrey submissively averted his eyes and managed not to react. The wolf tilted its snout and sniffed. Geoffrey stayed frozen. Nicolas bobbed up from within the wolf circle. Geoffrey slowly lifted his gaze. The wolf sat down, haunch muscles rippling. Geoffrey shuffled forward a few inches. Its ears twitched. Nicolas stared at Geoffrey.

'Hello, Nicolas. We looked after you in the cellar. Do you remember me?' he asked.

The child nodded warily. Geoffrey moved closer. The wolf gave a warning yap. Geoffrey manoeuvred into a sitting position, knees folded in front of him. It studied him, sphinx still. Raisin glanced around. Auberger and the commandos hadn't lowered their guns. If Geoffrey made one wrong move, they would shoot to kill.

Suddenly the alpha wolf hunkered down onto its belly; the rest of the pack followed, tails sweeping the air. Nicolas puckered up his face and squinted over Geoffrey's shoulder into the darkness.

'Where's Sarah?' he mumbled.

'She's with the man you saw in the garden. Do you want to talk to her?'

He gave a confused shrug. Geoffrey turned and waved at Raisin and Matt.

'He recognises you. Come quick,' he called.

Michelle raised her eyebrows at Auberger. He gave an irritated wave.

'Okay, go... but be careful,' she warned.

Matt draped his unhurt arm over Raisin.

'No more heroics, Sarah.'

'I just want to get him home safely.'

They squatted down next to Geoffrey. Muted growls rumbled from the wolves. The stink of infection from their wounds turned her stomach. She focussed on Nicolas.

'We've come to take you home,' she smiled.

He didn't answer. She caught his bewildered frown at her white robe.

'It isn't mine, Nicolas. I put it on as a disguise so we could rescue you. My own clothes are in the car.'

'Hello Nicolas, I'm Matt.'

'This man was with your daddy... do you recognise him?' Raisin asked.

He glanced uneasily at Matt's bald head.

'I... can't remember,' he stammered.

Raisin's heart tightened. He was too small, too alone, to be trapped in this violent nightmare. She twisted the Jupiter Seal ring around so it wouldn't frighten him and started towards him, but Matt stopped her.

'Let him come to us,' he murmured.

'Is *papa* with you?'

'No, but I'm going to take you to him,' Geoffrey said firmly.

Nicolas' eyes flickered to the weaponed commandos.

'Your daddy sent these soldiers to fetch you... there's no need to be afraid,' Raisin said.

Geoffrey carefully got to his feet. The alpha wolf jerked upright. Nicolas' lips trembled and a sob gulped out of him. Geoffrey edged forward. He was close enough to be savaged by the alpha male. The remaining wolves sprang up, chains rattling. Geoffrey flinched but didn't retreat. Raisin steeled herself for shots. Nicolas stretched his arms up to Geoffrey. He leant unhurriedly over the alpha wolf, scooped the child high into the air and crushed him against his chest. Nicolas buried himself in Geoffrey's neck. One by one, the wolves dropped to the ground and rested their heads on their paws. Nicolas and Geoffrey clung to each other, entwined, paralysed, as if the slightest move might tear them apart. Then Geoffrey turned and walked away from the wolves. Golden eyes watched him leave. Raisin let out a ragged groan. Nicolas was almost home.

Auberger cleared his throat. 'Leroux, give the kid a once over.'

The medic pulled off his balaclava, slid his backpack to the floor then gave his gun to the Special Services woman and showed Nicolas his empty hands.

'I just want to make sure you're okay,' he said reassuringly.

Nicolas twisted the buttons on Geoffrey's shirt and shook his head.

'You do it… he trusts you,' Leroux said to Geoffrey.

'But how? I haven't a clue what to do.'

'Don't worry… I'll talk you through it.'

'Is that okay, Nicolas? Can the doctor help me make sure you're not hurt?'

Nicolas didn't resist as Leroux guided Geoffrey through some basic medical checks. The boy's breathing was rapid but beginning to steady. He had dilated pupils, no broken bones, and no obvious wounds.

'That's enough. He needs his damn parents,' Geoffrey said impatiently.

'Okay?' Auberger asked the medic.

'Yes. Let's get him home,' Leroux replied.

'Good. Vincent and Michelle, let's try this again… take the civilians up. Leroux, lead them out and radio for back-up.' He pointed to Barbwire. 'Stay here with the prisoners. I'll take the rest of the unit and hunt down the woman.'

'What about the brigadier?' Michelle asked.

'Let him rot,' Vincent grumbled.

'Missing female first, then we'll deal with the prisoners and dead body,' Auberger said.

'What about the wolves?' Matt asked.

'They aren't a priority.'

'They saved Nicolas.'

'He's right… we're not leaving until a vet gets here,' Raisin said.

'You're leaving right now,' Auberger snapped.

Raisin looped Henri's wolf amulet around the tribeswoman's shell necklace and rubbed the two together.

'I'm staying,' she said.

'We're both staying,' Matt said.

'They're terrified and hurt…' Raisin mumbled.

'Michelle, please do something,' Matt insisted.

'They're right. I'll summon the vet to come here as soon as possible,' she promised. 'Is that okay, Captain?'

He gave her a curt nod then waved them away. 'You're wasting time. Go.'

Raisin obeyed reluctantly, half-tempted to leave Henri's amulet with the wolves.

'They're commandos, not gratuitous killers,' Michelle said reassuringly.

'I hope not,' Raisin muttered and tucked the tooth back under her robe.

The overhang softened the sun's blazing burn but didn't protect them from the seething heat. The air was windless and thick. It was hard to breathe.

Lieutenant Leroux checked Matt's arm and applied another layer of gauze.

'How is the pain?' he asked.

'Easing up. The tablets you gave me must be kicking in,' Matt replied.

'The bleeding's stopped but don't overdo it.'

'Shouldn't he go to hospital?' Raisin asked.

'It's a flesh wound, so no stitches needed, but get a doctor to change the dressing and prescribe antibiotics.' He inspected her palm. 'And get him to look at this too.'

He cleaned and bandaged her hand then made them drink water

before they started the short hike down to the police vehicles. No-one spoke as they passed the cup from person to person.

'Here… eat this,' he said, handing out energy bars.

Nicolas pulled a face.

'Go on, try it,' Geoffrey encouraged the child.

'Do you have M&M's?' he asked, eyeing Leroux's backpack.

There was a startled silence then an explosion of laughter. Michelle waved her mobile in the air with a wide grin.

'*Bon,* you're obviously none the worse for your ordeal. Eat your food bar, and I'll phone your mum and dad and ask them to bring M&M's to the police station. How does that sound?'

Nicolas' excited chatter floated around them like soap bubbles as they headed down the mountain. For the first time in days, Raisin felt light-hearted.

'I'm glad you're here,' she whispered to Matt.

He winked at her and lifted his bandaged arm.

'The things a man has to do to get his girl.'

Michelle and Vincent's yellow Suzuki looked toy-like next to the hulking Land Rovers belonging to Special Services. Raisin slipped behind the vehicles and changed back into the clothes she had borrowed from Matt. She bundled up the robe and gave it to Michelle, dropping the ring on top.

'This should be burned,' she said grimly.

'I'll take the kid from you,' Leroux said to Geoffrey.

Nicolas locked his legs around Geoffrey's waist.

'I promised I'd take him to his father, and I will. Why do you need to take him?' Geoffrey frowned.

'It's procedure. Special Services must take him to his parents, and the police will take you three home.'

'I'm not big on procedure at the moment. He's staying with me,' Geoffrey said tightly.

Leroux shrugged and swung his pack into the vehicle.

'Suit yourself. Get in.'

Nicolas clung to Geoffrey and refused to allow Michelle to buckle him into a separate seat.

'He's scared. Can't he sit on my lap?' Geoffrey pleaded.

Michelle ruffled the child's hair.

'Just this once. Don't tell anyone you were in a police car without your seatbelt, okay?'

'See you back at the forestry station,' Geoffrey waved through the window.

Raisin felt numb as the Land Rover disappeared. She still hadn't told him Mum was here.

30

'SHOULD WE DROP you off in the village or up at the forestry station?' Michelle asked.

'Village, please,' Raisin said.

'Sarah, we should first go to your mum and let her know you and Geoffrey are okay,' Matt said.

'She can wait. I want to get changed.'

She gazed out of the window. In less than an hour, Nicolas and his parents would be reunited at the gendarmerie. She imagined his overwrought mother trying to decide which of his favourite toys he would want most, and both parents desperately blocking out images of what might have happened to him during his kidnapping. Her own mother would also be frantic, but to hell with her, Matt was all she cared about.

'I'd really like to go home,' she said.

'Here, use my phone to call her,' Michelle said.

Raisin stared at the scratched Nokia, paralysed. She dropped it on Matt's lap.

'Please do it for me,' she murmured.

Vincent studied her in the rear view mirror. She scowled. Let him think she was cold-hearted. Matt tapped out the forestry station's number.

'Hello René, it's Matt. Yes, we did! He's on his way to his parents. Is Mrs Radcliffe there?'

He manoeuvred the phone between shoulder and chin, and leaned close to her ear.

'You're not alone in this, sweetheart.'

She pinched her eyes to hide the tears. The heat in the car was oppressive; she couldn't wait for the cool darkness of her fisherman's house.

'Hello… Jane. We just wanted to let you know that… yes, don't worry, Geoffrey's safe. No, I'm afraid not. He's gone with Nicolas to his parents and we're… yes, he really is fine… I saw him myself. Sarah and I are first going home so she can pick up some clothes, but we should be back at the forestry station soon.' He checked his watch. 'It's 12.20… so we'll probably be there around three o' clock. Yes, I'll tell him.'

He was pensive as he switched off the phone.

'She didn't even ask about me, did she?' Raisin mumbled.

He squeezed her hand and caressed her cheek with his lips. Michelle stopped the car just before the village bridge and double-parked in front of *Café Délice*. Vincent sprang out, shouting hello to the owners as he did.

'*Salut Serge, Loulou!*' He walked around the car to Michelle's window. 'I'd better go with them and check the house before they go inside. You never know.'

'That's okay… we'll be fine,' Raisin protested.

'Let him go with you… just to make sure,' Michelle said.

'But why? Rema's the only one who wasn't caught, and she isn't going to do anything stupid like come to the village. Hopefully Auberger already has everyone else locked up in jail.'

'Assuming we know who *everyone* is,' Vincent snorted.

'They've got a point, Sarah. What if there are more people like the brigadier?'

The rock with Nicolas' bloodied t-shirt flashed before her. She gave a resigned shrug.

'What about your car?' Michelle asked.

Raisin looked at her blankly.

'We found it on the forestry track and had it towed to the gendarmerie.'

'Oh God, I'm not thinking straight. Romul took my backpack… I don't even have keys to get into the house.'

'I'll get you in,' Vincent yawned.

'You might remember that breaking and entering is one of his specialities,' Michelle said dryly. 'Try not to *break* anything this time, Vincent.'

He poked his head back into the car, clacked open the cubbyhole and rummaged inside.

'Old houses are a burglar's dream,' he smirked, holding up a string of paperclips.

'Do you have a spare car key at home?' Matt asked.

'Yes,' Raisin said wearily.

'I'll let them know you're coming for the car,' Michelle said.

They walked in silence down the pedestrians-only *rue Pasteur*. She let Matt steer her through the sweaty summer crowd, feeling numb. She longed to talk to him, really talk, but now they were alone, she didn't know where to begin. She yawned; he caught her as she tripped on the cobbles and held her against him.

When they reached her little lane, even the rainbow colours of the houses failed to irritate her. It seemed a lifetime ago when she had dragged her suitcase to her indigo front door for the first time. She sat on the steps and watched Vincent elongate a paperclip and manoeuvre it inside the keyhole. There was a metallic click and he pushed open the door with a satisfied slap. Cool air wafted over her as they walked inside. Home at last.

'I'll start upstairs,' Vincent said.

They heard him clatter on the wooden floorboards then he was back, flipping a cigarette into his mouth as he clunked back down the steps.

'*C'est bon*, all clear, you can go up. But I suggest you get that window fixed. They're predicting thunderstorms in a few days.'

'I'll ask René to recommend someone. Thanks for your help,' Matt said.

'*Avec plaisir.*'

He waved and ambled off down the narrow street. Raisin followed Matt to the first floor.

'I'm starving and I'd kill for a cup of coffee,' she sighed.

'Me too...' He froze in the kitchen doorway. 'Damn it, Sarah. You could have been killed!'

'It looks worse than it is. We weren't even home when it happened.'

But she didn't blame him for his reaction. The room looked like an abandoned tenement. Shattered glass and dark soil clods crusted the chequered floor tiles, and the jagged window glistened angrily in the light. Grimy breakfast dishes cluttered the sink, but worst of all, his vine lay toppled on its side, leaves wilted, gnarled roots vulnerable and exposed. She cradled it in her palms.

'I'm so sorry. Geoffrey was desperate to check out the area around Massane, and I didn't want him to go on his own... otherwise I'd *never* have left it like this.'

'It'll survive, sweetheart. Go and get changed while I take care of it and make us some coffee.'

She nodded but didn't leave, peering listlessly out of the broken window. Down in the street, a young mother was trying to calm a screaming toddler while the father stood by, a dribbling ice cream in each hand. She wished she had never left London. Matt stood behind her and circled her waist.

'If I hadn't damn well come to France, Mum wouldn't be here, and Geoffrey wouldn't have to deal with her,' she moaned.

'If you hadn't come, Nicolas might not be alive,' he said, turning her to face him. 'She *is* here, and we'll figure out what to do... *together.*'

She smiled wanly, still struggling to believe that he knew about Mum and hadn't rejected her.

'I'm not going to lose you again, Sarah.'

Realisation that she would never be alone washed over her, warm as treacle.

'Matt...'

He kissed her. Soft lips, hesitant, then bold, hungry. Her arms crept around his neck, their tongues slid together, testing, exploring, demanding.

'I've missed you,' he said hoarsely.

She undid a button and held her hand against his chest. His heart thudded under her palm.

'How is your arm…?'

'Miraculously healed,' he said with a twinkle.

He ran his hands under her shirt and cupped her breasts, fingers teasing her nipples. They stumbled to the bedroom. She fell back onto the rumpled sheets and drew him to her, drowning in the familiarity, the known heaviness of his body. This man, this togetherness, was home. Their legs entwined, their hips joined, they rolled and surged, not once did his eyes leave her.

Stillness draped the room, velvet-thick with contentment. She twisted onto her elbows. Matt traced a finger along her nose. She smiled. He was happy, and she loved that it was because of her. They laced fingers and she rested her cheek against his hand.

'Didn't Leroux warn you to be careful?'

'I was,' he grinned.

'We should get you to a doctor.'

'It's just a surface wound, sweetheart.'

'You could've died.'

'We *all* could have died.'

A dustbin clanged outside, a dog yapped, yet the real world felt a million miles away.

'What are we going to do about us?' she sighed.

'Today or tomorrow?' he bantered.

'Matt, I'm trying to be serious. The thing is, I'm not… ready to go back to London. Not yet, Matt.'

'Me neither, sweetheart.'

'But…'

He held his finger against her lips.

'Shhh… I'm here till the end of September. Let's enjoy today and let the rest of the world worry about tomorrow.'

'Will you carry on staying at the forestry station?'

'Fret, fret, fret. Up there, down here with you… it doesn't really matter. Anything is better than being a thousand miles away.'

She dropped her head onto his chest. He drew hearts on her skin.

She nestled against him. What had possessed her to run from this? She muffled a groan. There was still Mum.

'A penny for them?' he probed.

'Mum probably thinks she can stay with Geoffrey and me, but I don't want her here. And I know Geoffrey, he'd rather leave than be here with her.'

'She can stay at the forestry station. Julien isn't back for at least another fortnight. There's plenty of room.'

'Maybe she'll get the message and damn well go home.' She disentangled herself from him and slid off the bed. 'If I stay here a minute longer, I'll fall asleep. We'd better get going.'

'And the mess in the kitchen?'

'We can do it later. I have to warn Geoffrey.'

On the way to the car, Matt popped into Café Délice and bought two pieces of apple tart and two *pains au chocolat.*

'I'm not *that* hungry!' she protested.

'You don't have to be.' He tore off a flaky-soft corner and fed it to her. 'Admit it… there's *nothing* this good in London.'

'Wait until I've finished my pastry course at the Perpignan Hotel School then…'

She clapped her hand over her mouth.

'Relax sweetheart! I'm not second guessing everything you say for hidden messages about our future,' he laughed.

'I'm sorry, I just…'

'You were never this good at apologising in London,' he teased. 'Look… there's your car.'

Five minutes later, the release papers were signed and they were back outside. She gave him the spare key.

'Please will you drive?'

It took him more than an hour to ease her little Golf over the rutted supply lane around the back of the mountain to the research station. Raisin eyed the jumble of buildings with trepidation. Would Mum come out to meet them?

'Why don't we check on Merguez and Cava first?' he said, parking out of sight next to the stone barn.

She jumped at the distraction. So much for the big confrontation she had planned with such belligerent confidence. If only Mum would simply go. Preferably straight to hell and without any goodbyes. She grimaced at her childishness. If only life were that easy.

They straddled the fallen stump in the cub enclosure and waited for Cava and Merguez to appear. She snuggled closer to Matt and wondered which of Henri's winds was blowing. Definitely not one of the good ones. This one felt like it was at war with the earth. Two ominous cloud disks hovered overhead like alien spaceships. She wondered where the wolf cubs were.

'I hope they're okay,' she worried.

'Me too.'

Her mother's presence chilled her like a shadow. She rubbed the bare spot on her ring finger.

'Matt, what did the feather mean?'

'You haven't figured it out yet?'

'Maybe… but I'm not sure.'

'Marriage is nothing more than a piece of paper, so if you don't want it, I don't either. The last thing I want is for you to feel caged… all that matters is that we grow old together, married or not.'

'Really?'

'Really.'

Her heart galloped. She had to tell him. Right now.

'Matt… I can't… have children.'

He paled, stunned.

'Sarah…? Why? What's wrong? Are you okay?'

She shook her head angrily, tears welling.

'I'm fine… it's not like that, and the last thing I deserve is sympathy. I… had it done… I chose to…'

Confusion, pain, love jumbled across his face. He rubbed his sore arm.

She shifted away. 'I'm sorry.'

'When Sarah? When did you do it?'

'Long before we met.'

She tried to meet his eyes but couldn't. Neither spoke. They sat statue still, too paralysed to reach out to one another. The wind stabbed her with icicle gusts.

'Why didn't you tell me before?' he murmured.

'I'm so sorry.'

'Am I that hard to talk to? That hard to trust?'

'No, it's not like that…'

'Well… what then?' he said bitterly.

'Matt, please… you always said you wanted children and I…' She glanced at the forestry cabin and her voice fell to a whisper. 'Ever since I was a child, I've been scared of having children. How can I tell someone who dreams of being a father that the idea of motherhood terrifies me to death? I couldn't tell you. I tried to, Matt. I wanted to… a million times over I wanted to, but every time I plucked up the courage to, I just couldn't go through with it.' She swallowed nervously. 'If you want to change your mind about us, I'll understand. I'm so sorry.'

'Stop apologising, Sarah. I love you for you, not for our… the babies we might have had. It's just… hard to digest. It hurts that you couldn't tell me.'

She shrugged helplessly.

'Would it really have been so bad if I'd known sooner?'

'It was bad back then… and it's still bad today.'

'People in love tell each other stuff like this. What did you think I would do, sweetheart? Leave you?'

'Won't you?'

'Sarah, of course not. Not now, not ever.' He cupped her chin. 'Is there anything else you need to tell me?'

'Maybe one other thing…'

Fear flinted his eyes.

She leant forward, her lips against his. 'Just that I love you.'

They kissed hungrily then he hugged her to him.

'Let's get this over and done with,' he whispered.

274

They walked hand in hand; the knot inside her began to ease. What could Mum possibly do to her with Matt at her side? But when she heard her mother's voice, she stopped.

'Who's she talking to?' she asked anxiously.

'Probably René. Be happy he's here… it'll help diffuse things.'

Chilli was pacing along the top of the deck railing.

'I wonder if a wild cat's been here because Chilli looks jumpy,' Matt remarked.

They climbed the steps to the deck and Chilli bolted off.

'She's not usually so skittish,' he frowned.

'I'd also be skittish if I had to live with her.'

'Stop it, Sarah. Stop torturing yourself.'

'I can't help it. I don't want to see her.'

'Raisin? Is that you?' her mother called from inside.

'Just relax, and remember… you're not alone,' he said.

'We have a visitor!' her mother exclaimed as they entered the kitchen.

René wasn't there. A tall slender woman leant against the kitchen sink, sipping water from a long glass. The blood drained from Raisin's face.

Rema.

31

HER MOTHER GRASPED Raisin in a ferocious embrace. She couldn't breathe for hair, too much bosom and the pungent stink of Opium. Her mind raced. She had to get Matt away from Rema. But she did nothing, frozen in her mother's arms, with Rema's eyes drilling into her back. What the hell was the woman doing here? Raisin tried to squirm free but her mother clung to her, hot breath searing her skin.

'Thank God you're in one piece, darling.'

Darling. The endearment pierced her soul. She teetered between longing and hatred then wrenched away. The dregs of Mum's love belonged in hell.

'Raisin darling, this is Rema, she was separated from her hiking group and ended up here… completely lost. Luckily she found the forestry station. You should have seen the state she was in when she knocked on the door. I even had to lend her clothes!'

Raisin hid her shock. So that was how Rema had weaselled her way in.

'How terrible for you. Is there someone you can phone?' Matt asked.

Raisin winced. *For God's sake, don't trust her.*

'I don't have any phone numbers with me,' Rema sighed.

'Matt is Raisin's boyfriend,' her mother explained.

Boyfriend. The word jarred. He was more than that, she wanted to scream, but said nothing. The less Rema and Mum knew, the better. Matt winked at her. *I'm right here,* the wink said. She frowned in despair. *If only you knew the danger we're in.*

'Hello, Raisin,' Rema purred.

Raisin searched the woman's smug face. What in God's name did she want? Rema threw a lazy look in Matt's direction and unfurled a knowing sneer. Raisin went cold, glanced at Matt, then quickly dropped her eyes, but it was too late. Rema's satisfied smirk told her she had given the woman exactly what she was looking for. Panic began to disorientate her. One wrong move and Rema would attack Matt.

Her mother's hand fell off her shoulder and Raisin inched away, unshackled from her mother, but still ensnared by Rema's hateful watchfulness. She gulped down tears. She couldn't let the woman win, but she didn't dare underestimate her either. Rema was a predator skilfully waiting for her prey to expose its underbelly. And she had just given her Matt on a plate. He slid his good arm around her and she was tempted to shrug him off. No point. Rema already knew what he meant to her. She leant into him, stiff as a board.

'Where is Geoffrey? And why didn't he come back with you?' her mother complained.

'He wanted to take Nicolas home. The *police* will drop him off here soon,' Raisin said, unable to stop her voice from shaking.

Rema sipped her water, unperturbed, steel grey eyes absorbing every ugly nuance between her and Mum. Raisin fought down her terror. She had to get Matt away, warn Geoffrey.

'The *police*? Good! They can give Rema a lift back to the village,' her mother said.

Raisin gripped Matt's hand. He smiled at her. She squeezed harder. *You don't understand.* He smiled wider. She wanted to curl into a ball and die.

'Matt...' she started.

She couldn't tell him about Rema. Not yet. Rema raised her eyebrows and gave a scornful grin. Raisin flinched. The bitch was in control and relishing every moment.

'Do the police know why those people took the boy?' her mother asked. 'It's beyond me why anyone would do anything so awful to a child.'

Bile rose in Raisin's throat. *But you did worse!*

Rema, her mother, it was too much. Hot waves of claustrophobia choked her. The two women were as bad as each other. They even looked alike. How had it all turned so ugly? Not even two hours ago she and Matt had been making love. She stared glass-eyed into the garden where the wind was mercilessly lashing Matt's willow trees. Even his goddesses couldn't protect them.

What if she simply walked out of the kitchen? No. Rema would never allow it. She wasn't armed, but that didn't mean a thing. Rema would find a way to stop her. And it wouldn't be pretty. Adrenaline crackled as she scoured the kitchen for a weapon. Nothing, not even a fork. How were she and Matt going to protect themselves? He sensed her disquiet and frowned worriedly at her.

'My son helped rescue the boy,' her mother babbled.

'I can't *wait* for him to get here,' Rema exhaled.

Her voice was so laden with violence that Matt grunted in shock, and her mother recoiled. Fear hit Raisin like an avalanche. Rema was showing her hand.

'I want what's mine,' Rema snarled.

'Sorry…you want…? I… what do you mean?' her mother stammered.

'Your son stole my escape from Earth, stole my son… and I'll make him pay.'

She smashed the glass against the counter edge and jammed the ragged spikes of its base under her mother's chin. Raisin screamed and hid her face in her hands. Matt lurched in front of her, pushing her behind him. Her mother clawed at Rema's arm. Rema dug the glass into her neck. Blood covered both women.

'Please stop, you're going to kill her,' Matt begged.

'Maybe I will… just as her son killed my son.'

'She's lying! *She* killed him… killed her own damn son,' Raisin cried.

'A *son* for a *son*. I will be redeemed. I will find Quirinus,' Rema howled.

'Let go of her, for God's sake!' Matt yelled.

'A son for a son. It isn't too late. Quirinus awaits! I have wolves… all that's left is the sacrifice. Just the sacrifice!'

'She's *mad*, Matt! Get the hell away from her!' Raisin screamed.

He paused, touching her cheek, as if reassuring himself she really was unhurt, then he turned back to Rema.

'Let her go,' he said firmly.

Rema swung her arm around her mother's neck in a chokehold, yanked open the drawer nearest her, snatched out a sharp vegetable knife and waved it in the air.

'Or you'll do what...?' she laughed manically.

'Matt, come with me. Let's get the hell out of here.'

'Leave and the old bitch dies!' Rema roared.

'We're not going anywhere,' Matt said calmly.

'*Please* can we go, Matt. I don't care *what* she does to Mum,' Raisin sobbed.

'You don't mean that, Sarah... just stay behind me.'

'She'll *kill* you! We have to get out of here,' Raisin begged.

'We can't leave her, Sarah. You'll never forgive yourself.'

'You stupid, *stupid* selfish bitch!' Raisin raged at her mother. 'She's one of them and you let her into the house! Isn't it *enough* that you ruined Geoffrey's life?'

Her mother shook her head in confusion, eyes bulging, hands manacled around Rema's wrists. Raisin didn't care. If she died right in this kitchen, right in front of her, she would step over her mother's body and not look back. Matt mattered. Geoffrey mattered. Mum could rot in hell.

'She killed her own goddamn son as a sacrifice but it didn't goddamn work so she wants yours. If she *knew* about you... she would kill *you* instead of him,' she shouted.

'Raisin...' Matt hushed.

Rema stroked her mother's cheek with blood-stained fingers, eyes gleaming with malice.

'But think about it, girl... losing a son will be *worse* than death.'

'Don't listen to her, Sarah,' Matt murmured.

Raisin waved impatiently at him, panting so hard her chest hurt.

'I hate her. I fucking *hate* her! I don't care what happens to her.'

'A son for a son. A son for a son,' Rema crowed.

Raisin felt buried alive. The woman was intent on killing Geoffrey. Her eyes glazed over. Geoffrey. This time she would save him. Even if it meant dying.

'Take me instead of Geoffrey,' she said hoarsely.

'Sarah, shut up.'

Rema leered at Raisin.

'I have a better idea. What about a *mother* for a *son*? Just give the word, girl.'

Raisin stared, dumbstruck, revolted, tempted. Rema sniggered and calmly sliced her mother's cheek with the knife. She screamed in pain. Blood bulged mesmerizingly slowly.

'Mother for a son? You *know* you want me to.'

Rema's blonde hair hung in dishevelled strands, sweat stained her borrowed blouse, madness skittered across her eyes. Raisin shrank away. She saw herself. Heard echoes of her own thoughts in Rema's crazed anger. Glimpsed herself in the woman's vindictive soul.

'No,' she rasped.

'Sure?' Rema said, digging the knife edge into her mother's jugular.

'*No*! I said *no*! I'm not you. Stop, for God's sake, *stop this madness!*' Raisin wept.

Laughter brayed out of Rema, so wild, so evil, the air turned unbreathable. Raisin crumpled against Matt. She didn't want Mum to die.

'A son for a son. A son for a son,' Rema ranted.

'Raisin... Matt... help me,' her mother pleaded, bloodied hand trembling like a dying animal.

Raisin slipped her fingers over the tribeswoman's amulet. How could she have been tempted to play God with Mum's life? For one terrible moment she had become Rema; crossed into an abyss where humans shouldn't go. She held the shell to her lips. She *wasn't* Rema, and she didn't want Mum dead. Geoffrey had been right. What she wanted was revenge. And revenge was futile. Let the law decide Mum's fate.

The bitter fury poisoning her heart crumbled. She took a deep breath, felt the pain ease. *Don't do anything stupid,* Matt's expression begged. She smiled tremulously.

'*Allô? Qu'est-ce qui se passe ici?*

'*Henri?*' Raisin gasped.

Rema whipped around, still wielding the knife. The old shepherd shuffled into the kitchen, *makila* staff in hand, Pastis at his heels, and Cava on his forearm. Raisin's eyes widened. Why was he carrying the wolf pup? Where was Merguez?

'Henri, no! Stay back!' Matt shouted.

'Give me my wolf!' Rema screamed.

Henri didn't flinch.

'So this is the monster who killed the cub,' he observed.

'Merguez is dead? What *happened*?' Raisin cried.

'Give me my wolf!' Rema screeched.

Henri lowered Cava onto the kitchen table. The wolf cub wobbled on her feet then collapsed. Raisin cried out in despair. He banged his stick on the floor.

'Free the woman,' he growled.

'Give it to me,' Rema screeched.

'Free the woman.'

He stood still, buckled over his stick, gnarled fingers curled over the handle, but Raisin saw the alert rigidity in his body. The old man knew exactly how dangerous Rema was. Rema must have stolen the cubs from their enclosure to attempt another ceremony. With Geoffrey as the sacrifice. How were they going to stop her?

'Help me. Please help,' her mother cried.

'Give me my wolf or the whore bitch dies,' Rema snarled, spearing the knife in Henri's direction.

Pastis sprang up and clamped his jaws over her wrist. With lightning speed, Henri untwisted his *makila* and plunged the stiletto into Rema's arm. Matt lunged for Cava. Rema screamed, her undamaged arm flailing for the cub then she crumpled to the floor. Henri yanked the *makila* free and pointed it at her.

'When a wolf attacks my sheep, I attack back, and ask questions later. *Madame,* what possessed you to kill an innocent wolf cub?'

32

'*Eric,*' Rema keened, back arched, face skywards.

'Her son,' Matt murmured to Henri.

She hissed like a snake and jack-knifed her legs against Henri's shins, but he skipped aside and her body skated past him into a chair. Raisin jumped back in fright. Henri snatched Rema's injured arm and twisted it above her head. Pastis sank his teeth into her ankle. She bellowed furiously and kicked him away, clawing at Henri with her free hand. He yanked her wrist higher.

'Answer me and I'll call him off,' he snapped.

'Quirinus. Quirinus. I can… I'm ready,' she gasped.

Raisin kept close to Matt. Cornered and hurt, Rema was more terrifying than a wounded animal.

'Help me,' her mother whimpered.

'Leave her to me, Sarah. Go and get help.'

'I'm staying with you.'

'Please go. Think about Geoffrey.'

'*Geoffrey*? Is he here?' her mother stammered.

Raisin glared at her. *Damn you.* Even injured, she wanted him more. She hid her distress, furious that it mattered, and let Matt lead her to the door.

'Raisin…' her mother called.

She stopped, turned, said nothing. Her mother reached for her with shaking hands.

'*Why* do you hate me so much?'

All Raisin saw were vermillion nails. Her stomach heaved. Those hands had done unspeakable things. She dug her back against the doorframe.

'You know what you did,' she said hoarsely.

Matt handed Cava to her. 'Here… keep her safe.'

She hugged the warm little body to her but couldn't move, staring at the broken old woman who had masqueraded as her mother. *Yes, I hate you.* Then guilt twisted like her barbed wire. Children aren't supposed to hate their parents. She shut her eyes, opened them again. Nothing had changed. She still felt revolted. Still felt hatred. Still felt guilt.

'Go Sarah,' Matt urged.

She obeyed in a daze, shuffling between the red armchair and René's rickety coffee table, and almost tripped over Chilli at the door. She eyed the sleeping cat with desperate envy. What wouldn't she give to disappear into a cocoon of oblivion?

In the garden the willow tree hissed like whips in the wind and a group of blue tits squabbled angrily over food. She was beginning to hate the way the Tramontane tormented summer here. She rubbed her chin over Cava's head and wished they were both a million miles away.

Her mother's accusing face invaded her thoughts like a prowling vigilante. She glanced behind her in panic. *Leave me alone.* But the flood gates were open, and she was four years old again, squirming under Mum's furious eyes. She smothered a sob and hunched over Cava, as if by protecting her she could protect herself. Her body shook. How could Mum still reduce her to this?

'*Quirinus! Quirinus!*'

Rema. Mum. She stumbled off the deck and headed for the green office behind the barn. Maybe it was open and she could call the police. She winced at how history was repeating itself; once again she was running to a shed to hide. She rattled the slatted door. Locked. A phone rang inside. She banged the door in frustration. Why have a bloody office if it wasn't open? Cava gave a pitiful whine. She stroked her stubby grey-brown paws.

'I'll make sure no-one hurts you,' she promised fiercely.

The wolf pup sandpapered her with its tongue. She twisted her wrist sideways to check Henri's watch.

Almost four, and still no sign of Geoffrey. Where the hell was he?

She sank down onto the steps and dropped her head against the door. If only she could turn back the clock and start the year over again. Not leave Matt. Not come to Collioure. Not have Geoffrey visit her here. Not remember.

She lifted her face to the sun and let out a troubled sigh. How on earth was she going to tell him?

I've got bad news, Mum's here. Too blunt. *I don't know how to tell you this, but there's someone here you don't want to see.* Too wordy.

However she said it, he would be furious she hadn't told him sooner. But how could she have with all the chaos and emotion around Nicolas?

She shifted restlessly and wiped the back of her neck. Damn this strange climate. Too cold in the wind, too hot in the sun. The smell of pipe smoke jolted her. Romul? Impossible. She stood up unsteadily just as René appeared around the side of the barn. He waved his pipe at her.

'*Tiens!* What are you doing here? Where's Matt?'

'René! Thank God you're here. Please could you open the door and help me phone the police! That woman from the cave's here. She attacked...'

'*Doucement...* slow down.'

She took a deep breath.

'One of the kidnappers escaped from the cave and talked my mother into letting her in the house. She's stark raving mad and determined to kill Geoffrey.'

'And where is he?' he asked briskly.

'I don't know... he's not back yet.'

'And Matt?'

'He's in the house with her... in the kitchen.'

'Are they alone?'

'No, Henri's also there. We have to get Captain Auberger up here!'

'*Calmes-toi.* Henri's good in situations like this.'

He knelt next to a tall Aloe Vera cactus at the bottom of the steps, fumbled in the soil and pulled out a dirty Ziploc bag that contained a key. Seconds later, they were inside.

'I saw a dust cloud on my way back… it could be your brother.' He held up the phone. 'How bad is your mother? What must I tell the emergency services?'

What a relief to surrender to him.

'We need an ambulance. Rema stabbed her… and Matt's hurt too,' she added huskily.

His head jerked up. 'How serious?'

'He was shot… down in the cave. It was my fault.'

'Shot? *Bordel!* Why isn't he in hospital?'

'The medic said it was just a surface wound. He bandaged it and gave him pain killers but it's not enough… he should…'

The rumble of a diesel engine thudded close by.

'He's here!' she cried.

René took Cava from her and opened the office door.

'Quick! Make sure whoever brought him doesn't leave. We may need their car.'

She ran outside and almost wept at the sight of the Special Services Land Rover coming towards her. Geoffrey sprang out of it, uncharacteristically jubilant.

'We did it! Nicolas is with his parents! You should have come, Raisin. It was *incredible!*'

The 4x4 reversed and started a three-point turn. She ran towards it, waving her arms.

'Wait! Don't go!' she screamed.

The vehicle skidded to a halt and Lieutenant Leroux popped his head out of the window.

'What's wrong?' he asked.

She pointed to the forestry cabin.

'Inside… she's in there! And people are hurt. Do you have your kit with you?' she wheezed.

'*Who* is in there? What the hell is going on, Raisin?' Geoffrey asked.

'The woman from the cave… the one who got away.'

The medic was already out of the Land Rover and unlatching the hatch at the back.

'How many injured?' he asked.

'Two… the woman and…' She glanced uneasily at Geoffrey. 'And my mother.'

Geoffrey hooted with laughter.

'Mum? Yeah right! Don't joke about things like that with men like Leroux, they'll take you seriously!'

'I *am* being serious.'

'Where are they? How badly are they hurt?' Leroux asked.

'In the kitchen. The woman has a… stab wound in her arm from Henri's stick… the top comes off and becomes a spike…'

Leroux nodded impatiently as he flung the medical pack over his shoulders.

'And the other woman?'

'She was attacked with broken glass… and a knife,' she stammered, eyes clinging to Geoffrey in abject apology.

He stared at her, ashen. Leroux unholstered his Berretta and sprinted to the cabin, barking an update to his unit through a two-way radio. René joined him along the way.

'Raisin, what the *fuck* is going on?'

'I'm sorry. I should've warned you earlier but…'

'How long has she been here?'

'Matt fetched her from the airport while you were with Nicolas. I didn't know she was here until…'

Geoffrey looked blindly at the forestry station, lips twitching as if talking to himself. She didn't know what to say.

'She's really here?' he mumbled.

'I'm afraid so… I'm sorry, Geoffrey.'

'*Why*, for God's sake?'

'The police asked Matt to warn next-of-kin that we had disappeared, and she got on the next plane to France…'

'Fuck,' he grunted.

'I should've told you earlier but… you were so…'

'Why did Rema attack her?'

She gave an irritated wrist flick.

'What do you care? I thought you never wanted to see her again.'

'I don't exactly have a choice anymore, do I?' He took a few steps towards the forestry cabin then stopped. 'Tell me what happened.'

'I don't understand why you're being like this.'

'Like what, Raisin? Not ready to lash out at her like you'd like me to? I don't hate her, and nor should you. It doesn't change anything. She'll never understand how what she did affected us, and you'll be the one left with a burning hole in your heart.'

'Don't tell me you've forgiven her?' she spat.

He backtracked and leant heavily against the Land Rover.

'No, I haven't, but forgiveness has nothing to do with my hating her or not.'

'So you're going to waltz in there as if nothing ever happened?'

He ran his hands over the vehicle's roll bar and her anger dissipated. What right did she have to judge him?

'I thought you hated her and wouldn't want to see her,' she muttered.

'See her, not see her, I don't really care.'

'She *ruined* your life.'

'No, you're wrong. She ruined *part* of it, not all of it. What she did never goes away but it does get easier.' He cracked his knuckles. 'That doesn't mean I don't have my demons.'

She toyed with the bandage around her palm.

'You mean that you're still scared of the dark?'

'That… and… those out-of-control rages when I… feel trapped,' he said awkwardly.

Apprehension rippled through her at his honesty. He looked her straight in the eye.

'The truth is, even after everything, it took years to stop longing for her to be a mother, a real one, but eventually I did, and then… I also stopped hating her. It didn't happen overnight… no Oprah-moment of à la carte forgiveness for me, but I did eventually, somehow, manage to disconnect from her.'

He had never been so open. Or so vulnerable. It was too much. She felt hot and uncomfortable and didn't want him to continue.

'When the desperation to confront her was gone, I started thinking about you.'

Stop.

'I didn't want you to be burdened by it like I had been all my life. We'd never talked about it, so I didn't have a clue how you'd coped, if at all.'

Her chest closed in. *Shut up.*

'My New Year's resolution two years ago was to talk to you.' He gave a sheepish grimace. 'I'm sorry it took me so long.'

The Tramontane wind shrieked over their heads like a poltergeist. She watched cloud flecks scatter across the sky like dry leaves. No wonder artists were drawn to this area and its violent beauty.

'Raisin…?'

'I had forgotten everything,' she said, unable to disguise her reproach.

'Souls never forget things like this,' he said softly.

'Mine did.'

She opened the driver's door and sat down. His voice became a dull burr. Since that night in the cellar, the memories hadn't stopped. Her own hateful Pandora's box.

'Raisin, it's too much to carry on your own.'

A tear slid down her cheek. She fought for the right words.

'I told Matt… about not being able to have children,' she faltered.

'And about Mum?'

She pressed her palms into her eyes. Why was talking to him harder than talking to Matt? Her heart felt mauled, as if Romul himself was ripping it out. He leant on the open door.

'Did you tell him about her?'

'Yes.'

'Good for you. And he doesn't love you less, does he?'

She shook her head.

'It's a relief, isn't it?'

289

'Yes. Yes it is.'

'I've been there, Raisin. I carried the shame on kiddie shoulders trapped in a man's body for way too long. Telling Chris took the load off that little boy, and made me determined to make sure you were okay. I'm your big brother, I had to do something.'

She nodded, choked up with love, fear, hope. He pushed aside the door and crouched in front of her, tears glistening.

'I missed you.'

'What happened to us?' she whispered.

He dried her cheeks with his thumbs.

'It's going to be the old us again... you'll see. This is just the beginning.'

She chewed her top lip and searched his face. Dare she believe him? She willed him not to look away. The muscle in his jaw spasmed and he blinked nervously, but his eyes stayed with her.

'We've a lot of time to make up, Raisin.'

He opened his arms and she melted into his embrace, sobs wracking her body. Geoffrey was back.

'I'm right here,' he soothed.

She cried for their lost childhood, the safe mother love they never knew, their father, the people she had hurt along the way, the babies she would never have. She drew back, wiped her face with her shirt.

'Why didn't Dad ever *do* anything?'

He stood up and gave the brawny tyre of the Land Rover a half-hearted kick. Grey mud clods crumbled to the ground.

'I suppose because he was never there. You know... when it happened...'

'He had no idea?' she asked, hope careening.

'Deep down... I... I think maybe he did...'

She gazed over the Land Rover's bonnet into the forest.

You're wrong. He didn't know.

'I remember so little about him from that time,' she sighed.

'You were only eight when he left.'

She heard a tremor in his voice, turned and for a moment glimpsed her frightened young brother again. He kicked the tyre again.

'When I was ten, maybe eleven, I was helping Dad fix the sprinkler system out in the back, near the washing lines...'

A shadow flitted across his face. She waited anxiously. *Don't, don't, don't say Dad knew.*

'In the same voice that he asked me to pass him a Philips screwdriver, he asked me if everything was okay at school...'

In the distance, the drone of a helicopter pummelled the air. They both craned their necks in search of it.

I don't want Dad to have known.

'I knew he wasn't really asking about school and that it was my chance to tell him, but I couldn't... so I somersaulted the screwdriver to him and he caught it mid-air. Our eyes met and everything seemed to stop... as if he was waiting for me to speak, but I just stared at him, desperate for *him* to say it, to help me. Then he patted my shoulder and began working on the damn hosepipe again. And that was it, my moment was gone. A year later they were divorced.'

'Maybe he left because he knew, so you could go with him, I mean, and be away from her.'

'Maybe, maybe not. Deep down, I always hoped he knew.'

'And what about when you lived with him, you never brought it up?'

He gave a sad shrug.

'I was still scared of Mum's threats, but I think I was even more scared of destroying my fantasy about him knowing.'

'But he did *nothing*. Didn't that make you angry?'

'No, believing he knew was enough comfort and made me feel less of a monster. And anyway, he *did* do something... it all stopped when we left home.'

'But surely you realise...'

He waved her silent.

'I only understood much later that he didn't save me, of course he didn't... but back then, I secretly believed that he left Mum to protect me... so I would be safe from her.' He laid a fist over his heart. 'I can still feel how good that felt.'

'Don't you think one of us should talk to him?'

'What's the point? He's an old man who's built another life.'

'We've *all* built other lives.'

'And where did it get us? God knows, I had the career, house, car, but when it came to facing those godawful memories, I was still fucking alone… my cosy life was a lie.'

'Enter Chris?'

'Enter Chris and the infamous Paula,' he said with a glimmer of a smile.

'I'm glad you found them, and that… you came for me…'

Her voice was drowned out by the thunder of the helicopter hovering over their heads. Four Special Services men leaped out before it had properly landed and raced towards them.

'Where's she?' Auberger barked.

Raisin pointed to the forestry station. 'In the kitchen.'

'Who's with her?'

'René, the man who phoned you, Henri the shepherd, Leroux and… and a second woman,' Geoffrey said.

'My… our mother,' Raisin said.

'Don't even *think* about following us,' Auberger snapped.

The commandos circled the cabin. Auberger and one of the men went around the back while the tall female commando and the fourth commando went through the front door. Raisin's heart lurched when minutes later, Matt appeared on the deck, followed by Henri and René.

'Thank God,' she cried, rushing towards Matt.

He held her tight. 'It's over, Sarah.'

She clung to him, not trusting herself to speak. Let him be right. Henri gave a polite cough.

'I'd like to take care of the little one's body before it gets too dark… so I need to get going.'

Raisin undid his watch and slipped off the wolf tooth.

'Thank you for making me wear it,' she said.

He smiled tiredly, looped his forefather's amulet over his head then ran a leathery finger over the names engraved on his *makila*.

'Perhaps the healing power of the *Linía de Llop* can do what it's meant to do at last.'

He waved his *makila* in the air and followed Pastis into the forest. Geoffrey shook his head in dismay.

'I forgot Pi's body,' he murmured.

'We covered him as best we could with leaves and twigs,' Matt said gently.

'I need to go back and bury him properly.'

'I don't advise it, Geoffrey. When I saw him on Wednesday, he was already...'

'I grew up on a farm, I know what to expect. I can't leave him there.'

'We'll go with you,' Raisin said.

'I think I'd rather go alone, Raisin, but would it be okay if I used your car?'

'You mean that red thing at the back?' René snorted. 'It'll never make it to that house. I'll take you. But you'd better go and see your mother before she's airlifted out of here.'

'Auberger said we had to stay away from the cabin,' Raisin said tightly.

They fell silent as two Special Services men came out of the cabin carrying a stretcher. A rope of white hair drooped like a snake off the edge. Raisin slipped her hand into Matt's. Mum. Lieutenant Leroux and the female commando appeared carrying a second stretcher. Broad canvas straps bound Rema's upper body and legs to the poles.

'I hope the only blue sky she ever sees is through the bars of Perpignan Penitentiary,' René grunted.

'I hope she rots in hell,' Geoffrey said.

Raisin wondered which of the two women he was referring to. Auberger paused on the deck, gave a curt nod then trotted after his men.

Minutes later, the helicopter's rotor blades roared to life. The machine lifted a metre off the ground, stabilised in a hover that blasted the trees, then circled to face the wind and climbed high before tilting to the right and disappearing.

A heady urge to applaud overcame Raisin. Safe at last.

'Are you sure you want to go alone?' she asked Geoffrey.

'I'll be fine. You two have a lot to talk about, but I do have a favour to ask...'

'Anything,' Raisin said.

'Get me on the next available flight to Chris,' he grinned.

33

FILIGREE SHADOWS DANCED on the ash grey granite inside the dolmen. Raisin wound the clamshell necklace around her fingers and showed Matt the breach in the stone wall. He stroked her cheek. She held his eyes, thankful he understood how badly she wanted to return the necklace to the tribeswoman.

He pointed to his torch, eyebrows raised. She nodded with some regret. They wouldn't be able to go further without light, but it didn't feel right somehow, like shouting in church. He switched it on, hand cupped in front to dim the glare. A warm glow washed over her. He respected the dolmen as much as she did.

They clambered through to the other chamber. Her neck bristled in the cold and she reached for her hair. Growing back, but still too damn short to cut the chill.

'I told you, I like it that length. It suits you,' he grinned.

'I look like a bloody boy.'

'A damn fine looking boy.'

'And compliments will get you everywhere,' she laughed.

She manoeuvred his wrist sideways and shone the torch on the statue. The wet stone gleamed silver bright.

'Meet St Francis,' she said with a flourish.

'I've just thought of something… wasn't there a legend about him and a wolf?'

'Yes, Geoffrey also mentioned something about that.'

'I remember something about him stopping a village from killing a wolf. Maybe St Francis is here to watch over more than just the caves.'

'Nothing surprises me about this underground world anymore. What made you think of that now?'

'I don't know, maybe the cowl-necked robe and the way he's holding the cross against his chest.'

He moved the beam over the objects lying at the statue's feet and picked up the tooth.

'It's only when we saw Henri's one that we realised these teeth could be from wolves,' she said.

'*Teeth...*? There's more than one?'

'Geoffrey also found one near the statue in the stairway cave.' She took the tooth from him. 'Do you think Henri built the shrines?'

'I doubt it. This statue was protecting the dolmen long before he was born.' He traced the calcified veins running down its length. 'These are from dripping water and they didn't happen overnight.'

'What about the wolf tooth, maybe Henri put it here?'

'It doesn't really matter, does it?'

It didn't, but the *Línia de Llop* still intrigued her and she longed to connect the dots. When the old shepherd had explained how silent guardians watch over what is sacred in the world, she had known instinctively that it was the way things were. Her experience with the enigmatic tribeswoman had taught her that much. And yet, now she was in front of the shrine again, she wasn't so sure anymore. If guardians protected what was sacred, why weren't they also protecting children? Surely children were sacred in their own way? She knew what Geoffrey's answer would be to that. He would snarl that it was safer to trust numbers than legends. Matt rubbed her forehead with his thumb.

'Big frown...'

'Just thinking about Geoffrey.'

'I thought you weren't cross with him anymore?'

'I'm not... given half the chance, I would also have run off without seeing Mum.' She ran her hand over the statue. 'I just wish I knew what it all means.'

'And what if there are things we're not meant to understand?'

Not in her world, she thought. But there was wisdom in his words. Trying to figure everything out was wearing her down.

'Where did we put my nail file?' she asked.

He slid his hand into his back pocket, pulled out the file and tapped it against his palm, eyes tender.

'Ready?'

She nodded and took the torch from him to free his hands. He rubbed the statue's right shoulder then positioned the tip of the nail file next to his finger. She watched intently, jittery with anticipation as he began to sandpaper the stone with slow careful movements. The hypnotic singsong of metal on granite filled the cave. Her eyes glazed over.

She had been livid when Geoffrey left without seeing Mum, and had been taken aback by how much she hated breaking the news to her. Her first taste of how worthless retribution was. Not that she didn't still have visions of Mum ending her days in prison, but she was slowly coming around to Geoffrey's way of thinking: Mum simply wasn't the point. They had to live *their* lives.

At least everything was out in the goddamn open, and Mum couldn't escape from the fact that everyone knew. She would probably never acknowledge their version of what had happened, but when she was alone at night, shame would be her gaoler.

Raisin picked up the clamshell and held it next to the shells on her necklace. Identical. Who had put it here? Had someone else needed guidance from her tribeswoman?

The cave fell silent as Matt stopped filing and ran his fingers over the statue's shoulder.

'Not quite ready,' he said.

She dipped her hands into their backpack and pulled out a bundle of soft red cloth. He caught her eye and smiled. She lifted the corners of the cloth and gazed at the tiny stone bird nestled there. A lump formed in her throat. So perfect, so vulnerable. *Back where you belong, little one.*

At last Matt gave a satisfied grunt and straightened up, slipping the nail file back into his pocket. She edged next to him, heart racing. He cradled her hands and their eyes locked as the red cloth dropped to ground and she let go of the bird. He balanced it on the statue's shoulder, rocking it sideways to test the fit.

'Will it work?' she whispered.

'Of course it will.'

He returned the sculpture to her. She kissed the top of its head, surprised at how warm it was, and glanced behind her. Was the tribeswoman nearby? Did she know Nicolas was safe? And did her watchful wolf companion know that the pack he helped rescue was thriving with baby Cava at the wildlife park in the mountains above Les Angles?

She smiled to herself. Of course they knew.

Matt wiped the statue's shoulder with his shirt, opened a red tube and smudged glue over the area he had just prepared. She held the little bird out to him. He shook his head and moved aside.

'You do it, Sarah.'

She crouched forward and gingerly positioned it on the monk's shoulder.

'Hold it there and count to thirty,' he said.

They counted together, voices melding into one. At thirty, she lifted her thumb, waited a beat, then lifted her index finger. She paused, too nervous to remove her hand. He urged her on with a nod. Still she hesitated.

'Let it go, Sarah.'

She chewed her lip and floated her hand away. The bird stayed perched in place, stubby beak parted as if thanking them.

Tears pricked her eyes. 'Geoffrey will be so pleased.'

She draped the necklace on the ledge next to the statue, unable to resist peering over her shoulder one last time. Would her goodbye be acknowledged? Matt curled his arm around her and they stood quietly in front of the shimmering shrine. She leant against him. Where was the tribeswoman?

But there was no cool caress on her skin. No flash of savannah wolf tail in the shadows. She gave Matt a resigned shrug.

'She knows you're here,' he murmured.

He helped her through the wall to the front chamber, and held aside the branches blocking the exit. The outside warmth was tempting, but she didn't move.

'I'd like to fix the wall, Matt.'

'Isn't this how you and Geoffrey found it?'

'No, we opened it up so we could get through. I'd feel happier if we blocked it up again.'

'Won't the authorities want to do something with the dolmen?'

'Nobody's bothered to come here since they caught Rema, so hopefully its existence is lost in a triplicate report somewhere.'

He studied the U-shaped opening in the old wall.

'Should be easy enough to do. We'll put the biggest stones at the bottom then close it up with layers of smaller ones. It won't be very stable though.'

'It doesn't have to be… just as long as it's not obvious that the dolmen has another part to it.'

Stone by stone, they put the broken wall back together, and within half an hour, the hole was gone. She jammed two small stones in the last remaining gaps and stood back.

Let no-one disturb you.

They squirmed between the branches and she carefully rearranged the foliage after her, heart light. St Francis could watch over the secret caves and passageways in peace.

Clouds hung low and a balmy breeze rustled the leaves overhead. She smiled. One of Henri's more gentle winds.

'Let's not go all the way to Massane to picnic. It's too hot,' she said.

He dropped his hat on her head.

'Here, wear this. Why don't we picnic right here, on the rock? Then you can show me the engravings at the same time.'

They climbed on top and explored the crosses and dimples on the dolmen's cap stone. She traced circles around the weathered symbols.

'I keep asking myself *who*… who built the shrines… who did the cave paintings… who left these engravings?'

'Someone with heart and that's all that matters. People think our prehistoric ancestors were different to us, but I disagree. We probably all have a kindred spirit who lived back then… a soul sister or brother in our image that walked the earth in ancient times. Your one was probably the clan's head cook, delighting in trying out meals with new roots and fruits.'

'And yours would have made poultices with the leaves and flowers mine couldn't use,' she giggled.

'They would have both marvelled at the same sunset... been fascinated by the same symmetry in a daisy...'

'Felt the same thrill in love.'

She lounged back, holding out her hand to him. He brushed his lips over hers. She stroked his face.

'The best thing you ever did was come for me,' she sighed.

'Life without you was never an option, Sarah.'

She flushed. Three months on, and she still loved to hear him say it. Thank God he hadn't let her run away. They lay side by side under the gnarled branches of the cork oak. A woodpecker tap-tapped nearby; so loud, she peered between the leaves for it, but as if sensing her interest, it stopped.

'Do you believe Henri's *Linía de Llop* exists?' he asked.

'I'm not sure. Do you?'

'We're in Collioure, and together...that's pretty powerful proof of something big at play to me.'

She rolled onto her side and toyed with the loose threads of a lost button on his shirt.

'But Collioure took me away from you! Oh, I get it... you're being a cynical scientist, aren't you? You don't really believe the *Linía de Llop* exists,' she accused sheepishly.

He tweaked her hat.

'You could have gone to any hotel school in the world. Would Geoffrey have visited you in a big city? I don't think so. And besides... last I looked, there weren't any forestry stations in Paris or Rome!'

Was he saying the *Linía de Llop* had drawn them all to Collioure? Could such a thing really exist? On the face of it, he had a point... so much good had come out of them being here. She and Geoffrey were close again. The terrible stuff with Mum was out in the open, and not as overwhelmingly scary anymore. And best of all, Matt was back.

Part of her was tempted to believe a greater sacred power existed, but another part rebelled against it. It felt safer to trust that she alone drove her destiny. She flopped onto her back and covered her face with the hat. It didn't matter. Maybe that should be her new mantra, and she should stop trying so damn hard to figure life out. Matt placed a palm over her heart.

'I'm just happy to be on this rock with you, knowing that we'll figure out what happens next… and we'll do it *together*. And as to whether I believe in the *Linía de Llop…*'

She lifted her hat a fraction and shushed him with a finger to his lips.

'It doesn't matter.'

Made in the USA
Middletown, DE
30 April 2021